DIVINE JUSTICE

Joanne Hichens

CATALYST PRESS
Pacifica, California

In North America, this book is distributed by
Consortium Book Sales & Distribution, a division of Ingram.
Phone: 612/746-2600
cbsdinfo@ingramcontent.com
www.cbsd.com

In South Africa, Namibia, and Botswana,
this book is distributed by LAPA Publishers.
Phone: 012/401-0700
lapa@lapa.co.za
www.lapa.co.za

First published by Burnett Media, South Africa in 2011.
FIRST EDITION

10 9 8 7 6 5 4 3 2 1
Library of Congress Control Number: 2020933807

Cover design by Karen Vermeulen, Cape Town, South Africa

PRAISE FOR DIVINE JUSTICE

※

"*Divine Justice* is both an intriguing mystery and a brilliant character study, presenting vivid snapshots of desperate people straddling the fault lines in contemporary South African society. A gripping narrative that rushes to a thrilling climax."

Roger Smith, best-selling author of *Dust Devils, Sacrifice and Capture*

"Hichens is a powerful writer...While there are gruesome and horrible murders throughout, some moments, especially the dénouement, are pure black comedy. Hichens has written a cracking good crime novel set in familiar landmarks in the Cape and Namibia. An excellent book to take along on holiday. It will keep you entertained even if the sun don't shine."

Janet Van Eeden Harrison, LitNet

"Joanne Hichens's *Divine Justice* is a wonderfully edgy thriller that sears a path through Cape Town's underbelly like caustic soda. Newly minted private eye Rae Valentine— and amputee ex-junkie—has morphed into one of those fortuitous fictional creations that one can only hope to see more of in future."

William Saunderson-Meyer, *Sunday Times*

THE PROMISE

*The city below him is sizzling in the heat;
the mountain above him is simmering,
a taste of hell's furnace.*

❋

One foot in front of the other, Heinz Dieter hikes up Castle Gate. He digs the walking stick deep into the charred earth. Through his thick soles he feels the heat from the scorched surface as he steps and sinks through the cinder crust, releasing clouds of ash.

He stops to placate his aching lungs and squints at the alien sun shimmering blood-orange through the smoke, a pall that obscures his view of Camps Bay and the elite suburbs on the Atlantic seaboard. He holds in a searing breath, the saliva burning dry on his tongue. He sips water from his bottle and applies balm to his parched lips. He repositions the wet handkerchief over his mouth, tightens the knot of the wide-brimmed hat under his chin, and eases the rucksack on his shoulders.

Near the summit, he passes the remains of two mountain huts now burnt to the ground. Where once he smelled fragrant buchu and plucked hardy ericas and proteas for his mother, the vegetation is reduced to little more than blackened twigs. Black as death.

He exalts in the silence.

Every creature, every life form, is burnt to a crisp.

Flesh of one flesh! Burnt offerings!

He chuckles. *Today there will be no wild flowers for you,* Mutti.

With the veld grasses roasted to their roots, it is

difficult to make out the path. It takes longer than usual for him to reach the upper cableway station, now deserted. At the view site, he is alone. He positions himself, stands close to the edge, the rock face a sheer drop to the smouldering slopes below, savoring what glimpses he can of sea and city through the tendrils of spiraling smoke. The air is greasy, reeking of cooked fat.

He'd asked for a sign: nothing could have directed him with more insistency than this Great Blaze, with its leaping tongues of fire, glorious shades of red and gold and orange and crimson.

Euphoric, his breath coming in ragged gasps, he stretches his arms to the Heavens, accepting whatever is to come. He has seen God's wrath with his own eyes. He has read the prophecies:

The mountains will split open to release a hail of rocks and lava and a blood red sea will rise to meet the devastation, silencing all sinners in its path!

He relishes the thought, anticipates the piteous shrieks of wicked children snatched from the arms of the weeping nonbelievers.

He is shouting now, conjuring the moment, gesticulating wildly towards the matchbox city at the mountain's foot; ships and cranes in harbor; skyscrapers, monuments, structures all as insignificant as playthings: "Your screams will rise over Sodom and Gomorrah!"

Tremors shake his body.

He clutches at the vial in his pocket; popping a pill under his tongue, he turns and prepares to descend.

Passing Maclear's Beacon, the highest point on Table Mountain, he makes his way along a flat path to the ravine above Kirstenbosch Gardens. The fires have not yet reached the leafy green suburbs, an Eden among the ashes. At Skeleton Gorge—how aptly named—he throws back his head in triumph and laughs out loud. But the laugh sticks in his throat. A sound of ripping canvas and a sensation of soft flesh underfoot. The laugh morphs into a scream. The snake strikes as he jumps, hitting the underside of the leather boot. His heart thudding, fit to burst, he recoils in disgust at the sight of the yellow and brown chevron patterning dulled by soot, a perfect camouflage. Swallowing hard he watches in captivated terror as the puff adder, fat, slow and repulsive, retreats lethargically to find shelter in the crevice of a rock.

This is the second sign.

God will punish him, His servant, if he does not act soon.

He drops to his knees on the filthy ground.

The unprepared will burn and be buried under rubble.

The seas will churn and rise to become one.

"Oh Lord!"

Screams will pierce the night as rolling waves crash along the shores.

Liquid fingers will drag under everything within grasp, reaching out for those that remain.

"So be it!"

The sun is low on the horizon when he reaches the contour path. Resting his pack on a boulder, he searches for the plastic bottle. He sprays disinfectant on his grubby hands, wipes the moisture from his forehead with a clean white handkerchief.

All indeed is well.

He will be home with Mutti before dark.

"Lord," he murmurs, "I am ready."

PART ONE

FIRE AND FLAME

❋

Anthony Durant drank in Rae Valentine over pasta and vino: dark hair spilling onto her bare shoulders, soft curls he longed to bury his face in. He wanted to stroke her smooth cheek, run his fingertips over her kissable mouth. Most of all, he wanted to keep his gaze from the zigzag scars at her throat and chest. He wanted the past to vanish, to wish away everything that had happened over the last six weeks.

"Heck, Rae, you're a vision."

She saw "Love" writ large. The night was young, and she smiled as she rotated the fork, slurping up the last coil of spag bol, a little of the sauce settling on her chin. She wiped the plate clean with ciabatta, pushed it away with a satisfied sigh. She looked at her man, big guy with a big face. Ten years older than she was and gray at the temples, he'd grown his hair, wore it back, but tendrils were loose, softening the roughness around the edges of an ex-cop turned PI.

"I adore you too, Tony Durant," Rae giggled.

He reached across the small table to clean her chin: "What's so funny?"

"Your pony, Tone."

"Well you wanted to French-braid my locks."

"Aw, you look so gorgeous." She leaned across, placed her hands on his cheeks and kissed him full on his wide mouth. It felt like old times tonight, with good memories flooding back, the comfort of togetherness starting to gel for them once more. The way they'd been. The way Rae Valentine wanted them to be: in love, cozy, comfortable.

"Hey, Tony," she said, making real the unmentionable. "I'm so flippin' glad to be done with that hospital hellhole, I can't tell you."

"Me too, babe." He smacked his lips, tasting olive oil and lip ice. "I'm glad you're okay. More than okay."

"You'll miss chatting up the nurses, though."

He made light of the mention of the more than well-endowed ward matron and her stout side-kick: "Yup, those buxom mamas with their booties squeezed into their uniforms really did it for me."

"Tell you what, Tone. I'll get myself a cute little ensemble, dress up in a tight candy-striped skirt and a cap with a red cross on it, and wear my outfit around our house—just for you!"

This was what he'd always liked about her. Sex was fun and food was foreplay. She liked to eat a good meal and then she took life by the balls. Busy now with the tiramisu pick-me-up, scooping amaretto-soaked sponge biscuit and mascarpone into her mouth till every crumb was gone—going *Mmmmmm, this is sooooo yummy!*—her good foot worked between his thighs, bare toes teasing his crotch.

"I'm stuffed, Tone," she sat back. "That's what I call a feast! Worst thing about the hospital? The food. Not exactly culinary delights. White it's sugar, brown it's meat, gray is everything else. I'd rather die than face hospital grub again."

Silence.

Her joke hadn't quite come off.

The why-for of the hospitalization—the attack on her body and the scars she was left with—was suddenly between them again. The truth was there'd always be a *before the attack* and an *after*. How did a man ever get over not being there to stop the woman he loved from being hurt? The crims had come after him, had got her instead.

The burnt-orange jacket Tony wore for the feel-good factor hung creased over the back of his chair, and what the heck had he strung on a tie for? He was sweating, partly on account of the heat, with temperatures rising over forty degrees outside and made worse by the mountains on fire these past few weeks, but mainly he was sweating on account of what he knew he had to do.

"Hey, doll," said Rae, sensing the shift of his mood, taking his hand and holding it close. "Don't worry so much, I'm feeling strong. It's all good." She flashed a smile and started humming along with the café's background music, Chris Brown's classic "Forever" playing on a compilation of love songs. She mouthed her version of the words, "Yeah, it's you and me, Tony, together, moving at the speed of light until forever!"

She squeezed his hand, raised her wine glass, and toasted: "To us!"

11:35PM

JP Cowart took a squizz out his bedroom window in the Origin Street digs in the Cape Town suburb of De Waterkant, near the old Malay Quarter. He could see the harbor and the lights of the swanky Victoria & Alfred Waterfront, and if it wasn't for the smoke from the fires he'd see clearly the flickering signal from the old lighthouse on Robben Island.

Then he tugged the curtains closed.

The house was a Cinderella waiting to be snapped up and done up and sold to some overseas Prince, but it was perfect for the Core. Even this rough bunch couldn't do permanent damage to the solid floors, yellowwood or pine, he couldn't tell which. But they'd made their mark, he smirked. The owner would shit bricks when he saw the inside walls painted a deep, mucky red—like living in a pulsing artery.

He shimmied into Levi's, caught a glimpse of skin in the cupboard mirror. With his shirt off was how God intended JP Cowart to be, his chest and one sleeve an artwork of tattoos—of skulls, swastikas, lightning bolts, snakes circling his arm. He raised a bicep, an eagle popping there. Was more than pleased with the results of months of pumping iron at cross fit. The days anyone called him a skinny weed were long over. So what, he was a late bloomer. His talent, in demand, was that he knew about computers and hardware and shit and he knew a whole lot of other stuff besides.

His hair, though, was way too long now; he looked like a nine-to-five workhorse the way it was styled, just about to curl at his neck. In the bathroom he brought out the electric clippers, mowed his head all over to black bristle the way he liked it and glistened it up with a smear of gel. He parted his lips, then clamped his mouth shut in a thin tight gash, not wanting to bare his ugly teeth. He wished his cheapskate folks had paid to get them straightened instead of forking out for psychiatrists forcing medication down his throat.

He slammed the door on the mess, wet towels on the floor, dirty laundry. Slammed the door on the memory of his father beating him with a cane.

"You feel the heat, JP?" Christoff Wessels asked. Curly carrot-topped, flaccid-faced, red-cheeked, he lay with his legs white as bread dough stretched in front of him, his dirty feet up on the couch stained and torn and singed from daily abuse. "Air's so thick it's like breathing in bath water, like drowning, man."

"City's frying," said JP. Then mumbled under his breath: "Why don't you get up off your fat arse, cray-fish-boy, and clean the place up instead of watching TV all bloody day."

Christoff mashed his Camel butt on the armrest, the acrid smell of burnt fabric tainting the air. With the remote he switched to an all-night news channel and upped the volume. He crossed his wrists behind his head, exposing his porcelain-white armpits sprouting ranga spirals, and leaned back, further flattening his unruly curls. "Jissis, check this out!"

"Can you see I'm otherwise occupied?" JP wiped off the sweat beading on his upper lip.

"On the news, hey," chirped Christoff, "a chopper's gone down fighting the fire on the mountain. Blade clipped the rock. Whoosh! Check the footage! Chopper's buggered. No use against those flames."

"City's burning all right. Our world is fucking doomed!" At the dining-room table, concentrating on the device, sweat glistening now on his pecs and tats, JP finished the fuse—spooned out the mixture of potassium nitrate and sugar into the tissue, rolled it like a marijuana joint. "Twisted tight as a virgin's cunt," he quipped, satisfied, smiling as he methodically filled the small tin with the precise amount of C4 explosive, did it just like he was supposed to, the info he'd found on the Internet stored on the Samsung right there in front of him.

He'd downloaded all sorts of useful bits and pieces: "How to make Bombs" from *The Terrorist Handbook* was helpful, but it was easier to go straight to YouTube, download the tutorial *Wonder How To* clips and see right there in front of you the finer craft of creating homemade explosives. He'd pored through the archived recipes, found one that suited his needs and followed to a T the oh-so-simple step-by-step video.

The third housemate, Dermot Glynn—dark haired, blue-eyed, pink cheeks, his claim to fame, "I'm from pukka Irish terrorist stock"—came in from the kitchen, bringing through a six-pack, dumping the beers on the coffee table. Fingering his rosary, swinging the thing about.

The beads and the metal cross tinkled, distracting JP.

"You want one?" asked Dermot, splitting the vacuum-plastic with his overgrown thumbnail.

"Derm the Worm, why bring 'em through if we not gonna down 'em?"

"I'm third generation," said Dermot, "no bloody worm me." He lobbed a beer at JP.

Christoff burped. "Ja, and for me too, Rooinek." He sat up, his grubby vest, tight over his beer belly, proclaiming him to be 100% BOER. Proud of his heritage, proud of being Afrikaner.

"This's so easy a monkey could do it," said JP. "Why people bother wasting time getting diplomas and degrees, worthless paper, is beyond me when there's DIY tips on the Net for whatever you wanna do."

"Where's the jobs out there anyways?" Christoff snorted. "If there are jobs they're anyways all going to swart boeties, our black brothers."

"That's why we creating our own opportunities," said JP, placing the finished masterpiece of a device on the newspaper in the center of the table. He stretched into a stand, pulled on the black T-shirt yanked off the back of the chair, the Celtic cross straining nice and tight across his chest.

"It's time," he said, picking up his handiwork. "Switch off that bloody box. Let's roll."

Dermot Glynn, the designated driver, freewheeled the Tazz through the tight streets of De Waterkant.

He kicked in the engine in Somerset Road, made for the city center. The skyscrapers were obscured and the streetlights haloed on account of the smoke pollution caused by zigzag flames licking at the slopes of Table Mountain. Fire engines lined the curve of Tafelberg Road; police cars cordoned off De Waal Drive, the route snaking between the slopes and the city, all the attention of officialdom focused on the devastation.

Ten minutes later Dermot switched off the engine and rolled the Tazz into an empty delivery bay at the entrance to Gardens Mall.

The plan was he stayed in the car watching—*thank you, Mother*, he crossed himself, forehead, chest, left, right, his foot poised to gun the accelerator—while the others got down to what they needed to do.

Christoff joined his hands in prayer, the way he always did, asking God's blessing on a clean job. Then he sprang from the car and went to work on the street-side ATM. Seconds ticked on as JP waited at his side, Christoff taking his bloody time prising open the mouth of the machine.

At last JP stuffed in the device.

"Holy Mother of God, we got company!" shouted Dermot.

He saw the security guard running towards them, making them out in the shadows, the old boy with salt and pepper curls, that earnest look in his rheumy eyes, yelling, waving his baton. *The misguided fool!* Panicked, Dermot jumped from the car, gestured to the others.

In the same moment JP flicked the Bic, lit the fuse, scurried well back, crouched behind a bin. The ATM exploded as the bullets started flying—*bap, bap, bap!*

The guard went down.

So did Dermot.

"Pick up the bucks!" spat JP. He and Christoff

scrambled for the money, pulling plenty of cash from the wreckage, dumping the bundles into the hatchback, pulling Dermot into the car.

"He's got blood all over him. A total utter mess this!"

"Just fucking go!" JP ordered, as Christoff fell into the driver's seat. "Get us the hell out of here."

They screeched from the scene, burning rubber.

"Bloody unbelievable!" shrieked JP.

"Sharp man!" whooped Christoff.

Dermot moaned, "I need help."

"You just keep saying your Hail Marys there, Derm, and stop moaning about a mere flesh wound," JP said, going on: "Guard didn't have a hope in hell of stopping us. Got what was coming to him."

"Unbeliever didn't even have a second to grab his walkie-talkie before you wiped him. Got him good! Fokken A!" Christoff smacked a fist into his open palm.

"Smith & Wesson put a load in his goolies where it counts," said JP, "an' a couple more in the heart, bang bang!" Then taking the piss, he half-turned to Dermot: "I almost killed you too, Rooinek! What the fuck were you doing out the car?"

They dumped the stolen Tazz in Woodstock, picked up the bright and shiny souped-up Mini Cooper with its twin-scroll turbo-charger and overboost function. Car drove like a dream but the chrome detail was way too flash for heists.

The trio headed back to the red house as they called it, with its blood and guts walls.

01:55AM

Detective Rex Hawkins jangled his car keys as he strode across the quad at Caledon Central Police Station, felt the sticky sweat at the armpits of his short-sleeved polyester-blend Chinese-made excuse for a shirt. Rail-thin Rex Hawkins, more than slightly stooped from years on the force, with a hard paunch puckering the buttons, had seldom experienced such intense heat.

"When's this hell of a summer gonna be over and done with?" he mumbled, folding his frame into the driver's seat. The constant fires, the pale ash settling on every surface. And the fury. When would it end?

He lit up, dragged on the Marlboro hanging from his lips as he pulled out of the police yard. He took a left on Barrack Street, rolled past the gentleman's club Mavericks where the action spilled out onto the pavement, strippers and jocks chatting it up, and Rex wished he too could find refuge from real life in the arms of a woman, or at least between her legs. If only refuge wasn't quite so pricey and short-lived.

He started up the hill towards the highway, the streets here almost deserted at this God-forsaken hour. He stopped at a red. Lit another smoke from the burning filter of the C-stick he'd just sucked dry, crushed the empty pack heavy with health warnings in his fist. Waiting for the lights to change, he checked out Table Mountain illuminated by spotlights and the ragged flames on the slopes. No one could do anything about the fire spreading, not at this time of night.

He sat through green, came to his senses as some bloke behind pressed his palm long and hard on his horn. As amber turned red, Rex accelerated, his tires squealing a *fuck you*.

Eyes focusing again on the straight and narrow, he took a left into Breda Street, made his way to the labyrinth beyond. He loved the city. Didn't love the spikes, barbed-wire curls, electric fencing atop every wall of every apartment block, house, shop. Over-the-top security spelled people trapped, spelled a current of crisis. This was Cape Town all right, billed as a top-ten beauty of the world, but the undertow was ugly. All the politicians in the land couldn't deny crime was at an all time high.

He turned left at the Gardens Mall, a tall block of mixed retail and luxury residential, all the million-buck rage to live in the city if you could afford it. He parked, slamming the door on his thoughts. Nodded to the saluting cop who'd caught the call. He was proud of his record; a reputation as the detective with the most "solveds" in his case file still meant something to some of the guys. He deserved the respect. He grunted an assent as the cop pointed to Rex's early-bird partner. Waiting. Expecting him. He deadened and pocketed the butt, then stepped over the yellow crime-scene tape. He listened in on the tail end of a civilian statement made to one of the cops working through the small crowd of urban flat dwellers: "… the commotion woke me and my wife. First there was yelling we thought was street people, you know, having a late night party, then this bang happened, helluva loud!"

"Howzit. Awake and aware at last. What took you so long?" Rex's partner, Adrian Lombard, took his eyes off the scene, gave Rex a quick once over.

"Top of the morning to you too, Adrian. Dressed to kill, I see."

Adrian shrugged. "Dep Com Moodley says wear police blues, I do what Moodley says."

Together they checked out the smoking remnants of the ATM, the guts of the machine, blackened wires and springs, spilling out all over the place; plus singed bundles of cash left behind. They checked out the body of the security guard, his hands curled into claws as he'd suffered the burn. A gust of hot wind stirred up the ash, blew a whiff of charred flesh Rex's way.

"Hell's teeth." Rex pulled Vicks balm from his pocket, streaked a smear under his nostrils. He'd never get used to the sweet smell of burnt human. "Hope to God the poor bugger was dead before his face was blown to hell and gone."

"Doc de Wet confirms he stopped a number of bullets before he was roasted."

They stomped soot off their boots as they stepped back over the yellow tape.

"How the hell do the cheeky bastards get away with it?" Adrian whistled, running his hand over his stress-pattern bald patch. Hardly thirty years old and he was thinning all right. This was what cop business did to you. "How the hell do these jokers drive right up close to a so-called secure parking lot, blow the machine to pieces, and fuck right off with the bucks? What's this, the fourth ATM these jokers have targeted this month?"

"Looks like the same C4 damage."

"With the explosion amplified by electricity connected to the safe. Still reckon security guards aren't paid off to look the other way?"

"This one wasn't." Rex turned away from the corpse, walked around the strewn rubble, the melted blue-and-white bank sign on the ground. One of the security guard's takkies lay just to the left of the scene. Rex contemplated the cheap sneaker: it didn't matter how tight the fit, shoes were kicked off with the shock of the final moment. "Always the shoes," he said out loud to no one in particular. He looked up. "Any video footage?"

"You kidding me?"

"I never cease to hope."

"Hell, why bother putting up state-of-the-art security cameras when banks are insured to the hilt? Besides, the crims wear hoodies, caps, sunglasses. Can never make out a thing."

Rex ran a finger along the spray-painted graffiti on the wall to the left of the burnt bank. A variation on the theme of swastika, a vile sign, something they'd seen before. His tips came away red, he wiped them on a tissue. "Still wet."

"Same crew clearly."

"Same red, black, and white. Forensics didn't happen to call with news on the samples, did they?"

"We're a priority..."

"Reckon tonight's shindig will get Pretoria working any faster?"

"'Cos there's a corpse? As you say, hope's not dead. Pity all the scientists have exodused to better prospects Down Under or wherever they've fucked off to."

"Wouldn't mind escaping Down Under myself. Problem being my age." Rex coughed, ratcheting up a glob of brown phlegm into the tissue. "And my good health. What I've got to look forward to here is my pension, if I ever get to claim the damn thing." For the umpteenth time he checked his Timex. "We're done here."

The night was not yet done with them.

02:10 AM

Rocco Robano was waiting. Rocco, the brains behind the Boyz, the brains behind the trio, JP, Christoff, and Dermot. He scowled when he saw the blood, wondering what the hell his crew had done now, helping them carry Dermot in, laying him on the couch, the guy groaning, saying, "JP did it."

"He took a bullet, Boss," said JP.

"Yeah?" said Rocco, pulling back Dermot's sodden jacket, seeing the hole at his shoulder.

"Shot him by accident," JP sniggered. "Fool shoulda

stayed in the car like I told him."

"Christ, JP, there's always complications." It wasn't the first time Derm the Worm hadn't listened.

"I need a doctor," croaked Dermot.

Rocco ran a freckled hand over his scalp bristles, his fingers moving like a spider's legs as he looked down on his wounded lackey. He glowered now, fingers pulling at the tuft of hair under his lip, replied, "Doctors report bullet wounds. We'll fix you. This business calls for versatility. On the other hand I shouldn't have hired a weak piece of rubbish like you who keeps causing problems." In one movement, he grabbed a pillow from the couch and his Colt Python from the holster at his hip, rammed them together beneath Dermot Glynn's right ear and pulled the trigger: a muffled thud, and blood and brains splattered against the red wall, the blood a deeper, brighter crimson than the paint job.

"What the fuck're you looking at?" He stepped towards JP and Christoff, the two idiots spooked like buck in the headlights. "You two got nothing to say for a change? Good. Derm the Worm here had no staying power, no stamina, no feeling for the job. Was a serious accident waiting to happen. You agree?" He moved around to the front of the couch, surveying the scene. He kicked Dermot's leaking corpse. "Plenty to choose from where he came from." His yellow eyes honed in on his remaining team. "Don't you two ever forget that. Now clean up."

03:00 AM

Detective Rex Hawkins checked his Timex once more: he no longer envied ex-cop and one-time friend Tony Durant.

"Hawkins, am I clear?" Deputy Commissioner

Chas Moodley barked over the cellphone, a rabid dog frothing at the mouth. "I repeat, d'you hear me, Hawkins?"

"Clear as a bell, Dep Com."

"I'm warning you, Hawkins, you stuff this up you'll be off the force faster than–"

Rex disconnected. Weary of crime, of all the violence out there, and mostly weary of cop politics, he sighed and pocketed the phone. He hated the fact that he was at Moodley's mercy 24/7.

The partners walked together, the smell of Adrian's menthol wafting under Rex's nostrils. "D'you have to smoke that crap? Makes me sick to my stomach."

"You're sick to your stomach with what we're about to do."

"What a waste. What an absolute bloody waste."

"We still have jobs. Moodley'll take us down if we don't do this."

"As if bloody Moodley doesn't have his hands full with this shit going down, armed robbery, malicious damage to property, contraventions of the Explosives Act..."

"Now murder."

Rex coughed again, wetly, into his hand this time. He felt the trickle of perspiration down his ribs, smelled his body odor. "Let's go. Moodley'll be snapping at our heels if we're late."

On a heat-saturated morning like this, with air so dense you could take a bite right out of it, Rex knew it would be a lifesaver out there on the sea.

That was what they'd planned to do, Rex and Adrian and Tony. He knew Durant would be ready to head out fishing, would have the ice chest packed with cool drinks, beers, sandwiches. The plan was to pull a yellowtail or two or a plump Cape salmon from the sea for the braai.

But that wasn't about to happen.

He fired up a Marlboro from a fresh pack and looked back at the bunch of rookie-cops stamping evidence into the ground. He looked up at the burning mountain, a hint of the famous tablecloth there, wispy cloud rolling over the top, white in the moonlight, the edges tinged with orange from rising flames. If he was a religious man he'd send up a prayer in awe of the sheer terror of it, and beg for rain. But he didn't believe in a goddamned thing any more.

Here he was, a part of Dep Com Moodley's pathetic plan, cringing at his lack of self-respect. He looked across at Adrian. "This job is about to become a whole lot more distasteful."

03:10AM

JP got the booze from the kitchen. He needed this drink, for sure. His hands wilted from the wet cloth, from the hard scrubbing of the couch; the whiff of bleach stung his nostrils. He sloshed a couple of shots into the dirty glasses on the coffee table in the living room: "To the Boyz!" Or what was left of them.

"Amen!" Christoff threw back the Klipdrift Gold and saluted JP in return, felt the zing of the brandy at the back of his throat. They each took a seat, warily avoiding the couch where Dermot's body, now wrapped in a blanket in the garage, awaiting disposal, had recently slumped.

Again JP toasted, "To a successful collection."

"We've done well this month."

"Fuck yes." JP slugged back another tot. "We're working towards a worthwhile investment."

"Jissis, though, times when I'm fingering the bucks," said Christoff, "it's bloody hard to keep the faith, bru."

"Trust, boykie, the Core's operation calls for trust."

Because Rocco Robano is not a man to be crossed —JP's thought went unsaid.

This wasn't the time to be stealing the funds, or skimming off the top for shiny shoes and leather jackets, just the sort of stuff Christoff was in to.

Rocco had offed Dermot just like that, cold, clean, the dude never knew what hit him. Thank God the walls were red. Didn't show up any blood splatters they might have left behind. Would make a good advert, he smiled, a couple of guys effortlessly wiping blood off a fancy, stain-resistant paint job. Yup, all round a successful clean-up.

"How about breakfast then?" Christoff sat up. "Eggs and bacon. You want?"

"No," said JP, irritated with the guy always stuffing food in his gob, snacking no matter what the time, as if the dude's belly wasn't fat enough.

"Seker?"

"Ja, I'm bloody sure, if I eat eggs now I'll puke."

JP needed a couple of hours' sleep. He pissed in the potted palm, the fronds brown and wilted, in the passage outside an open bedroom door and noted the empty bed and Dermot's useless Bible on the pillow. Tough takkie. Win some, lose some. Derm the Worm had lost out big time.

03:20AM

Ratatatatatat!

Tony Durant heard the spray of machine gun fire. He twisted off the rise onto his haunches, oozing sweat from every pore as the searing heat of the thatched hut ablaze shriveled his skin. He smelled scorched flesh, felt his battering heart about to break free of his chest...

Then he realized he was in his own home, his flash-back to border-war days fading as he focused on the dark shapes he recognized: the TV, the cabinet. This was no Angolan war nightmare. Hell, this was his lounge. He tripped over his tog bag as he grabbed the ringing cell phone, whacked his shin against the coffee table—bugger!—checked REX on the screen, saw the time, 3:21 am, answered, "You're way too early."

"Tony, can you get out here?"

"I'm coming, I'm coming." He disconnected. Stumbled into the kitchen, confirmed the time on the yellow wall clock. At the basin he splashed cold tap water on his face. Cleared his mind as best he could. Dried off with a sour-smelling dish towel.

Guys were scheduled to go fishing this morning. Cape salmon were running and Tony wanted nothing more than to chill out and chew the fat the way he could with Rex and Adrian. But they were a bloody hour early, the pick-up planned only for four-thirty! Everything was spot-on ready: his beloved boat *Aunt Mary* was hitched to the Isuzu, the cooler box packed with Cokes, Castles, sandwiches. The good Lord knew he needed to get out on the ocean.

Only a few hours back in the mom-and-pop Italian café, Rae had crooned like a besotted teenager about love with a capital L, had drained her glass and looked at him like he'd be in her life till death do us part.

Tony knew the truth of it: there was no rhythm of ecstasy.

Hell's bells, it was the word "us" that had really freaked him.

Another rapping sequence. "I said I'm on my way! Don't break down the bloody door."

He stopped briefly to check himself out in the hall mirror. Had dark rings under his eyes. He slapped his cheeks, drew his wild hair back into his pony. Then through the spy hole in the door he confirmed this was no misunderstanding, the two cops were on the stoep.

"What the heck, guys?" He unbolted, unlocked, slid back the chain, opened the door. "It's well before sparrowfart." Well before a man had a chance to finish working through his nightmares. "What the hell're you clowns doing here?"

And why in police blues?

Then he heard a familiar voice boom from the dark: "Good morning, *Mister* Durant."

Had to be another bad dream. Except Deputy Commissioner Chas Moodley's sharp features were right in his face now, his dark brows knitted, his lips wet and twisted in a snarl.

"Sleeping in your clothes are you, Durant?"

"Going fishing," yawned Tony. You had to be ready.

"My, my, how the mighty have fallen."

"To what do I owe this pleasure, Moodley?"

"Anthony Durant," Moodley barked, handcuffs dangling from his left hand, his right loosely placed on his piece in its holster, "you're under arrest for murder."

"What kinda joke is this?"

"You never kept up with the police procedure manual, did you?" Deputy Commissioner Moodley smirked. "Slap the cuffs on him, boys."

"What the heck's going on? What bullshit're you spouting, Chas?"

"With your rough justice you're a law unto your own. That's right, Durant, there's such a thing as the Gun Act, and several others you'd know about if you'd ever bothered to do your homework. The rules, boy, you're always bending the rules into pretzels."

Tony, trying for reasonable, said, "Is there something we have to sort out?"

"You know as well as I do, Durant, that you can't go around shooting people in this country without showing just cause. You're not a cop any more and this isn't the Wild West. This is South Africa. Criminals have airtight rights here. You can't kill them without facing the consequences. We're taking you down to Caledon Square."

"You serious?" He'd shot the men in self-defense, defending Rae.

"C'mon, boys, do it!"

Tony shook his head. Why today of all days? "No need for cuffs, Moodley." So far neither of his henchmen had volunteered to snap their ex-buddy in the metal.

"Ag, don't be so goddamned difficult. Questions need answering." Moodley flexed his thumb backwards. "Don't give us grief. Just get in the damn cop car."

Tony scratched at his crotch. Registered his furry tongue like a small animal trapped in his mouth. "Give me a minute."

Moodley turned back, came up close, ranting: "Tell him, Rex."

"For Christ's sake, Moodley," said Tony, "I need to lock up, take a piss, brush my teeth."

"Detective Captain Hawkins, tell *Mister* Durant what serious shit he's in! The cop who couldn't take the heat, the guy jerking our wires. Some heavy fall-out's coming your way, buddy." Moodley swung about and strode down the short path towards his sleek Mercedes SL parked in the street.

Tony wiped Moodley's spit from his cheek.

Rex said, "There's a baton up his arse, or a pineapple." Then turned shame-faced to Tony: "Best make it quick. We have to take you in."

"Whatever you say."

In the house he tidied himself while Rex checked the dirty dishes, the clothes heaped on the floor, the pillow and the twisted sheets. "You still dossing on the couch, pal?"

"You're calling me pal? Bedroom's got too many memories, you know that."

"Best sell this place soonest. Get over what happened here."

Tony ignored him, closed and bolted windows, turned off the lights, the scene of the attack just weeks ago still fresh in his mind: *Rae naked on their bed, crouching. Her hands tied behind her back, blood trickling, her stump leg drawn up beneath her, her face pulped, her breasts cut, blood soaking into the sheets. The stench of urine, of human feces...*

Instinct kicking in, he lurched for the crim with the gun, lashing backwards, grabbing the Beretta, the two of them wrenching at it, till it went tuktuktuk! and the man fell back, bullets to the chest, and Tony turned and before the second bastard could swing his knife, Tony pulled his Police Astra and put a load in the attacker's skull...

He'd held Rae as she'd keened in tune to the sirens in the distance. Held her till a host of cops arrived and stormed through the door, till the ambulance took her away.

He flinched now as Rex touched his shoulder: "Play along, Tony. Moodley's on a witch-hunt. We'll sort this out soonest."

"I'm to be made an example of? Payback is what it's all about."

Tony fingered a stray mint chew in the pocket of his denims, didn't look back at the house as Rex escorted him to the cop car. He popped the chew, sucked off the lint. "I need a decent lawyer."

"It's sorted."

"You didn't get me some Legal Aid nitwit, did you?"

"I put in a word with Natasha Armstrong. The lady's got a good record getting crims free."

"That the way you see this? I'm a criminal now?"

"Not me, Tony," Rex jerked his head in the direction of Moodley's Merc. "You nailed two low-life scum. You deserve the President's medal, not the fucking third degree. Guy still nurtures a grudge, hates you for being a better cop in the dark than he is any day, has a chip on his shoulder the depth of Glencairn quarry."

Adrian Lombard, at the car, stared at his boots.

"Et tu, Adrian?"

"Sorry, man."

"Right then," said Tony, resigned, as he got into the car with the two cops. You knew it was a scam. You went along with it. What else could you do?

Dep Com Moodley, leading the cavalcade from the wasteland, added the siren to the flashing lights. Tony was hanging for a joint, a long drag of a head of dagga to take the edge off. If only.

From the back of the cop car, he said, "When your friends show you who they really are, believe them."

"Huh?" said Rex.

"An old Zulu saying." Tony stared out the window at the gray dawn. "Let's sort this out then, shall we?"

"I'll call Rae and let her know," said Adrian.

"Don't do that, pal."

"You two not talking again, or what?"

"Something like that," he muttered.

Last night, just hours before, over the empty pudding dishes, Tony had looked into her eyes: "You and me, Rae...I need my space." He'd blurted it out, so

27

bloody clumsy!

"What?"

He'd given it to her straight: "It's over, Rae." The way he ended it. Snap! After nearly two years.

"You're dumping me, Tony?" Rae had snatched her hand back, blinked. "After all we've been through, you're dumping me? You're really doing this to us?"

"I can't do 'us' right now, Rae."

"I don't believe what I'm hearing."

He'd seen the worst, blood and snot streaking her cheeks, he'd seen her vulnerability, her fragility. "Babe–"

"Spare me, Tony, don't you dare give me the 'it's not you it's me' excuse."

"This is gonna–"

"And don't you dare fucking tell me it's going to hurt you more than it's going to hurt me!"

With her fingertips she'd killed the flame of the candle in the Chianti bottle, pushed back the chair, hoisted her rucksack on her shoulder and walked into the night.

03:40AM

JP lay naked on top of the duvet. In the heat, sleep did not come easy. He closed his eyes, tried winding down, but the potent mix of adrenaline and explosives he sniffed on his fingertips kept him tingling. The smell of the burn, of the melting plastic and metal, the smell of the chemicals, like Guy Fawkes, turned him on.

He switched on the Samsung, clicked on his favorite site, Stormfront, where he scanned Best Quotes edited by Eagle Eye, read a comment by one Schweitzer putting it blunt: "*White* the superior, and *they* the inferior!" Clicked around till he found a challenging thread he could pick up on. SnoWhite saying, "I wont eva go with brown boys. Why would any white girl want to?"

JP, on his fancy cell, typed his reply to his kind of gal, his fingers tap-tapping at the keys. He appreciated this sort of intellectual challenge, putting across his opinions out there on the Net: "no ways im in 2 the lartay cupachino nutmeg story or any kind of brown. i like whiter than white simple as that. who cares if im prezident and i fuck up, but if i say i like white chicks liberals ready 2 give my country away 2 hethens r all over me!!"

On YouTube he checked out a classic music video some Stormfront trooper had posted, of Heidi Klum and Seal. So steamy, sexy, even got JP blushing, with Seal black and slick and self-satisfied as a seal sunning itself on the steps in Kalk Bay harbor, Heidi on top of her lover, blonde curls bobbing and tumbling at her breasts as pale as cotton wool. "Heidi," JP said aloud, fingering his cock, "you could have snapped up anyone you wanted, yet you settled for the darkest of nights." To top it, Heidi had hosted a TV show for faggot fashion designers! It hadn't stopped there, from Khloe Kardashian and Lamar to Harry and Meghan. The world had gone nuts! And this sort of mixed-marriage travesty was rife in God's own country! Never mind a proliferation of Caucasian single-mom bleeding-heart lesbians adopting black babies, schlepping them around like designer handbags.

He scanned the White Nationalist News, checking out extremist killings happening worldwide, not only here in his homeland, then logged off, patted himself on the back for being in good company. He jammed earphones in his ears. Found his music. Turned the volume control right up, the band Skrewdriver, yeah, getting his blood pumping. "Tomorrow Belongs To

Me," yeah, the day was coming when the world would indeed belong to the Core, the chosen people it was meant for.

He tickled his balls, stroked his cock, hard with the success of tonight's blast. A good job left him extra horny. A real plus factor, the extra turn-on, was the look of surprise in the ou-toppie security guard's eyes as JP had shot him, those eyes turning dead as glass before he fell apart, blood and pieces flying. Now he fisted his boner turned diamond cutter, jerking off, squirting over the sheets, breathing in the heady mix of adrenaline, explosives, jism.

What a triumph of a night it was!

The future was theirs.

All hail the Core!

The future, indeed, was his! No question!

And he didn't mean the Lord's.

"The future," he hissed, "*is mine!*"

Hate: *n.* a deep, enduring, intense emotion expressing animosity, anger and hostility towards a person, group or object; strong aversion, dislike; an emotion of dislike so strong that it demands action.

PART TWO

WIND AND WATER

SIX MONTHS LATER
THURSDAY: NEW HORIZONS

The first thing Rae Valentine had done once she'd got over the break-up with Anthony Durant after their last supper, the way she thought about it, was trade in the Liquid Bullet self-defense spray she carried in her rucksack on Tony's instructions for some proper fire power.

Everything legit, she'd had the paperwork sorted in record time, the competency form a bit of a stickler, but her contacts on the force—Rex Hawkins and Adrian Lombard—had come in useful, plus their complicity in Tony's predicament had worked to her advantage. She'd settled on a second-hand Colt 1911, an unusual 9mm with the grip of a .45. She turned out to be a crack shot, wielding the handgun with confidence at the gun range. From fifteen meters she could nail a bullet in the black and send home what was left in the magazine through the same hole. Well, almost. Her grouping was accurate, to say the least.

Truth be told, after counseling, after healing, semi-healing, not a day, hardly an hour went by that the attack didn't somehow flash in Rae's mind, the details of the near-rape, the smell of feral aggression, the weight of the man on top of her. It was times like this that she opened the center drawer of the office desk where she let the pistol rest during the work day, and ran her fingers along the cold length of the barrel.

Some days it felt like yesterday. She flinched with

the physical memory of the punches, the pain shooting though her neck, her chest.

...Her face hurt, her head, her back. He grabbed her under the shoulders, dragged her across the threshold into the bedroom. He threw her onto the bed, as the other one pissed on the carpet. The men stared down at her, one thin, in a sweatshirt, waving a gun, the other in a striped polo, the gold hairs on his arms catching the light as he brandished a flick knife. She eased up on her elbows, realizing then he'd slit her T-shirt from waist to neck, sliced through her bra. She cried, "Fuck you," trying to cover her breasts, and she kicked out, snagging his crotch. He grunted and smacked her face, the sting not as terrifying as his breath scorching her ear, his words: "Now you've had it."

She collapsed, her split lip releasing blood in her mouth, the taste of rust. She wanted to scream, scratch out his eyes. But if she was going to get out alive, she'd have to control her rage, her fear. Do whatever they said. She vowed: I'll make it.

He tied her hands.

He placed the flat edge of the blade against her skin. "How lovely."

Heat seared at her breast as he cut her flesh. The blood spurted. He sliced off her denims.

"Well, well, what have we here." He tapped the prosthesis attached just under the knee of her right leg. He pressed the release button on the inside of the knee, gawked as the leg came off. He tossed it down. "It's got red toenails."

"My favorite shade," she croaked.

The knife now on her again, the tip scratching its way above the stump, up her thigh. Helpless, at his mercy, bile rose in her throat.

She heard the front door open.
Tony home early from work.
He called, "Rae?"
The man with the gun said, "We got company."
She pulled up her leg and stump, curled up, protecting herself, but the man with the knife pounded two fist-strikes to her gut.
Gasping, she heard gunfire.
She felt blood on her neck, her body.

Now, she wrapped her hand around the grip of the semi-automatic, lifted it from the drawer, felt the heft of it, and relived the moment she'd sworn to herself she'd never again be as helpless as she had been that day.

"You mess with me"—she played Dirty Harry, aiming at evil—"C'mon, make my day. I'll shoot you right where it matters most."

Rae grabbed the ringing landline, snapped, "What?"

The woman's voice at the other end came over strong, a German accent: throaty, guttural, formal, addressing her as Fraulein.

"Yes, I am still a Fraulein," said Rae. *Not for lack of trying.*

"Is this the correct number? For Durant and Saldana?"

"Durant, Saldana *and* Valentine."

A slight lull before the woman introduced herself as Rosa Dieter. "Your agency has been recommended to me by a friend, a Mrs. Kapinski. I require the services of your Mr. Durant ."

My Mr. Durant? Rae parted her lips in a snarl.

"Are you there, Fraulein?"

"Anthony Durant is tied up with a big case"—his own bloody prosecution—"but you can take your chances with me and my associate, Vincent Saldana."

The woman hesitated for a breath only. "I have an emergency."

"As I mentioned, if you want Anthony, he's not available."

"This Mr. Saldana is the gentleman who was stabbed several months ago in an incident involving poaching in a game park?"

"The very same."

"I read about it in the paper. Poor man. So he is alive?"

"Last time I checked." Just about. If you could call what ex-cop Vince Saldana did *living*. It was more like Vince, now her PI partner, escaped life by being in a perpetual stupor. He was ex-cop on account of life happening all around him: his near death, his early retirement, and she knew from his complaints that he couldn't stop the nightmares. Which cop could. Couldn't stop using alcohol to numb the memories. She didn't condone it, but she understood.

"And are you possibly the Ms. Valentine I've read of? The counselor, the motivational speaker?"

"That's me."

"You're to the point, aren't you, Fraulein? I'm certain you can do the job."

"So how can we help?"

"It's a theft, of a personal nature."

"Yes?"

"Of my jewelry, Fraulein. When can we discuss the details?"

A voice in her head warned: Rae, get out of this business. You're more-or-less a rookie. You'll make a plan, sell time-share or create mosaics or teach yoga, whatever. Another voice countered: take it on, you need this job, the rent is due. You'll do fine.

A time was made, the receiver replaced.

Rae put the Colt back in the drawer, shivered in the cold of the Long Street office. She had to calm down, didn't want to blow any job by letting her anger seep through, had to store her personal hassles in a box, unpack it only when she saw the shrink. It was time for forgiveness. She knew—her anger scared her—she had to forgive herself, let go of her pain. She'd been attacked but it wasn't her fault.

She turned to the window, raised the blinds, looked up at a sky as heavy as new laid cement, then looked down three stories to the wet street below. Normally Long Street was vibey and bohemian, a mix of sophistication and in-your-face Africa, a cross between London and Lagos, New York and Nairobi. But the street was quiet today, the hounded refugees and asylum seekers opting to stay hidden on account of the storms breaking: the bad weather and another spate of hate attacks on anyone labeled "different." All too aware of her own mixed roots she abhorred this fear of the "other" and mourned for Cape Town that couldn't change. She hardly believed this was happening. The panic, the frustration, the misplaced anger of resentful citizens had welled again, the citizens blaming the refugees and asylum seekers, pointing fingers at any foreigner, for stealing jobs and women.

These last few weeks the city was a far cry from the images on commercial postcards, of street parties, beach sunsets, bathing beauties in bikinis, quaint townships and urban game parks—all the fun and sights the city had to offer. Where usually she checked out the mix of locals—admiring the billowing traditional direh dresses of Somali women, their hijabs and head-to-foot jalabees, the Nigerian men's agbada attire of loose pants and long flowing tops—today there was no color, no head-ties, shawls, wrap-skirts or shirts in bright ethnic prints. Today the pedestrian traffic was restricted to men in heavy overcoats and women hoisting umbrellas, heading for inner-city office jobs. Lola's Grill, Mama Africa Café, Zula restaurant and the rest were all closed; no vendors setting up food stands, no comforting smells of borewors and chops cooking on open fires wafted up to her window, no aroma of corn on the cob or fried whitebait.

A short queue of refugees ousted from their township homes by fists, pangas, and bullets, milled outside the Anglican Soup Stop diagonally opposite, some of them reduced to wearing doled-out blankets to shield against the bitter weather. This was the in-your-face tragedy of xenophobia. She couldn't take it, it made her sick, that people treated each other so disdainfully, so dreadfully, without compassion, without recognizing shared humanity.

Like the tides, like the seasons, you knew the cycle of bitterness and violence was repeating, but you hoped that once it had played out, the rainbow, a small miracle, would once again grace the skyline; you hoped that tourists, with their crisp dollars and tele-photo-lens cameras and Hawaiian-print T-shirts, would flock back in summer after the hateful winter was over.

She rubbed her hands, flippin' freezing, the office needed one of those fancy gas heaters. She popped her head through the hole of a wool poncho. Not exactly a fashion item, but warm. Then sat back in the roller chair, rolled up her pant leg, and took off her prosthesis, the prototype her doctor had asked her to try out, the good man raking in the money with limbs he churned out for casualties of Angolan landmines. "For you though, Rae, something more advanced, more versatile, the knee joint and ankle joint have a smoother action." The leg had no calf, just the rod, hardly a beauty, but state-of-the-art. The cold affected her stump. She rubbed it, trying for proper circulation, worked it as she stretched her good leg under Tony Durant's desk, in what was once Tony Durant's office.

The reasons she'd ended up in this hot seat were all due to her pig-headedness induced by self-inflicted guilt. After Tony's arrest, on account of shooting dead the scum who'd violated her, and having his license suspended, he'd needed her to keep the business going while he was stuck in his court case. Sure, his partner, Vince, was back in the picture after *his* recovery, but he was a wreck.

Her volunteer counseling stint at a local drug rehab center could wait. Addiction was going nowhere. For now she felt more than a little obligated to keep Tony's sorry-arsed PI show on the road. She felt the pang still, that he'd dumped her. She hadn't recognized the signs, had resolutely forced herself into what was his home, his life. But despite the humiliation of that last meal, she'd vowed to do her bit.

She'd said, "I'm joining your firm, Tony."

"No, you're not."

"Yes, I am."

"You don't have a PI license."

"I'll get one."

And she'd done just that. Did a one-month online training course and registered with the Security Industry Regulatory Authority. She had no criminal record, only her driver's license fingerprints in the system, and plenty of people vouched for her integrity— yeah, with emphasis on "ex"-addict.

She manned the phones, kept business ticking over. She'd done Google searches, credit checks, mainly inconsequential desk jobs. The sort of cases they could count on were seedy insurance scams and exposing spouses having affairs. Rae'd seen first hand how easily undying love flew out the window when someone better snapped his or her fingers. Hence the various videotapes of fornicating cheaters stacked near the dented filing cabinet along with the crime novels she'd bought at the local second-hand store and read in the off times.

She'd got tips from the best of them. Sue Grafton's Kinsey Millhone the perfect role model. Rae had read as far as *U Is For Undertow*; had noted early on the author and the heroine had both been dumped unceremoniously by their lovers. Anna Blundy's Faith Zanetti was cool; Stephanie Plumb was a hoot. What she'd learned was women sleuths took the bull by the horns. You believed in yourself. You did the job.

She flicked a business card between her fingers: DURANT, SALDANA & VALENTINE — Private Investigators. She slotted the card back in the Carroll Boyes pewter stand in the shape of a naked woman, the ephemera that had cost her a day's pay from a tourist-trap gift shop. But what the hell, she wanted the place to look nice. She'd even bought an Art Deco vase, put flowers in it. Now past their prime, her latest offering, of lilies, drooped. So much for the touch of class.

She'd done other things too. She could still make out the smell of the paint job, and she'd bought a coffee machine, an imported number that did fancy Affogato, Americano, Corretto, Crema, whatever you wanted. No need to order out all the time.

"But once a dump, always a dump," she grumped.

She had to get going, punched speed-dial.

Mrs. Saldana picked up.

"Hey, Mrs. S, how are you? Is your son awake?"

"Vincent? Lazy boy. I get him for you."

She heard his mother call in her sing-song Mandarin accent: "Vincent, you lazy like a vaglant, sleep every day tirr midday...You have too much beer again last night?"

In the thirty years since she'd come from Mainland China and been a South African citizen, Mrs. S had never quite mastered English. As for Vince, she could have called him Hong or Chang or some other Chinese name but here he was, Vincent, the patron saint of wine and vinegar. How appropriate.

"What's up?" His voice was hoarse and he sounded far from charmed. She could just about see him run his fingers through his jet-black mop, scratch his scrotum, bloodshot eyes blinking painfully at daylight; the olive skin, inherited from his fisherman father, would be sallow with booze abuse. Sad to think that before he'd become the better half, which wasn't saying much, of Durant & Saldana, he'd been main-man with the anti-poaching unit, trapping gangsters plundering endangered abalone from the sea, flying to game parks, protecting rhino, doing his bit.

"Gonna see you today, Vince?"

"D'you really need me to come in?"

"We got a call. We haven't worked a proper job in a while. It's time to roll."

"Rae…I had a rough night…"

Vince, like a hamster on a wheel with his drinking problem, like a thousand other PIs before him, had been clean for a couple of weeks, lying in intensive care, till a spunky nurse got taken in by his specific brand of wounded-soldier appeal and more than willingly snuck in booze as therapy. Didn't even disguise it in his IV drip. Colluded to pour alcoholic contents straight down his gullet.

"Thing is, we need to be on the job. Keep our fingers nimble, our minds occupied. So you're coming in."

"Don't snap."

"I'd appreciate the pleasure of your company."

"I'll be there."

"Try not to sound so damn excited."

"Yeah, sure," he groaned through a yawn. "Give me half an hour."

"And shower, okay? I've set up a meeting with a potential client."

"Whatever you say."

"We lost the last client, remember. That chi-chi wife clutching her Dior handbag too tight, and her nose, saying thanks but no thanks 'cos she couldn't stand your BO?"

He was in the middle of asking, "What's up with you?" when she put down the phone.

A walk down to the office from Kloof Street would wake him good and proper. Till he arrived, with time to kill, Rae reached for the remote and switched on the portable TV positioned on the trolley she'd got cheap from Cash Crusaders. She channel-hopped, turning up the volume on the news: "... a foreign-owned shop in Cross Roads was targeted last night by an unknown gang, the owner and his wife and children hacked to death with a panga..." The hate was not about to abate. She switched channels, got the weather: "...with seasonal snow on the Hottentots Holland mountains and heavier than usual rainfall on Table Mountain, Western Cape Rescue is on high alert..." Clips showed frothing oceans, windswept streets, the weather man pointing at the next set of spiked cold fronts approaching from the Arctic. The city, making it through a summer as hot as hell, was now suffering the tail end of a harsh and unforgiving winter.

She switched off. More to life than doom and gloom.

Rae Valentine, well known for getting her breasts slashed, was hardly as respected as the teacher Alison who'd lived to write of how she was hijacked and left for dead at the side of the road, her throat slit, intestines spilled, but as a one-legged ex-druggie who'd hit rock bottom, who'd made a comeback after drug addiction, who'd survived a vicious home invasion, Rae certainly had a story to tell. She'd signed with a publisher for a memoir, a money-spinner. Or so her publishers reckoned it would be. Not that she was doing it for the bucks. The writing was a way to deal with the pain. Right?

Who was she fooling? She'd welcome the cash.

She reattached her bionic leg. Turned back to the task at hand. Took a deep breath. Started the letter the therapist reckoned she should write.

Shrink had said she was ready to *process* what had happened to her, the attack, but especially the mortal wounding of the break-up. As if it would help to stuff her shredded heart back through the mincer—might it come out whole?

God, she could hardly bear doing this.

Dear Tony...
I see you, the way we were, in the garden at the house. I'm in my red bathing cozzie, the one you said was like a second skin. You couldn't take your eyes off me. You couldn't help yourself, pushing up your baggies with your hard-on. You nearly singed yourself there at the braai! And I can smell the yellowtail and the garlic butter you splashed on the fish. I can taste the sauce I licked off you after we were done. I miss you, Doll. Your smile. I want to run my hands through your hair, tug at that pony. I want to wrap myself around you...smooth the muscle at your jaw that tightens every time we make love...show you how much I...

No way. This would not do. She tried a more removed approach:

I pushed you too hard, Tony. Going on 35, I wanted a baby. We women and our biological clocks, right? You were terrified. I didn't see it.

I remember our first meal as if it was yesterday, the fish you fried up, what a feast! And our last dinner at the Italian place, I couldn't have been happier, believing everything would be okay—then you told me it was over.

Her mood turned, from dark to blue, the way it did these days. Unresolved issues will trip you up, the shrink had said, as if she didn't know.

"Insight is the easy part," she reminded herself, spinning now in the roller chair, catching a glimpse of her reflection in the window. She puckered full lips, accentuating her high cheekbones. She was firm, fleshy, strong, her curls pulled back in her customary ponytail; had clear skin. Had lost some kilos since the trauma, but her breasts had stayed a generous size and she had a bum J Lo would approve of.

After the attack, though, Tony had hardly touched her, had treated her as if she was made of porcelain, as if she'd break if he came near her. She couldn't shake the memories, the two of them spooning in bed, his hands cupping her breasts.

"From one day to the next I go from being your lover to part of a business deal?" She addressed Tony's likeness pinned to the corkboard. She threw down the pen. Tore the letter from the pad and balled it into a tight wad.

Aimed. Missed his face. Zero points.

You're driving yourself crazy.

She breathed deep, trying to work through the melancholy.

She punched in his home number on the cell.

His landline rang long.

At last he picked up.

"Hey, Tony?" She bit her lip.

"You want Anthony?" said some sleepy woman's voice. "Just hang on a minute…"

Rae slammed down the phone. She'd recognized the voice, the harsh bark she'd heard commanding attention in court. Tears welled, slipping down, burning her flushed cheeks.

So you're fucking your defense lawyer?

Rae imagined Tony's big hands at the small of Natasha Armstrong's back, pulling her to him, saw his dazzling smile as his mouth came down on hers.

Fuck you, Anthony!

Tony Durant listened to the flat-line of disconnection.

"So what's your ex with the peg-leg have to say?" Natasha Armstrong asked, coming back to the bedroom with coffee.

"Not a thing." He gently replaced the receiver on the cradle and lay back in bed.

He watched Natasha sip the coffee, her eyes hooded. She put the coffee down, and in reverse strip-tease she eased silk stockings over smooth legs, over skin almost blue-white with the veins so close to the surface. She zipped up her true-wool pencil skirt, slipped on a cashmere top, high-heeled pumps. Scraped back dyed-blonde hair from a high forehead, into a chignon. Dressed for success. Natasha was one hot-looking woman in a skinny-model sort of way. Ambitious. Ruthless. A Johannesburg special. LLB suma cum laude from Wits University, plus a string of successful defends to her name.

Their understanding was this was mutually beneficial, nothing more than a casual affair.

Tony was going to keep it that way. Heck, no good ever came of getting close. The way he saw it, you got close, you got burned. Commitment with a capital C was an invitation for grief to come calling. Best to stay on the outside looking in. Best not to have the wife, the cat, the girlfriend.

Rae.

Look how that had turned out.

Even now, six months later, there were moments he could hardly stand being in this bedroom. Though he'd had every centimeter, every crack professionally vacuumed, sprayed, disinfected by crime-scene clean-up with their ammonias and acids, he reckoned if CS techs scanned the room with ultraviolet flashlights, the indelible blood spatters would show blue against the walls, the floor, everywhere. No escaping the stains. Nor the tactile memory of slippery blood on his hands.

Natasha prodded him with the tip of her shoe: "See you in court in a few hours?"

Not a question.

"Prick Moodley's really eeking this out."

"Justice system's at fault. It's a bloody traffic jam." Natasha stretched her thin lips, rolled on gloss, then lined her ice-eyes with kohl.

"It's bloody Moodley tying my cock in knots."

"As long as it unties for me." She sidled close, clutching what was between his legs.

"It's self-defense tarred with the murder brush, that's what it is."

"Of course it is. The posturing is just a game. You'll get through it. You have to ride the ups and downs."

"A six-month roller-coaster ride?"

"You're lucky it's not longer. Let's hope this time we can get the charges dropped."

She leaned over him as he lay back against the

wooden headboard of the new king-sized bed, kissed him full on the mouth, lingered there. Then pulled back, leaving the odd mix of coffee, spearmint toothpaste and the smack of sticky gloss on his lips.

"Be on time for a change, and keep your cool. Oh and Tony," she looked at him, "two things. Blow-dry your hair. If you insist on sporting a hairdo worn with pride by an out-of-date hippy, at least try to tame it. No hair hanging in your face. Hardly creates a good first impression. And that orange jacket looks tatty. Time to go shopping." She picked up her black briefcase with the gold trim and combination lock and left the bedroom without looking back. All business. The way it suited him. Even when it came to sex she was to the point. Natasha loved a quickie, was emotionally removed, sex was exercise, a release, a convenience.

As soon as he heard the door slam, he got up, shivering, quickly drew on trackpants over his Superman boxer shorts, a gift from Rae. Put on a sweatshirt. In the kitchen he scrambled for a spliff at the back of the knife drawer. None ready, he got out the Rizla plus a baggie, in it the buds crushed to a decent texture. Pushing the mix into the paper, he rolled the joint, licked the edges of the paper, sealed the seam. Lit up. Dragged hard. Sighed deep. Exited to the front stoep where the winter chill slapped him in the face. He kicked at the weeds splitting the slasto paving. The "for sale" sign rattled on the gate as the wind whipped. He'd committed to one sole-mandate after another; now the sale was an estate agent's free for all and still no takers. He couldn't stand living in this house. This house that was once supposed to be their house. His home, Rae's home.

His cellphone vibrated in his pants pocket.

A "please call me" from a new doctor, an intern at Groote Schuur Hospital. One right weirdo who hid in the hospital museum in his spare time "to relax" he said, to get away from the mayhem of the trauma ward, preferring to hang out with jars packed with pickled eyeballs, slivers of heart, lung, liver, whole fetuses in ethanol.

Tony called back. "So what can I do you for?"

"D'you have something a wee bit stronger, something that not only smooths the edges but keeps me going?"

"You're changing your order?"

"I need more. Add Dexies or Bennies, all hell's broken loose here."

The good doctor was turning out to be a serious addict.

"See what you can do for me."

"I can understand working ER must have knife edges but I'm not really into that line."

"I'm on shift for the next thirty-six hours."

"Non-stop?"

"You said it. And it's extra fun here with the non-stop commotion. Knife wounds, gunshot, axe-slashes. The life of a trauma surgeon. I need my stuff."

"Right then." Tony disconnected. His new client for sure a little too needy for his liking, but what the hell. No judgment. You had a shit job, you got desperate. He simply supplied the remedy. If it wasn't for this delivery business handed over as a gift from a grateful politician some years back, and his growing list of clients needing help at all times of day or night—a little dagga, maybe a little E to keep them sane—he'd be on shit street trying to keep up the mortgage payments on this house he no longer wanted.

He let his favorite regular, Sarah, know he'd drop off her order too.

She texted back: *Much appreciated. Till next, Anthony.*

He liked her, a professor of classical whatever, polite to a T. Coming across ladylike even when she met him at the door in her housecoat, her gray hair loose on her shoulders, like she was saying *take it or leave it, this is who I am*. It amused him, the way she, every time, gave him a quick peck on the cheek when he took his leave. He'd catch her another fish at some stage. If he ever again sailed the *Aunt Mary*. Seemed like a hundred years ago since he last went fishing on his beloved boat. He felt the pang at his heart and sucked deep, pulling Durban Poison way down into his lungs.

Back inside, he hauled his bones over to the CD player. Wavered over Springsteen, Cash or Cohen. Lying on the new couch, a cheap Furniture City special, he listened instead, for old time's sake, to one of Rae's CDs, Joni Mitchell singing about hating and loving someone.

He rubbed his face, felt the two-day stubble. At last squashed the life from the roach in an abalone shell ashtray, wondering what mother-of-pearl had ever done to deserve such a fate.

He shaved. Showered. Washed the melancholy from every crevice of his body. Tried to, at least.

He slotted *Blood Sweat And Tears* in the boom box, perked up with "Spinning Wheel" as he dressed in neat chinos with boots, a crisp white shirt straight from Bubbles Laundromat. Yeah, talking about your troubles was a crying sin all right. Tony checked himself in the mirror. Squeezed Eyegene into his bloodshot whites. Slicked back his crowning glory, which looked fine to him, maybe a little frizzy at the temples, and the split ends needed a trim, but not something he cared to do a thing about. Then he pulled on his burnt-orange jacket. Natasha had no idea the color inspired confidence.

If you could face the day, this was about as good a start as you could get.

"Heck," he chirped. "I feel better already."

※

I ride and I ride...

She rode the swivel chair. Damn thing would break in half one of these days.

Didn't people have jobs to go to, criminals to pander to?

Tony and *that woman* sounded as if they were cuddling in bed, if Natasha was capable of any tenderness.

"How stupid can you get, Rae?" With her good foot she kicked the desk. Fuckit, she was stuck in this business when she was supposed to be counseling, and had a commitment to get on with her memoir; she knew the PI stuff was a distraction from looking closer at herself. Knowing herself. She stared at the phone, half-expecting, half-hoping Tony might call back. But it wasn't about to happen. She ordered coffee plus a selection of Danish delights from the downstairs deli; would keep down the feelings with pastry.

Twenty minutes later, some filing done, the intercom tinkled.

Rae buzzed in the waiter in his branded black shirt, with the cappuccino and treats and a double espresso.

"Don't you guys ever use your machine?" He eyed the Jura.

"Forgot to buy coffee. Besides, old habits die hard." She scrawled her X on the bill.

"Oh, Miz V, about this. The manager wants to know when you're gonna settle your tab."

She stared him down as he turned and scooted towards the door. Cute guy. Corn-row braids and big white teeth, tight buttocks on him, held in denims.

She pushed herself up, adjusted the blind. Cold light cut through the slats. In the background was Table Mountain obscured by menacing cloud as dark as her mood; in the foreground the wind chased trash down Long Street. She turned back to watching TV rather than doing the filing—jeez, it could wait—relaxed again in the chair, channel-hopped with the remote, settled on a true-crime retrospective featuring the Bladerunner, handicapped South African sportsman Oscar Pistorius. Guy'd had both legs amputated before he could crawl. For him legless was normal. Here he was in the doccie, streaking to one of the countless victories of his career, winning gold on gold every chance he got, at every competition, in every country. He'd even managed a silver at the able-bodied Olympics before he ended up in a crowded cell for shooting his girlfriend, Reeva.

"Another fallen hero," said Vince, stepping through the doorway.

"Drink." She handed him the cooling coffee. "Wake up good and proper for our meeting. At least you look half decent." Today he passed muster. He'd cleaned up nicely, was good-looking, with his half-Chinese half-brown genetics, was lean, taut and lithe on his feet. In his chinos, he too had a tight butt on him. Involuntary pleasure played at Rae's lips.

"So you're in a better mood?" Vince slumped in his chair, sipped at the coffee.

She noticed the subtle tremble of his fingers. "Show must go on."

"Queen."

"Don't you start." It was catchy, Tony's trick, teasing out lyrics as a guessing game. "We have to work, that's the bottom line."

"So long as the client's not another hormonal wife

with menopausal delusions. I'm not gonna follow around some browbeaten hubby like you got me to do the last time, week after week, only to have you recommend the wife go see her GP for hormone replacement therapy."

"We do whatever it takes to pay the bills."

"Like that crazy woman paid the bills?"

"Lay off, Vince, my mood hasn't improved *that* much."

He shot her a look. "You missing Tony?" He reached out, touched her arm. "Me too."

She drew back. Truth was there wasn't an hour of the day the state of her personal affairs didn't gnaw at her soul with razor-sharp teeth.

He knocked back the espresso now less than lukewarm. "Maybe you'll still get it together."

"When hell freezes into a winter wonderland."

Aware again of her anger seething under the surface, she turned from Vince before saying something she'd truly be sorry for. As far as she was concerned, Anthony Durant should get on his knees in gratitude that she was in this with him. As for Vince, he couldn't organize a piss-up in a brewery. He couldn't before, now it was worse. Both men should get on their knees.

Vince sighed, "So what's our case then?"

She turned back to him, her voice steady. "Some German aunty's jewels have been nicked."

"How'd you know she's a Kraut?"

"Accent. And she kept calling me Fraulein."

"Sounds like a character from a crime novel."

"Vince, that your ex-cop skepticism talking? Hey, I can still smell the booze on you," Rae warned, putting an end to the conversation. "Here…" She tossed over a pack of Chiclets, grabbed her army jacket, headed for the door. "Chew half a pack of those and maybe Rosa Dieter won't notice your breath. Maybe, just maybe, we'll make us some money for a change."

They took the three flights of rickety stairs to the ground floor. Vince tripping down, Rae following slowly, her limp pronounced as she took every step with care.

⚜

Sitting comfy in Rae's beloved almost brand-new Jeep, a demo vehicle she'd got discounted off the floor and had a mechanic friend customize, moving the accelerator to the left of the break to suit her leg, Vince asked, "So, where to?"

A terse: "Sea Point."

Five minutes later they were heading towards one of Cape Town's elite suburbs, a short drive from the Central Business District, along the outward bound boulevard.

Vince saw heavy cloud, over the neck between Lion's Head and Signal Hill, now cascading fast and furious over the slopes and apartments and fancy mansions of the Atlantic seaboard west of the city. While Rae parked, he checked out the wild sea rolling in with a vengeance, wave on wave of murky green-gray topped with scum, breaking over the promenade. He whistled. "Concrete's being washed away like it's made of sand."

The sheer force of the stormy ocean had lifted chunks of the retaining wall, plus dislodged a stretch of aluminium railing. Yellow tape was strung at the site and signs erected warning joggers and dog-walkers of dangerous gaps.

"You've seen tsunami footage," said Rae. "That's the sea for you…"

"…a monster, rising, undulating…"

"Keep your epithets to yourself, Vince."

"Huh? What's an epithet, Rae?"

"Let's just get there, okay?"

Rae secured the gear lock, climbed out of the Jeep, leaving the cubbyhole empty and open, and clicked the central locking. She'd parked across two spots on Beach Road.

"You're overcautious, Rae."

"She's my baby." She felt more than a pang of guilt at conceding that men might be better reverse parkers. "I don't want some incompetent princess banging right into her paintwork."

She pushed a strand of wet hair back from her forehead, caught Vince in the act of checking her out. "Windswept and lovely enough for you, PI Saldana?"

"You always look great to me, Rae. I can look, right."

She felt the spray on her face, sniffed the sea air, the refreshing smell of ozone, through a nose as cold as a dead relationship. She pulled her army jacket tightly around her body, but still the wind cut through, chilling her to the marrow, as they made their way past what was left of the three-meter wide retaining wall.

Vince took her elbow, steadying her against the elements. "Mother Nature's making her point."

They struggled against the wind, the rubbish blowing past their ankles into gutters; branches and the contents of bins blown over, even seaweed had been swept into the street.

"Thanks, Vince, weather's bracing."

"Your attempt at gratitude?" His voice rose as a gust masked his words.

"Hoping for blessings in return."

"This the place?"

"48 Beach Road."

The single-story Edwardian, one of the last of the original homes on the strip, was set back, with a tidy garden out front and a Norfolk pine at the gate.

"A house, whaddaya know."

"Unusual for the condo strip."

Every which way was luxury; Green Point and Mouille Point one way, Bantry Bay and Fresnaye the other; and inbetween Sea Point's high-rise apartment blocks with ground-floor shops and restaurants. All of it spelled progress, wealth, sophistication; here if you picked your venue right you'd see the likes of Charlize, Kanye, Taylor or Halle.

Vince pushed open the gate, pressed the brass bell, said, "Not much security. Sure sign it's a geriatric living in hope till the last. Then some developer's gonna earn millions sticking a fancy block of flats on this land once the house is flattened. Must be worth some dosh. Let's hope Mrs. Germany's loaded."

"Would make a difference for a change. But assets don't always translate into hard cash."

"Which is what we need to be paid, right, Rae? No feeling sorry for the old bird."

"Just remember, make nice with our client, Vince. You're not a cop on duty and this isn't an interrogation."

"Yes, Ma'am."

Rosa Dieter—spruce, lean, straight as a plank, in a chic ensemble of snazzy navy Chanel skirt and jacket with a cream blouse buttoned high—opened the door and ushered them out of the wind. Her outfit, deceptively simple, spelled money. Her hairdo, a Cruella de Vil style, dead black, streaked with white, and sprayed in place, framed her face plump with the firmness of a much younger woman. Her style hinted at a core of steel, a life of order.

"Willkommen." Frau Dieter drew back meager lips painted crimson, stretched them across her pearly white dentures. Maybe implants. She held out her hand, Rae keeping in check a twitch of revulsion as Rosa drew back her scratchy grip.

"Come," Frau Dieter ordered, leading them down the passage like a pair of trusting puppies.

Rae made a quick assessment. The house looked in good nick, had high ceilings, wooden floors. Trapped in a time warp, the furnishings were ball-and-claw imbuia and stinkwood, the drapes heavy brocade; the smell of the place a combination of boiled kale and suffocating potpourri.

Ushering them into the dining room, Mrs. Dieter pointed towards a set of upholstered straight-backed chairs at a table laid for guests.

"Tea." She poured the brew dark as coffee. "Biscuits. Help yourself." In the flesh her German accent was less pronounced.

They drank politely.

Rae broke an awkward silence: "So what can we do for you, Mrs. Dieter? You mentioned a theft of valuable personal items?"

From her briefcase Rae fished out her notebook, jotted notes as Frau Dieter talked, ensuring a check list to go back to. She'd studied the PI profile in detail. In general PIs invariably had briefcases, notebooks and pens on hand—and Kinsey Millhone had cards.

"Tell me, Fraulein," said Rosa Dieter, "at my stage of life what good are magnificent baubles like a noose around my neck? All they are is a connection to a past I don't want to think about. Did you know in Europe displays of ostentatious wealth are considered poor taste? As for South Africa, wearing expensive jewelry is an invitation to be violated." She shuddered. "A gold chain is a death sentence. They will throw me down in the parking garage and cut my throat for it. So I said to my jeweler, to Sol Anderson, if the price is right, sell." She stopped short, a dream-like stare in her eyes as if looking into the future, or the distant past perhaps, who could tell?

"Ah...And then?" prompted Rae. *Keep asking questions*, the basics of detective work.

"My son delivered the jewelry."

"Your son?"

"Heinz Werner. I wasn't well. I empty the safe deposit box. Heinz takes the jewels to Sol. Heinz shows me the receipt. Then I wait for the money. Sol does not call, so several days later I phone Sol. He begins to cry like a child. Tells me something terrible has happened."

"Let's guess. It's all gone?" said Vince, ignoring Rae's glare and a sharp kick to his ankle.

"I want them back. My mother's diamond solitaire, also a sapphire ring of the most royal blue. The jewelry is my security blanket."

"That so?" Vincent put his stale Lemon Cream back on the plate.

"Pieces of enormous sentimental worth are *missing*, and a gift from my father—" snapped Rosa Dieter "—uncut stones of great value."

"Uncut stones?" Now she had Vince's attention.

"A handful of valuable stones my father hid from the Nazis." Rosa Dieter leaned into Vince's personal space. "He worked with a diamond merchant in Hamburg before the war."

Vince drew back from the sour smell of her breath, from the squinty eyes.

"How many stones?" asked Rae, her pencil poised above the notepad.

"Around thirty. I kept them in a velvet bag."

"A velvet bag?" Vince raised an eyebrow. "And

you don't know the number precisely and you don't have insurance, is that right?"

"The cost of insurance these days is like throwing money down the drain. There is no way a woman of limited means can keep up insurance."

Limited means? He wasn't too sure about that. Vincent pushed, "What about this Sol Anderson? Surely his shop is insured?"

"I told you," she clucked. "The man is extremely upset, although he says not to worry. You talk to Sol. Find out what's going on. Find my jewelry."

She sipped her tea, her pinkie flexed.

Vince looked up, blinked, asked, "Have you at least been to the police?"

"What can they do?"

"The police should know."

"Will they care?"

"There can be no justice if no one reports crime."

"What good are the police? You tell me."

Vince sighed, stood up, asked, "Boy's room down that way?"

As he disappeared down the passage, Rosa Dieter looked directly into Rae's eyes. "I prefer working with women, Ms. Valentine. Women mean what they say and they get the job done. Men spoil everything with their testosterone." She leaned forward, hissed, "When the thing between their legs gets hard, their brain"—she tapped her temple—"goes soft."

Taken aback, Rae twittered: "My mother always used to say, if it's got tires or testicles, it's guaranteed to give you trouble."

Rosa Dieter patted Rae's hand. "I definitely want you on the job."

"There's the matter of the fee."

"Cash is the way you private investigators prefer it, isn't it so?"

"Six-hundred an hour, plus costs." Hell yes, bucks had to be made. "All invoices submitted at the end of each week."

"I've read a detective novel or two in my life," sniffed Rosa Dieter. "See how far this will take you." She got up and went to a roll-top desk in the corner, another expensive-looking antique. She handed over a wad of newly minted hundred-rand notes pinned with a paper clip.

Rae counted, made out the receipt for five thou, thinking Frau Dieter had obviously not read the right kind of detective novels. Where would this insignificant contribution get them? They'd better work fast... She stashed the cash before Vince made re-entry.

"And we need a precise list of the stolen items, Mrs. Dieter, and the receipt from the shop you talk of."

"Sol Anderson and my son will help you there."

The partners sprinted through a belting downpour.

"Here, use this to dry yourself." Rae tossed Vince a hand towel. "Don't get my seats wet."

As she fired up the engine, Vince turned on the heater, adjusted the blast of warmth to his feet and torso, said, "That was a waste of time."

"How come you say that?"

"Jesus, Rae, give me some bloody credit here. You forget conveniently I was a cop. The theft, the stones, it's not legit."

They drove in silence, the only sound the rain on the roof of the car, the swish-swish of the windscreen wipers, before Rae said, "We're taking the job."

"No way."

"We have to do this."

"Mrs. Germany's a nutcase."

"Her money's green, that's all that counts. And it's

in my briefcase."

"What!"

"A done deal, Vince."

"There's something screwy there, believe me. I checked out the house when I went loo-ways and every single door was locked. Either she didn't trust us or the mom and son don't much trust each other."

"Take this seriously, please, will you, Vince?"

"My bet is the only jewels are probably cheap diamanté paste hidden under big beige panties in the top drawer of the old frau's dressing table. And if jewelry's dinkum been nicked it's probably in some fat cat's safe in Khayelitsha by now. Or it's been melted down, sold for the limited value of the metal. What's the use?"

"Come on, Vince—"

"The Case of the Missing Stones—like the title of a Tin-Tin comic."

"—go easy on the cynicism."

"Thing is, Rae, you can walk into a jeweler's shop with a big rock in your pocket and you can get cash for it, walk away and never look back, simple as that. Or get rid of it over the Net. Check it out"—he held out his Sony—"right there on Alibaba.com. Open Sesame, you can buy or sell whatever you want. In three seconds there's diamond agents, diamond dealers, suppliers, sellers, buyers, from Cape Town to Cameroon, Hong Kong, India, Vietnam, Armenia, wherever you look there's a market. And every site has a community: Forums, Ask It, Price Watch. Plus a measure of 'I got screwed' stories. This is one of those. Maybe Rosa Dieter got screwed, bet is *we're* gonna get screwed."

"She may not be entirely traditional, Vince, but I can't see Frau Dieter pulling out an iPhone and selling anything on line. Let's just see where this takes us."

"Fair pay, fair job, fair conscience, is that it?"

"As always."

"No fair conscience this time," he sighed. "What about those hands? Like props for a B-grade horror movie."

"Whatever happened, it's not pretty."

On her right a criss-cross of faded scars marked Rosa Dieter's knuckles, the last joint amputated off the fourth finger. On the left, two fingers were gone, the ring and the pinkie sheared off at the second joints, the lumps white and deformed, but all intact arthritic fingers were tipped in sharp nails lacquered with a glossy turquoise varnish, a nod to a streak of youthful spunk left in her.

"At least she has a pinkie intact to flex while she's drinking tea."

"Vince," said Rae, "where's your compassion?"

Truth be told, Vince had no compassion, no energy, no nothing. What he wanted was to flop down on his bed. Stare at memories of boyhood and be comforted.

A roll of thunder split the sky, a flash of light illuminating the skyscrapers, dulling the neon signs. He turned up the heat, hunched near the blast of hot air. "We gonna bring Tony in on this one, Rae?"

"What're you asking?" Her voice cracked.

"We're partners, or supposed to be, that's what partners do. Keep each other abreast of what's happening."

"You echo my sentiments exactly. Problem is, where the hell is Tony these days? Either at court or pomping his slutty defense-attorney chick."

"Okay, okay, I get your point. Slow down, will you? Roads're dangerous in this rain."

Rae paid no heed, skidding to an abrupt stop outside the Hot Wok in Kloof Street. "I don't owe Anthony Durant a damned thing."

"Okay, let it go already."

"All these months," she sighed, "that's what I've been trying to do. So if you bring him into the conversation, I'll kick him right out again. *You* won't let me down, will you, Vince?"

"No, I won't let you down. Though you know as well as I do this job's a fucking dead end."

She tore a page from the notebook. "Here."

He took the scrap from her outstretched hand, Heinz Werner Dieter's cell number scrawled there in Rosa Dieter's spidery script.

"Go see the son, Vince."

"Yeah, yeah, what's one more lousy interview? One more dysfunctional family. I'll talk to whoever you want me to, a son, a pet goldfish, whatever. But I don't trust Mrs. Germany. Cops know when they're being scammed."

She ignored his wisdom. "Just don't blow it, okay?"

"What's to blow? We're doing it by the book, your book."

She swung a U-turn. The Jeep had a small turning circle and she handled it like a pro. In her rearview mirror, as she drove off, she spied Vincent, saw him stop at the door to his mother's take-away restaurant, the Hot Wok, hesitate momentarily, then pirouette on his heels, pull the collar of his denim jacket up at his neck to protect against the driving rain. Saw him hail a minibus, watched as he assisted a mama into the taxi then squashed in alongside her. Rae knew he was off to Roeland Street, to the Kimberley Hotel, to the sleazy bar recently renamed Deon's Pub and Bistro for the fancy factor.

"Vincent, you bloody soak."

If ever there was a nuclear explosion, it'd be the cockroaches and Deon's patrons who'd survive, so well pickled were they. She shifted into third, then second, stop-starting down the hill congested with cars, trucks, buses, taxis straining on the slick streets. This job had to work out. She wasn't about to go so far as to use an iota of her compensation money to save the firm.

She forked out a ten-rand note for a damp *Cape Times,* locally known as the *Cape Crimes*, from a street vendor clad in a makeshift raincoat of black plastic refuse bags.

The newspaper was full of it; the heavy cloud over the Mother City meant more rain, wind, floods; and of the misery of refugees caught in a double bind, a cold, mean-hearted city.

She thought of Frau Dieter's mangled hands. She thought of her own disability hidden under her pant leg. The amputation had been a turning point, she'd come to realize that she had to change, had to stop hurting people, and herself, that as she lay in hospital, about to lose part of her, she knew for certain she'd make a comeback.

Using bluetooth she punched in Sol Anderson's number on the dash.

No answer.

Life was cruel. And seldom fair.

Vincent Saldana stood outside the Hot Wok for about four seconds, weighing up facing his Ma or heading to the bar. Kimberley or Ma. Ma or Kimberley. Got a glimpse of the long afternoon stretching ahead and decided no contest. It had to be the Kimberley. "Just"— he promised aloud—"for one brewski."

He'd been living at the Hot Wok for months now, had moved back in with his mother, into the flat above the takeaway and restaurant. After his father's fishing boat was lost at sea, what felt like a hundred years ago when he was a kid, his mom had opened the five-table restaurant and takeaway that had stayed a five-table place, and her sheer guts had kept the Hot Wok going. Last week she'd redone the décor, had red tablecloths now, and candles, and little pots of Chinese umbrellas as a cute touch.

His ma had said, "This will arways be your home."

But he had no home.

Amber was dead.

He sidestepped two destitute women wrapped in sodden blankets, standing under cover of a shop front with their parcels and boxes and sad eyes, a resignation he recognized from staring at himself in the bathroom mirror. That life wasn't about to get any better. All he wanted now was to get to the damn pub, to drink, to obliterate every thought in his head.

"You've peeled off how many labels, Vince?" The barman slid another Castle down the counter.

Oh yeah, a brewski or two chased by a Springbokkie, the crème de menthe and amarula liqueur mix sweet on the tongue, helped Vince Saldana feel he could face what was left of the day.

"You have to move on sometime, Vincent."

Vince checked out the beer labels he'd torn and ripped into confetti, next to the empty bowl of peanuts. "This supposed to mean I'm sexually frustrated or what?"

"She wouldn't want you to be like this."

"Yeah, sure." He and Amber had talked about hopes and dreams, of having kids, like couples do. He said the first one would be a belly dancer. Just like her mother. She said it'd be a boy and he'd be a cop like his dad. "She was proud of me, y'know?" All that crap they'd talked about, how the child would be a chip off the old block, dressing up in jingly bells and pink tutus if it was a girl, shooting water pistols if it was a boy.

There is no Amber. Never will be kids.

He ached for Amber and he missed his job with the anti-poaching unit.

...In his mind's eye he saw the road-block, saw himself approach the back of the freezer van, pistol out. He gave the order to open. The van was full of bags of the shells, of the endangered abalone, the sea snail, the ear-shaped spiral, with its iridescent interior, the haul destined for Chinese markets where, in weight, it was worth more than gold.

He slapped cuffs on the men driving the van, the work horses, the lackeys, knowing the prize was the gang leader supplying direct to China where men who wanted stiff dicks would pay top dollar for powdered abalone to get them in a sexy mood.

He liked to think it was his father's fisherman's blood that kept him caring about the sea...

"How can I move on?"

He didn't want to move on.

Was forced to move by Rae, on inconsequential jobs.

He pulled his cellphone from his chinos. Hesitated. Played Knot Fun, but hell it was too complex. Tried Candy Crush, but the reward of those slick sweets couldn't keep him interested.

The Dieter case for sure was some sort of con. Another of Rae's nut-job old ladies, stringing them along till the dame told the truth about *really* wanting Rae Valentine to chat about her upcoming memoir at some Third Age book club. *Give us all the juicy details puhleeze, of your life doing drugs and what happened next.* Women were supposed to have a sixth sense about these things. "Where's your bloody instinct,

Rae?" He burped into his hand, the pungent blast briefly sobering.

He moved away from the bar, slumped in a stall, worked his tongue in his mouth to get it working, punched in the number printed on the scrap. What else was there to do?

Drink more Castle. He signaled for another.

A voice answered: "Heinz Dieter."

Vince sat straighter, kept his tone interested, professional: "Mr. Dieter, name's Vincent Saldana. I'm a private investigator working for your mother..."

"My mother?"

"Mrs. Rosa Dieter, I believe?"

"You're a private investigator?"

Like the guy was taken by surprise. So far none of his mother's German accent coming through. Just his name hinting at his ancestry.

"What's this about?"

"Your mother's asked us to look into the theft of her jewelry."

No response.

"You there, Mr. Dieter?"

"Yes, yes. Of course. Most unfortunate, this whole affair. When shall we meet? Can you make it now?"

Rae's rule book called for face-to-face, read-the-body-language shit.

In this bloody weather?

Stuff that. No way.

Rae might have his balls for breakfast if he didn't pitch for a full-on interview, but hell, who was the ex-cop here? Who knew a thing or two that didn't come from crime novels? He could handle this with his eyes closed.

"Let's see what we can do over the phone," he said, not giving the guy a chance to object, going straight into the preamble: "Have to get on to this right away.

I'm needing to confirm as much background as I can. You never know what details count when you're looking at the bigger picture."

"Yes, yes, certainly." The voice came across as strong, sonorous, but the words were guarded, hesitant. "I understand. Just a moment." Vince heard Heinz Dieter talking to someone butting in on his end: "Yes, yes, give me five minutes." Then the squeak and click of a closing door, and a quieter atmosphere.

"Go ahead, Mr. Saldana."

"Your mother's what, early seventies?"

"Actually on the wrong side of three quarters of a century," Heinz Dieter said, "which she insists is the new middle age. Pensioners these days know how to get what they want from life. Isn't it commendable?"

"Your mother says you handed certain items over to a jeweler, one Sol Anderson, is that right?"

"She asked me to deliver them. She had just had her eyelids lifted. You know how women are, too vain to leave the house with dressings on their scars."

Was why-for Mrs. Germany's features looked tight as plastic. What more? Botox, liposuction, implants? This was sounding better and better. A geriatric living a fantasy. Evading aging and death, as if that was possible.

"My dilemma," said Heinz, "is that my mother, whether she admits it or not, won't hear a word about getting on in years. She makes decisions without consultation. Certainly not with me. And more often than not her ill-conceived plans backfire. I won't be surprised if she wanted cash to fund some or other wild adventure. Investing on the stock exchange for instant wealth, or booking a cruise believing she'll meet the man of her dreams."

"She looking for love?"

"Companionship, she says."

"You think some gigolo type's taken her for a ride?" Heinz Dieter sounded agitated enough to believe it. "Pushed to get his hands on her cash maybe?"

"She's independent. A force to be reckoned with. She's always saved, made sure there's money for her old age. Now she lets it leak though her fingers like rain. I'm concerned, Mr. Saldana. She could live another ten, fifteen years, God willing, and she's diminishing her assets. Look, she's entitled to do what she wants, but it seems to me as if her judgment is clouded. I have a job, I can't focus all my attention on her. I can't force her to stay home. It's her life, but I won't be shocked if you tell me there's a man involved."

"Any possibility it's the jeweler she's romancing?"

"Sol Anderson? Nothing surprises me anymore. But, no. We trust him. A con man preying on a misguided pensioner is more likely."

Vince registered a drawn-out sigh. A son at his wits' end. Vince not near pissed enough to miss the edge of disapproval. Mommy was doing her own thing and Heinz was less than happy about it.

"Bottom line is, you're confirming the missing items, right?"

"I tried to convince her not to sell, but she wouldn't hear a word. I gave the box to Sol right in his hands. He went through the pieces, listed them as I watched. He signed a receipt. Now the consignment's been stolen right from under his nose."

"She...your mother mentioned uncut diamonds."

"Stones? Yes." A hesitation. "Her collection is worth a small fortune, I can assure you. Two dozen or so stones. Plus the rings, brooches, several other items. Tell me, is there actually a possibility of finding any of it?"

"If the items can be recognized, if we can trace them somehow, then maybe."

The truth, Vince thought, *even if this story's kosher? None whatsoever.*

"Thanks for your input, Mr. Dieter."

Vince disconnected.

Maybe Mrs. Germany was just another victim of brazen robbery, in whatever way it had happened, like two thirds of the good citizens out there. Some would argue three thirds. But his first bet still stood. That she'd hidden the paste, if it existed at all, in the toes of her stockings, and she and the shop owner and maybe the son had concocted some sort of ploy, whatever it was.

He mumbled to himself, "You gotta get off your backside after all, Vince."

What he wanted was another beer.

"Gotta cut down," he said aloud, pinching a role of fat at his gut. "Gotta get back into the habit of love, life, and everything else." He caught the barman's eye. "Deon, one more."

That's it, boykie, one for the road.

He doled out cash for his sixth Castle.

But who's counting?

Late Thursday afternoon her therapist's office was warm, womb-like, Rae felt safe, though the Gustav Klimt print on the wall, *The Wedding—so beautiful, so full of whimsy*—tugged at her heartstrings.

Her shrink was a neutral sort of man with neutral looks: brown hair, deep-set eyes she couldn't quite figure the color of; he let her talk, he nodded at the right intervals, was overall the rare kind of mental-health pro who genuinely tuned in and listened to every word, aware of every nuance.

"You could fool just about anybody with that leg,"

he said, not for the first time.

He waited as she settled, a little too tentatively today, the leg giving trouble in the cold, the slight swivel of her left hip giving the game away.

"You know, when I tell people I'm an amputee, they're usually more shocked and upset than I am over the whole deal. Really, I've got over it. Though I do have good leg days and bad leg days." Rae tossed her hair, crossing one ankle over the other.

She pulled a folded sheaf of paper from her rucksack beside her on the couch.

"The letter didn't work. Then I tried making the list you suggested."

"Would you like to share what's on it?"

She unfolded the foolscap page, started reading out loud: "*I miss your smile.* That's always at the top of the list. It's true. He smiled and I melted. *I miss the way you kissed me, so tender.*"

"What else?"

"*Your tolerance, your loyalty.* Then again where'd that evaporate to?"

"So what *don't* you miss?"

"I was duped. I let him see into my soul. I let my guard slip. I don't want to live with walls. I honestly thought he wanted me to move in with him. That we'd have this wonderful partnership, that we'd be a family, have a family. I was so deluded I convinced myself we wanted the same thing."

"Things change, don't they?"

"Do they change that much?"

"Sometimes."

"So you're saying?"

"*Your* smile is pretty stunning too."

"You flirting with me, Doc?"

"I'm reminding you that you've got a lot going for you."

"Thing with women, Doc, is we're always looking on the inside to see what it is we did wrong. Hell, not any more."

He nodded. "How's your memoir coming along?"

"Mulling things over in my mind. I want to inspire! With honesty, you know?"

"That's positive."

"It's on hold, though, I'm on a case." She'd have to get on with it, reflect on her life, on what she'd learned, but right now she couldn't quite confess she'd hardly written a page.

"Oh yes? You up for it?"

"Have to be. Need the bucks. I already spent the advance the publishers forwarded. Put the advance and a chunk of the compensation money, you know, the blood money, from the asset-forfeiture deal, from selling the scumbag gangster's flat"—*the crim who'd cut her, sliced her, the filth who'd soiled her dignity*— "towards paying for my Jeep, and I ordered a new couch."

"I'm glad you treated yourself."

"Suede, in blue. Soft to the touch."

"Like Elvis."

She laughed. "Now I just *have* to write the damn book."

This was life, paradox and contradiction.

Back at the Long Street office, Rae detached her prosthesis. Rolled off the sock, massaged the stump, admitting to herself the negatives of this state-of-the-art bionic model. A state-of-the-art pain in the leg with all the techno problems she was going through fine-tuning the wearing of it. The chaffing had to do mostly with the cold, she reckoned, rubbing the tender stump on the inside of her knee, where it hurt most. She'd been through a few models since her first government-issue fibreglass and resin leg. She'd had no medical aid at the time of the amputation and under the circumstances, mom and dad weren't ready to fork out for anything better. But that old leg had charm, with it's shapely calf in skin-tone silicone. This new one had great mobility, and she raved about the sophisticated joint at the ankle which made the foot more mobile.

But still she limped.

She got comfy on Tony's chair.

"Time to get your own chair, Rae." Maybe get an upholstered armchair for the slow times, the fiction-gorging times. When the money rolled in, she'd buy an IKEA kit, chair and shelves, nothing too fancy, but easy to assemble, easy on the eye and practical.

She checked the answering service. Niks. Tried calling Sol Anderson's shop once more. No answer. Likewise on the cell. Left a message: "If you could please get back to me as soon as possible I'd appreciate it."

She switched on the computer. Checked email. Sixteen new incomings, bang bang bang.

Blue pills will help your lifelong fiesta of sexy fun.
Hey, hot man, wet woman is waiting for you!
No need to have small wiener!

Delete, delete, delete.

"Ag shame. Poor men with their special needs."

Next, she made a couple of Internet payments: rent, Telkom, the plumber's bill for unblocking the toilet down the hall, the Victorian number with a pull-chain and the stench of urine coming at her whenever she dared go in there. Couldn't Vince, or Mandla from the next-door office, bloody aim straight?

She re-invoiced bad debts. She hated to admit it, but the firm would never see the money. "You're right, Vince," she said aloud, "gotta be more careful about taking on dodgy jobs. Okay, okay, dead-end jobs, the jobs *I* take on. At least this one's money upfront."

Rae checked her website. Her publishers insisted she have one. "Up your profile on the Net," they'd said. She hadn't even delivered the damn book and they wanted her to have a writer's Facebook page, do Twitter, Instagram, create a buzz. All about marketing. Ra ra ra!

She scanned new comments. Yet another idiot asking if he could meet her: "*Disabled women r so boootiful to me…You r soooo stunning…*"

He wasn't interested in her survival, not in her experience, nor her wisdom.

"Some hectic weirdos out there…" She'd had her trouble with oddballs, that's for sure. The devotees, the pretenders, the wannabes. She'd pored over reports and descriptions of all sorts of fetishes when she'd first become aware of the pervs out there who adored her only for her stump.

She was on the meat market all right, except it was her disability this kind of voyeur was into, this kind of freak-stalker, sending bizarre messages she could do without.

And how was this request from *Fascination* magazine?

Dear Ms. Valentine. We'd love you to pose for photographs. Not completely naked of course. The pictures will be tasteful, the editor will assure you of this, but we would like to prominently position your stump.

She considered suggesting a crude caption: "This stump is worth a hump…" but replied instead:

My disability is not something I want to exploit. My

drug addiction, starting in my teen years characterized by confusion, cost me so much, in so many areas of my life, that to turn my amputation into a sexual fantasy is to totally discount who I am as a "whole" woman and would minimize the value of what I have lost. I can't emphasize enough that if I could have my leg back I'd choose to have it back. If the surgeons knew how to do a leg transplant, I'd ensure my name was placed first on the list.

Pressed send.

Now what?

Check in on Vince.

The ringing of the landline at her elbow startled her, brought her out of her reverie.

"Vince. Think of the devil…"

"You want feedback. You love your feedback."

"On your meeting with Rosa Dieter's son, I take it."

"The very one. What's with the tone, Rae? You're getting steamed up."

"I saw you sneak down to the Kimberley—am I right?—when I dropped you off. Reckoned you'd be there till the wee hours."

"I did not *sneak* in, I walked in tall. Call it a lunch break."

"If you say so." From the background buzz, she could tell he was back at the bar.

"I'm doing it by the book. Union rules." He belched.

"So okay, you went to see Heinz Dieter already. I'm impressed. Where're you now?"

"Rae? You're breaking up…Rae?"

"For heaven's sake, don't jerk me around, Vince."

"Gimme a break, Rae."

"Just fill me in, okay? What'd he say?"

"Well, he says"—an almost indiscernible slur a giveaway to his state—"his mother's spending money like water. More than that, he reckons some toyboy might be squeezing her dry, encouraging her to spend more than she should."

"You buy that?"

"Yeah, maybe some user's romancing the old bird, hence the selling of her stash of trinkets, or whatever plan she's concocted to cash in. Clearly she's on a ski trip."

"Spend the kid's inheritance type of thing?"

"You got it. Anyways, on the surface the theft pans out. He has the receipt for goods delivered to the jeweler."

"Nice work." She pressed END CALL.

Who would have thought it? Vince pulling his weight. *Miracles never cease.*

Not yet five, she tried Sol Anderson's shop once more, then Sol's cell. On both counts nada. Now no voicemail, no message machine. Too late to go by the shop, she'd never make it before closing. Better wait till morning.

She smoothed out the stump sock, clicked back the prosthesis.

Was time to head home.

Though thinking about it, her apartment didn't feel like home, piled the way it was with boxes she hadn't had the heart to unpack. She hardly knew what was in them any more, wasn't sure she even wanted them unpacked. She'd come to enjoy the sparseness and utilitarian quality of her living space. The white walls, the empty spaces. She used a box as a bedside table, another as a foot rest while watching TV. She'd had to cancel the lease signed with the student for her apartment, had coped with the student all huffy about it till she heard what had happened, the attack and all.

She picked up a ballpoint pen, aimed between the eyes of the smiley photo on the corkboard, enlarged courtesy of Zip Print: of Tony in his baggies, pulling in his gut as if he was confused about the fact that he wasn't Brad Pitt with a six-pack under the padding there. Holding a big fish. Yellowtail. Good on the braai. From the days they were making plans to seal the deal.

When're you going to let it go, Rae?

Thwack. The pen hit Tony's left cheek. If he was pock-marked before, now his face was crater city with everything and more that had been been tossed at him.

She locked up the office.

The rain had let up. Only a lull for sure, a respite from gale-force winds and flooded streets. Perhaps, she hoped, even the xenophobia would abate.

First she paid her dues at the downstairs deli where the excessive tip for the waiter bought her a cheeky nod of the head. Yes, nice teeth. Then she walked the couple of hundred meters up from the office to the Long Street Baths, past the few shops that remained open; a trickle of business starting at Kennedy's Cigar Bar, Hip Street Lounge, the usual punters settling at Bob's Pub and Grill. The Baths were open, the historic Art Deco Turkish Baths and Indoor Public Pool at the top of Long Street, where she regularly let off steam, got her exercise, kept trim.

The silence under water was something she loved and looked forward to, doing lengths a neccessary ritual. Submerging into the temperate blue, she swam a half-length along the bottom, her fingertips slipping across the tiles. Then surfaced, setting up a natural freestyle rhythm, breathing left then right, hand over hand over hand, for forty laps of the pool, the tightness easing in her shoulders. Forty laps equaled her prerequisite kilometer.

You put your head under water and it blocked sound. You got in the zone, you forgot about bills to pay and difficult clients with missing fingers. The disappointments of love were eased. You forgot about the news, the murders, man turning on man. A sort of meditation, the swimming brought into focus what truly mattered: *I am alive.*

You even forgot you were triply disadvantaged: you were female, had brown skin, and were disabled on top of that. Their PI biz definitely fit government specs for equal opportunity.

She backstroked now, staring up at the cantilevered roof, the rain coming down again, beating hard against it, but in here she was cushioned, felt strong and vital.

In the changing room she peeled off her suit, squeezed out the water, took a quick shower, dressed.

Messaged Vince: *Call me if u need me.*

Took a detour on the way home.

What else was there to do? Enjoy a Millhone moment.

She parked down the road from Rosa Dieter's house. Considered briefly the madness of sitting in a cold and lonely street as she switched off the engine. Switched on the radio for company. A chat show, instantly heavy.

…many of the Somali Muslims targeted in the violence are well educated, Vusi. In the townships where there's dire poverty, the Somali business acumen is not appreciated.

What about police though, Lindiwe, are they helping or hindering?

Well, Vusi, the attitude exists that police are culpable, have in fact stepped back and have allowed attacks on foreigners to happen…

She switched off. Slotted in a compilation flash drive.

Annie Lennox sang how some people never say the words "I love you." She listened to more love gone wrong, Adele singing about love hurting so bad, then local Louise Day with "Slowdance," *how you can't help the feeling that you've been defeated by this thing called love*...misting up her windows with nostalgia. This was stakeout, the numb bum, the cramped legs, the gnawing hunger, the pressure at the bladder. *Squeeze, girl.*

At least she was warm enough, the Jeep reasonably well insulated, and on top of that she kept a throw in the back to cover her legs during this sort of long-stay in the vehicle: forty minutes and counting.

She wiped the windscreen clear just in time to see Mrs. Dieter arrive home in a new Kia, perfect for a glam-gran, zipping into the open gate at the short driveway. Frau Dieter, lugging her Woolies bag to the front door, did not look at all like a woman who'd have the wool pulled over her eyes by anyone. Rae could hardly see her heating up a tasty Woolworths meal for two. But who knew? Maybe Rosa and her man planned sitting close, watching TV, watching *Masterchef*, maybe repeats of the bloody kills of *Dexter*. Life being stranger than fiction. Then she saw a figure running through the thin rain, letting himself into the house. The man was tall, slightly stooped, hair black as jet, probably in his early forties from what she could tell from this distance. Wearing a brown jacket. The gigolo? About to share that cozy supper with Rosa?

Not likely. Had to be the son. Heinz Werner Dieter.

Eva Cassidy crooned an original Sting number, about how she never made promises lightly, her soul-ful voice resonating with Rae's own melancholy.

Rae'd had enough of the downer tunes and switched off. She waited another half-hour listening to the wind whistle through the air vents, then reckoned no lover boy was about to arrive. She'd bet Rosa was spending her evening a single gal.

As was Rae Valentine.

She reached for her cell and punched in Vince's number, muttering, "What're you calling Vince for, Rae? You so lonely you're calling a drunk, are you?" Voicemail answered: *The subscriber you have dialed…* She threw the cell down on the passenger seat. Chitchat about the job or anything else would have to wait till morning.

One thing Rae knew for certain was she had to stop listening to sad love songs. Found *Paradise In Gazankulu* on the stick, turned up the volume on the perfect pick-me-up, Harry Belafonte singing "Global Carnival," Rae bopping along to the chorus of trumpets, percussion, the Angels on backing vocals, feeling the music, feeling the beat, feeling better, feeling upbeat.

"Hey, you gonna answer that, Vince?"

"Deon…" Vince looked up, bleary-eyed, knew the guy who was shaking his shoulder, knew the barman's name was Deon but hardly used it. Better that way. Less personal. Wasn't as if he spent half his life in the place. "Whaaasup?"

"Your cell's jangling, buddy. Gonna pick up or what?"

Lifting the cell, focusing.

RAE on the screen.

"No way."

He let it ring.

He rubbed his eyes. Checked his watch. "Shit, it's after seven."

"Maybe your doze there did you good," quipped Deon.

"Yeah, yeah." At least there was still a whole lot of golden liquid left in the bottle. The echo of Rae's imagined lecture cut through his consciousness: *Vince, your one brewski's turned into a binge of hard tack, that first beer was what, how many hours ago?*

"Ah, shut it, Rae."

"Talking to yourself there, Vince?" said Deon.

Vince laid his head back on the stall countertop. Focused on the horizon in the two-thirds-full bottle of Jack Daniels, pleased with himself that he hadn't drained the lot, had self-control after all. Morons saying he had a booze problem were talking bullshit. No way Mr. In-bloody-Vinceable Saldana was AA material!

He burped. "Excuse me."

"You've been in this spot for the best part of the day. Time to head home, buddy."

The Kimberley felt like home. Inviting. Warm. Reluctantly Vince peeled himself from the stall seat. Exiting the pub, he pulled up the collar of his denim jacket, an excuse for protection against the wind and the persistent rain. He thought briefly of heading for a gentleman's club and the distraction of foreplay, though any thought of getting physical seemed a betrayal.

Amber in his head again sobered him up.

The colors of a car crash.

He walked the back streets to the Hot Wok.

He let himself in, bowed from habit in front of a shrine his mom had set out: a stout jade Buddha, plastic flowers, a bowl of fruit, red and gold paper lanterns, all offered for good fortune.

The beef chow mein his ma had kept warm for him settled the nausea at his gut, but no way he could face her like this, see the sorrow in her tired eyes: *You drunk again, Vincent.*

He grabbed a fortune cookie from the jar, cracked it: *In God we trust; all others must pay cash.*

He heard the slap of the mahjong tiles on the card table in the restaurant section as pieces were dealt at his ma's weekly game, heard the strains of old world Mandarin as she gossiped with her regulars, Chris and Hulan.

Vince climbed the stairs to his bedroom; didn't brush his teeth; lay in his clothes reeking of smoke, on his side, on the rickety pine single, too short for his length. He placed his hands between his thighs, stared at grade-school artwork his mother had framed: a pencil drawing of a Ferrari, a portrait of his first dog. Teen posters were presticked to the walls: Led Zeppelin, Deep Purple, Nirvana, Pearl Jam, Madness; in the bookshelf his reading material went from *Beano, Buster,* and *Boy's Own* annuals to *Zen and the Art of Motorcycle Maintenance.* His treasure was propped in a corner, a cricket bat scrawled with signatures of players of the national team, from a time his single mom had sacrificed to take him to an international match. Yeah, he'd been into sports. His mother all the time telling him, "You can be whatever you want to be, do what you want to do." She'd assured him that race classification was a load of bullshit. Always his mother building him up. What happened? Life happened.

He listened to the rain battering the tin roof, wishing Tony had left him for dead when he'd found him after his last anti-poaching stint.

...On his next job, the sun rose orange over the horizon, he blinked, unseeing, as a poacher stood over

him blocking the light. "I should shoot you in the head for all the trouble you've caused, but this is your lucky day. Or is it?" He'd exhaled, heh, heh, heh, heh. "I rather like the idea of leaving you out here to take your chances," and they both knew there were no chances. Vince was about to die; the rhino was dead, the rangers were dead. If he didn't die of blood loss, the hyenas would find him and rip apart his flesh and the vultures would finish off, tearing the meat from his rotting carcass...

He couldn't stand lying there a moment longer. Checked his watch. Got up, zapped his fermented breath with Listerine. Five minutes later was heading out the city, weaving his rust-bucket Cortina down Kloof, blearily negotiating the curves of De Waal Drive, swerving across the double white line, pulling back, slowing down. In his head was Tony's voice: "You wanna kill yourself, Vince? What good will that do. Vince, talk to me, pal! Why not take a fucking Uber, pal!"

In her flat perched above the city, Rae nuked a single-portion box of instant Thai green curry in the microwave. She stood looking out at the view from the double glass doors separating the lounge from a small porch. City lights had been activated early on account of the weather. Cape Town harbor a scene to die for, even through the drizzle: illuminated container ships, cranes, cruisers, lights reflecting off the black water, glittering like spill on spill of sequins. Belafonte's lyrics riffed in her head, how Cape Town had, has still, a flaw in her sparkle...

Absent-mindedly she spooned globs of sticky rice and bamboo shoots into her mouth, the appetizing picture on the box a predictable lie. She tossed the noodles in the plastic-lined bin, would rather go hungry than eat cardboard. In for the night, she double-locked the door, secured the bolt. Unstrapped her custom-made shoulder holster, put the Colt on the table. Took off her leg, changed into a tracksuit and flopped on the couch, trying to block Tony and his touch from her mind, focusing on the clatter of rain, the wind turning gale force once more, ripping through the gaps in the window frames.

What she needed was escapism: maybe a good series. But turning on the TV, flicking channels now, she got a whole bunch of inane reality: *The Bachelorette, My Perfect Wedding, Farmer Seeks a Wife*, everybody trying for pathetic love.

On SuperSport, she caught the tail end of a special on handicapped sports. A Paralympic basketball team thrashed around the court as wheelchairs like hardcore bumper cars spun, crashed and toppled; followed by a profile on Natalie Du Toit, the Laureus award-winning amputee, the "flying fish" who'd swum the China Sea and competed in the pucca Olympics. On screen, Nat, with the South African flag draped around her shoulders, bowed for another accolade. This was more like it. A reminder of all Rae herself was capable of.

She made coffee. She'd get moving with the job first thing in the morning.

She tuned in to *Law & Order*, enjoying the structure, learning from the plot points, and praying in the ad break that between the two of them this was one case she and Vince—legit diamonds or no legit diamonds—didn't fuck up.

Heinz Dieter plucked the note from the letterbox, hand-delivered, like the others. With no postmark, just his name neatly printed in block letters, the way a child would do it, on a crisp white envelope. He didn't dare open it in the dim entrance hall; he folded it into his pocket.

He switched on the light, checked his digital watch: 7:35 pm. In the kitchen he poured himself a glass of filtered ice water, then checked the shopping from Woolworths. The lettuce was pre-washed, the dairy products RSBT-free, the foodstuffs organic.

Good for you, Mutti.

In the dining room he saw the evidence on the table of the earlier gathering: three gold-rimmed tea cups and saucers, washed and stacked, waiting to be returned to the dresser, and a neatly folded embroidered cloth. And a business card. Surreptitiously he helped himself to a ginger snap from a plate of shop-bought biscuits set out on a doily and protected with a lace cover. Mutti never baked. Nor was she one to offer treats.

Where was she now?

He scowled. "*Mutter?*" he called. Louder: "Mutti?"

He pocketed the business card. The threat.

He pulled out the envelope.

From the writing desk in the study he took the ivory-handled letter opener. In one clean swipe he slit open the seam and removed the note, this one concocted with an assortment of letters cut from magazines and neatly pasted on bond paper.

No time to waste. He who hesitates is lost!

He walked quickly to the window, looked out from the crack between the red brocade curtains into the empty street. Saw no one lurking under lamplight, no one mad enough to be out in this storm. The wind raged as never before, issuing its warning; and the sea, a portentous shade of green in the floodlights across Beach Road, crashed over the crumbling retaining wall.

God no longer cared to hold back!

He drew closed the curtains.

"Aaah," Mutti's voice penetrated the silence, "here you are, Heinz."

He stuffed the note into the pocket of his jacket, turned quickly to respond, stumbling over his words: "I-I-I had a call from a private investigator today."

"So they're on the ball."

"Why bother calling investigators? The gems have probably been plucked from the settings by now, and the gold already melted down."

"Don't say such things, Heinz," his mother scolded.

"Don't build your hopes up, Mutti, please. The stones are long gone by now."

Her voice turned cold: "Are you implying that I should give up? I should let my own property simply disappear into the ether?"

"You've been distressed enough as it is. I'm sorry, Mutti." His voice broke and faltered. "I don't mean to upset you."

Her sharp tongue cut like a shard of glass: "But you do, you do. I sacrificed everything for you. I pushed you from between my thighs, with gritted teeth, the agony you caused. And now you rub salt in the wound."

"It'll be all right."

"I wanted the money for you, for us. I held on to those stones for years as my insurance policy. You said it yourself, Heinz, we can no longer afford this house, the expenses. I'm not ready for an old-age home, unless that is what you want? Is that how you plan to repay me?"

"N-n-no, Mutti, never, we are comfortable together."

"I want to live a little adventurously, Heinz. In style, in the last years left to me, with you at my side."

"Yes, Mutti."

"We are not personally insured, Heinz, and what can the police do? We need help to get them back, or at least be compensated." Her voice suddenly soft as cotton wool, and as smothering, she whispered, "Do you understand, my poor, dim Heinz."

She ran a finger down his cheek, brushed her pinkie-stump against his lips. He saw the fine hairs covering her chin, smelled the powder on her face as she kissed the corner of his mouth. He wanted desperately to wipe off the residue of smeared saliva.

"My Henizie, what will I do with you?"

She shook her head, smiling as if sorry for him. He looked down at his shoes.

Rosa Dieter lifted her son's chin. "Look at me when I talk to you."

She slapped him.

The humiliation stung more than the blow to his cheek.

"Oh, and do you know, one of the detectives is a woman?" She went on as if no insult had transpired. "And has only one leg. Lost it from using drugs. She's a motivational speaker now, and writing a book." Then lowered her voice: "She's a cripple. Disabled, just like your mother." Rosa Dieter held out her damaged hands, placed one on either side of her son's face. "In my day disability meant struggle, especially with a young child to bring up. But I doted on you, Heinzie."

With another sudden movement of an ugly hand, she pinched his ear till it bloody well throbbed.

He sucked in his breath. Would not cry out.

"Now off you go. Clean up before supper."

His fury rose, a storm at his throat threatening to break out to match the storm outside. He wanted to scream, to howl, but held back, his throat constricting, scared now to tell his mother he was going out after dark, stuttering, "M-M-Mutti, I'm on late shift at the pharmacy this evening."

"Well, come straight home when you're done." Her eyes seared into his. "There's no need to keep your mother worrying unnecessarily. It's selfish, Heinz. I worry when you stay out on night shift, let alone on these courses you insist on enrolling for."

He retreated to his bedroom, heard her clucking and complaining: "Mrs. Kapinski, you know how I despise that busybody, will have to keep me company yet again. While you galavant, Heinz!"

He unlocked his wall safe, the only privacy she had reluctantly allowed him, the small safe he had insisted on because of the drugs he sometimes collected or brought home from the pharmacy for delivery. That's how he'd explained it. Always he had to be so careful with her. She watched him like a hawk watches a fat little mouse it's about to gobble.

Ensconced in the safety of his room he retrieved the other notes from the safe. Four of them altogether, the notes were a tease, a taunt, a chastisement, as if he was taking too long, not keeping his eye on the clock.

The inconsistency of the notes irritated his sensibility: one in italic lettering on feather-weight airmail paper; another typed on scented card with an ancient typewriter; two of them simply printed off a computer.

Now this one. Like a kindergarten project.

"Dear God above!" He closed his eyes and pressed his palms together. "Anyone who believes I do not take my calling seriously is misguided. So wrong!"

He retrieved the vial in his pants pocket, fumbled with the childproof lid, dropped the vial to the ground in frustration. On his knees he gathered the spilled pills, then pushed a double dose to the back of his throat and swallowed dry—never mind they'd been on the floor, Mutti kept his floor clean enough to lick—gagging, the bitter aftertaste of the pills rising to his esophogus. He waited for his pulse to calm, took several deep breaths until it no longer felt as if his heart was about to jump out of his chest.

He hung up his jacket, gathered his kit, walked quickly to the bathroom, the voices coming at him, the shrieks that passed as wind.

The season of fire is over; now the lashings of wind and rain are a manifestation of God's wrath.

And the killings.

The city beset by man on man, malice and murder.

So many signs!

In the bathroom he caught sight of a thread on his shirt. Not a thread. A rust-tinted curly hair. His gut spasming, he plucked it off, rolled it in toilet paper and flushed it. Yanked off the contaminated shirt and squashed it in the washing basket.

He scrubbed long and hard under the scalding spray of the shower, turning on the cold tap only when he could no longer bear the intensity, his chest and thighs on fire from the boiling, disinfecting heat. He trod gingerly onto the bath mat, dried with the fresh towel, vigorously scrubbing off dead cells. He caught a glimpse of himself in the mirror. Button nose in a moon-shaped face, small straight teeth, raven-black eyes, blue-black hair combed back. A double chin was evident under his jaw, even as he clenched his teeth to heighten the definition. He concertinaed his soft face, the skin smooth as a baby's, into his neck. The perks of working at a pharmacy were the face creams and the vitamins he brought home, for Mutti, and himself; the moisturising masks and firming ampoules to smooth onto his sagging jowls. But still there was no change. This one physical trait bothered him—this flaccid flesh with no muscle tone. He was a man of purpose. God should have given him a strong, square jaw line. Like Mutti. One couldn't have everything. He wiped the misted mirror with a cloth, then stood naked, staring at his whiteness, at his penis shriveled like a dead baby bird fallen from the nest.

Sucking in his lips he turned away in distaste, pushing from his consciousness the thoughts his mother forbade him to entertain. Heinz Dieter stretched out his fingers. His hands were whole, smooth, free of those ugly age blemishes, and his fingernails impeccably filed and buffed with an emery board. He winced now as he scraped the point of the file too roughly under a nail to loosen a pinhead of dirt. He washed his hands again, then rubbed on hand cream. Applied fragrance-free anti-perspirant, and sprayed his soles and toes with Lamasil to prevent athlete's foot.

Back in his bedroom, cleansed and composed, the intensity of the rage abated, he lectured himself: "Nothing is impossible." He dressed in pristine cotton underwear and vest, a pressed shirt, freshly dry-cleaned brown suit and patent-leather shoes. As this evening called for pomp and ceremony, he knotted a claret bow tie at his neck.

The message: *I take my calling seriously.*

Reaffirming his sense of purpose, the gnawing hunger for his New Order, he stood straight as a flagpole. Not a hair out of place. In control, power surged in his veins.

He checked the business card again: DURANT, SALDANA & VALENTINE.

While Mutti dished up supper he called his right-hand man from the landline in the study.

Rocco Robano would fix everything, just as he always did.

※

"Shut up!" Rocco raised his voice. "I want quiet, Boyz, zip the lips." He answered, "Hey, Pastor Heinz."

"I'm afraid I have to give you the heads up on a complication."

"What's the problem?"

"My mother called a private investigator about the theft."

"She did what?"

What the hell was the old bat thinking?

"She hired a PI firm."

"For Christ's sake"—and here they thought she'd do nothing on account of the stones being the spoils of war—"what the fuck she go and do that for?"

"Watch your language, please, Rocco."

"Pastor, forgive me." Dammit, he'd had enough of watching his tone and language with Heinz, was sick of keeping up appearances, the efforts he'd had to redouble to seem sincere, to keep in his good graces.

"Collect me. Your Pastor is ready."

Heinz disconnected.

Rocco bounced his fingers over the bristles on his scalp, dyed a white-blond now, though the strawberry showed at the roots and the orange hairs on the back of his sinewy hands were a dead giveaway as to his ginger status. Not that anyone would dream of pointing this out to him.

What the hell had Heinz's old lady gone and done? Hiring in bloody bozo PIs.

No matter. He'd sort it. Always did.

In the kitchen, he opened the fridge. Fuck all to eat. They'd have to get takeaways. He poured himself a tot of Klippies to take the edge off as he listened to the Boyz singing again in the Godawful carmine lounge, the crooked vein. Kitted out in shiny suits and bling, they couldn't get more conspicuous and rowdy, now belting out a tuneless a cappella version of "Praise My Soul The King Of Heaven." Enjoying choir practice, they sounded worse than goddamned cats on a crap night. Alex Silver, the new driver, had close to a strong voice, some resonance to it, and Christoff wasn't half-bad, but JP was tone deaf.

...to my feet thy tribute bring!

Oh yes, tribute. Money, checks, bequests, the hard cash in bundles, whatever contributions he and Pastor Heinz could get.

It wasn't all bad.

Heh, heh, heh, heh, he snickered.

Ransomed, healed, restored, forgiven,

Who to me His pay should bring!

He'd soon be singing the praises of the Lord as loud as the rest of them.

Yes, there was much to be thankful for.

He popped the cap off a Windhoek Lager for his supper. Pastor Heinz could damn well wait ten minutes. What couldn't wait was Rocco's desire for the money he'd make from the sale of the diamonds.

As he left the house he called, "Don't be late."

The Boyz were notching up the volume, going wild with the singing...

Mine eyes have seen the glory

Of the coming of the Lord!

...getting out of hand, bellowing out lyrics JP had printed off the Internet:

Glory glory hallelujah,

We will fight till we subdue ya,

Don't resist or we will shoot ya,
Our cause is marching on!

❂

Alex Silver, the third member of the Core since Derm had copped it, said, "You heard the boss." He stood up now, straightening his tie, smoothing back the blond fringe from electric-green eyes taking in the scene, his one leg bouncing, nervous of these trigger-happy half-wits and how it could all backfire. "We gotta get going, and watch out, you don't wanna end up later singing the wrong words to sacred songs."

Sitting in the blood lounge, at the table covered in newspapers, on it spills of nails and wires, plus a cake of C4 right smack in the center, JP fiddled with his latest device. "Heinz wouldn't even click. Pastor is fucking off his trolley."

"Ja, when we gonna be done with him?" piped up red-faced Christoff.

"Rocco's told us practice patience," said Alex.

"Patience is a virtue. We none too virtuous," hooted JP.

"You nearly done there?" nagged Alex, dangling the Mini's car keys from his fingers.

"Why don't you come and help me, Alex?"

"Just get a move on, JP."

JP tossed a box at Alex, grinning at the sheepish soft boy's face as he grabbed for it, dropping the keys, his pretty green eyes wide with fright.

"You thought I tossed you the C4, huh Prettyboy?"

"You paying attention to the bomb there, JP?"

"You nervous I'm gonna blow you to hell and gone? Don't worry so fucking much, bro."

"Don't want any accidents happening, is all."

"Take it easy, Alex, watch your nerves there or

you'll need a nappy change."

"You ready, Boyz?" Alex barked, ignoring the goad. "Let's go."

Vince Saldana couldn't miss the surprise on Tony Durant 's face as he opened the front door.

"Howzit, Vincent."

"You gonna ask me in, or what?"

"You shit-faced?"

"Not yet." Vince popped the leftover whiskey from his jacket. "Something to look forward to."

Tony held the door wide, motioned a red-eyed Vince to the kitchen where he had a joint lit up already, the rough strains of Johnny Cash on the boom box filtering from the lounge. So much for his peace; if you had any to begin with, if you could hold on to it if you had it.

He handed over the roach.

Vince dragged deep, sighed on the exhale. "You got tumblers for the Jack?" he asked, pulling open a melamine cupboard, finding some freebie Johnny Walker glasses he'd given Tony a couple of months back.

The men, the roach, the perlemoen ashtray, the whiskey—all in the lounge now.

"So how'd it go with the court case?" Vince kicked off his wet trainers, stretched his legs out on Tony's new couch.

"Heck, Moodley's got me hamstrung. Had to hang out for hours at the courthouse this morning and it ends with another postponement and another bloody wasted day. Natasha keeps trying to broker a dismissal."

"Bloody six months down the line."

"All takes time."

"Been tough, hey."

"There a note of concern in your voice?"

"When we gonna see you back?"

"Like at the office?"

"Thas right. Still your nameplate on the door outside."

"Soon enough."

"You been saying so for months."

"Soon, buddy, soon."

"Right. Is it the suspension of your license or Rae perching at your desk that keeps you away?"

Tony pursed his lips, scraped back the only other seat in the lounge, a desk chair, rode it, put up his feet on the coffee table, broke the silence. "So Vince, what's the update then?"

"Rae's capable. Done with the GI Jane course she was on, that fitness course, running around with sand bags on her shoulders, building up muscle."

"Yeah?"

"Adventure boot camp for women I told you about? You shoulda seen 'em, mommies and students, all dressed up like a buncha Rambettes. Rae in that army jacket of hers, even had camouflage leggings to match, all learning the leopard crawl, the lunging squats, how to smack a magazine in a pistol. Coupla lethal self-defense moves they were trying out too when I watched."

"What the heck did I unleash?"

"She's caught on quick all right, eye-gouging, testicle rearrangement, an' I tell you, she's got the knack for following cheaters. Done some nifty footwork with that leg of hers, ducking behind cars, hiding behind newspapers, points the video camera in the right direction. Wasn't for cheaters there'd be no rent money."

"S'true…"

"An' she's got an eye with her Colt. Ay ay ay… You two ever gonna talk things through?" Vince waited for an answer. None came. "You and Rae, Tony, you'll have to sort it out."

"You must be well pissed, buddy, doing social work here. This why you stopped by?"

"I want you to know what we're doing. Sometime you're gonna have to take on your share of the bullshit."

"All right, all right." Tony fired up another joint.

Vince stretched for the roach. Sucked long before passing it back. "An' we got a new client," he slurred. "Nother nowhere job."

"Work is work."

"Rae taking orders from hormonal women is one thing, running around at the instructions of a nutty old bag with missing fingers will end badly, I'm telling you, Tone. So this old bird Rosa Dieter read about you in the paper, how you were dedicated, she wanted Tony Durant on the job. Gotta admit, you do have a certain reputation."

"You're telling me—as a failed cop, now a murderous PI."

Vince shook the dregs from the bottle, the Jack long gone, and *dronkverdriet*, the remorse, arriving. "PI bullshit's sordid…Don't you miss the cops? Hey?" Vince turned on his side on the couch, his face towards the cushion, curled his feet up, closed his eyes, cupped his crotch. "Oh for the chase of a hijacking, or tracking heisters or investigating straightforward murder for a cellphone. None of this family intrigue bull… Where'd it all go wrong? All those free abalone steaks, hey, 'member those?"

"Finger licking good nicely fried up." Tony followed suit, closed his eyes. "Superb with mayo."

"Yeah, from when I was on the anti-poaching unit, bringing home the bounty of the seas. An' you were a cop…"

"Those were the days." Except for being at Chas Moodley's beck and call.

The doorbell rang, a jingly tune. A woman's voice called out: "Hey, Tony, I'm home."

He snapped open his lids. "Natasha."

"The very same. What the hell're you doing, Anthony?" She walked into the lounge, saw the two men stoned, good and proper.

Natasha didn't like Vince, liked the dope less. You could do what you wanted in your own home, but she didn't approve. She threw down her briefcase, went to the kitchen, went for one of her soya milkshakes in the fridge.

Vince got himself upright. "Don't worry, I'm on my way."

"Vince, pal, stick around," said Tony. "You're pissed, man. Doss here tonight."

Natasha returned, sucking from a cardboard straw in the glass bottle. "Where's your friend going to sleep?"

"I'm okay, m'fine. Got my car back, parked right outside. You have twenty for gas?"

Vince heard Natasha gripe as she latched the door: "I can't believe you do business with that loser!" Then Tony, defensive—"He's my friend…"—before the roar of the northwester drowned out the rest of it.

Vincent skipped his mother's place, couldn't stand the anticipated third degree, his mom's voice already ringing in his ears: "Vincent, you stink like a vaglant! Where you been, Vincent?" Weaving his way practically blind-drunk through a dark and treacherous city, he headed for the office. He'd crash there for the night.

✳

On stage at the Milnerton Scout Hall, faded velveteen curtains drawn closed were an attempt at a dramatic backdrop for Pastor Heinz Dieter standing behind the lectern at the edge of the stage.

He shouted, "Hallelujah!" His glistening baby face staring at the Core members in chairs arranged in a half-moon in front of him. Behind them a good eighty souls had streamed in, Heinz Dieter's reputation preceding him in the circles of the disillusioned, the righteous, the gullible.

"We praise you God for the opportunity to stand up for each other, to be there for each other, to support each other. We thank you for the opportunity to build a community that will not succumb to the future of the world. We thank you for Aurora!"

"Hallelujah!" echoed Rocco Robano. Yes, thank you, God. For this tremendous opportunity. The potential Rocco recognized in Heinz was his fervor, the way it came naturally to him to rub the collective sore, not only about the state of mankind and its impending doom, but of the foreign influence, the "other" taking over. Heinz loudmouthed about all that was unfair, disgraceful, about everything that could be set right and *how*—and a certain kind of folk were mesmerized by Pastor's feverish gabble.

Rocco had convinced Heinz he deserved a community of his own, a haven for the like-minded loved by God. And Heinz fell for it, allowed himself to be groomed, calling for the Dawn of the New Order, the building of his Aurora.

Heinz Dieter spread his arms as wide as Jesus had on the cross, held up his palms in supplication, waited for silence, raised his eyes as if he, the crazy fuck, could see through the stained ceiling to the heavens above and beyond, then raised his voice: "I revive the courage of those with repentant hearts! I will lead you like no other!" Pastor cried: "I will lead you from the rain of fire, from God's damnation, from the flood of God's tears! I will lead you to salvation!" The energy loosening in him, flowing in him, his wax-white cheeks flushed with the burn.

Rocco was pleased. The audience, the fools, the brain dead with glossed-over eyes, desperately wanting someone to lead, to take charge, to show them the way, were stirred and gripped by the intensity of this black-eyed prophet.

"Whom will you serve? Before whom will you surrender?"

Wow! The man had power.

He patted himself on the back for organizing the glut of appearances. Heinzie telling his mommy he had to go up country for pharmacy courses, or had to work late, when he was really sermonizing at small churches, town halls, Scout halls. Putting the word out. No paperwork involved, no pamphlets, no signs. People with nothing else to believe in flocked to hear the Good News.

Heinz Dieter shrieked, "You are here because you are searching for purpose, for reason to carry on! You see the trouble in this world and you know it is time. You want the Grace of God!"

Oh yes, he loved the flush in Heinz's fat cheeks, the way his tongue darted from his wet lips. He loved the way the punters lapped up Heinz Dieter's crap.

"We are Family!"

With a capital F.

"The greater the *donations* to build Aurora, our community, the sooner the Chosen will be Saved to live together, to live out our blessed days in harmony!"

Rocco sniffed at the smell of warm bodies, the smell of fear and anticipation that got the good folk bringing out their purses and wallets.

"Seek and ye shall find!"

The punters had found their Pastor.

"Sow and ye shall reap!"

The good citizens were all the same, giving cold hard cash for a brighter future.

"Smoke will curdle in the sky, the seas shall become one. But we will be safe. Money is a necessary evil in these times. You have come to pledge allegiance. Help us bring this united community to fruition! *Together we will build a home like no other!*"

By the time the police figured it out, if they ever did, Rocco Robano would be long gone. So what if he had to pamper Heinz, drive him around all over the city, the country? He had Heinz in the palm of his hand. The rest too: JP, a psycho-geek pretty sharp with the computer, his mean streak a bonus. And Christoff, staunchly Afrikaner, a pukka platteland rock spider, feeling the loss of his country to the new dispensation. Even Alex, with his nowhere arts degree, was wrapped around his little finger; a self-absorbed specimen so pretty, with his green eyes and deep dimples, that the artist Tretchikoff might have enhanced his reputation by producing a portrait of the guy: "You're smart, Alex," he'd joked during the screening, "you could find employment."

"You heard of affirmative action, employment equity, black economic empowerment, Mr. Robano? I'll never get a job. I know that. I'm a realist."

Yeah, all the Boyz were right wing racial realists, just the kind of freak weak-willed deluded young bucks he could play with and use and would feel fuck all about when the time came to put them down. And he knew it took someone like Heinz to inspire the eager punters in the hall, to fire up their passion, make them believe in an opportunity, a future, as all sorts collected to build the New Order of Aurora.

Hallelujah!

"Opportunity knocks but once!" encouraged Heinz.

A woman, skinny, gray, dressed in white, had to be an old-maid disgruntled virgin clutching the Good Book, was swaying, ululating in tongues, in gibberish.

"The more ye give, the more ye shall receive!" Heinz's black eyes transfixed, mesmerized, sucked them in, the message that infiltrated: *Salvation is yours.* For a price, of course.

Ka-ching ka-ching, the mamparas, a bunch of suckers, couldn't wait to contribute. Men in checks, women in shapeless skirts, all of them stooped, stressed—feeling lighter and unburdened as they tossed their pledges into the box. He saw cash and envelopes. From personal banking accounts, from savings accounts, from under mattresses, it didn't matter where the money came from.

Heh, heh, heh, heh.

And finally Pastor Heinz Dieter, his eyes glinting, lit from somewhere deep inside, quieted the group, bringing them together as one.

"*Oremus!* Let us pray."

Videre est credere! Seeing is fucking believing! Oh yes, Heinz had fallen for his own lies.

The crowd burst into song.

Praise the Lord the King of heaven!

The Boyz sang in well-practiced unison.

Rocco reckoned that Pastor Heinz most probably believed the notes left in the post-box were from God himself. God with access to magazines, scissors and glue.

But the writing was on the wall. Punters would

only keep giving for so long. They had to move, and he was not averse to helping things along a little.

When it was done the assembly shook hands, hugged, threw their arms around each other, men and women bonding. Men and women awaiting promised pamphlets of an update on Aurora. Men and women filling in sheets of personal info, then guzzling biscuits, swigging tea.

"You were inspired tonight, Pastor Heinz." Rocco lowered his head in deference after the last congregant had left.

"Surely we have enough now?" enquired Heinz now sitting in the back seat of the Land Rover, composed and pensive, spent, his manicured hands crossed neatly in his lap. "All these people giving and giving countrywide, surely there must be plenty?"

"This is most certainly the last phase," placated Rocco.

"So when will we relocate?"

"Aurora is nearly set up. The buildings so close to completion. I want to pay off the bond, cancel the loan with the bank. Aurora will be truly independent. As soon as we sell the diamonds, Pastor, we won't have to rely on a soul." *Not even God.* His heh, heh, heh, heh he kept to himself.

"Pity my mother wants her jewelry back," sighed Heinz.

Rocco saw it clearly: his view of the future, when he first started this deal, was to lay his hands on as much cash as he could get. Cash idiots gave freely and cash the Boyz stole. Add to that the value of the antique trinkets, and the diamonds Mother Dieter had hidden, a lucky packet of rough-cut pebbles, and he'd be a made man. No matter that De Beers said you needed authentication and certificates of origin, there was always a market for stones a skilled cutter could transform from rough hewn to dazzling gem. Fire and ice any way you cut it: oval, rose-cut, cabochon, pear, marquise, emerald, brilliant, a diamond was a diamond and every woman, and man, wanted one.

Heinz better not start fucking backtracking. Letting mommy get under his skin.

"See your gift as a final investment, Pastor. The rewards which will flow from such a gift, setting up Aurora in His Name, will be countless!"

"As always."

"Don't worry about the sale. I'll take care of it. And don't fret about the PIs either. A minor hassle is all," he said, dropping Heinz home.

※

Mutti was waiting up. "Where've you been, Heinz Werner? I've been worried sick! Selfish as ever! You don't think of me, do you?"

She pummeled his chest.

Her ardor spent, she kissed him goodnight.

He waited for her incessant gargling to stop, the toilet to flush; he waited for the click of her door, for her to sleep.

In the quiet of the night Heinz turned to his safe, to his secrets. He sat on the edge of the bed, leafed through his magazines. First his travel periodicals where yellow Post-its marked several spots he'd thought suitable for his haven, his Aurora.

Namibia was heaven on earth. Mutti had always told him she was meant to live in Namibia, with her people, her Germans. Namibia had oil, water, resources were plentiful there, Namibia was the new Saudi Arabia some said. The prophecies predicted her survival through epidemics, earthquakes, tsunamis, nuclear explosions.

*In the night the wicked will see the sun and the
half-pig man.*

Chaos, shouting, screaming in the sky.

The lifeless beast shall speak.

From the West will blow toxic clouds of dust…

But we in Aurora will be free!

He paged through a photo essay of Luderitz with
her stunning colonial and German architecture; the
spoken language was his birthright.

In his second set of magazines, his extra-special
magazines, he pored over well-thumbed articles, and
touched the glossy pictures. He knew every inch of
flesh.

He placed his fingers at the base of his throat to
ensure his breath still came, and felt the plump carotid
beating vigorously, vital blood pumping. It was midnight before he changed into fleecy pajamas. At last,
his hands folded over his chest, he slept, dreaming of
the Promised Land.

FRIDAY: MISCHIEF

Five after midnight, on Friday morning, Christoff
crowed, "Hallelujah!"

"Praise the Lord!" echoed JP.

"Guys, guys," said Alex, "cut the happy clappy."
He'd had close on enough. JP was a madman, the
heating in the car was oppressive, and the bulletproof vest tight at his chest restricted Alex's every
movement. At least if anyone retaliated he wouldn't
end up dead. His aim: stay focused, get through this
without a scratch. Make sure these brain-dead excuses
for human beings get what they deserve. The racism,
the hate, it riled him in a way he never thought it
would.

"What a sweet night," said JP, hyped up after the

meeting, rocking back and forth in the Mini Cooper passenger seat, jamming to Aggressive Force on the boom box, the lyrics screaming out: *Time we had our freedom, time we had our say.*

"The night is newborn!" shouted JP. "Let's start the fucking party. Let's do it, let's get it on! This is our time!" *My time.* The world would one day belong to him, just as Pastor Heinz had promised, nutcase or not. "Let's ride, Alex, up the city's backside! The night is but a pup!"

Twenty after midnight, the three men cruised the empty streets, the gray skies threatening to break.

"Perfect night for this job," said JP.

And he was right, with the wind whipping, causing havoc, bins overturned, rubbish flying, tree branches ripped from trunks, they could just about cause whatever mayhem they wanted.

At the red light, Alex checked out his reflection in the rearview mirror: his blond hair a number two he'd got used to; he'd lost weight, the red-rimmed eyes staring back at him spoke of exhaustion. He couldn't wait for this gig with the Core to be over. They never slept, were all go go go, blam blam blam, his nerves were shot.

He took the Nelson Mandela Boulevard out of town, away from Table Mountain. He drove the scenic route, along the winding country avenue through the leafy Southern suburbs past double-acre dream homes and Pollsmoor Prison and private schools and stables, all an ironic mix, before turning onto Tokai Road, then right at the traffic lights at Main Road, heading for the seaside suburbs.

The ATM in the down-and-out seaside village of Muizenberg went *whoosh!* The blast lit up the black sky with a tower of orange flame and smoke.

JP gawked. "Like bloody Hiroshima! How much

fucking C4 did you pack in there, Christoff?"

"Did it just how you showed me," said Christoff, wide-eyed. "Jissis, maybe I stuffed in a bit extra, like a slither, man, like a pinch extra, that's all, JP, I swear."

"Fricken hell," hissed Alex, "the money's on fire!"

Christoff and JP scrambled for free-falling cash, grabbed handfuls of notes that weren't yet incinerated. Alex cowered from the blaze behind a cement pillar.

"Help us, Alex!" shouted JP. "Get your lily-white arse out here!"

For a frantic moment they gathered their toasted spoils before dashing back to the car.

"How'm I supposed to know it'd blow like that?" whined Christoff.

"Let's just get outta here," yelled Alex fifteen seconds later, back behind the wheel and willing Christoff to finish his bloody graffiti already. "Shoudn't have done this in the Mini in the first place. We're too fricken obvious in this thing."

"You always know better don't you, Professor? C'mon, Prettyboy, say the word *fuck*. Fuck fuck fuck!"

Two minutes later, speeding on the Blue Route highway into town, JP in the back counted the money, too much of it singed.

"So what did we manage to get from that disaster? C'mon man, tell me the bad news," groused Christoff.

JP snarled, leaned over the passenger seat, klapped Christoff a stiff blow to the side of the head. "Maybe three grand if we lucky. You and your fucking overkill."

"Most of it as valueless as toilet paper," said Alex.

"Just small change in the ATM anyway," said Christoff. "Handfuls of tens and twenties. Monopoly shit."

"Would've been plenty if it hadn't all been cremated, you douche bag."

"We mos should've stuck to doing the banks in town, JP, or maybe tried the winelands. ATMs where there's proper bucks. There's no money in that shit hole, ek sê," said Christoff. "All the Nigerian refugees are there, selling coke and crap, leading good citizens into a life of drugs. They don't put their drug bucks in the bank, I tell you."

"When you gonna get it through your stupid heads there's no Nigerian community there in Muizenberg? It's Congolese, man," said Alex.

"Prettyboy," said JP. "You lecturing us again. You say there's a difference? They all look the fucking same."

"Dudes, let me help you get it right. Muizenberg's a Mecca if you're homeless and into night shelters. Nigerians sell drugs in Sea Point on the Atlantic where the sun shines, where yuppies can afford to buy the shit. Somalis start shops in the townships. Malawians live in Westlake, and on this side, the Indian Ocean side, is where Congolese live, get it, trying to make a living at whatever."

"You taking the piss, Prettyboy?" JP leaned over and pinched Alex's dimpled cheek as he drove.

Alex jerked his head sideways. Treading on thin ice, he played the game. "Just putting the facts straight."

"It's foreigners draining the system, that's what it is. And best of it all, this xenophobia shit is darkies killing darkies. How's that for poetic justice? I say let it happen." JP whooped. "Homeboys driving *foreigners* back to where they came from, Nigeria, Somalia, Timbuktu. Makwerekwere stuffed up their own countries, now they wanna come and stuff up here. No way!"

JP, with cash—though he could have done with more—and his gun in his pocket, felt as powerful as God himself. "Umshini wami! Bring out your machine gun! Kill the bobbejaan, kill the baboon!" Heading home to the red-veined house, doubling back past the Sea Point Scout hall, JP watched the streets go by. Saw, even in this weather, a refugee group huddling outside, taken to the city safer than staying in the townships. "Look at 'em, as if it's safer here than wherever they came from. Thinking if they kip in school halls and shelter at churches the principal or God'll protect 'em."

Christoff started singing, "De la Rey, De la Rey! Sal jy die boere kom lei! General De la Rey, Come lead the Boers! *My home and farm are burnt to embers, I've got flame and fire burning deep inside me!*"

"Let's get it on with the fucking war, man!" JP felt the Smith & Wesson in the front of his pants, alongside his semi-hard main vein. Was singing along, checking himself in the rearview mirror, belting it out like a rock star, with Christoff shredding now on his air guitar in the passenger seat. "For my country... Right or wrong!" whooped JP.

A block down, in a side street, another group of men, had to be refugees, leaned towards a dull flame flaring atop a tin drum, warming their hands.

JP unwound the window, yelled at the strays, "You've outstayed your welcome! Go back to bloody Africa where you came from! And if you won't go home by bus, go home by pine box!" In one swift movement, he pulled out Smith: *bam, bam, bam, bam!*

Alex swerved. "What the hell you doing? You lost your mind? Cops'll hear that ten blocks away!"

Christoff, exhilarated, nervous, said, "Ja, JP, d'you forget to pop your Ritalin this morning, hey?"

Alex muttered, "This I bloody well didn't sign up for."

"Ag, you pussies," said JP. "Aw, an' I missed too, boo hoo."

❄

Back at the red house Rocco waited up for the Boyz, sitting up like their goddamned daddy. He guessed they were going wild. He was losing control. He could have detoured to the Cape Grande, but no, here he was, waiting up for the idiot kids to come home.

"Where you been?" he said, as soon as JP et al walked through the door, Alex down-at-the-mouth, the simpleton Christoff flinging his podgy self down on the couch. Even his knees had cellulite. Rocco knew this was crunch time with the Boyz, had watched JP getting too big for his Doc Martens, with his dead eyes, his skulls and lightning bolts etched under skin. And Alex, too clever for his own damn good, was competition for any idiot savant. Funny, how it was all coming to a head: a scabrous head, a crusty boil he'd better lance ASAP or it'd be too late to excise the infection. He stared at JP scratching his balls, the red walls casting an eerie glow on his face; the look of him unhinged.

"Jesus, what drugs are you guys on?"

"Chill, Boss, we've had us a night on the town."

"Yeah? You score funds I take it?"

"Hit a machine in Muizenberg. Crap score, I tell you."

"What did you lot go out there for?" Then changed his mind about knowing the sordid details. "Forget it." He turned on his heel, back to his room, paused, turned back for a moment. "You three"—he pointed a single finger from one to the other—"keep the noise down, or I'll have you. I need my sleep."

The Boyz noted the mood swing. Were used to it.

And they knew what happened when you fucked with Rocco when you shouldn't be fucking with him.

"Let the big man get his beauty sleep and do likewise," said JP, fingering his Samsung, the screen lighting up with a design in red and black, the three-sevens swastika mutating on the white screen, a dance in front of his eyes.

"One thing for sure, Boyz," said JP.

"*Whatsit?*" said Christoff, slurping the brandy.

"There has to be a better way to crack ATMs. Less hassle. Less mess."

JP headed to his room, needed a dose of his phone. As he pissed in the potted palm outside his bedroom door, his usual spot, he heard Alex yellow-belly close the door to the room across the passage. Time was ripe, he'd know how to deal with dead-weight Prettyboy.

Lying on his bed, JP's fingers flying over the keyboard found a decent YouPorn clip: a video that turned him to wood in a flash. A blonde in leathers, in straps and collars and a tight corset, with blue eyes like the water of an over-chlorinated pool. Skin as white as ice crystals. He touched the screen, touched those heavy breasts with nipples tweaked hard as bolts.

He clicked in closer. Wanted to squirt all over her face, but no way he was gonna fuck up his new phone, like he did the last one, the fucking thing had short-circuited. It's all about control, he thought to himself, unbuttoning his jeans.

5:45 am Friday morning Heinz Dieter arrived at the Sea Breeze Pharmacy, a steel and glass new-fangled double-decker building on Main Road, Sea Point. As a trusted assistant, with access to keys, he unlocked the security door, pushed through the turnstile, hurried past counters of medicines, creams, pills, hairbrushes and health bars, and punched in the alarm code.

In the storeroom at the back he sat in front of the computer, cleaned the screen with Windowlene, switched it on, and listened to the reassuring hum of the hard drive come alive. He fingered his meds, refilled a vial of pills from the stock, tucked one under his tongue before placing the sealed container in the pocket of his white coat.

Calm and clear, he ran his fingers over her name on the pilfered business card, then Googled her. Clicked onto her website.

He caught his breath as a picture of the lovely Ms. Valentine popped up: in denim jeans and pumps, and a linen shirt with buttons and collar, her bare throat a near-flawless stretch of flesh, marred only by the scars of her past which of course he could forgive. Relaxed, her left foot was firmly planted on the pavement; her right, the knee bent, was raised on a pock-marked cement block, with just a hint, a glimmer, a glint of hard steel peeping from under the cuff of her jeans—something bionic at her ankle. The photograph was too street for his taste but he could forgive that too. The site was simple, her shelf page told of her forthcoming book, *If You Really Knew Me*, with comments and details of talks she'd given on drugging and the consequences, the loss of dreams and limb. He pored over the screen, spellbound by her shining eyes, her cheeks glowing with health.

How beautiful you are!

The warning tweet sounded at the front of the house as support staff arrived through the glass door and he was rudely called from the storeroom. With his heart racing, he braced himself to work with the sick, offering cold capsules, flu meds, vitamins, hot-toddy sachets. His first client, a woman topped with wild and coarse gray spirals like steel wool, asked, "My children have got lice. What can I use to nuke the little bastards? The lice, of course…"

He could cope with handing over antidepressants, women coming in for HRT, but this… His head started itching, his skin crawled. He pointed out the shampoos: Control Lice, Paralice, Quellada, any shampoo with gamma benzene hexachloride so heavy-duty it was little more than a pesticide that caused cancer, though it scarcely mattered, as long as the parasites were dead. At the staff toilet he covered the toilet seat with tissue paper. He had to purge. Could hardly bare to defecate. He scrubbed his face and hands with soap and Wet Wipes.

Calm at last, his ragged breathing under control, he stole a spare moment to get back to the storeroom. The printer groaned as Ms. Valentine's likeness, her splendor, was loosed from the machine. His ardor heightened when he had her in his hands. He folded her image twice over and sealed it in an envelope which he placed in the breast pocket of his coat. Close to his heart. He pressed his palms together, closed his eyes, thought of all he'd accomplished in this short time, and gave thanks.

7:00 am. Rae reached from under the warmth of the duvet into the chill air, slammed off the alarm.

Oh God, the night is too short.

The quicker she forced herself upright, swung her one-and-a-half legs over the edge of the bed and faced the day, the better. She felt her foot on the cold tiles. The Persian prayer mat, which for years had been at her bedside, remained rolled up. She had to get real, unpack the boxes she'd brought back from Tony's place. Get out the carpet to soften her first waking step, for the remainder of the winter.

She stood up. Hopped two steps to the window. Pulled back the blinds, saw the flat gray slab of the sky over Cape Town, the mountain invisible under the shroud.

She showered, lingered under the hot spray, then grabbed her towel, dried off, making sure the stump was dry as dust, before sitting on the toilet seat, smoothing on the stump sock and attaching her leg. In the bedroom she dressed in dark jeans and a white fleece top, a gray wool jacket plus scarf and cowboy boots. She scraped back her hair in a neat ponytail. She brushed on eyeshadow, rouge, a little powder. Smooched at the mirror. With make-up on she looked more like a PA at a law firm than an ex-junkie. As a motivational speaker she had to look the part, smart-casual. And the pay was good and getting better as she was more and more sought after on account of her straightforward, personable style.

First, though, to business.

Sol Anderson picked up this time and after introductions and small talk, his voice frail, sounding broken, he agreed to a meeting. "Make it 10:30."

A little before 9:00 am at Hillcrest High, Rae Valentine stood on stage in front of a hall packed with chirpy private-school "learners" as they called them now—who was the genius who'd come up with that term?—sitting upright on chairs; girls with stockinged legs, knees closed tight, hair pulled back off scrubbed faces; boys in neat chinos and knotted ties looking her way. Some of them not shy about pointing at her leg, the original, which she'd propped against the table. The one that looked real, the government issue, with foam built up over the rod connecting ankle and knee to resemble a calf, the one that looked like her skin. She'd painted the toenails in the shade she preferred for now: black.

She used to roll up her pant-leg at these gigs. Used to pull off her boot as she waited for the teenage chatter to die down. She'd put her fingers to her mouth, let rip an ear-splitting whistle. Then she'd push the button at her knee, pop off the prosthesis, call "Catch!" and toss the leg into the crowd. Usually some ball player on form would rise up, clutch the leg to his chest, then more often than not, drop it on the wooden floorboards as if it was a live grenade.

She didn't need to do the leg toss any more. Her reputation preceded her.

As for the leg she'd certainly moved on since then, had a few legs to choose from, mostly wore a sleek shape with defined toes that made her foot appear natural, and of course the bionic number she wore now.

"You're wondering," she started, "what I can possibly tell you about drugs that you don't already know." Yeah, probably half these kids' parents, brothers, sisters, were slaves to some sort of drug, popping Ritalin or Redupon or snorting cocaine off polished glass coffee tables in their designer lounges. Or just hit the booze.

"Check it out!" She pulled up her pant-leg, showing the kids the new model, the steel rod a polished piston shining under the stage lights. The last of the chitchat fizzled. She had their attention.

"Spiking up between my toes did this to me," she said. "With all that smack in my veins, they collapsed. Doctors had to chop off my leg. Bottom line, you do heroin, if you don't lose your leg you'll lose your dreams, maybe your life…"

Then on target, she lightened up and joked about the government issue leg, how she'd upgraded. "On the bright side, I'm sure to get a movie deal with this bionic limb! I'll be the first disabled Shero!"

After applause, the kids with chutzpah, or the ones on undecided street, came to her with more questions: *Smoking weed's okay, isn't it? D'you feel phantom limb pain? How do guys like you, Miss?*

"They seem to like me just fine." Best left unsaid that a whole lot of sleazebags got a kick out of her stump status. Best left unsaid how she'd been dumped. Worse.

She blinked, held the flashback in check.

She barely made it out of there. She got in the Jeep, locked the door, sat shivering uncontrollably, all of it coming back in a rush: fear clutching at her throat...

...the bastard running his tongue up her cheek, his sour breath coming at her as he held her down, pushing his rough tongue into her mouth, a flick-knife slashing...

She scratched at the itching scar tissue that ran from neck to breast.

She could feel the bulk of the Colt in the holster under her arm, she let her fingers drift over the comforting shape.

You're a survivor.

As were four-fifths of the population out there.

You are not alone.

She called the shrink. Voicemail.

Called Vince. Voicemail.

Wanted to call Tony. Couldn't.

Where are people when you need them?

Wanted to call family, but couldn't. If the "learners" could see her now, they'd understand: *When you drug, you lose people. You alienate everyone who ever loved you.*

It's a bloody hard road back.

Twenty minutes later, Rae talked herself into driving to Sol Anderson's Gold Extravaganza. Was lucky enough to find a spot for delivery vehicles right in front of what had to be one of the last independent stores off Adderley Street, the oldest city thoroughfare linking Cape Town central to the sea. Small enterprise had mostly been eaten up by big retail business, or had retreated to the safety of the underground mall below St George's or the squares of Greenmarket and Grande Parade. On top of that, the city was turning mostly residential. The order of the day was conversion of office space into loft apartments selling at the "affordable" millions quoted on swank billboards. As everything did, the city was changing.

The window of Gold Extravaganza was empty. The shallow trays lonely-looking without their wares. She imagined what might be there once Sol opened shop: gold wildlife brooches, pendants, assorted charms of lion and zebra, elephant-hair bracelets, rings of tanzanite the bright blue of Tony's eyes. Engagement rings, wedding bands, you name it. Maybe even baby pins, like the one her mother had pinned to her lacy dress at her christening. Did people still do this? Give silver spoons and cash boxes? Naaa, all disposable nappies nowadays, and baby-grows, and bath foam and Rescue Remedy for New Mom. She looked down at her bare hands: not even a pale tan-band on her ring finger.

"Let go your fantasy," she said aloud. "So Tony didn't want the same thing."

Took your house and your bird getting fucked over before you plucked up the courage to walk away. Right, Tony?

She held out both her hands. At least the shakes had stopped. She needed to see the shrink again, soon.

She buzzed the intercom.

About to push the glass door open, the two cops came out.

"Well, what do you know?" said Rae, as Rex

Hawkins and Adrian Lombard walked out the store. "What's up, guys?"

"Could ask the same of you. Though Sol told us there was a PI involved. Just didn't think it'd be a rookie."

Not about to make up some bullshit, she told them straight, "A client's jewelry's disappeared. Sol Anderson signed for it. Gave it to a dealer who's—poof!—gone. Client wants her baubles back."

No need to mention the uncut diamonds.

"Yeah?"

"You're not here about the same thing?"

She saw Adrian glance at Rex, saw the tacit agreement formed to keep her in the cold, then saw Adrian focus on her hands. "Find a nice guy yet? Pony-Tony's a mule."

"Don't give me a hard time, guys. Stick to filling me in on what's happening. How'd Anderson check out?"

"Sol Anderson's clean, Rae, clean as a whistle. But today's probably not the best day to chat."

"I'll see for myself if you don't mind, thanks very much."

"Suit yourself. Though you're wasting your time, girlie."

"Watch the patronizing bullshit, boys."

The cops sauntered off, she buzzed again.

Rae had expected a small man from the nervous sound of his voice on the phone, but Sol was a gentleman of some bulk, in a creased tailored suit, cracked gold-rimmed bifocals perched on a bulbous nose, a yarmulke atop a scalp of icing-sugar-white fluff.

Sol Anderson scrutinized Rae Valentine's ID as they stood on the pavement, kept looking left, right, then left again; jittery, drawing her in, as if expecting trouble. From the look of his face—bruised, his lip stitched—trouble had already come calling.

"Come in, come this way," he said, his voice a thin rope of pain.

"What happened?" asked Rae. "You all right?"

"I'm alive. My shop was hit yesterday. Robbed. I was assaulted."

"My God." She stared at the ruined interior, at smashed glass cabinets, splintered drawers. What must have been a neat and sparkling showcase of a shop was a wreck, deliberately bulldozed. She noticed the mangled security camera.

"After you, Ms. Valentine."

He followed her into his studio and closed the shattered glass door behind them. His certificates of expertise, the frames smashed, the paper torn, but revered enough to save, were leaned up against the wall.

"Please, have a seat." He pulled out a chair from in front of his desk. He sat alongside her. "I've never had so much as a shoplift in thirty years. I have better security than most, I have trusted staff. And now I suffer two incidents on either side of a week."

"I'm so sorry," comforted Rae, a gentle tone to her voice.

He spread his palms. "What can I do? A sign of the times. At least I'm alive. I read in the papers the criminal element is chopping off the ears of Somali shop owners, burning their body parts in pyres in their spaza shops. I've fared better than most."

"I can't bear it, either. Good people getting hurt."

"Breaks my heart, Ms. Valentine, the refugees under every canopy..." Sol Anderson ran a palm across his yarmulke, kept his hand atop his head and winced as he looked past her towards his store, and beyond, his eyes sunk in the hollows of a haggard face, the skin around them blue and raw. "Anyone who's different, the *other*, is in the firing line..." He wrung his hands. "Look what they did to my place!"

"So what happened?"

"Near closing yesterday afternoon, two young men came by. Dressed smartly, in ties and leather jackets. I believed they were from the diamond squad tasked with the annual inspection of the shop. They come this time of year, every year."

"You asked for identification?"

"They flashed ID, who knows what. My assistant Stella let them in. One minute she's busy sorting new stock, beautiful pieces of tiger's eye, jasper, aquamarine, semi-precious stones the tourists can't get enough of, the next a man's holding a gun to her head. He demanded the safe keys. They forced us to the ground, pulled cable ties around our wrists. They took everything: cash, rings, chains, everything."

Sol Anderson whispered, "One of them called me a dirty Jewboy. A kike. He slapped me, kicked me." Sol leaned forward, took off his yarmulke, the tears forming in the corners of his eyes threatening to spill over. "Look what they did. Why all this hatred?"

She winced at the bloodied rip in his scalp, the ugly bruising at the receding hairline.

"Thirty stitches they sewed in me. The hospital wanted to keep me in for observation, but I couldn't stay, I had to get back here."

"What do the police say, Mr. Anderson?"

He looked up again. Focused. "The criminals, damn them, were caught briefly on camera before they smashed the system. The police have the tape."

"Did you give a description?"

"I told the police already." The sadness of his pathetic response not lost on her. "One with dark hair, one with red curls. Both white."

✳

Tony Durant checked the screen, saw the name there, thought maybe too much dope smoking had addled his brain at last. He answered his cell. "Rex, my my."

"Long time no talk, Tony."

"To what do I owe the pleasure?" Tony drew long and hard, stars bursting behind his eyeballs as he held in the smoke. What the hell was Rex phoning for?

"You there, Tony?"

"What d'you want, Rex?"

"We're on our way over."

"We?"

"Me and Adrian."

"What for?"

"We'll be there in twenty. For an overdue chat."

"Let bygones be bygones, that it?"

"About time."

"And I'm s'posed to welcome you. I don't hear from you in six months and now you two're coming over to chew the fat."

"Something like that."

"Right then, you gonna tell me what's going on?" Silence.

Tony stared at the dead phone.

Natasha came into the bedroom. Stood there in a fuchsia camisole and matching panties, towel-drying her hair from the shower, water droplets glimmering on her bare shoulders.

"Tony? Was that *Rex Hawkins* on the line?"

"The very one."

"You're not getting involved in something you shouldn't be, now are you?"

"You know me." He drew her to him on the bed, nibbled her nipple through the silk cami; the towel dropping from her hands, they pressed together, her body still warm, Natasha's mouth on his, devouring, teeth on teeth, nipping at his tongue.

She pulled back. "Pony-Tony Durant is always getting into something he shouldn't. Don't sink yourself back in shit before I've hardly pulled you clear, Anthony. Your case is a priority, the negotiations at a sensitive stage. Could mean permanent dire straits for you if things get complicated."

Dire Straits. *How long, how long.*

He let her go. "Natasha, listen to yourself. I have no clue why Rex's coming over."

"Well, whatever it is, don't froth up the storm."

He drew her back to him, put his hands in her panties. "I hear you...I'm not about to do anything to jeopardize my case...apart from make love to my lawyer...which is somewhat...unethical...not so?"

She pushed him away. "You've already made me an hour late this morning."

Twenty minutes later, on the dot, Tony's cell rang.

REX on the screen.

"We're at your front door."

He spied the two cops through the peephole. Rex, on edge, shifted his weight from foot to foot. Both wore civvies. Rex had on a checked shirt, his regular Marlboro hanging from his lips. Adrian, spruce in white T-shirt and denims, held a conciliatory six-pack of beers.

Tony opened the door. "Déjà vu."

"Crosby Stills Nash?"

"And Young. You put foot."

"You gonna ask us in?"

"You gonna arrest me again?"

"Been there done that."

"So you gonna bring us in from the cold?" Rex

this time.

"Le Carré," said Tony, stepping aside.

"You're not just a pretty face, are you?"

Bloody hell, the Judases had crossed the threshold!

"Now tell me, what's going on?" Hard, stony.

Rex asked, "You still sore, Tony?"

"You set me up!" The lilt of disbelief trailed the men heading towards the lounge where the sweet smells of sex, coffee, and dope still mingled, hanging in the air.

"My friend," said Rex, "my job's worth a coupla hundred thou a year. Paltry sum, we're agreed on that. But making a choice between you and pay, my medical aid plus full pension, my good buddy, meant I had to save my skin."

"So you went right ahead and fucked me over."

"Don't be so melodramatic. You were fucked no matter what we did. You can thank Chas Moodley for that."

"And now the court date gets pushed back with every appearance."

"You'll get off, Tony, you know it, I know it. Moodley knows the state doesn't have a leg to stand on. You'll probably get a major payout for wrongful prosecution. Make a killing."

Tony said, "The system's a blocked drain."

"What can I say? Hang in there, like the rest of us wading through piles of crap."

"Yeah? And in the months it's taking to get sorted, what do I do, Rex?" Tony sighed. "Heck. So what's up then? You're not here to dop and chat about chicks, or what?"

"In fact," said Adrian, "we did come to chat about women. One woman in particular."

※

A Charlize Theron lookalike, with turquoise eyes, fine blonde hair and ski-slope nose, but shorter, plumper, brought in tea for two. The assistant no doubt.

"Thank you, Stella," said Sol. Then to Rae: "At least they left me the kettle and mugs."

Rae played mother, poured.

Stella interrupted, shy and introvert, saying, "Sol, okay with you if I run? I want to be on time for my counseling session."

"Absolutely, you go ahead."

Sol sipped at the tea, his head bowed, his hands trembling. "So Rosa Dieter said you were coming. She thinks you can do a better job than the police. The police will handle this robbery," he winced, "but as for Rosa she doesn't believe in their ability. Who can blame her? Rosa said the stones might as well have been sourced from the local Scratch Patch for all the good they did her. She wanted cash, wanted to splash out, book a berth on the *QE 2*. How do I get over this?"

"You will, Sol, you will."

"The stitches are driving me crazy." The jeweler scratched his head and Rae saw, as his cuff slipped back, a faded blue number stamped on his forearm and wondered at the kind of hate he'd already suffered.

"You must understand diamonds are a gentleman's game. Agreements in this business are made with a handshake and the worth of your word. I am an honorable man, Ms. Valentine. I don't insist on paperwork. I acted in good faith as I always have over the forty-five years I've been in the trade. All indications were the sale was in order. And I have never in the last eight years had a problem with my dealer."

"Your dealer?"

"A sort of a middleman. In this case a woman, Trudie Kellerman. I set up a meeting with her. She told me she had a buyer. I met her at the Cape Grande as I've done before, did everything exactly as before. I handed over the jewelry, pre-war European treasures. And the diamonds of course." Sol coughed, clutched at his hurt ribs, struggling as he regained composure. "The set gems mere baubles in comparison with the value of the uncut stones from Grandmother Dieter's husband's days in the trade. As I said, everything was in order, every item authenticated. Trudie handed the consignment to the buyer. It's as simple and as terrible as this: the wire transfer never came through; the buyer disappeared." He dabbed at his weeping eye, controlled the tremor at his lip. "There are no documents of proof. Trudie is as devastated as I am. A centuries-old tradition of trust is now a flaw in this business. And now the shop is targeted for everything else."

"So what do you know of the buyer? How do we *trace* him? Assuming it's a male?"

"Or not. That's Trudie's department."

"How did you advertise the sale?"

"I didn't." Wringing his hands. "Again, I left it with Trudie. More and more people are selling up, it's nothing unusual. Now Rosa is threatening to sue." He cleared his throat. "For the family heirlooms, the actual jewelry, you understand." His knowing look not lost on her.

Whatever Vince had surmised, the kind of emotion in Sol's soft eyes, his unsteady hands, spoke of torment, betrayal. No make-up story this. Even if the diamonds were undeclared. Whatever it was, her gut said this was a genuine double-whammy deal gone wrong. Her job was to get the items back to the owner. That's what she was being paid for. After that, let the police deal with the irregularities and illegalities.

He continued: "She's understandably furious. She says it's my fault. My good name is now called into question, though what does it matter?"

He gestured lamely towards his ruined life—the trashed shop, the monstrous red, black and white graffiti on every wall: three-pronged variations of the Nazi swastika. The paint raw and symbolic of hate.

❈

Rex grimaced. "No better coffee than this? Still sticking with the cheap stuff?"

"You didn't pop by to talk beverages. And instant's all you'll get."

"I care about you, pal, whether you believe it or not, our times on the force, our times fishing…"

Tony shrugged. "I'm hardly crying 'cos it's over. You said this is about a woman."

"Rae Valentine. Your ex-girl's new job she's taken on. A job too big for her."

"Rae knows what she's doing."

"But taken to carrying a piece—"

"She's entitled, she's licensed."

"—and was dressed today in an oversized army jacket like she means business. Her hair tied back, those full lips on her, man, Tony, she reminds me of the unstoppable chick in *Tomb Raider*, 'cept this is no flick. What's her name? Lara Croft."

"Angelina Jolie."

"Yeah, yeah."

"So what're you saying? She's doing the sleazeball stuff, same as me and Vince were doing. And doing it well by all accounts."

"She's in over her head this time."

"Vince said some pensioner's had her jewelry nabbed. Sounds like the kind of yawn Rae's well able to handle."

"Seems there's more to the jewelry thing than meets the eye."

"Yeah? So what d'you want *me* to do about it?"

"Talk to her. Find out what she knows."

"Then tell you, is that it?"

"You've got a good understanding of the situation, Tony."

"Aw, and I thought you guys really did miss me."

"Life's not the same without you."

"So tell me, why don't you talk to her yourself?"

Adrian cut in: "She's proving she can do it. Fiery, gutsy, not about to share a thing."

"Call Vince then, guys."

"When he's soaked he's impossible, you know that," said Adrian.

"He needs AA before we can have a conversation with him," added Rex. "Seriously."

"You're his mentor, right?" said Tony.

"It's for some people." Rex drew on the Marlboro, coughed harshly, his lungs solid waste. "Not Vince. We all have our habits," he warned Tony off from pushing more buttons. "And at least I can still do my job."

"So, Tony," chirped Adrian. "How's about you encourage your partners to step back from this one? How's that sound?"

"C'mon, *pals*, you want help, spit out the rest. This obviously isn't some straight theft, so tell me what's really going on."

"Jesus Christ, Tony, if you must know. Yesterday a couple of hate-crime bastards left a nice mess at the very store Rae's investigating as part of her job, including the owner's blood all over the show cases. All we have are shadows on surveillance to go by."

"Killed?"

"Beaten pretty badly. But he's a big man. Big spirit."

"Heck, this sounds straight down the line."

Adrian shook his head. "No man, ordinary people are turning on each other. It's shit publicity for the Rainbow Nation. In the early hours, right here in the city, a coupla Malawians doing nothing but standing outside the Sky Street People's Church were shot at. Middle of suburban Sea Point. Potentially anyone who's a citizen of another nation could end up a victim. You might be a loaded tourist, but you just look like you don't belong, you wear the wrong clothes—a veil, a scarf, an ethnic print, a yarmulke—you might end up dead. This rubbish has people spooked. People in high places are worried."

"So it's about keeping up appearances?"

"Hell, it's about more than looking good."

"Bottom line," interrupted Rex, "this incident is one of a few that points to a right-wing group planning trouble, to some real nasty pieces of work capitalizing on the instability to cause serious crap."

"And you know this how?"

Adrian jumped in: "The War Room's worried. We don't want Rae or Vince spooking a Nationalist group hellbent on destabilizing the country before we've got a handle on things. They'll go underground. You hear anything you'll come to us, right, Tony?"

"Who else would I go to?"

Soon as Rex and Adrian were out the door, he rolled a spliff, deftly and expertly, lit it, drew the smoke into his lungs. It wasn't about keeping Rae and Vince safe, it was all about Rex and Adrian protecting turf. That War Room talk just a load of horse shit.

Bastards!

He ignored the tick-tock but heard it all the same, the cheap kitchen clock marking empty time. He pulled deep, till he'd reached the short end, felt the sting at the back of his throat, held in the smoke for a couple more beats, exhaled. Then went out to the garage to check out his latest investment: hydroponic cultivation of imported seeds at one hundred bucks each from the Netherlands, with special lighting, extractor fans, heating and tubes for suctioning air in and out. The blue-green glow emanating from six 25-Watt four-foot tubes set a meter apart on the ceiling was soft and nurturing, the hum of the lights comforting. The temp maintained at a warm 22 degrees Celsius. He checked the nitrogen, phosphorus and potassium ratios in the mix and sprinkled the base of the plants with soil food. You had to be careful using synthetic chemicals; you didn't want to risk killing off any potential clients with contaminated leaves. Then he watered the plants, in terracotta pots, with a sports-drink bottle, saturating the earth around the babies. No good letting your weed investment die of dehydration, but you had to be sure not to overwater either.

His grandmother was right about gardening. It soothed the soul. He had come to understand this. Especially when there was profit to be made. As soon as the plants were a good two feet high and budding, he'd prepare for the ritual of picking, drying, trimming, crushing and packaging. The business was small scale but satisfying, and profits would leap to the next level now that he was growing more of his own stuff. Was a matter of time before selling was legal. Till then, he still had to earn his keep. And no doubt about it, he looked forward to smoking his crop.

Back in the house Tony pressed the landline speed-dial but cut the call before the last of the digits had completed the sequence.

What're you doing, boykie? If your ex answers, then what? Leave Rae alone, for Christ's sake. She's a grown woman.

Rain came down heavy on the tin roof. He emptied the bucket under the leak in the lounge, thought of helping himself to one of the lagers his pals had left behind, but booze before dope wasn't a good plan. He rolled another stop. For old time's sake slotted Rae's Joan Armatrading in the CD player, lay back on the couch and listened to just one song: Joan singing about breaking hearts and losing pride, her gravelly voice striking a chord. Nothing to beat the classics. Pity you couldn't turn back the pain.

"Talk to me," he said to the emptiness, his voice creaking with the hit still in his throat. This was what loneliness felt like, and waste…

He drew long and hard, obliterating thoughts rushing like the wind.

Kickstarting her flagging spirit, Rae breathed in the new-ish-car smell of the Jeep. She couldn't get Sol Anderson out of her mind. He hadn't been able to stop weeping—mourning. It was more than the stolen jewels; it was the sudden and tragic loss of his wellbeing cultivated over all the years he'd believed he belonged. He'd allowed her to hug him, stroke his arm, but she knew only too well the trauma of what he'd been through, the desperation, the rocking of his emotional world. She empathized even as she knew he was doing deals under the table. Had to be. Something about his story didn't gel. She'd got nothing more helpful from Sol apart from a scribbled hotel name, a no-brainer to look up the Cape Grande.

She activated the Bluetooth.

"Hi," she said jauntily, confidently, arousing no suspicion, "put me through to Ms. Kellerman in room 712."

"We have a Trudie Kellerman in room 814."

"Trudie Kellerman, yes, thanks."

"Ms. Kellerman is unavailable," the receptionist came back after half a minute on hold. "You're welcome to leave a message."

"No worries, thanks."

Rae pulled out into the slow stream of traffic. This was city-improvement for you, inner-city congestion, an endless frustration manifesting in hooting, swearing, showing finger. When the attacks were over, road rage'd still go on strong.

She called Vince: "Where are you?"

"At the office."

Midday only and Rae heard the gruff in his voice. "You're kidding me."

"Nope. At your service, Rae. Whassup?"

"Order up a couple of coffees. Sounds like you need a triple espresso." She could just about see him slumped on the couch. "Try sober up before I get there, if you'd do me the honor."

Newspaper headlines loomed large, on posters tacked to poles:

HEAVY WEATHER WARNINGS

FOOD CHAOS PLAGUES HOPE REFUGEE CENTER

MORE CITY BOMB BLASTS

She drove down Adderley towards the foreshore, past the iconic Standard Bank, and the alley where the famous Flower Sellers of Cape Town sold their blooms; past OK Bazaars and the Golden Acre and then the station on the left; past all the modern structures erected after the Victorian buildings had, long since, been torn down; past, on the right, a tiny memorial to Scott of Antarctica, and past Van Riebeeck's statue. Getting closer to the foreshore's sea-front buildings, Rae spied crime-scene tape near the fancy fountain at the juncture of Adderley and Heerengracht, saw the blue lights flashing. No wonder the traffic was backed up. With every vehicle slowing down for a gander, five minutes later the Jeep had crept only two blocks further along. Curiosity may kill the cat, but satisfaction brings it back, Rae sighed, as she too slowed to a crawl to check out the debris-covered pavement, yet another ATM blasted to hell and gone with the guts of the machine spilling out. Yeah, another one down, another one bites the dust, she tapped out the rhythm on the steering wheel. CSI had to be done scouring the scene. Workers were already sweeping the mess from the road.

Then she spotted it: the graffiti. A three-pronged swastika similar to the one sprayed on the walls of Sol's shop.

Something more here Rex and co aren't sharing.

Her cell buzzed, jolting her to reality. No caller ID, but she pushed green.

"Ms. Valentine, what progress have you made?" Rosa on the line. Damn! She hadn't added Rosa to her contacts.

"I've just chatted with Sol Anderson at the shop." Rae wondered if Frau Dieter knew about the attack and the looting but she wasn't about to share over the phone. "Mrs. Dieter, there's a matter I need to discuss with you."

"Come. Now."

Just like that.

Rosa expecting service on the double.

Rae took a left at Heerengracht, towards Somerset Road; past St Andrew's Church; past the old Catholic church, past the Salesians Institute and the old Gallows Hill just above the Breakwater Prison; then saw the commonage with the landmark Cape Town Stadium looming ahead; a goddamn awful ugly-as-sin edifice resembling a giant toilet bowl, a blot on the mountain backdrop, and costing ratepayers a bomb to service. *It* should be bombed; at least the architect should be forced to work on a chain gang. The talk now on the news was that the stadium may be converted into a refugee center.

Traveling on Beach Road, she drove through Three Anchor Bay, then got to Sea Point.

Waiting at a traffic light she pressed the icon for "office landline." "You had your caffeine boost yet, Vince? Yeah? Change of plan. Give me an hour. I'm on my way to Rosa Dieter."

"What d'you want me to do in the meantime?"

"Drink more coffee."

"Get serious, Rae."

"I am. Get yourself together. Sit tight, have lunch. Let's see what Frau Dieter says."

Rae wanted clarification; in her mind's eye she saw a list of questions.

One: who else knows about the jewelry apart from you, your son, Sol and Trudie Kellerman?

The thief of course.

Two: is there anything about the provenance of the diamonds you need to confess?

Three: is there indeed a gigolo type sucking you dry?

In answer, in the flesh, Rosa replied: "Yes, Heinz knew about the jewelry, as did Sol Anderson, and of course several of my friends." She introduced Mrs. Kapinski, packing away what Rae swore were holiday brochures, at the dining-room table.

"Sit. Pour the sherry. I trust my friends."

"You don't think any of us had anything to do with the theft?" Mrs. Kapinski put the file in the basket of her Zimmerframe and downed her glass. "We encouraged you, didn't we, Rosa? Live a little we said! Always so stiff upper lip! Always looking after that son of yours!"

Rosa Dieter saw her friend to the door. Rae heard Mrs. Kapinski shuffle out with gusto, the gutsy senior calling back: "Ms. Valentine, tell Mr. Durant I send my regards."

Another woman obsessed by Tony...

Rae sucked it up, got quickly to the point when Rosa took her seat: "I had to ask, Mrs. Dieter. And I have to ask too about the history of the diamonds?"

"The only things left to me apart from a likeness of my parents"—she plucked a photo from a drawer, handed it over, a frayed memento of loss—"were my mother's precious things." She sighed. "Sehr schön but I had a right to sell every piece, and I have explained how I came by the stones. They're no blood diamonds. My father was a lapidary."

"A lapi- excuse me, Mrs. Dieter?"

"Pour me another," the old woman instructed. "A diamond-cutter, at his Hamburg diamond shop. He sorted stones, diamonds in the rough, into sands, smalls and carats, then he polished and cut and sliced the facets. I used to watch him sometimes. Such concentration it took to use the special cutter. I tried it myself one day. I was only a child, five years old. The result was not positive." She held up her disfigured hands. "The stones were my father's legacy. He was supposed to meet us in Namibia, but near the end of the war a bomb killed them both, my mother and father. Hamburg was all but destroyed, razed to the ground. I was suddenly an orphan and put on a ship to South Africa."

Rae kept her expression neutral, her hands still in her lap, her notebook to one side, as Rosa leaned into her personal space and recited deadpan: "There were many of us, crammed in like cattle. We wore life jackets, suffered seasickness. Yes, we were looked after by nurses, but I missed home. We thought we wouldn't survive. It was the mines we were afraid of; at any moment the ship could hit one and we would be blown up or burned or drowned." She looked almost vulnerable, her eyes clouding. "Got 'im Himmel, we were so afraid of the mines…" She slumped a little. "There were many good people on that ship but also thieves and rapists. I kept the diamonds safe. Days before my parents were killed, my mother sewed the jewelry in the hem of my coat; I watched as her fingers zipped in the treasure, listened as she whispered instructions. I never took off the coat, not even in the heat when I first arrived. My parents were dead, my hands itched in the bandages. I was to go straight to Nazareth House. The nuns would have looked after me. But my benefactors were waiting for me on the dockside. I had nothing else to my name apart from the coat."

Rosa smoothed her mutilated hands over her thighs, stroking, comforting herself. "And I never let it out of my sight. I would not allow them ever to take it from me."

Rae interrupted, "They took you in?"

"Oh yes, I had a loving foster family." Rosa's mouth tightened, her eyes narrowed. "I grew up in this house, this very house. When my stepmother died, I stayed on with my stepfather. Mein Vatti. He was surprisingly gentle with me, showing his love." Sarcasm tainted her tone. "I had the baby, Heinz, in my very own bed. The blood, the suffering…Have you had children, Ms. Valentine?"

"Not yet."

"It's a drain. From the moment the child screams and takes in his first breath, from the time he bites at your breast as he sucks you dry and raw, it is an ordeal, a cross to bear." She clucked her tongue, her façade once more in place. "I'm not interested in any man."

Unaccustomed to women divulging their secret shame quite so readily, Rae found herself reaching for Rosa's hand, that mutilated hand. She held it, as rough as sand paper, between hers, the stumps stiff and cold in her gentle grip. The older woman allowed it for seconds only, then withdrew as if the warmth was too much to bear.

"The unpleasant business is long in the past. To move forward is always a good thing, you agree? And I have Heinz, after all, a lovely boy."

Rae headed out, shivering as the cold hit her, the hint of Frau Dieter's pain still on her skin as she made tracks back to the office, knowing that she had learned a little more, but not the whole truth. Rosa had been through hell, but what had Tony warned her about way back? *When the client tells you what you haven't asked about, when you're bombarded with more information than you need, that's when a PI gets curiouser and curiouser.*

Rosa Dieter had done just that, played her.

But what's the game?

"You gonna join me, Mandla?" asked Vince passing the open door of the adjacent office, seeing the lawyer stooped over his desk.

"Kentucky Fried? Don't mind if I do." Mandla stretched, got up like an old man, all creased and stiff from poring over files, making notes, being there for other people.

Vince guessed he was in his late twenties. A young, driven lawyer, hip with his designer suit and shirts, his natural Afro a soft two-centimeter cushion. Had soft eyes. Wanted to change the world, believed he could do it, spent long hours working at it.

In the PI's office Mandla glanced at the makeshift bed, a camping mattress in the corner. "I sleep in too, when it's too late to go home."

"I sleep in when there's no way I can go home," Vincent replied, picturing his ma's face drawn in angst.

Vince pulled out a chair for Mandla and the two of them tucked in as they sat opposite each other, tearing at the drumsticks, sucking marrow from the bones, slurping, smacking greasy lips. The lawyer brought out a flask, pouring them each a healthy tot of whiskey in the tea cups Rae kept for clients.

"To you, brother, you saved me. I was starving. On me next time."

"You doing okay next door, Mandla?"

"Hey, it's not too bad spending a night or two in the city. I could get used to it."

"Why d'you live in Khayelitsha anyway?" Vince scooped coleslaw from a tub with a plastic fork, went on with his mouth full: "Guy like you could leave the township for good. Could buy a house in a top neighborhood, in the safe southern suburbs."

"It's where I grew up, home, you know?" Mandla talked of the narrow streets, the shacks of corrugated iron, the poverty he couldn't turn his back on. "Now developers are finding out there's money to be made there, even me, I'm looking to invest in an epic apartment block going up near my council house. Apart from that, my wife works with AIDS orphans. Helping the community's her life. She wants to make a difference."

"Some would say that's what it's all about."

"It's tough, you know? With all these troubles we're having, I get threats from locals saying I'm helping foreigners steal their jobs." He downed his drink, let out a neat burp. "Will be a relief when all this bad feeling, this violence out there, quietens down and I have space to breathe." He pulled up the bottom of his jersey, revealing a designer-beige bulletproof vest. "Bloody expensive, this!"

Vince popped an eyebrow, nodded, "Lawyering's a dangerous business!" He ripped the corner off a tomato sauce sachet, squirted ribbons over the fries. *Yeah, go ahead, try change the world, till you bust a gut, then live knowing it's all futile.* "World needs people like you, Mandla." *People like you don't last, Mandla. Bulletproof vest or not.* He wanted to warn the guy: *You'll burn out trying to change human nature. There's your own limitations, Mandla.*

"Gotta get back to the grind, Vince." Mandla wiped the grease from his fingers with a serviette.

"Before you head off, can I ask you something, without getting billed?"

"Sure, my brother, go ahead."

"Know anything about the illegal diamond trade?"

"I don't know the difference between a diamond and a cubic zirconia. I swear I paid over-the-top dollar for my wife's ring. Vince, seriously, you know as well as I do it's a cold, impersonal business. You heard of the Kimberley Process? Was set up by the United Nations in 2003 to prevent conflict diamonds from entering the mainstream rough-diamond market. But hell, that's for buyers and sellers with consciences, not your wheeler-dealer types."

"So legalities around provenance mean nothing?"

"Problem with provenance is if the diamonds are

old enough, the story dies with whoever knew it in the first place. Diamonds seemingly fallen off the face of the earth easily land in the hands of a private dealer, they materialize with a new sales pedigree, can end up in auction rooms for legit sales. Problem is diamonds can't be traced with sufficient court-proof accuracy. It's white-collar crime. Now I really gotta run. Have to file last minute papers before I'm due in court."

"Thanks, man. Don't kill yourself with your heavy workload, now."

"I'm representing a Zimbabwean couple. The wife lost an eye in a beating. They've put in an emergency application for asylum in Canada."

"Even though our government want refugees to stay?"

"But what do the refugees want? My job's to help them with what they want."

"Mr. and Mrs. Zim don't wanna go home?"

"You serious? To what? She's a doctor, he's a bean counter. Husband says he and his now half-blind missus'll starve to death with Zim gone from bad to worse. No work, no food, the currency collapsed."

"Till later, then," said Vince, kicking back in Tony's chair as Mandla disappeared out the door.

Yeah, yeah, Mandla, hang in there with your passion, your caring, your heart of bloody gold.

He spun round a couple of times, kept half an eye on some inane crime crap on the small TV. After a long swallow of Coke, he polished off the soggy chips. Gnawed the last of the flesh from a leg. Found a stray wing at the bottom of the KFC bucket, sucked off every morsel off flesh and tossed the bone back in the bucket and belched.

He picked up a copy of *Noseweek*, uncovered the .357 Magnum he'd laid on the desk, a double action Taurus. He picked it up. Big gun, heavy. He pushed in a single bullet, clicked the cylinder in place, spun the wheel of fortune then shoved the muzzle under his cheekbone.

What were the odds? It had nothing to do with luck. It had everything to do with the law of averages. Thing about Russian roulette, there was only a one in six chance, not even seventeen percent, of shooting yourself. Odds were in your favor.

Vincent's heart was pumping.

He'd had a satisfying last meal.

He sniffed at the rank smell of his shirt, the adrenaline turned sour. Couldn't get the vision of Amber, bloody and broken, out of his head. Her car-crash death no accident. His wife targeted on account of his cop work, on account of the scum he'd put away.

He pulled the trigger.

Click.

Fucking nothing.

His heart racing.

He pressed the muzzle to his temple.

You might survive if you do it this way, boykie.

With brain damage.

So do it right.

He opened his mouth, jammed the pistol under his palate. Felt the cold ring of steel, his tongue curving under the barrel; his finger pointed straight along the slide, about to slip to the trigger.

He heard steps on the stairs.

Gagging, he rukked the revolver from his mouth. Replaced the gun in the top drawer, thinking *not yet my time*, as Rae came through the door.

"Yuck," said Rae. "D'you have to eat takeaway rubbish in here? Place stinks."

Plus the reek of alcohol breath and stale body odor gave the game away: Vince was a hungover wreck. The restlessness, the tapping foot, the twitch at his lip. Sunken eyes. A bruise starting under his cheek.

"What you been up to, Vince?"

Wouldn't be the first time he'd got himself mixed up in a bar-room brawl, usually coming off second best as if he *wanted* his heart beaten right of him.

"Waiting for you, Rae."

She sighed, tossed her rucksack on the desk, sat on the warm chair. Watched him put his feet up, swivel back to the mute CSI rerun on TV.

He broke the silence: "Blame these dudes for complicating the issue. Now every bloody client expects techs to meticulously sift for pubes, take nail scrapings and penis swabs and get the results overnight. Don't people click it's fantasy? Miami, New York, LA. Hollywood. All that temperature taking, checking for bugs 'n' slugs. Coming to definitive conclusions." He laughed hoarsely. "What's wrong with the South African way? The guy's dead. Stick the guy in the morgue and let him rot. Forget the evidence. Who cares who did it."

"And TV cops look way too good." She made light. "Perfect make-up every time."

"Yeah." Vince blinked rapidly. "When last did I get my hair blow-dried and wear eyeliner on a case?"

"My, you're in a positive frame of mind." Rae could only handle so much of Vince's booze-fueled bad attitude.

"So what can *you* tell *me*, Rae? Two hours ago you let me know you were on your way and you only rock up now? Mandla ate your lunch. I was gonna save you a drumstick, but it's all gone."

She registered the bones and mayo smears in a polystyrene plate in front of Vince.

"D'you want to know about the job or not?"

"If you must."

"The jewelry got to the shop all right," she confirmed. "Take a look." She tossed over photographs Sol had taken of Rosa Dieter's collection. Fourteen items in all. Several engagement-type rings: a brilliant cut of a sought-after tanzanite in a platinum band; a Kate Middleton sapphire surrounded by smaller diamonds; a solitaire diamond in a gold-claw setting a mile high; a ruby pendant with a drop-pearl; an emerald brooch; an engraved fob chain; and more; and the uncut, rough stones, spilling from the velvet pouch.

Vince whistled.

"Twenty-eight stones to be exact, according to Sol. A tidy investment in anyone's books."

"Worth a fortune. But those photos could be fake."

"Maybe, but why would Rosa lie? Heinz brought home a receipt. Sol claimed his middleman Trudie Kellerman's a woman he's worked with for years. Problem arose when Trudie handed over the diamonds to a buyer and the all too willing buyer absconded."

"Or there never was a buyer. Stuff's in Sol's safe. Have to consider every angle, Sherlock."

"See what you make of this then, Watson: Sol Anderson's shop was hit yesterday."

"You're kidding?"

"Major robbery. Sol and his assistant, Stella Whoever, were tied up. He was beaten and the shop smashed up and vandalized."

"A planned hit? Your sixth-sense telling you it has some link to Mrs. Germany's story?"

"Sometimes the obvious answer is the right answer." Rae left her cell in her pocket, with the pics there of red and black three-pronged swastika bleeding down the jeweler's wall. "Here's another theory: it could be connected to what's going on in the streets. Maybe Sol's just another casualty of the bad feeling out there."

"What's the craziness out there got to do with an old white Jewish jeweler?"

"Different is different."

Vince went on: "If you want my two-cents worth, my sense is still cherchez la femme. I'm telling you it has to be Rosa has your answers."

"What about Trudie? There's a femme for you. She knows the game, knows Sol's business is based on a handshake, on trust. Knows there's no paperwork to track, and till we talk to her, all we have is conjecture. That's where we have to look."

"What d'you know, just maybe," a true smile played at Vince's lips, "this might shape up nicely after all. Maybe it'll work out more promising than a severe case of senile greed."

"She may be greedy, who knows, but there's no flies on Rosa, Vince."

"So tell me. She say anything about the boyfriend, the gold-digger sonnyboy fears?"

"She's adamant there's none. Acted insulted we'd even consider the possibility. I didn't want to press her. She told me things...a lover's not a realistic option."

Rosa had held her hands in front of her, as if protecting herself, droning about her foster father raping her all those decades ago. Rosa knew and now Rae knew. And she'd keep it to herself. Some things you didn't have to broadcast.

"So what about you, Vince?"

"Nothing we don't already know. Sonnyboy went on about the toyboy. Which you say mummy denies. So there's nothing to tell. Heinz Dieter gave the diamonds and sparklies to Sol, got the receipt, Trudie had it, handed it over, now it's gone, back to square one."

"Square one being a pearl-in-an-oyster-at-the-bottom-of-the-sea search for engagement rings and a pouch of diamonds."

Vince couldn't help laughing. He swung his legs off the desk, sniffed. "You need coffee, Rae?"

"I'll call down."

"I wanna stretch my legs. I'll get it."

"You sure it's coffee you're after?"

"Don't start now with the drinking problem crap. Let me be."

"So go. Go," she said. "Go on!" Who was he kidding? Of course he was gonna make his stop at the Blue Bottle for his hair of the dog. *I understand! How couldn't I?* But the thought didn't stifle her disenchantment.

Vince grabbed her over-sized camo jacket, said, "Bloody cold out there."

"Any time. Help yourself." She watched as he pulled the collar of her fleece-lined jacket up around his neck.

"Rain's beating down. I'll be back in ten."

"Why the hell don't you splurge for a decent coat, Vince?" His sodden denim jacket hung on the back of the chair. "Just go. And get it right this time, Vince. My order's an Americano." Sometimes it felt as if Vince was stunted in every part of his life.

Rae knew first hand you had to hit the gutter before you could help yourself. But what the hell was rock bottom for Vince? He was hurting, Rae saw it in the way his body sagged, as if he'd lost height, a wretchedness about him she wished she could ease. Rae was a pro at airing her angst, but Vince couldn't talk, wouldn't talk.

She also knew she was scared. Truth be told, she didn't have a clue how to handle a case like this and she was too damned proud to phone Tony. He'd know what to do, would give good advice—but she wasn't going to ask.

There were always her role models. Ha! According to Kinsey Millhone, when stuck you make a list. In what Rae thought was a determined fashion, she picked up a pen and pulled the A4 pad close, started scribbling:

Rosa Dieter—blows hot and cold, is calculating

Heinz Dieter—anxious and worried son, but hiding something

Sol Anderson—injured, distraught, disbelieving

Stella Whoever—to interview

Trudie Kellerman—trusted diamond dealer with a difference

The thief—???

She waited for the kind of deep insights this activity produced when it was completed by fictional PIs. Not a damned thing. Other than make a list, she might get more info if she went to see Stella. Plus, she'd send Vince to see Trudie. Had to wonder if it was as simple as the lot of innocent, trusting people out there, like Rosa, Sol and Trudie, who knew about scams, but were, surprise surprise, getting ripped off by bad people.

Rae called Stella's number. Got her mother on the line saying, "Poor Stella's not back from the trauma counselor. My little girl was so shocked at what happened to Sol, such a dear man. Can she call back?"

"No problem. I'll try later."

Then tried Trudie again. Not available. Didn't leave a message.

Said to herself, "On the upside you haven't checked out, have you, Ms. Kellerman?"

According to Sol, Trudie was a brassy brunette in her forties.

Knows diamonds, so Sol said, and he trusted her

implicitly.

Well, this was one bit of trust that could bear some scrutiny.

Like so many other bits.

My husband would never cheat on me.

My wife, my mistress, my dog, my hamster would never cheat on me.

I would never cheat on them!

She'd learned another early lesson in the PI business: it was Tony who'd told her to always check the phone directory. "You want a phone number, a home number or business, you let your fingers do the walking in the White Pages, the Yellow Pages, a lotta times you get lucky."

A more successful method, Rae had learned, was if you had a name, you Googled it. You found more than simply phone numbers. "Tony, you Neanderthal," she said aloud, turning to the computer, "I could teach you a bloody thing or two." Nine times out of ten you found info on the Net. You found so much info you didn't know where to start scratching.

Trudie Kellerman had a web page with the usual stats and facts. Trudie was more than just a dealer. She called herself a freelance diamond merchant, an authority on gemstones, a jewelry connoisseur, with descriptions of deals made. Sounded legit. No pictures of Trudie though.

She opened Facebook. Who out there did not put their lives out on social media in this day and age? Maybe Tony the technophobe, still thinking a mouse was something you set the cat on. But for the rest?

Bingo!

Hardly a challenge now, was it?

There she was, in all her glory. Sweet.

"You might know stones, Trudie, but you have no sense of reservation or self-preservation."

She was more than seductive; a hedonist, a woman who didn't seem to know you shouldn't put pics of yourself on the Net that may seem a trifle inappropriate. The screen filled with Trudie Kellerman— resembling a plus-size model in racy, lacy lingerie, her double-F breasts spilling from a push-up brassiere way too teensy-weensy, barely covering deep-coral nipples—in a photo taken at what must have been an intimate shoot and should have been kept way private. And this her profile pic! Facebook was where people inadvertently gave the game away, with updates and tagged photos. About who they were. Who they *really* were. Rae sent a friend request; most social media extroverts so keen to build up their friend base they'd say yes to anyone.

And there it was too, a cell number.

She punched in the sequence, hung in there for long moments before the ringing reverted to voicemail: a heady, throaty voice. German? Austrian? OTT Swiss Miss suited the persona on screen. Rae didn't leave a message. With any luck Trudie would call back. Trudie looked the type who didn't want to miss out on any damn thing.

The harsh ring of the landline jolted Rae from her voyeur status. "Hello?"

"Ms. Valentine?"

"Speaking."

"You saw my mother yesterday about her missing jewelry?"

"Oh yes?"

"My name is Heinz Dieter. I'm Rosa Dieter's son."

"Ah, Mr. Dieter. What can I do for you?

"Please, call me Heinz."

"So what can I do for you, Heinz?"

"And may I have the pleasure of calling you Rae?" he crooned in a voice soft as butter, but timid, as if chatting up women wasn't his thing.

"Yes, of course."

"I've been thinking increasingly of my mother. I wanted to communicate my anxiety, I'm desperately worried about her."

"We're on the same side, Mr. Dieter. There's nothing much more we can do at this stage. We're following up on various leads. And I'll be liaising with the police, too, especially after the attack on Sol Anderson yesterday."

"Attack?"

"You didn't know?" *Why am I the one to break the news?* "His shop was targeted, burgled, he was pretty badly hurt."

"I'm devastated. Sol is a good man."

"He's tough, he'll be fine. So to get back to your mother's case..."

"Yes. There might be something more to this. Something that has nothing to do with the missing jewelry." His voice obsequious, persuasive, compelling. "I don't understand what's happening, but my mother is in trouble. This is where you come in, Ms. Valentine." He hesitated a moment; she heard him draw breath. "Rae, I'd like to hire you in my personal capacity. Of course, while Mr. Saldana may be an excellent detective, I would require a woman's touch when dealing with my mother."

How to say this tactfully? "Uh, I'm not sure what you want me to do, Mr. Dieter. As my client, my first responsibility lies with your mother."

"I've made clear she may not be fit to handle her financial affairs any longer, and of course I can't say it to her face. I need you to simply follow her for a few days, see what she gets up to, see if her behaviour is in any way erratic or self-defeating. I'm sure Mr. Saldana has told you of her *independence* let's call it, but frankly, it's her state of mind I'm worried about."

"We're not social workers, Mr. Dieter."

"Call me Heinz, please, I insist."

"Heinz."

"My mother is her own worst enemy, running around like she's ten, twenty years younger. She looks in the mirror, sees a youthful woman. If she's at all... vulnerable...I fear she'll end up destitute. Of course I'll pay the going rate. More. All I want is a report on the details of her days."

Rae hesitated, considering the conflict of interest. Was it unethical to follow her primary client? She'd done it last night, sitting on Rosa's doorstep, on Rosa's tab. Could she lose her license doing this?

"Ms. Valentine, Rae, can we at least get together to discuss this?"

Not committing to any moonlighting just yet, what was the harm in seeing the guy? "What about first thing tomorrow?"

"How about this afternoon sometime, Rae?" His tone ingratiating.

"I can't make it till later, but I'm happy to meet you say, at 6:45?"

"Oh?"

The guy expected some explanation, Rae felt obliged to provide it: "I have training before that. My swimming. At Long Street baths." Damn, she should have said she was meeting another client at least, give the impression theirs was a hotshot agency.

"No, this evening won't suit, I'm afraid." He sounded suddenly hoarse. "I suppose our meeting will have to wait till morning, after all. What's one night more? Could you come by the house? My mother leaves early on a Saturday. You can collect the receipt Sol left with me. Mr. Saldana said you'd like to have it. I found it in my files at last."

So what's so wrong with taking his money, Rae? Bucks are bucks. And there's the issue of the outstanding office rent.

"How does 10:00 in the morning sound?"

"I look forward to meeting you."

"Till tomorrow morning then, Heinz."

Something screwy was going down.

As far as Rae was concerned, Rosa Dieter had all her faculties and then some.

Sure, Rae'd meet Heinz, though she was nowhere near inclined to pay a third visit to that intensely depressing house.

※

Rocco Robano had waited since before noon at the address on the card. He'd spotted the chinaman with nine lives arrive at the Long Street office with KFC. He'd seen the chick come in close to 1 pm, watched her struggle just like a woman to reverse park her Jeep, saw her head for the door where the sign said: DURANT, SALDANA & VALENTINE—PRIVATE INVESTIGATORS. She was wearing an army jacket, the in-your-face message crystal clear: don't fuck with me.

It was them all right. Confirmed indeed that Rosa had employed the bozos Saldana and Valentine. Vincent was a drunk. Valentine was damaged goods. As for Tony Terror Durant, who'd been too hot on his tail for years with Vincent Saldana, he was out of the game. Problem was, if these guys were at a loose end, he sure as hell didn't want the idiots interfering with his new gig.

What the fuck was this lot doing back in his life? A bunch of strays sniffing around his operation, a pack of mangy dogs. And if they cottoned onto something, got their teeth into something, he'd have to make like invisible but fast.

If Pastor Heinz was looking for signs here indeed was the mother of all signs. This was a complication Rocco could do without. Why hadn't he told his minions to kill Vincent when they'd had the chance? As for Durant, he'd get rid of him when all this was done.

The bottom line: time for action.

In traffic, on automatic in the Subaru, Tony Durant munched through his peppermint chews.

First drop-off was the order for Sarah: "On the house."

"Oh, you really shouldn't, Anthony. This's your business."

"Please, I want to."

She leaned into him, gifted him with a kiss on the cheek.

He blushed, imagining curvy breasts under the housecoat, as if she was into a little no strings attached action, said, "No problem, my treat, enjoy."

He tossed the smelly Prof's order through the letterbox. On the way to Long Street he turned up *Neil Young's Greatest Hits*, "Harvest Moon" getting him mellow.

He pulled into Long Street, idled just outside the office. After the warning from his ex-buddies, it was time to pay the business a little hands-on attention. The bugger in the Land Rover took his time pulling clear from the spot Tony eyed. The driver, clearly not the type to dole out charity, leaned out his window, swore at the unofficial parking attendant wanting his few bucks for letting out the bay.

Tony's blood pressure dropped a mile and his heart skipped a couple of beats. Despite the dye job, the

Van Dyke facial hair, some weight loss, recognition was instantaneous. He knew the ginger-haired hunting spider gone spiky blond could only be a face from the past. A cold-blooded killer. The invisible man coming back to smack Anthony Durant upside the head. This guy was either Rocco Robano or his twin-brother, and Rocco didn't have a twin brother.

The bloodied gash at the rhino's head swarmed with flies, the horn sawn off; Tony saw the bullet holes, the poor creature pumped full of lead; he saw her calf on its side, mewling, dying. He saw the dead game rangers. He saw Vincent lying in a pool of his own blood. He knew Robano was responsible, the sadist, the murderer, but no one could pin him down...

Forgetting the office, the parking, ignoring the attendant with the outstretched palm, he got on Robano's tail. You had instincts, you learned to trust them. Or your friends got hurt. Or you got hurt. One thing for sure, when evil personified came into your life, there was a reason. So you didn't take your eyes off that evil, *evil that had way of nipping you in the balls, a way of ripping them right off.*

He followed the Land Rover up Long Street, right into Buitensingel, to the top of the hill and back towards Green Point. Tony followed him every inch of the way, right up to a compact semi-detached house in Origin Street.

Hunting Spider parked and jumped out. Had a key to the door. Let himself in. Tony waited. Popped a chew, anything to relieve the bad taste of unfinished business. He checked out the quiet street; a Harley Davidson in the spot outside the semi-detached cottage with one entrance to the street; he checked out the silver council caravan parked opposite the property; the workers on break in orange overalls, seated on stools, playing dominoes on a child's plastic table;

a couple of male prozzies hanging out in doorways; a woman running after her enthusiastic Whippet straining at his lead; people out and about with wisps of sun showing through brooding cloud. He wanted his emergency spliff, wanted dope in his lungs, to soften his nerves, his fear.

Rae and Vince could handle adulterers and fornicators and fraud. This missing jewels case was a bit of a joke till now. But a psychopath-murderer-mercenary all rolled into a ghost of the past? No way his partners were up to it.

This was the thing with unfinished business: you didn't deal with it, it reminded you it was there. It didn't let you go. It came at you in your nightmares. In your waking hours. It reminded you it was hanging about ready to beat you down.

Rocco Robano in the mix made for damn dangerous handling. Vince and Rae, like kids tossed a live grenade, didn't have a chance in hell.

No two ways about it, this was a Bad Man about town.

This was something police needed to know.

Rae buzzed Vincent in, waited for him to clear the threshold, was about to mention she was on first-name terms with Heinz Dieter, but it clean slipped her mind as the scent of freshly baked goods wafted into the office.

"What smells so damn mouth-watering, Vince?"

"Toasted croissants with melted Ementhaler over smoked ham and rocket."

"Wow. You still hungry after your junk food?"

"I couldn't resist. And here's the paper." He frisbeed the news onto the desk.

"What's the *Cape Crimes* saying today?"

"City's suffering."

"Hate and fear, Vince, a perfect combination for loaded headlines."

She paged through the paper. No way a looted jewelry store would feature near the front pages when maniacs out there were torching their fellow men, hanging tires around their torsos and setting them alight. The city was wide open for the ruining. And the taking. Another ATM blast got decent coverage.

Vince made no secret of lacing his coffee with Jack from a four fifths bottle in a brown bag.

"What're you looking at? This's just a boost to see me through a lazy afternoon. I'm not hiding anything. I reckon I've got another two years to go before I'm swimming in my vomit, forced to become an AA disciple."

"You're already making love to the toilet bowl."

"Lead a clean life or die, right?"

"That from my website?"

"One of your favorite slogans."

"Why wait if you know it's coming?"

"Trying to get in all the fun I can."

"It's your life, Vince."

"You said it. So what now, Boss Valentine?"

"You'll have to man the fort. I've got my appointment with the physio."

"What happened to that work ethic?"

"I can't miss it, otherwise my hip plays up."

"Your hip?"

"What's left of the leg causes problems. The strain on my hip is killing me."

"And the job then?"

"As far as Sol goes, poor guy's distraught, not much help. I'll head for the assistant's flat after the physio. See what she can tell me."

"So what do I get to do?"

"You get to check out Trudie Kellerman."

She brought her computer back to life with a wiggle of the mouse.

Back on Facebook: friend accepted. Whoopie, one more!

She motioned Vince over to inspect Trudie on screen, larger than life.

"I have to wonder how dignified Sol Anderson can trust a woman in a get-up like this."

Vince stared.

In the pic—part of an album, and one of several—auburn curls spilled over Trudie's cleavage; between black sexy panties and bra were tires of flesh; her plush red lips pulled back from big teeth; she held a flute of sparkling wine. Pic two: Trudie lay on a couch, her legs up, bent, her hitched up skirt revealing stockings on ample thighs, held in place by frilly suspenders. Pic three: Trudie Kellerman, her tongue peeping out between moist lips, had placed her hands on either side of her breasts in a low-cut top and pushed them up, a provocative pose with more than a hint of the promiscuous; she leaned into the camera, filled the frame, clearly having fun.

Taking a wide-eyed peek over Rae's shoulder, Vince whistled. "She's one meaty woman. And not exactly a choir girl."

"Too much of a handful for you?"

"Definitely not my type. I prefer my women a little more reserved, if you know what I mean."

Rae didn't much feel like a chat about Vince's sexual preferences, said, "I've tried the Cape Grande a coupla times. She's unavailable but apparently still checked in. Room number 814. Go hang out and do the wait-and-see thing."

"For how long?"

"'S'long as it takes."

"Follow the breadcrumbs."

"First you have to find the trail. If you get the chance, ask her some questions."

"Find out who's got the stuff?"

"Yeah, it'll be that easy."

"I'd like a share of Mrs. Germany's geld for operations. For Uber fare. Too expensive to park the rust-bucket. And for maybe a toasted sandwich."

Rae shot Vince a look, handed over a couple of hundreds.

"What's this? The tip for the doorman? You better hand over another few bills. Cape Grande's not cheap."

Hell of it was, Vince was right.

"Take this," she sighed, slow to hand over the credit card, hoping she wasn't throwing good money—money they hadn't even earned yet—after bad. She shot him a warning snarl for good measure. "Don't lose it, partner. Keep your spending in check. And keep the slips so we can claim from the taxman."

Back at the house, Rocco popped a light beer. The Boyz lazed around in various forms of consciousness. JP was on the couch, his thumbs streaking over the Samsung.

Rocco asked, "Where's Christoff and Alex?"

"Asleep."

"Still?"

JP grunted.

"Figures," said Rocco, "considering the havoc you wreaked last night." As if they reckoned he didn't know they were pulling odd jobs on their own, the stupids. They could do what the hell they wanted out there, he didn't care. But at the rate they were going, this bunch of loonies were bound to get themselves in the shit. And shit attracted more shit.

JP smiled, as if he could read his mind, said, "Nothing to it, Boss."

In the kitchen Rocco chased a double shot of Peach Schnapps—all that was left of the spirits—with a Castle. Fuck the light brews. He tossed the beer bottle into a crateful of empties. Sink was filled with crusted dishes, a godawful rancid stench rising from the drain. He kicked aside a lone cockroach on its back, stared at the uselessly revolving legs. His Boyz were spoiled, their mothers never taught them a thing. Always had a mommy or a maid to do chores for them.

In his back room, the bed was made—he was in the habit of smoothing every crease since his army days—and he had his bag packed, on the ready to get out. He lay on the bed now, stared at the ceiling like a movie screen, and replayed in his mind the last six months.

He had done the poaching thing, too risky, though he'd itched for blood…he'd narrowly avoided arrest. He'd tried sitting in the bush and running African safaris for wealthy international contacts, all the high fliers, his bad buddies, now dead, had known. His ex-Beijing-chief, after the abalone poaching had come to a head, had gifted him the game farm in consolation, had been more than generous. He mentally lit a joss stick in the man's memory. But keeping a game farm running was hard graft. Work load too high, margins too low. Licking the tourist arse not his idea of time well spent.

Thing was, Rocco was greedy, even if he said so himself. *Heh, heh, heh, heh.*

Greedy for women and money. He itched for the hunt still, but didn't miss the mercy killings he was forced to execute for Americans, Argentinians and

Germans, the spoilt tourists who couldn't shoot straight.

...He was eight. Had his first buck in his sites. Dropped it with a single shot. His father was slapping him on the back, the buck was kicking, not yet dead. He'd progressed to bigger things. His daddy, his mentor, proud of him, a teenage son who'd done good. He remembered rocking in the chair, on a farmhouse wrap-around porch, the walls hung with the horns of blesbok, kudu, buffalo....the trophies left behind when his family abandoned the farm.

Killing was in his blood, the hunting, whatever form it took.

On the upside, he'd met Heinz on one of the second-rate safaris he'd organized...

He, just as his father had done, slapped Heinz Dieter on the back, Heinz on safari with his pharmacy colleagues on one of those bonding weekends that businesses thought so essential. Heinz talking about the end of the world so that even Rocco started believing the Apocalypse was about to hit, like yesterday. Heinz an anomaly: preaching blood, fire and brimstone, but carrying around his hand-cleaner wherever he went, squirting on the disinfectant, the wacko wanting others to get their hands dirty for him...

Heh, heh, heh, heh.

He'd sat with Heinz Dieter, the loony toon's eyes ablaze as he rattled off his twisted views of the world. In a flash of inspiration, suddenly knowing he was in the presence of his future, Rocco had egged Heinz Werner Dieter on, supported him, telling him what a grand plan he had.

"You need finance for your Aurora," he'd encouraged, for the Dawn of the New Order the way Heinz described his dream haven. "There's ways and means."

Rocco'd had an epiphany all right: Heinz had a talent. And he was waiting to be used.

Rocco had a vision of a very good life indeed.

Then from one small advert in *You* magazine he'd got half a dozen men looking for work. Men with names like Dirk, Pieter, and Cornelius, not about to find any sort of job in the Rainbow Nation. There were plenty of young men out there to whom life was nothing but a disappointment. Men salivating for blood. Alex, Christoff, Jean-Pierre. Dermot. The more fucked up the better. Men—boys, really—warped and angry and insane and deluded, seeing their particular dream of the rainbow come to fuck all. No pot of gold at the end of it.

But the bullshit was piling up so high Rocco needed angel wings to fly above it. *Apocalypse now!* The movie soundtrack's "Ride of the Valkyries" echoed in his head. He'd never been able to shake it. Nor the reminiscences of war, when men were men, not mommies' boys…

…he's in a tank, covering the bridge for a meeting, a détente. The dirt road is quiet.

Then a spook comes from nowhere on a bicycle, the man too lanky for the child's bike, guy's knees knocking his chin as his legs go round and round, he's coming from the fields, pedaling and taking a turn towards the village with a basketful of corn on the handlebars. He has to go over the bridge. His back is in Rocco's sights. The red light flickers, the gun is live. Rocco's finger hovers above the button. He presses down, lets rip, blows the terrorist dressed in khaki shorts, on the kid's bike, right to kingdom come.

Of course, he loved the kills. Didn't faze him if he shot a man in the back. But the most satisfying was being close…*seeing the whites of the victim's eyes, the beast, the man, as he realizes he's trapped…*Hunting called for precision...

Heh, heh, heh, heh.

Was always thoughts of the good old days that centered him. And got him randy.

But what he wanted now was to fly. And if anything could give him angel wings, it was the diamonds.

The diamonds had been authenticated and valued. And they would be his shortly. Happy days.

He got on the cell to his woman: "See you later, Sweetcakes?"

"I can't wait, Big Boy." Trudie Kellerman panted, wanting him, like she always did.

Tony would have to talk to her face to face. He didn't want Rex and Adrian with their rough manners breaking the news to her. A hunting spider was in town and she was about to be trapped in his silk.

One thing he knew: she wouldn't appreciate being patronized. He could hear her snap, "Tony, back off, I'm a big girl."

He turned to the spliff first, for courage.

Heard, "Yoohoo!" as the front door opened, Natasha waltzing in, hissing, "Damn, I forgot a file under the bed," still working her cellphone, going, "Uh-huh, uh-huh..." mouthing, "Make me tea."

He snuffed the roach in the abalone ashtray, wished he could at least twak in peace. Reached for his antidote.

From behind, she wrapped her arms around him.

"Anthony Durant," she sighed, "the minute I turn my back, you're at the stash. And you think munching garlic will disguise the smell?"

"Garlic's good for me, Natasha." He always called her Natasha, never doll, or baby, not even Nat. He drew her close, kissed her so she'd lighten up, so he would too.

Rae would never pull a face at the sweet scent of dagga or the delicious pungency of raw garlic. Thing Tony missed about Rae was it got her all worked up to see him sweat at the stove. She loved her food. She loved him cooking food for her. And yeah, she knew garlic was great for the manhood.

He boiled the kettle, poured the water in her special thin-lipped mug.

Natasha was all health shakes, smoothies, filtered H2O. Green tea. Where was the eating? What a joke!

He squashed the teabag, pulled it clear. Floated a slice of lemon in the brew.

"Thanks." She disconnected. Leaned against the counter, tapped her well-heeled foot on the floor, sipped at the piss-water.

Never sat down, was all go go go.

"Who's been round, Anthony?"

"Say again, Natasha?"

Heck, here it was coming, the lawyer talk, the third degree.

"Anthony, what's going on?" She looked at the empty bottles. Rex and Adrian couldn't function without their beers. She kept up the inquisition. Tell me, tell me, tell me. Then the lecture: "You have to stay out of any kind of trouble. Moodley is ready and waiting in the wings for you to trip on your shoelaces."

How'd this happen?

Yes, he liked her well enough, but how'd she end up with a set of house keys? Came and went as she pleased. *How the hell had it come to this?* He felt the weariness course through him.

"And now you're distracted. Have you listened to a word I've said?"

"Am I? Distracted?" Of course he was, he had to

get to Rae. *But how?*

"I know how to get you focused," she softened. "C'mon, let's forget it, lover…"

He watched as she stripped, giving him a show. Unzipped her skirt, unbuttoned her silk blouse. Kept on her heels. He felt the silkiness of her camisole against his fingers as she pressed herself to him, the two of them against the counter, her hand at his crotch, feather light…

Long moments later, she pulled her hand away. "Is there a problem, Tony?"

"No, no." He pulled her towards him, kissed her hard on the mouth. Her hands were at his crotch again, teasing, rubbing.

She pulled back again, from the softness.

"Heck," said Tony.

"Don't worry. Happens to the best of them."

"It's not you, Natasha."

"Of course it's not me, Tony, I'm ready for you," she breathed into his neck, close again, touching him, trying once more to knead a rise.

"I've got things to do," said Tony.

"Never kept a good man down before."

"You're probably right, then. I'm distracted."

"It's the damn weed."

"Nothing I can't handle."

"Damn it, Anthony, I want your one-hundred-percent attention. I hate the way you hang for your fucking toke, and smoke during the day, all hours. I hate to think you can't do without it."

He ignored the dig.

"Look," she said, slipping on her clothes. "Don't lie to me."

"Christ, what d'you want from me?"

"I'd like to fuck you, but it's patently obvious you're not in the mood for spontaneous action." She turned her back.

He heard her in the bathroom, she came back waving her toothbrush, heading for the door. "I deserve to know if this has something to do with your ex? She calls once and now you can't get it up?"

"Aaaah, Natasha, don't do this."

"There's something more going on here." She stalked out. "When you can tell me, call me."

Apart from the gentle lovemaking, and the way they cooked and ate together, there was another thing he missed about Rae: the subtlety about the way she walked, a mesmerizing slight limp.

The insidious smell of chlorine stung like a fist as Heinz Dieter pulled open the double doors to the public baths at the top of Long Street, the foot-long brass handles damp and sticky. He felt the earth shift under his feet. He brushed past a jungle of palms and ferns in large ceramic pots in the entrance hall; he cut through the air, moist and thick, his throat constricting as he strangled back a cough. Rising damp bubbled the murals on the walls of the Turkish Baths, the pink and blue art deco interior decorated with scenes of yesteryear, of 1950s swimmers and lifesavers frolicking in caps and pantaloons. In places the paint had flaked off on to the tiles.

Heinz walked gingerly towards the changing rooms, withering at the thought of what he was about to do. He felt the blood drain from his face as he cut through the steamy air warmed by the heated water and semi-naked bodies.

He changed into the black Speedo he hadn't worn for years. A size too small, the elasticized waistband cut into the soft white flesh at his belly. The bathing suit was too tight at his testicles. He pulled the new silicone cap over his hair, tucked in every last strand, and settled a pair of tinted goggles at his eyes, the goggles very nicely distorting his face, pushing his eyebrows up, his forehead squashed in creases. He'd secured cotton-wool wads in his cheeks as an extra precaution. He walked through the changing room towards the pool, averted his stare from a pair of abandoned jocks.

He tried not to focus on the dirt caked in the grouting of the tiles at the edges of the pool, or the used Band-Aid that caught his eye. He'd had the presence of mind to bring sandals. He forced himself to breathe through his mouth, evenly and controlled. Above all, he had to look as if he belonged. He did not want to draw attention to himself.

With the navy bath sheet protecting his shoulders and torso, he sat on the stands and waited impatiently, staring at the clock above the pool, following the second hand tick, panicking that perhaps she'd changed her mind. It was close to 6:00 pm. His knuckles showed white against the blue of the towel.

On her site she said swimming kept her sane, kept her fit.

On the phone she'd just as good as invited him here.

And then he saw her.

Adrenaline ignited his fingertips.

She entered the pool area, a striped towel around her hips. She looked straight at the water, not left or right. At the deep end, she unwrapped the towel from her waist, exposed one strong, shapely leg; the other still had the prosthesis attached. Sitting on a diving block, she bent forward, removed the prosthesis, and leaned it against the tiled wall directly behind her.

The leg, perched on top of her towel, gleamed

there, the steel rod burnished and hard, connecting foot and knee the exact shade of her skin. The futuristic business made it all the more titillating.

How vulnerable she was without it.

Her good leg dangled down to the water, toes testing the temperature. Her stump stuck out straight in front of her, the end of it tight and shiny, like the glistening head of a penis. No, no, Heinz shook the distasteful—disgusting—image from his head, reworked it: the stump was pale purple, the mauve of a ripening plum. Yes, that was it, a strange fruit.

Oh God, oh my God, how much more enticing was she in the flesh than in the two-dimensional printout.

This woman was indeed a sign from God, *the sign*, for which he had been waiting!

Heinz pinched the mercury mounds under his little fingers, made fists. Blinked fast. Wished he could go up to her.

He wanted her.

He ached to have her, to reach for her.

He bit his lip. Tasted blood.

He watched her push her body from the block and dive in. He watched her exercise, a sports trainer working with her in the water, the two of them chatting, the trainer touching her, holding her from the back, his hands around her slender waist.

Thing about swimming lengths, once the physio was gone, was it gave Rae time to think over what had gone down earlier in the day. Also what had not gone down. Damn it all, she hadn't yet told Vince about the meeting with Heinz Dieter. Yes, there was something unethical about setting up a meeting with the guy. That gut feeling grinding, telling her she should think twice. She was learning to rely on instinct, to trust herself again. *Post attack, post Tony.* To know what she stood for, what she'd fight for. What she'd invite into her life. In this case though, even if Heinz Dieter was questionable, he had money, and what better proof of a thriving business—to show Anthony Durant, Hey I can do it!—than a positive bank balance, especially in this dwindling economy. Durant, Saldana & Valentine needed income, and more of it.

For the moment she'd put it all out of her mind, Rosa, Heinz, Sol, the theft. She swam in rhythm now, breathing smoothly, one breath for every three strokes, in out, in out, turning her head to either side, in the cool water.

But she couldn't get work out of her mind entirely. It wasn't the missing jewelry so much that bothered her; it was the haters trashing Sol's store. The ugly swastikas, the gashes of red and black dripping down the shop walls.

The same swastikas she'd seen at the destroyed ATM. Another fact she'd not shared with Vince.

Heinz wanted to shout *Hallelujah,* he wanted to thank God for the gift, the vision before him, as length after length he glimpsed the different parts of her body break from the water.

Then when she was done, he marveled at how she pulled herself from the pool, hopped on to the steps one at a time, muscled arms lustrous, holding and pulling herself up using the railings.

He stood up, quickly headed for the changing rooms, holding the towel against his erection.

He dressed, found Rocco outside waiting to take him home.

"So, Pastor," asked Rocco, "you did lengths or

what?" The crazy's hair was dry, the whites of his eyes clear. No chlorine contamination. "Why the interest in physical activity all of a sudden?"

"I need exercise."

"That so?" Didn't take a brain surgeon to know Heinz couldn't pack away his damn phobias long enough to put his big toe in a public piss-up.

"My body is a gift from God. The home of the soul."

"How about germs, Pastor? Those places are breeding grounds for athlete's foot, flu, with all those half-naked plebs together in the nice warm water. Didn't it worry you?"

No answer.

Heinz was shivering now, wiping his hands over and over with Wet Wipes, on the brink of losing whatever composure he had left. This was more like it. The Heinz he knew. Wearing his fears on his sleeve. Showing how easy he was to manipulate. But what niggled was the idea of Heinz on some mission he knew nothing about.

※

Friday early evening, cocktail hour and Vince Saldana soaked in the buzz of the Victoria & Albert Waterfront, a tourist Mecca of note, pumping with shoppers and party animals. Privileged, beautiful Cape Town, partying no matter what, no matter the bleak sky, no matter the hardship, no matter the killings, the burnings, the lootings. This was one playground—despite the rain and cold, despite the trouble flaring—where luxury living and spending never ceased.

He'd got to the swank Cape Grande in the heart of the V&A a couple of hours earlier, drinks time. But he'd paced himself. Paged now through a sightseeing pamphlet as he played tourist sipping at a margarita, enjoying the tang on his lips left by the salted glass. This was PI business he could get used to. Beat a police stakeout hands down, getting a frozen bum and pissing in a cool drink bottle, while you waited in a cold car in a sordid back alley not knowing if and when the boredom would be relieved. And Mrs. Germany was paying for this jaunt, *so it's all good*.

The V&A dated back, he read in the pamphlet, to the 1860s, when Prince Alfred, Queen Victoria's second son, started construction. Hence the first basin was named after him, and the second after his mother. Vince remembered back twenty years when this working harbor, with shipyards, cranes and dry docks, was mostly populated by Filipino and Taiwanese sailors on shore-leave looking to hook up with Cape-Malay prozzies sporting their legendary passion gaps—no front teeth, easy access for cock.

Now the Waterfront was a premium up-market haven for the wealthy hanging out in malls and hotels and yachts. Vince, playing the part of hotel guest—in the bar, where else?—reckoned this life wasn't half bad. And what a great bar to hang out in! With a fire. Relaxed, in a comfy couch-style, he checked out, to his right, through floor to ceiling windows streaked with rain, the view of a sheltered dock. Catamarans, yachts, speed boats in mooring, bobbed on the water. No one was going out in this weather. On his left was a view of reception, decorated in shades of green and maroon, with gold trim. All in all, a rather decent change from Deon's.

Was dark before Vince could get a handle on Trudie Kellerman. For sure Vincent Saldana would get the job done. He stuck to his stakeouts like a pro. Was a pro. He stuck to his watch, seeing the cloudy sky turn from blue to black. His mark wasn't hard to spot. He saw her come from the lift into reception, probably from her room. Brassy auburn all right, and as voluptuous in the flesh as she was on screen. The soft-looking woman, dressed to kill in a beaded kaftan-style dress, cut low in front, clearly didn't feel the cold with the extra pounds on her. A chunky necklace of gemstones disappeared in the depths of a cleavage where a grown man could drown his sorrows.

Vince watched Trudie Kellerman for an hour or so. She sat at the bar counter, ordered champagne, no less, kept yack-yacking on her cellphone; kept checking the glittery time piece almost lost in the folds at her wrist, making coy turns, glancing towards the door, clearly expecting someone. He reckoned he'd hold back on making contact with Ms. Kellerman, see first who she was meeting. If no one came, he'd approach her, but for now he snapped his fingers for the waiter. Time for another double cocktail. Though his tongue was already sticking to his teeth.

What was he supposed to do? Order Rooibos tea? *Bloody hell no!* Existence was rather pleasant right this minute, living the life of the rich and famous, or infamous. He ordered an "Asian Bloody Mary," its claim to fame a twist of chopped chili and soy sauce. Healthy.

Then came the moment Vince was waiting for: he saw the lady shift off her stool, grinning, as she embraced and engulfed a thin, blond man with a dark tache, tickler and beard, from what he could tell. Trudie could hardly keep her hands off him.

The couple didn't stop blabbing, Trudie lapping up every word the guy was saying, leaning into his space, patting his arm, stroking his denim-clad thigh. Suggestive, sexy.

His cell rang. "Yeah?"

"You still at the hotel, Vince?"

"The wait's paid off. Ms. Kellerman's in my sights as we speak."

"You introduce yourself?"

"Wanna get a handle on her movements first. Before she becomes defensive. Gotta say she looks pretty happy for someone who's had a deal gone badly wrong."

"Tells us something."

"Yeah. Especially as she's cozying up to some blond dude at the bar. Looks as if they're ready to get it on."

"So you're gonna wait, is that what you're saying?"

"Preparation is a process, not an event."

"Of course it is. Just don't stuff it up, please, Vince."

"Relax, Rae. Don't call me, I'll call you."

"Immediately, if anything pans out."

"Yes, ma'am."

The waiter brought Trudie and her plus-one drinks: a beer for him, looked like a cosmopolitan for the girl about town, a pink cocktail with a cherry in it, plus Japanese paper umbrella.

Vince held up his phone, as if needing to check a text without spectacles on, took a video clip. Not great quality in the low light. But he'd leave with a good sense of the couple. Smiled at the thought of Tony sticking to an instamatic. Durant would have to graduate when—if—he got back to the biz.

Hey, hey, what's this? Vince paid attention to stiffening body language, the wiry guy digging fingers into Trudie's fleshy upper arm, jutting into her space, like he wanted answers.

Her mouth quivered. She whispered something as the two of them got up, the guy's arm at her waist now, as far as it would curve around her girth.

Vincent knocked back his juice, rolled up the travel mag he'd got from the rack, followed discreetly behind, saw the couple get into the hotel elevator. As the doors slid closed he saw Trudie all over the thin guy, swallowing him in the folds of her flesh. They must have made up. The jock might be an hour, or he'd be there till morning. Either way he was staying.

Either way there was time for another cocktail. Vince made himself comfortable in the reception lounge, crossed his legs, exchanged the travel mag for the *Cape Times*. He hardly read a newspaper any more—did anyone? Ay ay ay. All over the pages were more pics of the disenfranchised, the disheartened, the frightened out there; the reports were updates of attackers clobbering black brothers and sisters from over the borders, and Indians, Bangladeshis, Orientals, any ethnicity the conservatives deemed didn't belong; whether a citizen or not, a pukka resident's identity document didn't mean a thing.

He called his mother.

"Vincent, that you? You on the cell, Vincent?"

"Hey, Mom, don't shout." Something his mom had never got right— still believing a cellphone without wires was something you had to yell at in order to be understood down the line.

"When you come home, son?"

"Look, Mom, I think you need to turn off the neon sign outside the shop. Put up the "closed" sign. Some wild stuff is going on in the streets. I don't want you targeted, Ma, you hear me?"

"I do what you say, my boy."

"Love you, Mom."

Vince upped the game and ordered that cognac he was hanging for. Swirled the golden liquid in the snifter, sipped at it while paging through the Arts section: Bret Baily's *Orpheus* advertised at the State Theatre; a review of *Swan Lake* at Artscape; a Ladysmith Black Mambazo tribute at the Baxter.

While refugees and victims went sleepless on the streets and once-good citizens were chopping up Somali spaza shopkeepers, culture vultures lapped up difference. And while Blondie was burying himself in Trudie's cleavage, the Cape Grande, with the blazing fire, with waiters bowing in deference and in service to the cash card, was as good a place to be as any.

Rae Valentine parked in front of a six-story apartment block three roads down from her own. She checked the address on the scrap of paper: 21 Felix Court. Close to the Gardens Mall. Stella Whoever lived here. She reminded herself that the surname was not actually Whoever, but Botha. The apartment would also have spectacular views of the city, just like her place, and of the harbor beyond, once you lifted your sights above the razor wire spirals. She rang the bell, announced herself, was buzzed in. Limped up the flight of steps to Stella Botha's flat.

Miss pretty-as-a-movie-star peeped through the crack of the open door, slid back a heavy-duty chain. Minus heels she was even smaller than Rae remembered. She looked like a schoolgirl in her winter fleece nightie and gown and fluffy slippers, her baby-blonde hair, fine and flyaway, drawn back off a scrubbed face.

Rae asked, "Hey, sorry to be here so late, you heading for bed?"

"Soon. This whole thing's left me really whacked, you know?"

Stella's red-rimmed eyes darted to *True Blood* re-run on her laptop.

"That any good?" asked Rae.

Stella pushed pause. "I've seen it like a hundred times. Real escapism, you know?" Stella hesitated, then asked, "Would you like a hot chocolate or something? Wanna watch?"

"Yeah, sure," said Rae. The two of them stood at the tiny counter-kitchen of the bachelor's, eyeing the milk boil, then sipped the chocolate, sitting close on the bed-cum-couch watching the tail end of a carnal scene: Bill bursting from his grave, he and Sookie getting it on. What woman didn't hanker after a vampiric bad boy? Bill biting, blood squirting. Young girls today reckoned life was a series. Wanted what they saw on the screen. Wanted sex, money, devotion; to be the center of attention. Yeah, just what your ordinary vampire male was willing to provide.

"You doing okay?"

"Sol's closed shop. Don't know if he'll ever reopen."

"Maybe when he's recovered. When things get back to normal."

"If he doesn't I'll have to find another job."

"We didn't get a chance to chat at Gold Extravaganza," Rae explained.

"So what d'you need to know?"

"Anything you can tell me. Anything at all. I want to know about the theft of Rosa Dieter's consignment."

"That wasn't my business. I never met Mrs. Dieter. I really can't help. Poor Sol." Her voice quivered, the tears starting.

"You need a tissue?" Rae dug one from her rucksack. "Sol's tough. He's gonna be fine."

"What doesn't kill you makes you stronger, right?"

"That's about it."

"If you say so."

"Hey, I should know." Rae, trying for some common ground, lifted her pant leg and showed the rod of her prosthesis. "What about Trudie Kellerman. Did you ever meet her?"

"She knows her job. She breezes in and out the store, like larger than life."

"That a smile? Something I should know?"

"Wait till you meet her. Every man wants to date Trudie."

"Sounds like a lovely lady." Then said gently, "So tell me about the robbery."

"I hate talking about it." Stella sniffled.

"Terrible thing to go through."

"I lay on the floor just like they told me. I was so scared." The waterworks factory was now in business, tears welling, spilling over her lids and down her cheeks. "I thought they'd shoot me. I'm the one who buzzed them in. I feel so bad. It was near closing time. They tore the place apart. I couldn't even cry I was so petrified. They trashed everything. And the names they called Sol, he didn't deserve that."

"What else d'you remember?"

"My mind went blank. Like when the TV goes on the blink. A blur. When I knew they were gone for sure, I called the cops. They stole a lot of stuff, more than a million bucks worth, Sol says. And what they did to him? He's an old man, why'd they hurt him, pick on him like that?" Her eyes flickered back to the screen, to icons for the latest shows, all grist for Stella's perfect universe, and her Prince Charming. "Police tell you you're supposed to notice the shoes the criminals are wearing. I can't even remember if they had shoes on," she wailed. "It all happened so fast. They were out of there and there was just this sickening smell of paint in the shop."

Stella let fly little howls cutting between the wails of her sentences: "Then there were the hooligans, looters, just coming off the street, helping themselves to what was left, the silver, semi-precious stuff, just taking it, stealing it."

She wasn't one to give up easily, but Rae didn't do wailing and howling. Separately, maybe. Simultaneously? Too much snot and tears.

"Hey, hey, take a breath, that's right." She rubbed Stella's back while the girl blew her nose. She gave her a help-line number. Twenty minutes after she'd arrived she was gone.

She stopped in at the local superette, bought sustenance, finally pulled in to the covered parking area at her building.

Inside her apartment she switched on the heater. TV news said electricity usage was high. *Please use responsibly.* She had a responsibility to herself to keep warm. She nuked the meal for one. Macaroni and cheese. Yeah, just like Stephanie Plumb, she ladled wood glue into her mouth.

She popped a bag of buttered corn, for roughage, in the microwave. Screwed open an Appletiser, would do as a fruit. This had to be a low point in feeding herself, a fleeting nostalgia clouding her mind now, her thoughts of Tony, how he'd classed her as a foodie, a connoisseur of the beautifully prepared and delicious.

Last point of business for the day was to go online, check her website, that sort of thing. "Thing about networking," the publishers said, "you have to take it seriously, you have to keep up with the fans, with the requests." Publishers wanted you to connect with the world, show them who you were—or better yet, the fantasy of who you were. She posted a brief motivation—*It's not that I never fall, it's that I try to rise every time.*

Rae deleted junk mail. Makro specials. Exclusive Books promos for fad cookbooks, rubbish self-help guides; she opened a recommended Olive Schreiner biography, scrolled down the text to a photo of a dead baby—read that Schreiner built a fantasy nursery in which she kept her daughter's coffin. Now *there* was a reason to be a drug addict...Rae scrolled a bit further...clearly South Africa's first literary author was a drug addict if her medicine cabinet was anything to go by.

Went on to Facebook. One of forty-five notifications looked interesting: an invitation to attend the premiere of a visiting dance-group sensation called GIMP.

...In this new show, which took New York by storm, dance and disability merge magically, shattering preconceived perceptions. The show provokes people to think about body image and disability and beauty in an entirely new way...Dancers with shortened arms and legs move gracefully, a space is created where dance and disability and differences coalesce...

Attending? *Interested.*

A whole lot of "friends" had sent messages, emoticons, stickers.

No thanks.

The most distasteful of the day, a friend request from Ampman: *Dig your stump Big Time.*

One guy who would *not* slip past her nutter radar. *Request denied.*

She'd bookmarked sites on weirdo fetishes and an endless host of body dysmorphic disorders. Like teratophilia, the desire for deformed people. She'd read up about the "missing phallus theory": "The site of the missing limb, which to some men looks like an alternative sexual organ similar to a penis head, becomes an ideal erotic symbol for latent homosexuals."

According to Rae, a stump was a stump.

She got up, stretched, looked out the window at the unrelenting wind and rain, the trees and bushes cavorting in the gusting northeaster, and punched in

Vincent's number on her cell. Maybe he'd got further than she had.

"You still there, Vince?"

"Love birds've gone to roost."

"How long you gonna stick around for?"

"S'long as it takes."

"See you bright and early?"

No answer.

That implied yes, right?

Maybe she'd work on her memoir.

If you really knew me, you would know that every day is a challenge, every day is a struggle, every day I start by putting one foot in front of the other. If I don't fall down I keep going...

Rocco groaned, his penis scraping his belly button. "I wanna fuck, Trudie." He wanted to lose himself in her fleshy naked bulk spread on the bed made up with specially requested satin sheets. But first he had to make sure she'd dished the truth. He extricated himself from her arms.

"Stop playing games, sweetheart," he said. "I can't get it on with my mind going crazy. I want the stones, Trudie." Surely she had to know he'd come to claim the uncut diamonds, the rocks worth a small fortune. "Where are they, snookums?"

"I said I don't have them."

"You've got the verification and certificates, we can get rid of 'em with one phone call. Fact is, you've got a buyer lined up already, right?" He dug his fingers into her forearms.

"Rocco, please...that's hurting!"

"But you were having me on, right? C'mon, Trudie-toots, don't yank my chain."

"Rocco, ouch! Please, I'm telling you I gave them to Heinz." Her voice trilled. "He's the boss, whether you like it or not."

He let her go. "Sweetchops, let's get it straight," he said, "you gave the wacko man the gems, that's right?"

"To keep him happy."

"You gave him everything? The uncut stones as well?"

She nodded. "We've been through it, big boy, now's time for fun." She reached for her bag of tricks.

He pushed her onto the bed and lay down alongside her, nibbled her ear lobe, sucked in the flesh at her neck, then bit into it.

She squealed. "What'd you do that for?"

"You just handed them over?"

"What's the problem, baby?"

"You tell me you gave his mother's shit *back* to Heinz, how d'you think I'm going to react?" He pushed away her sweaty, heaving body. He'd lost his erection.

"Heinz asked for them. Who am I to say no? I had to do it. He'd have smelled a rat otherwise."

He got up, walked over to the window.

"You were supposed to give them to me, Toots."

He parted the cream and gold curtains, looked out at Table Bay. At the black sea. The glint of lights reflecting on the water; he heard the clang-clang of a collection of yacht masts coming at him, and the protracted sound of a foghorn as he opened the window to drag icy air into his lungs.

"What does it matter?"

Trudie came over to him, lifted his shirt and trailed her cerise-painted and glittered fake nails down his naked spine, goose-pimpling his skin. "You'll get the stuff back from the weak bastard anyway. No way I could say no to him. He came all the way in a taxi. Was adamant he needed it all back, counted every single stone. Stop worrying about it and come to bed," Trudie whined.

"First write me another note."

"I want you, babe."

"Write the note, sweetcakes. I'll top you up."

"Must say, I'm a pushover for Miss Molly," she twittered, throwing back the last gulp of bubbly in her glass.

He shivered, closed the window and turned back to Trudie, watched her waddle across the room to the desk. Once he'd got her obsessed with his love tool and onsides, Trudie had played along so nicely. She'd done what he said, produced the notes when he'd wanted her to. But handing over the haul to Heinz? What a colossal fucking disaster! What had she been thinking?

He dictated the words. Trudie formed the neat cursive, then folded the letter, slipped it into the matching envelope, licked the gummy seal—her pointy pink tongue darting between full glossed lips. She patted it closed.

With her brassy curls spread against the cream pillows, she relaxed on the double bed, arched her back and opened her thighs. "Now get over here, lover boy. Come taste my sugar."

His heart thumped hard. He was randy all right. "Me first."

She rubbed against him, kneaded his cock, worked him, then rolled off the bed, knelt down on the carpet, her tongue turning circles on his head as he lay taut as a cello string. She licked and teased, talked to his dick, telling Big Boy, "That's it, baby, wake up good and proper for mama."

Trudie climbed back on the bed.

He moved sideways, then kneeled over her, bringing Big Boy up to her mouth. Trudie sucked at the stiffness as if her life depended on it, insatiable. He called on every ounce of willpower to pull back. "Slow down. I want the best..." He reached for the accessories.

He mounted her. He clenched his buttocks. She moaned as he parted her, swollen and sticky, and went in, a mass of nerves, thrusting at her throbbing, middle-aged flesh surprisingly tight and wet, giving the bitch the time of her life, reminding the stupid bint who was in control after all. She groaned and writhed, matching his lust. He gripped her soft arms, squeezing as Trudie pummeled and kneaded his arse, twisting a finger up his anus. He clutched her closer, his nails digging in; the studded collar was all but lost in her fat rolls. He heard her moaning, her frantic gasps; he leaned forward, his weight now on one hand, and used the other to pull tight at the lead attached to the headboard, depriving her of oxygen, squeezing the breath right out of her, knowing this was the best orgasm of their lives.

"Coming, coming," he groaned with the intensity of his bursts, one, two, three, four, his jolts of pleasure beyond intense—"Thank you, Jesus!"—leaving him spent, ecstatic. He collapsed alongside of her, panting still.

Her head flopped his way and he looked into Trudie's glassy eyes. Trudie, snuffed with her last throes.

C'est la vie.

Heh, heh, heh, heh.

He'd find a new pomp soon enough.

"Thing about Jesus," he said aloud, "he comes in handy in orgasmic throes, not so?" Not that he'd get an answer. He settled back in his body, his wild heartbeat under control.

He showered, got dressed. The only sound in the room the hum of the heating unit. He straightened his pants, put on his jacket. Pocketed the note she'd written.

He helped himself for oulaas, *for remembrance,* to a tiny Jameson's from the minibar: "To you, sweet-cakes." Rocco toasted Trudie Kellerman, a woman truly satisfied once and for all.

He'd drop off the letter on the way back to the red house. Spook Heinz one last time.

"Yes, that's right, honeybun," he whispered, "the game is drawing to a close."

He blew her a kiss from the door.

On the point of finishing his mojito, Vincent Saldana—back to the fun of tasting fancy cocktails, mellowing to the jazzy piano tunes of a suited Abdullah Ibrahim wannabe—noticed the good-looking hotel employee sitting at a table across the marbled hall. Looking every bit the professional in her maroon suit with gold buttons and a badge pinned to her ample chest, she smiled at him, cocked her head. With even teeth like the proverbial pearls, her pink lips plump and sensuous, skin black as the night, her whole being spoke of deep delight. And it was a long time since Vince had experienced that sort of loving connection.

Was when Vince nearly missed the wiry blond come from the elevator, his back to Vince, Blondie's hair wet, slick, as if he'd just got out the shower. The guy checked his watch, headed towards the revolving doors.

Vince shrugged at his hot chocolate as ready as he was: *maybe later?*

"Aaaaaw," the woman mouthed.

Vince hurried past her, said, "Give me fifteen?" In that moment Amber's face flashed in his consciousness, for just a second, before the rum washed it away.

"I'll be waiting…"

Vincent shook his head, snapped out of it—followed his mark, keeping well back. Saw the guy disappear into an underground parking lot. Had only one entrance, doubling up as the exit. He hung back, weighing up his options: get Trudie up for questioning, though it didn't seem right at this time of night, or spend the night following Blondie, the surveillance costing a bomb in an Uber. He could of course call it a day and head back to town, chew the fat with Mandla no doubt still working late, roll out the sleeping bag back at the office and hit the sack…*or…*

Would be a travesty to waste his chocolate mousse. Had been a long time since a woman had looked at him like that, sending a clear message: come taste. Trudie was still checked in, he justified, and might come back to the bar any minute for a nightcap.

He fingered the credit card, had plenty of buying power. Just needed Amber to play along…

"Hang in there, baby," said Vince, scribbling down the license plate number of the silver Land Rover as it exited the garage. Blondie, just discernible behind tinted windows, hellbent on getting out of there, barreled over the speed bumps like a 4x4 should, turning left towards Sea Point.

Vince did a purposeful about turn back to the Cape Grande.

"My name is Princess." The woman in the maroon suit offered her très elegant hand. She had an intoxicating French accent. Before he could change his mind, he followed her to a room, his mouth was on hers, confirming that her lips were as delicious as he'd imagined.

You want me to move on, I know it, Amber, my one love.

He'd catch up later with Trudie et al.

JP Cowart had looked up on the Net the best way to rip off a stand-alone ATM: If you had access to heavy machinery, you forklifted the thing up and away. But where the fuck was the heavy machinery? So the Boyz had come up with an even more ingenious method. JP had done his research. He'd canned using C4 to blast ATMs—too messy, too noisy. Was now using hoses and gas cylinders. You pumped gas into the ATM and blew up the machine from the inside, bending the safe all out of shape, releasing the cash without three-quarters of it getting burnt useless.

Was all happening pretty damn satisfactory, JP had to grin.

Tonight, with the wind and drizzle kicking in, the way it'd been for days on end, the populace holed up inside, it'd be easy. And any stray souls out there who got in his way, Smith was ever ready to take a few pops.

Dressed in black to match the night, his Nelson Mandela mask strapped on his face, the smell of rubber in his nostrils, JP kicked open the stiff door of the old Merc—a crock they'd boosted that he prayed wouldn't break down on them—and ran across the main road.

Shht shht, Christoff spray-painted over the eye of the overhead closed circuit television camera.

JP got to work.

Christoff made his art.

Hi-tech systems with Internet connectivity were

supposed to monitor ATMs twenty-four seven. In theory. In Cape Town nothing fucking worked! Ha! Tonight was a breeze. Spray the eye, pump in the gas, hear the woosh! See the ATM fall apart, get the money, skedaddle.

"Fokken A, man!" whooped Christoff, collecting the notes now, running back to the Merc.

"Let's move it, Boyz," said JP, the tunes playing in his brain, the words rolling out, how it's okay to be white, securing what's sacred.

Alex, a steady hand at the wheel, got on the highway, detoured past Groote Schuur and made in the direction of the red house. He chewed his lip, biting down on the words that wanted to come. For how long could this go on? Problem was JP. The heist wasn't enough for him anymore. The guy was on the brink of being completely out of control. Like now, the closer they got to the city, the more hyped-up he was, ricocheting off the interior, like he really was off his schedule-six ADHD meds.

"Where's the fucking action, man?" spat JP.

"We've had enough action for one night, surely?" Alex eyed JP sitting in the passenger seat, the dude bouncing up and down like the Duracell bunny on speed.

"I miss the flames of a good blast, Al my pal."

"It's all about the money, JP. We got the bucks, let's go home," said Alex, taking the turn-off towards the Foreshore, driving on the outskirts of the city, a ghost town over the last few nights not only with the kak weather and the xenophobia but with the random pop shots JP'd been taking. People were warned to stay off the streets. He propped his tongue between his molars. Knew the only way to get through this was to keep his cool. "I'm saying," he tried again, "it's late, JP. I'm ready to hit the sack is all."

"Party pooper, party pooper, Prettyboy's a party pooper!"

Alex brightened. "So we going home now, JP?"

"You taking over leadership, Alex? You telling me you've got better judgment? No, we not going home. Let's find goffel-wogs out there for target practice," said JP opening the window, hanging out of it. "Keep your eyes open for the *muds* is what they call 'em over in the US of A. Like they rose from the depths, from hell. It's where they belong, is what I say."

"My pa said Satan created darkies," declared Christoff from the back. "Was why the creator expelled him from heaven."

"Where the fuck're the darkies hiding?" JP stared out the window into the black night, tapping his gun on his knee. "I need me a coal face for target practice."

"They all holed up in church halls and schools and camps and stuff," said Christoff.

"No worries, we'll find 'em," cackled JP. "And kill 'em!"

Alex, praying for an end to the gig, insisted, "There's no one bloody out there."

"God's wrath is falling from the heavens all right," roared JP, leaning out his window, staring at the sky, letting out a volley of shots, cracking the night. Back in the car he said, "Alex, you always putting a fucking dampener on things."

Yeah, no way Alex wanted any innocent person just minding his own business, whatever it was, to get blasted. No way this was the time to pick a fight with JP already so tight sprung. "What if the cops stop us? Close the bloody window, it's freezing."

"So tell me, bro," said JP, now holding the weapon to Alex's head. "Where's the fucking cops? No one's gonna stop us." His voice rising, touched with hysteria. "You see our leaders out there, in their brigadier uniforms pinned with medals and their aviator sunglasses and private zoos with mangy lions in 'em called Simba, you see them making a stand? They wanna get rid of the vermin foreigners as badly as the people do. Why not help out I say. The beauty of it is no one fucking cares!"

Alex swallowed hard. "Let's just go home, man. Please. I wanna get to bed, Jean-Pierre. And stop fooling with the gun, man."

"Jissis, that a Frenchie name you got there? *Jean-Pierre*. Your mother one of those Hottentots from France, man?"

"A Huguenot, Christoff," Alex corrected, his nerves still jangling. "Religious persecution of the French Protestants, and all that."

"Yeah, she was white, you fool," said JP. "Cultured. A believer. Driven from her own country."

"Let it go, dudes," said Alex. "Let's just get back to the house."

"When we done cruising, party pooper, when I'm fucking done!"

Alex tuned in to the rain falling, the windscreen wipers swishing, JP tap-tapping his gun on the window.

Too blustery to see much, Alex drove through midtown up Strand Street, kept his twitching eye on JP brooding, still bouncing about like a Mexican jumping bean.

No prey tonight.

"You watch out, Prettyboy, maybe I'll use the gun on you."

Of that Alex was certain.

SATURDAY: PLAYTIME

In the white light of dawn, though he was dressed in

flannel pajamas and bed socks, Heinz Dieter lay shivering. He was wet; he felt the smear at his stomach, the sticky emission cold and clammy.

...*The troll visited Heinzie in his sleep. Forced him into an icy sweat, pulling at his thing till it was rough and raw. He winced and moaned but those rough hands tweaked and tugged and would not stop. He drew his soul back slowly into his body from the corner of the room to where it had retreated...*

Overcome by panic he ran to the bathroom, puked up a bitter string of bile.

The reflection of a small boy—his face flushed, his bottom lip trembling—stared back at him from the mirror. He squeezed his eyes closed.

How can you do the work of the Devil?

It is evil to touch yourself, Schatzie.

If you touch yourself, Heinzie, the troll will chew off your piddler.

Softly moaning, sinking to the cold tiles, he wept till there were no more tears.

When he stood up and looked again in the mirror, the child had disappeared.

Heinz Dieter gave himself an enema. Then stood under the shower for long moments, till his fingers and toes resembled albino prunes. He had purged the disgust, the shame. Now he gargled with Listerine, swallowing a capful, the chlorhexidine sure to disinfect. For good measure he scraped his tongue with the ridged back of his toothbrush. He was clean inside and out.

Sanitized.

Purified.

Ready.

Confidence restored.

His Aurora now back in the forefront of his mind: the final destination.

The signs had most certainly aligned for the Dawn of the New Order.

Lord, I am ready to lead the Core!

"Life could not be better, Heinz Werner Dieter." He talked himself up as he dressed especially carefully in his usual crisp white shirt and freshly dry-cleaned brown suit. South Africa's home-grown Nicolaas "Siener" Van Rensburg, although a lesser prophet compared to Nostradamus, had foretold of a man in brown saving the world. Heinz buffed his patent leather shoes. He tightened the elasticized bow tie at his neck, pinned the carnation bought from the florist the day before at his buttonhole, leaving aside the cream and pink orchid in a small test tube— for *her*.

He checked his watch. Not yet seven.

He held back a corner of the curtain. Through his salt-encrusted bedroom window, he saw the council notice boards secured in drums, prohibiting the public from the promenade where entire sections had been destroyed. The sash window rattled. The wind whipped the waves over the walkway. Heinz Dieter witnessed a brilliant flash of light, the electric finger of God cleaving the gray skies. He heard an unstoppable roll of thunder.

"*God, how powerful is your wrath!*" he whispered. Another section of the retaining wall had disintegrated, the slabs of concrete lifting as if constructed of Styrofoam.

Finally, with care, he made up his solid oak bed, smoothing flat the creases of the spread; he meticulously straightened every model tank, every metal soldier on the shelf; he'd not had many toys. Mutti called toys clutter. He aligned the pictures on the wall. A blocked poster of a lightning bolt zigzagging from the heavens across a black and ominous sky, splitting a tree trunk right through to the roots, hung next to portraits of the great prophets of the world, of Stalin, Jesus, Nostradamus. He repositioned a miniature trophy on his desk, which, many years ago, had been presented to him for school service.

Lord, I am now in your service!

The room was respectable.

He could not help himself. He retrieved the box from the safe. To while away the time he chose his favorite magazine, his fingers trembling as he thumbed the pages of issue 49 of *Pharmaceutical Monthly*.

He'd had plenty of real-life sightings at the pharmacy. He'd seen women on walking sticks, in plaster, in wheelchairs, women with damaged arms and legs, women without fingers, like Mutti. But in the pictures he could examine them closely. He pored over stories and photo spreads of polio survivors, accident victims, lingering over the photo spreads of amputees.

With hours to go, he lay fully clothed on his bed, clutching his glossy magazine. And though he shivered with sinful pleasure at the images, he knew no two-dimensional photograph could compare with what he wanted: a flesh and blood wife.

He controlled his paws—he vowed never again to touch himself—and squeezed his eyes shut, his lips moving in supplication.

An hour later he heard Mutti rise, heard her in the kitchen, switching on the kettle for her morning constitutional of boiled water. No lemon.

He sucked a Strepsil, loosening the constriction at his throat.

Forty-five minutes later she left, as usual, to do her Saturday morning shopping, calling up to him first, "Goodbye, Heinzie."

"Goodbye, Mutti," he squeaked.

He had the house to himself.

In the dining room he set a tray, selected two good

cups from the set of eggshell Harlequin of pastel pinks and blues and yellows, with porcelain edges swirled in gold. He would offer tea from the silver teapot. He would serve. He would worship.

He'd always been certain he'd recognize the woman for him when he saw her, a woman of class, breeding, one who'd suffered, but a woman with more to give than Mutti.

It was only a matter of time before the perfect woman graced the table.

She'd already set foot in his home. She'd been sent. A gift from God. A woman who would obey as he obeyed God. It could not be clearer that she was meant for him.

In his mind's eye he saw Ms. Valentine's glistening arms break the water, her taut body ascend from the pool. A goddess rising more sensual than Boticelli's Venus, as she raised herself on the steps, water flowing off her form, her leg.

He sat at a dining room chair.

He watched the clock.

Trembling.

Waiting.

The signs were most certainly aligning.

"I've ordered you a double espresso," said Princess, "and requested room service to add a dash of whiskey to kickstart your motor. Est-ce que tu ecoute, Vincent?"

The way Princess said his name, in that French DRC accent, made her seem like a dream, a kind of fantasy woman, a woman to be turned on by. But Princess wasn't having more of it. She pushed him down on the bed. She kissed his forehead. "Au revoir, cherie."

Was only when Vincent was up and searching for his wallet that he clicked she'd left with all but the change of the five grand he'd drawn on credit last night. And left him a bill for the hotel room in his name. He dialed the number on the business card she'd slipped him, got through to an escort service. Fuck, she was a hooker!

"And you thought she worked for the hotel. Bloody fool!"

He had a hangover from hell, a hefty two-grand bill, no less, plus no news on Trudie.

"How'm I gonna explain this to Rae?" He groaned, lay back, held the pillow over his head. Didn't have to check out till eleven.

Back in his darkened bedroom, curtains tightly drawn, he hung his jacket neatly on his chair. The incessant tick-tock of the hall clock, every jarring chime on every quarter of the hour, reminded Heinz Dieter of time creeping at its petty pace, of wasted opportunity …He sat facing the window, saw the sky turn from gray to solid white, no streak of sun breaking the cloud cover.

"What sort of a test is this, God?" He sat immobile at the desk in his bedroom, facing the closed curtains, his hands crossed in his lap.

God did not answer.

Rae had not come.

The front door closed behind his mother, back from the shops, back from bridge with Mrs. Kapinski, back from her Saturday morning gad about town.

"Heinz?" she called, from the vestibule. "Why didn't you open the drapes? I know you are there, Schatz."

He heard the floorboards creak as she got closer.

"Say hello to your Mutti."

He registered the hard rap at his bedroom door.

"Heinz. How was the pharmacy? Answer me," she ordered, opening his door.

"I-I-I didn't go in today, Mutti. I felt sick."

"If you are ill then why is the table laid for tea? Are we expecting a guest?"

He blurted his news: "Yes, Mutti."

"I don't like surprises. I like to know when we have guests, Heinz." Then teased: "And here's a letter for you-oo-oo..."

He held his breath. A letter from Ms. Valentine. Explaining why she had not come. He couldn't bear to think of Mutti's hands, those hands, touching the letter.

"My my, look at you, Schätzlein, sehr schön. All dressed up and nowhere to go," she mocked, the letter pegged between her broken fingers.

He got up from the chair, reached for his note.

"Not so quick, my Heinzie." Skittish, she held it at arm's length. She picked up the letter opener from his desk. "Is it from a woman, Heinz? We can read it together."

"Mutti, my name is written there." He could easily read Heinz Dieter flowing in feminine cursive across the dusky blue-gray envelope. His nostrils widened at the perfumed scent rising as she flapped the envelope in front of him, snatching it back before he could reach it. Then he glimpsed, in sharp focus, the dull knob of what was left of her second finger *pointing right at him.*

"You will not dare involve yourself with another woman, Heinz Werner. You will not dare use your *thing* against any woman! I won't allow it!"

"Please, give me my letter." He reached again. She

hid it behind her back.

"You disappoint me, Schatz. Who would come for you? As if my Heinzie can ever have anyone of his own. It's ludicrous."

It is only the troll who will come, always the troll.

"You'll never leave me, Heinz, I won't let you leave me for another woman."

Pleading: "But she'll be my Regina, she will love me like you do. You'll like her, Mutti, you've already met her. You'll be Queen Mother. We'll be happy!"

He saw her lips close, a red streak across her face, a crossed-out answer. Then her stare shifted to the spill of stones on the bed.

"My God, are those the diamonds, Schatzie? You got them back for me?" The set of her mouth softening.

"For you, Mutti. And for my Regina. To share."

"How dare you?" she screeched. "I'll kill her, I won't share you or anything that belongs to me!" She drew breath, said coldly, "I knew this was coming, Heinz. I have ways of dealing with what displeases me."

She turned, smirking.

Repulsed, he suddenly felt dirty, indescribably contaminated.

The troll will come, the troll will eat your piddler. The troll will devour you!

"Mutti, what have you done?"

You destroy everything, Mutti, every time I turn to the flesh, you ruin it.

"You are ridiculous, Heinz." She laughed *at him*— a full gurgle from the back of her throat, she wouldn't stop.

Her spittle, like sparks, singed his skin.

"You will always be my little boy!"

An intense heat spread from his groin up through his chest, his neck, to the very tips of his smarting ears as he listened to her putrid words.

"This," she said, holding the letter aloft, "I will read then burn in the kitchen sink."

He could not allow it. "Give it to me!"

"You will not have it!" she shrieked in return.

Turning away, ripping back the brocade curtain, allowing in the sheer cold white light, the contested letter slipped from her hand and fluttered to the ground. Together, mother and son lunged for the prize.

He pushed her back. She turned on him, letter opener raised high, and he grabbed her wrist, twisted until the blade pointed at her chest. They struggled. Her feet slipped from beneath her on the polished floor and they fell together, Heinz on top. The sharp tip plunged through her blouse, through her skin thin as crinkle paper, pierced muscle, rebounded against her clavicle.

He straddled her, wrapped his fingers tighter around her fist, pushed the blade deeper, deeper, twisting. He saw blood, blossoming, spreading thick and red over her stumps clutching at the letter opener now firmly embedded in her chest.

With a satisfied grunt, Heinz sat back on his haunches and watched her clawing at her heart, a look of astonishment in her widening eyes.

He saw things plainly for the first time.

She went limp.

He blinked.

Vince tumbled from the bed, showered, was leaning on the reception desk shortly after 11:00 am, asking for Trudie Kellerman.

"Not answering at this time. Leave a message?"

No message.

Vince called Rae. No answer. Left no message either.

He reckoned he may as well head for the brekkie still on offer, but as he got closer he couldn't stomach the smell of eggs, sausage, grease; he kept control of his gag reflex; no way he could eat. He'd fucked up! Only thing for it was to numb the self-blame. He snapped his fingers for the waiter, "Bring me a Castle!"

No Trudie Kellerman surfaced for the buffet brunch or graced the restaurant for early lunch. He tried Rae again. This time she picked up.

"Hey, Vince." She yawned. "I just spoke to you five minutes ago. What kinda time is this to phone? Can't a girl get a decent night's sleep?"

"Rae, it's nearly 12 o'clock. Like in the post meridiem. You had a rough night, I take it."

"Shit!"

"What's the problem?"

"I've bloody overslept."

"I called a coupla times already. D'you pop a pill or something?"

"Took something for the pain in my hip, must've knocked me out."

Rae, coming back from the sleep of the dead, scrolled through her missed calls. "Damn! Fuckit!" She punched numbers into her cell as she went off at Vince. "I've overslept by four hours!"

"And I thought I had a mega night."

"You didn't cross the line with Trudie Kellerman, did you? Don't tell me, Vince–"

"I didn't cross the boundary with the bloody woman, give me a break. So what's up with you?"

"Don't ask."

"When you say don't ask, I wanna know."

"I set up a meeting with Heinz Dieter, okay? For

this morning and now I've gone and bloody missed it."

"Yeah? When were you planning on telling me?"

"It was just recon. He wants me to follow Rosa. Implied she has a screw loose. He wants a woman's touch. No harm in hearing what he has to say. How bloody unprofessional, incompetent!"

"Take it easy there, Rae"

"Don't tell me take it easy. I've screwed up."

"We'll talk later." Yeah, wait till she heard how *he'd* screwed up. "What I'm doing is letting you know, since you're settling the tab, is I'm at the hotel as we speak, waiting for Ms. Kellerman to surface. Got video footage to show you too, from last night, Ms. K getting lovey-dovey with a skinny blond dude."

"Vince, I've gotta go."

She put down before he could confirm Trudie's room number...804...803? Close, he reckoned, but he'd better have another beer, and a couple of peanuts to go with it, to oil his memory.

As soon as Rae was done talking to Vince, she called the Dieter residence. Got voicemail. Damn. Telling Vince off all the time for being pissed and stuffing up, and here she was trying to unglue her eyes.

Then she tried Heinz Dieter's cell: *The subscriber you have dialed is currently unavailable...*

She remembered smearing fish paste on semi-charred toast; remembered watching reruns of her once-favorite TV hero, House, limp around, rub his leg, lose his cool. She remembered hitting the sack, how she'd massaged her stump, had tried listening to Sadhguru to get her in a better frame of mind, but couldn't gel with the message of Universal Love. Had tuned in to The Trio on her iPod—Linda Ronstadt, Emmy Lou Harris, and Dolly Parton—the songbirds in sweet harmony, singing a woman's a fool for weeping. Too bloody right! She'd fallen asleep with the lyrics in her head, about a man's flattering ways, about his lies.

Yes dammit, Vince, I slukked a sleeping tablet!

And was grateful at least that the Stilnox had given her a few hours' solid respite from obsessing over Tony, respite from feeling downright pissed off with the guy, respite from replaying shit like an addict.

And now, as she forced herself out of bed, it was 12:05 in the bloody afternoon.

She checked herself out in the bathroom mirror. Thank God she had a face that woke up well, even after pills. She drew her hair back into a ponytail—no time to fuss with the hair straightener—and splashed her face with winter tap water a few degrees from frozen. She dressed fast in jeans and sweatshirt. Still raining and Vince had her jacket. She settled for the black leather. Tried to reach Heinz again on his cell as she drove. Still no answer. No Rosa Dieter picking up the landline either. The phone rang and rang, echoing in what had to be an empty room.

She called the office.

"Vincent? You there, Vince? Pick up."

Of course he wasn't there, shit, he was at the Cape Grande! Get a grip, she told herself, thinking that missing meetings was a sure-fire way to lose clients, especially unofficial clients like Heinz Dieter. This might have been easy bucks and she may well have blown it.

She felt light-headed, felt a low-grade throb gaining momentum behind her eyes. Punched in the number for the shrink. Put the phone down before the call went through.

What's this calling the doc whenever there's a bit of a hassle?

Enough already! Get out there! Do your job! Everybody oversleeps, fucks up even, it's not the end of the world!

She couldn't stop castigating herself—with plenty of exclamation marks.

She pulled over, breathed deeply, got a grip, and made it to the office.

Just calm down. Get sorted.

It came naturally to Rae to clean up after men. Seemed like she'd been doing it her whole life.

She'd nursed her biological father in his rented council flat before he died of a broken heart after decades of pining for his childhood, for the Victorian-semi and shop his folks owned in District Six. The mixed suburb on the edge of Cape Town city was declared "for whites only" in 1966 by the insane laws of the time. Every building, apart from a couple of churches and a mosque, was bulldozed, demolished, and its sixty thousand people removed to the wastelands, to the wind-swept sand dunes near the sea. He never got over it. That and lamenting his younger brother hanging himself in prison, an activist arrested at a protest against apartheid. As for democracy, a quarter of a century after the first free election, the "new" government had turned out as corrupt as the last.

She'd cleaned up after Tony when they were an item, picked his dirty clothes off the floor and dumped them at the laundry. Came like a whirlwind into his house, pulled up her sleeves, whizzed through the dishes, the vacuuming, setting things straight. And now she was doing it for Vince, still a bloody mommy's boy leaving his empty pizza boxes lying around for the cleaning fairy to toss. His jocks were on the floor, his damp socks and chinos strewn in the corner, the lid was off the toothpaste leaking over an invoice pad. She bundled a stinking shirt and the rest of it in a plastic packet and stashed it in his desk drawer. Saw the empty bottle of Jack Daniels. And Jesus, his revolver just lying about. Ex-cop, yet she'd have to set him straight on the gun laws.

She got on the cell. "Vince, when you gonna stop sleeping, or rather living, in the office?"

"Is it that obvious?"

"No comment." What was the point. "Look, how long you still gonna stake out Trudie? I need you here. We have to talk, plan, you know, connect the dots."

"If there're dots to connect."

"So how long will you be?"

"You know how it goes. Different client, different habits. D'you get hold of Mr. Pharmacist yet?"

"Zilch. Nor Frau Dieter. Can't raise them on landline or cell."

"Tut tut."

"Don't rub it in."

"Mrs. Germany's defs the one we should be keeping an eye on, I'm telling you, Rae. Alarm bells go off when you cross Morticia with Barbie."

"Our job is to get her jewelry back."

"Which is why I'm waiting for Trudie. If there's nothing else to report I'll get back to work if you don't mind."

That what Vince called it? She could picture the lush at the hotel bar already. She pulled the A4 pad on the desk towards her. Scribbled a mind-map this time, of what she and Vince had, looked long and hard at the bubbles.

Missing jewelry.

Mother. Son. Jeweler. Dealer.

Graffiti. Spoiling Sol's shop walls and at a blown-up ATM.

She drew the symbol on her notepad: a three-pronged swastika, three bent arms spreading from a central point.

She went straight to Google, typed in "three 7s swastika," read what she'd guessed already, that it was the symbol of a hate group: The AWB, the White Brotherhood of South Africa. She knew this movement first came to prominence in the 1970s, led by a crazy named Eugene Terblanche. She scrolled down, clicked on another site:

The three-sevens emblem of the Afrikaner Weerstandbeweging, the Afrikaans Nationalist Uprising, symbolizes supremacy over the Devil. The sign is the Biblical number of finality and final victory in and through Jesus Christ our Saviour.

She rocked in the roller chair, wiped off perspiration dampening the hollow of her neck, her fingers settling briefly on ridges of scar tissue.

Back to the screen, she pored over pics of bearded granddaddys and their male descendants, cohorts in khaki uniforms, sunglasses and badges, wielding rifles and the three-sevens emblems; men sat atop horses trotting down the main street of a small town; a group of khaki-clad brothers waved about the defunct Vierkleur, the old apartheid South African flag; supporters, mothers and sisters in long skirts and head scarves, cheered on their men; Rae saw the collective Afrikaner holding on to the past—to apartheid—in the name of God, Ons Hemelse Vader. The call was to the youth, to take up Nationalist arms, to defend *What is Ours!* It frightened her, this rampant Nationalism, this fear of the other, this inability to share, the continued exclusion, the desire for oppression.

She called the Dieters again. Nothing. Called

Vince. Service temporarily unavailable. Had probably switched off his phone. Scrawled a sticky note and stuck it on his desk: *Check out this link. Serious stuff. How does this fit in?*

Certain sectors of the population would never let go of apartheid, of white supremacy. It made her sick to her stomach.

She got up, shook the repulsion from her.

Now, with everything on hold, with the skies clear for five minutes, what else was there to do but to shift her own clouds?

The moment she fired the ignition, the ride was part of her being, an extension of her senses, not just nuts and bolts connected to the leather-bound steering wheel, an absolute pleasure to the touch. She settled into the driving, knew her stuff. All the *Top Gear* episodes she'd watched had not been for nought. She drove like a pro. She ran fingers over the leather seat soft to the touch, real luxury. And the Jeep handled impeccably on the wet roads.

She breathed deep, the thought crossing her mind that the down payment had been paid with her blood.

She drove on the highway, the Blue Route, then along the curves of False Bay, through the southern suburbs of Muizenberg, St. James, Kalk Bay, Clovelly, Fish Hoek, Glencairn, with the Indian Ocean to one side, mountains on the other.

Forty-five minutes later she signed in at the Glencairn Quarry, a spectacular setting for the gun club, the orange stone a steep backdrop to the ranges. She showed her ID and membership card; went directly to the handgun range, cracked a nod at the officer on duty in his red cap. She secured her earmuffs, fixed on the goggles. An afternoon of shooting was just what she needed. Never thought, ever, she'd be a shooter, had never approved of guns and what they did—made holes in people. Still didn't. Was conflicted. But as a past-time, a sport, it beat golf or book club... If she had women friends she'd have recommended it, scoring high on targets a real satisfaction. But that's what addiction did to you, even years later: you were alone, on your own, picking up the pieces of your life.

Vince Saldana inspected himself in the wall-to-wall elevator mirrors: his man bag over his shoulder, his Ray-Bans hiding his bloodshot eyes, he looked every bit a guest of the hotel. Sure, one who'd been on the tiles partying, one who'd had a heavy night. Was what tourists did with Table Mountain shrouded, the seas rough as a hangover. The last how many hours was basically a blur. He remembered leaving the bar; he'd seen Blondie leave the hotel; he remembered coming back, checking in as a guest, signing the register. He remembered worshipping at the feet of his Princess, remembered his tongue teasing and probing the slight and sexy gap between her square front teeth. They'd ordered room service. They'd fucked. She'd left with his cash. End of story.

He'd settled the bill. With the card. Ouch! Three-thou-nine-hundred-and-fifty for a room he'd hardly slept in. He had indeed fucked up. Did he care? Not particularly. But Rae would. About time to do a recon. Find out what Trudie knew. He'd waited around long enough.

What he liked about hotels was you were anony-mous, the whole idea being no one wants to know who you are, nor wants to know your business. He padded down the carpeted passageway to Ms. Kellerman's room, checked out the maid's trolley laden with clean towels, those little bottles of shampoo, conditioner, body lotion…Heard a scream, saw the maid running from the room, going "Woowooowooooo," as she knocked right into him, Vince stumbling sideways. She didn't stop, wooowooowooo, and kept on running.

It was the smell that hit him next, a heady perfume mixed with the acrid stench of human waste. Standing in the open doorway of room 814, Vince saw Trudie secured to the headboard with a leather thong, her neck swollen from a studded collar digging into her double-chins, her distended naked flesh. From under a rumpled sheet, one petite podgy foot pointed outwards. The tiny nails, on toes as plump as chipolata sausages, were painted a bright cerise. Her lips had turned purple. Gray tongue protruding. Her face blue. Maybe asphyxiated. By the collar at her neck. Had to be a sex thing.

Her clothes—a lady suit hanging on the back of a chair, high-heel pumps under it—spelled business. Seeing the magazines and food brought in, he calculated she'd been a guest a week or so, and had resorted at some stage to snail mail. Pen and blue-gray notepaper were laid out on the desk-cum-dresser.

Back in the passage he called Rae. Voicemail.

He was too late to interview Trudie.

Worse than that, she'd been murdered while he, ex-police, was fucking a prozzie down the very same passage. Choking on his remorse—he'd betrayed Amber, Trudie was dead—he cleared reception.

For long moments, as he lay on the floor alongside her in his bedroom, he stroked Mutti's cheek, the skin as fragile as parchment. He heard the phone ringing ringing ringing but could not leave her.

At last he carried her, light as a fallen bird, to her room.

"This is for the best, Mutti."

He settled her on the bed, cleaned her with cloths and towels. He wiped the blood from her hands, the trickle from her nose. Covered her legs with a throw.

"Schlafen Sie gut, Mutti. You'll feel better in the morning."

He swallowed a concoction of tablets and welcomed the seeping numbness, a cool disconnection he felt first at his tongue, then through his body.

He packed away the cups laid out so precisely, lovingly, at the dining room table. He placed the especially bought orchid back in the box and stored it in the fridge. He found disinfectant and bleach under the kitchen sink. It didn't take him long to clean up; there was surprisingly little blood on his floor. A little from where it had seeped from Mutti's breast. He breathed in the fumes of Jik and Jeyes fluid as he scrubbed the boards, heard the phones ring again, intermittently—the landline, and his cellphone ringing once, twice, thrice—as he rubbed methodically back and forth till the marks were bleached away.

He washed every crevice of his body.

At his desk, his hands clean, he steeled himself to study the rescued note.

Tentatively he picked it up. Carefully opened the envelope, gingerly unfolded the delicate paper, read:

Lead your men from the city before it is too late.
Before the waters overwhelm.
You are the chosen one.
For what are you waiting?

Not a note from his Ms. Valentine, after all.

The hot blush spread from gut to groin.

No doubt there was a logical explanation for her absence.

He tweaked the curtain and looked briefly towards the horizon, gasping at the breathtaking sight of crepuscular rays slanting through the clouds. "A veritable Jacob's ladder," he said out loud. He spread his arms, held them to the heavens. "Heinz Dieter, godly warrior of the people, a man of purpose, you have weathered many tests—fire, serpent, storm. *You will prevail!* His Light shines upon you."

Breathy, trembling, he slid out his most cherished copy of *Fascination* from the bottom of his precious collection in the safe. He slid it from the plastic sleeve, held his breath in anticipation, bit his lip in case he groaned and woke Mutti. He paged to the centerfold.

Ah, there she was, Miss Homemaker Amputee of the Year, leaning on her crutch, accepting her crown with grace. Her leg was gone from below the knee. She had such a radiance about her. There were other photographs too: one seductively posed over a vacuum cleaner, using it to keep her balance, the muscles of one strong thigh exposed; in another there she was at a stainless-steel sink, the basin filled with bubbles, sparkling dishes on the drying rack, the stump just visible beneath the frill of the white apron.

Heinz packed his things: his pills, bottled water, two changes of suit. He plucked the stones off his bed, dribbled them from hand to hand, the diamonds resembling nothing more than bits of glass swept up from a shattered windscreen.

He called Chief Disciple Rocco. "The time is now!"

"Eyes and ears, folks," warned the RO. "The range is hot."

Rae loaded her magazines, shot ten rounds at fifteen meters, five at a time, *bam, bam, bam, bam, bam*, blowing away the center portion of the target.

"You sending every bullet through the same hole there, Rae."

Not a question, a statement.

"That I am."

"Nothing left of the A-section."

"Right through the heart."

"No doubt about it, you and that Colt of yours are a formidable team."

With twenty-twenty vision, one leg giving her a steady platform from which to fire, she smacked in a full mag this time, shot the ammo into the black bull's-eye of a clean target, set at twenty meters, in under half a minute.

"Great gun that 1911. Good grip for a nine mil."

"Don't ever let anybody tell you that size doesn't count," Rae joked.

The RO shot back: "Then again, it's what you do with the bullets."

"Touché."

She took a break, scrounged around for the brass that got away, found it underfoot and in tufts of grass, slotted it back in the boxes for reloading.

She worked her way through another two boxes of ammo, then collected more brass, her targets, packed her toolbox, got the RO's John Hancock on her logbook.

"Now holster up," he instructed.

Ah yes, the Colt felt in place, fitting snug in the holster under her arm.

"You staying for a boerewors roll?"

Sausage in a bun. Her kind of treat. "Why not?"

After guns had been abandoned in favor of lunch and rugby, fans going mal at the TV in the clubhouse, "You beauties! Come on, Springboks!", after the snack and a drink and chewing the fat over police incompetency, the backlog of licenses, upcoming competitions and where to head for the best hand-tooled holsters and cheaper reloads, the conversation turned to the xenophobia. "When's it gonna end?" "How can people do this to each other?" "The rand is plummeting!"

"Right then," said Rae. She took her leave, the chat threatening to dampen her mood. Back in the Jeep, she packed away her gear, always got a kick out of the door pockets and cubby holes, perfect hidey-holes for her gun and spare mags. She felt recharged. Refreshed.

She could appreciate the view over False Bay to Cape Agulhas one way, Cape Point the other; she could once more, one hand on the steering wheel, one hand at her neck running fingers over her healed scars, appreciate her luck.

"I'll see you ASAP, Pastor Heinz."

At last we're on the same fucking page.

Yes, Rocco Robano had USE ME tattooed across his forehead. He'd etched it there himself. He'd do whatever needed to be done to keep Heinz meek and mild, but he didn't plan to be the dogsbody chauffeur for much longer.

He fired up the Harley. To hell with global warming and the Dawn of the New Order. He wasn't about to give up his earthly delights, his Landie, the Piper Warrior, certainly not his Dream Machine purring now between his thighs. He revved the engine, shifted gears, felt the sense of rush the bike provided. He got to Pastor Heinz in under ten. The pastor opened up, quickly closed the door behind him.

"Keep the lights off!" snapped Heinz as Rocco flicked the switch.

"Why not let the light in, Pastor?" With the curtains drawn closed, the place was dark and chill as an industrial freezer. Reeking of antiseptic, it was more like a morgue than a mansion.

"I've known this day was drawing close," said Heinz.

"Good, good…your mother know you're leaving?"

"Mutti has met with an unfortunate little accident, Rocco."

"Oh yeah?"

"She is in her room. Resting."

"So let's move then, Pastor."

"My worldly goods I bring are few. My suitcase is at the door."

"There is just one pressing matter."

"Yes?"

"The diamonds."

The wackjob didn't flinch.

"I need cash to settle outstanding bills."

"So Trudie mentioned that she returned the consignment to me?"

"I'm sure you're keeping the diamonds safe. Perhaps you'd like to hold on to them. But it comes down to costs, Pastor. The eco-settlement is on plan to being superb, with every finish of convenience. Solar panels, underfloor heating, air filters. I've got to settle the invoice for a small plane, a Piper Warrior, for easy transport, plus the rest of the arms as our defense."

"Every note given by every believer has gone to fund the cause, Rocco."

Rocco kept his heh, heh in check.

Actually, every tithe, every check, every note from

every ATM, every heist, is lining my pocket, you dumb fuck.

He felt the twitch at the corner of his mouth, the grimace straining to break free. With a dead body—poor Trudie—they'd have to move fast. Hotel staff would have his description, undoubtedly caught on the security cameras too. He said calmly, slowly, so the words would sink into Heinz's sponge, "It boils down to needing cash flow, and I have a buyer lined up."

"Tell you what, Rocco. You can have the gems in exchange for Regina."

He couldn't wait to hear what the crazy stupid was about to come up with now. Do this, do that, wipe my butt, suck my dick. *I'll do what I have to to get the stones, you arsewipe.*

"Who, or what, is Regina, Pastor?"

"My prayers have been answered, my deepest desires made manifest in the flesh."

"Yes?" *Say it in plain English, you mad fuck.*

"The woman who is to be my Queen, my Regina, has been sent by God himself. I want this woman as my partner at Aurora. It's for her I have collected the jewels."

He allowed the pleasure finally to stretch across his face. "Ah, right. And who is this lucky girl?"

"She's the final sign I've been waiting for, thanks be to God."

Rocco would show him a fucking sign if he wanted one so badly, stick his Colt Python right up Heinz's arse.

There were too many signs for his liking. Signs that things were about to fall apart. The signs he was reading loud and clear were his Boyz causing havoc, getting impatient, doing reckless, thoughtless stunts on their own out of sheer idiocy and lack of impulse control. And Heinz, the mad crazy fuckwit, had fallen further from the narrow ledge of reality he was clinging to.

"Her name is Rae Valentine, and I want her." His small mouth scrunched tight as a sphincter.

"The PI, Pastor?" He bit his tongue on a snigger.

"See, Rocco." Heinz brightened. "You know her too. It is meant to be. It is God's will that she be with me."

"Of course." *And it is God's will that I be a rich man.* The handful of stones were as good as his; he stroked his chin, pulled at the tickler under his bottom lip, agreed: "You'll have her, Pastor." He lowered his eyes in deference as he backed out of the room. "Your will be done."

Yes, indeed, the time is now!

On his way out, the astringence of antiseptic tweaked again at his nostrils. Hesitating at first, mystified as to how Heinz would explain his sudden holiday to Mommy, he retraced his steps, pushed open the door to the old bat's room, nearly skrikked out his skin thinking he was in a scene from *Psycho.* The old girl was laid out on the bed, her dead eyes staring right at him.

"Jesus wept!"

Well, well! Heinz had indeed flipped. He controlled the urge to take out his gun and pop Heinz between the eyes and lay him alongside his deceased mother.

He wanted the diamonds.

And if Heinz wants to swap the gems for pussy, then who am I to say no?

He steadied himself on the Harley, barked into the cell: "Alex, we're moving out. Got some details to finalize, then we'll be outta Cape Town. We're going shopping. You're gonna fetch Heinz. Put JP on."

Alex said, "Yeah? Why we moving all of a sudden?"

"Just give the cell to JP, Alex. And be ready for me in five goddamned minutes."

Seconds later heard, "What's going down, Boss?"

"JP, you compos mentis?"

"Compass fucking what?"

"For Christ's sake, just listen to every fucking word I say, and get it right."

At least Heinz would be in good hands with Alex. The bozos JP and Christoff would get the girl. Sorted.

Then he called Johannes. "Hulle kom môre, they'll be there early tomorrow, old man, and Johannes, make the place extra nice for Pastor Heinz."

Heinz lifted Mutti from the bed. Propped her in her chair in front of the dressing-table mirror. He placed a red shawl at her shoulders, wrapped a silk scarf around her neck. He brushed her hair one hundred strokes, as he was accustomed to doing in their nightly routine. "So sad you won't see Aurora now, Mutti."

He applied lipstick to her mouth and buffed her face with powder.

"There, you look pretty, Mutti."

He kissed her on her cool cheek. He adjusted her position to make her more comfortable, tightened the scarf at her neck, yes, to keep her head upright. He crossed her hands nicely in her lap. Yes, like that. He placed the remembrance there. Just right. She sat now like a lady. He thought of closing her eyelids, but she did so love to admire her reflection.

Rae saw on her cell Vince had called. She thumbed his number. "Come on, Vince, answer, you bloody alkie."

Voicemail. Damn, kept missing each other.

SMSed: *Called you back.*

Called Rosa, called Heinz.

Nothing.

No point in going to the office then.

She'd mellowed with the cider and sausage savored at the gun club. Only thing to do was go home.

Back in her lounge, she put her feet up, switched on the TV news: civil war in Syria, rebellion in the Middle East, African genocide, riots in Europe, gun violence in USA. Hate and racism the norm the world over, people struggling to live in peace, couldn't respect each other's differences.

In her home country—what had promised to be the Rainbow Nation with every race and creed coming to the party twenty-five or so years back, after the first democratic election—government was a hot mess. Officials were setting up refugee camps in major stadiums in every province; there was more on the plight of refugees swamped in the mud; a cholera epidemic had broken out in one makeshift camp—winter sludge and cramped space and poor hygiene spelled rampant disease; Red Cross was calling for donations of blankets, food, money; weather man said to expect more of the same: unremitting rain and floods.

She hopped channels—from one inane TV reality rubbish show to the next. *Big Brother* bullshit. *BridalPlasty* was enough to put you off marriage. The Kardashians sprouting crap, Kim asking Kourtney, "D'you prefer licking your boyfriend's balls or his arsehole?"

No wonder the world was messed up.

She switched off. Her own reality kicking in. She streamed Regina Spektor, singing about her sweetest downfall. Was true, she'd loved him first all right, beneath the stars, between the sheets, in the back garden of his crummy house in the northern suburbs; she'd loved his long hair, trawling her hands through that thickness—didn't care that he looked like an aging Axl Rose. "Lends you style and panache," she'd said, tweaking his ponytail.

But that was then.

The future alone she had some control over. She had strengths. Had to connect with herself above all. Bloody ridiculous to be mooning over Tony.

As for busting a gut over his business, it could wait. She switched off her cellphone, fuck 'em all, at least for an hour or so. She kicked off one boot, eased the other off her prosthesis. First thing Monday she'd call the specialist. Turned to Netflix now, scrolled for something fun.

Alex, trussed up in a checked shirt, with tie, corduroy pants and suede veldskoene, left the lounge, saluting JP and Christoff on his way out.

JP whistled, said, "Prettyboy's all neat and tidy for the Pastor."

Christoff set the razor on the number-two grade clip-guard, which, run through his hair thick and dry as rust, gave him the look he'd always wanted: as short as he could make it but not bald. He bounced his palm off the ranga bristles. He scooped up the red curls from the basin, flushed them, and washed the residue down the drain. He liked what he saw in the mirror: standing there pink and naked, cute, like a newborn. Ja, he'd settle on a patch of Aurora, but he'd prefer it if his people took over the whole land, from the Cape to the Zambezi, wishing the Heavenly Father, with a click of his fingers, would free the Volk! As for Pastor, he cared more about the prophecies and getting to his settlement with a community who'd worship *him*.

"Aurora," he said, "leastways a kif name for the

place. The breaking of the Dawn! Maybe it won't be too crap." He pulled in his boep, dressed, laced up his boots, preened—"Ja, I smaak the new me"—and joined JP in the blood-red living room, the vein of life, where JP sat Googling their target on the Samsung.

"Oh yeah," said JP, "give me a legless chick any day of the week. A couple Rohypnol, flunitrazepam to knock out the central nervous system, then she's mine. Just lookee here, Christoff." JP checked out Rae Valentine's profile. "There's major hardware happening here."

Christoff peered over JP's shoulder. "She Wonder Woman or something? Tell me, what kinda name is Valentine anyway?"

"Tainted blood," grunted JP. "The cherry's got white blood. Some indecent boer-farmer fucked his maid on Valentine's Day a hundred years back."

"Pastor's for sure one testament short of a Bible."

"No accounting for bad taste. Why Pastor Heinz wants a brown chick is beyond me."

Rocco had impressed on him to deliver Rae Valentine in good condition. The Boyz would get their turn with her, no doubt, but no, they wouldn't mess with her…just yet.

In the office Vincent yanked open a drawer, then another, searching for Disprin, Panado, cough syrup, anything to relieve his mother-of-a-head-splitting-ache still pounding at 6:00 pm. He found a sheath of Nurofen Rae used for period cramps, washed down four with a swig of Jack. How the hell was he going to explain over five grand down on the card to the dragon lady? Trudie he didn't even want to think about.

Vince collapsed in his chair. Put his head in his

hands. Shaking. He'd messed up. He'd ignored the mark, a woman was dead. He hadn't paid attention. Yeah right, he'd got pissed, and got fucked, while kinky Trudie Kellerman was murdered.

Then heard, "You there, Vince?"

"That you, Mandla?"

"Or a walking talking order of Nando's coming up the steps." Mandla stepped into the office. "My treat. Flame-grilled peri-peri, marinated twenty-four hours."

"You're advertising like the CEO."

"Chicken Excellence Officer—that I am, Vincent." He put the box down, loosened his tie, rolled up his sleeves; sat himself at a desk, helping himself. "This's a step up from KFC," said Mandla with his mouth full. "You all right, my brother? You look washed out."

"Check this out." Vince played the clip: Blondie and Trudie, the two of them into each other in the hotel bar, Trudie alive and well.

"Not great quality," said Mandla. "Could have done with HD."

"Yeah, yeah. So these two are having it on, though the way he's holding the woman's arm, something's not right."

"This yet another marital gone wrong? Is it the hubby or wife you spying on?"

"Look how this develops..." Vince played the second clip.

"Bad stuff," Mandla whistled, eyes wide at the next grainy video starring Ms. Kellerman spread and dead on the Cape Grande Hotel bed, her neck in what was little more than a vice, her face crumpled. "You told the cops no doubt."

"Not me."

"You musta told Rae."

"She's at the range."

"For God's sake, you have to call the police."

"They know. Staff discovered her before I did."

"But you've got the killer on screen."

"I'm ex-cop, Mandla. I don't trust cops. Me an' cops is another world, another lifetime, another story. They'll wanna know why I was there."

"Then I'll make the call. You can't ignore this. I know some people."

I bet you do. Vince checked out Mandla in his natty suit, pale-blue shirt with white collar and cuffs, gold cufflinks. Even on a Saturday night the up-and-coming human-rights lawyer would be connected.

"Be my guest. Just keep me out of it."

"What about the illicit diamond dealing?" asked Mandla, rising, hurrying. "That enter into it?"

"Like you said, diamond dealing's white collar. This isn't about a box of gewgaws. Our job has fraud written all over it. How a killing comes into it, if it does, who knows, Mandla."

Rocco dipped a chamois leather into the water, squirted shampoo on the fuselage, washed the Harley, then rinsed and wrung the shammy out in the gutter.

Soaping the Harley got him randy. Yeah, he missed Trudie's lusty flesh. Her ferocious sexual appetite. Bottom line was Trudie had betrayed him. She deserved to be vrek. Indeed he had a whole list of fuckers he'd like to see dead. Fuckers he'd take out himself. Something he'd learned: payback was sweet. And he couldn't wait.

He rubbed the Harley down with a soft cloth, got a superior shine on the gas tank. Superbly waxed, Arno revved her.

The Boyz, thank the Lord, had fucked off. As for

Pastor—"*Rocco, Rocco, Rocco,*" he mimicked Heinz Dieter's nagging, "*come here, do this, do that, take me here, take me there, nibble my tits, suck my balls*"— he couldn't wait to shed the parasite.

He locked the door of the red house.

He walked across the street, knocked on the door of the silver caravan.

The two council workers—nudge nudge, wink wink—had been outside playing dominoes, cards, dice on a plastic kid's table whenever the weak sun had shown itself these last few days, eyes only on winnings.

The men had stuck out as sore thumbs. Had to be Law Enforcement. Now one of them, the shorter guy, already pissed, bleary-eyed, taking his job oh-so seriously, opened the caravan door. *Pop*, Rocco shot him with the silenced Colt Python. *Pop*, got the second officer as he stood, the guys spewing blood and beer all over the interior. Shot them another time each. *Pop, pop.* Did the cops really think they'd nail him? For poaching, for fraud, for hate, for murder, whatever. The stupids.

There you go, Pastor Heinz, counting Trudie and your mommy, and Derm the Worm too, between us that makes five sacrificial victims for Aurora!

There'd be more.

Heh, heh, heh, heh.

He mounted the Harley, held his gloved hands firm at the handlebars. He reveled in the vibrations as he rode, becoming one with the engine, feeling the power between his thighs, energy surging through his muscles. Rocco Robano, in touch with the perfect ribbon of highway, was at last on his way to the airport.

Sick to his stomach over Trudie Kellerman, Vincent

couldn't eat. Sure he had to tell Rae, but if Rae didn't call him, he wasn't calling Rae.

He re-read her note. Checked out the right-wing AWB stuff on screen, the ugly take on the swastika, the triple-seven graffiti. Didn't see the relevance. He knew that deep in conservative up-country towns, a revolution was supposedly brewing, a revolution to keep the land as it had been in the eighteen hundreds, white and pure, to keep the native as slave. But no way this could be connected to Rosa and Heinz.

He read on screen:

...Where ploughs cut through fields of quivering cosmos, where silos breathe dust of maize and young boys still flick donkeys to action from the seat of the rattling cart, there's War on men's minds...

In his mind's eye, Vince saw the fanatical disenfranchised white men taking a break from their horses and ploughs, saw them gathered, caucusing at the local Wimpy roadhouse in their caps and khakis and battered boots, discussing war over French fries and fizzy drinks.

He knew about a group of incarcerated conspirators in local prisons forever making escape bids. Nationalism was a dangerous concept fueled by increased polarization, especially in trying times. But this job was something other than Afrikaner unrest.

If he could get his mind working, he might make sense of the video clips. What was he missing? What still didn't mesh for him was a diamond deal gone wrong.

He went over the story so far: Sol allegedly gave the trinkets to Trudie, they got nicked and she was killed by the lean wiry guy, a man any number of people in the hotel, certainly the barman, could easily describe, surely, the way the two—had to be true, opposites attract—had been making out in public. What Vince remembered were the spikes on Blondie's skull shimmering gold in the light of the bar. The sinews contracting on toughened hands as his fingers had bitten into Trudie's flesh. Mystery man's face was a blur, except for Vince's memory of facial hair.

His twenty-four-hour hangover showing no signs of abating, he got up, adjusted the blinds to soften the street light. He'd rattled off the partial registration plate he'd remembered from the Land Rover to Mandla, a vanity number: NEW something or other. What more could he do? Mandla knew some people, right?

At his desk, he opened the drawer. Drained the whiskey. Looked long and hard at the Taurus. A bullet in the brain was one way to cure a headache for eternity.

He closed the drawer. Offing yourself took energy. Energy he didn't have.

The taste of Princess had soured at his lips. He'd let Trudie down. And there was Amber, always reaching for his gut, brain, heart. The Kimberley would be in full swing despite the rain and trouble. Only way to get the peace he craved, to escape the crowing of his own guilt, was to glug from a bottle.

He pulled on Rae's camo jacket, called to Mandla, "See you in a bit, brother."

"When's it gonna stop pissing?" said Christoff, sitting in the Landie parked a half block down from the PI's offices in Long Street. "One thing for sure: gotta be a load warmer upcountry." He smacked his gloved hands one into the other, stomped on the mat, pumping blood to his cooling extremities.

"Oh yeah, our new home," JP snorted, drew a smiley face on the inside of the fogged window. "No

Rabinowitzes in yarmulkes, no Khumalos in African print, no Abdullahs in turbans. No darkies or unbelievers of any kind."

"Jissis, shoulda done job this earlier when there was a bit of sun. Can't we close the windows all the way up, man? It's like cold storage in here. My balls're turning blue."

"I don't wanna know about your balls, Christoff, that's faggot talk."

Christoff leered. "Let's go up there, slap her round a bit, get her meek and mild like a woman should be, show her your massive gonads, JP."

"Sit tight."

Christoff took the torch from the cubbyhole. Played Morse code with it, checking it worked. "City's supposed to be all razzmatazz, all glitz and neon lights, but it's dark as being up your own arsehole out here. Like the city's closed down."

"Switch that fucking thing off," snapped JP. "There she is." The collar of her camouflage coat up around her neck, against the rain, her black beanie pulled low over her eyes.

JP exited the Landie, into the pissing rain, stole up quickly behind her, taller than he thought she'd be. He grabbed her quick and solid, mashed cotton wool soaked in chloroform—courtesy of Heinz Dieter Pharmaceuticals—to her face, hard over her mouth and nose. Had to sucker punch the feisty bitch a couple of times in the side, bitch going down, still hitting out, squirming, as JP with super-strength wrenched her arm up her back, heard a pop at her shoulder.

"Christoff, get out here! Chick weighs a fucking ton!"

Christoff pulled off her beanie. "'Cos she's no chick, JP."

The dude moaning now, trying to sit up, struggling.

"Don't tune me grief or I'll fucking kick you to death." JP smacked his skull with the Smith & Wesson.

"So who's this Chink joker?" said Christoff.

"One of the partners maybe, Saldana or Durant. Both ex-cops, so says Rocco."

"Jissis, the pigs're gonna be all over this one."

"Be like flies at a pig farm. No way we can leave this idiot here like an invite for cops to come after us."

Christoff and JP lifted Vincent Saldana, stashed him in the back of the Landie, folded in his legs, secured duct tape around his hands, feet, mouth, hiding the dude in darkness under a tarpaulin.

Back in the car, JP checked the printout left on the dash, the pic of the brown cherry. "Wearing that camo jacket like she's in the army or something. Fuck, how we supposed to know it wasn't her?"

"What do we do now?"

"Pastor Heinz wants his sugar. This offering"—he jerked his head towards the trussed up body—"won't do. Whatever religious maniac he is, Heinz, as far as I know's no fudge-packer bum bandit."

"I'm freezing my boude off," whined Christoff, "who the hell knows where's she's at?"

JP dialed 1023, requested the office number. Phone rang till the message came on. No one at Durant, Saldana & Valentine. "We gonna go up there. That's where her address'll be."

The first desk drawer JP pulled out yielded a nice surprise—"How's this!" He plucked up the .357 Magnum. "Double-action Taurus. You gotta have strong hands to work this baby. Sweet, bro." JP walked across to the window, sat in the swivel chair behind the oak desk which looked as if it came from a bank or someplace. He stubbed out his smoke on the worn green leather top. "There's a bit of history for you," he said. "I've made my mark." JP upended the drawers. Just paper, headache pills, paperclips. "You find anything?"

"Nothing," said Christoff, scratching through an obsolete Rolodex, throwing it across the room in dyslexic frustration. "Let's just get the hell outta here before some idiot calls the cops."

"We're not leaving till we know where to look for her next."

JP turned to the computer. Punched at the blue-sky screen saver, saw password protected. Was when they heard footsteps on the boards, a voice calling, "Vince, what're you doing in there? What's the bloody noise?" This guy just opening the door then, strolling in, as if he owned the joint, as if he belonged. "Vince?"

The Taurus in hand, JP barked, "Look what we have here. A darkie in a suit is still a darkie."

"No worries, I'm outta here." Head bowed, hands up, Mandla edged backwards.

"Where d'you think you going?" JP bounded from the chair.

"Back to my office. Home. To my wife. Just minding my own business."

"Empty your pockets."

Jittery, jumpy, he put cellphone, wallet, small change on the table, said, "I don't want trouble." Eyes down, sending a message: *I'm not looking at you, I won't ever recognize you.* Slowly backing away with his palms up in front of him. "I'm a lawyer. I can help you with whatever problems you have, free of charge, my card's in my wallet."

JP cocked his head. "How is it a black man's palms are so pink? What kind of lawyer are you anyway?"

"Human rights...for all..."

"Tragic isn't it, these attacks on foreigners in the city. People're so callous, so inhumane to fellow human beings, just 'cos they from Pakistan or Mali or Malawi. In your case, you from where?"

The lawyer stumbled over his explanation: "I'm homegrown, born and bred in South Africa."

JP plucked four two-hundred-rand notes from the wallet, read from the card: "MANDLA UBUNTU. Ubuntu? That's the humanity shit our Bishop Tutu sprouts about."

"That's it," the lawyer's tone upbeat. "So you know about that."

"Don't get your hopes up. Only the fucking criminals have human rights in this country."

JP lifted the Taurus, pulled the trigger.

Click!

"No bloody bullets in the gun," JP guffawed.

Christoff sniggered, "Your eyes just about popped out your head, Ubuntu."

JP pulled the trigger a second time.

The muzzle flashed, the lawyer blasted back out the door, slumped on the boards, clutched at his chest, gasping, blood spurting.

"Holy fuck!" JP looked at the smoking gun in amazement, let out a triumphant cackle as Christoff shook up the spray paint, added the finishing touches to his trademark triple-seven, then added the shape of an eagle, the beak looking too hooked, the bird looking more like a chicken. "What the hell," he hooted, "we was here!"

"Now let's get our fists out our arses," said JP, "and go get Heinz his cunt."

Rocco Robano had ordered Alex Silver: "You head on out with Pastor Heinz before the crazy changes his mind and tells us we have to hang around another six months for more fucking signs. You look after him." And now Alex was stuck transporting his ray of sunshine while the Boyz were doing Rocco's bidding, whatever the hell it was. Rocco treated Pastor with kid gloves, Pastor the key to whatever was going down.

The road was straight and long, the emptiness of the land was one thing that struck you, you passed stretches of farms where the buildings you saw were desolate cottages, maybe two or three Cape Dutch-style farms in oases of green, palms and fruit trees kept lush with borehole water; the people you saw on the road were farm hands hitching.

Alex said, "Shall we talk to each other or what?"

The response from Pastor was to tap Alex on the shoulder and hand him a flashdrive.

Alex adjusted the volume, resigned himself to hours of what threatened to prove to be a never-ending dirge of Gregorian Chants mixed up with solemn hymns.

Even with the trailer attached, the souped-up Mini Cooper drove like a dream. She stuck to the road like an ant to an aardvark's tongue. Alex avoided speeding on the open road, stuck to the 60k-speed limit through God-forsaken one-horse towns named after dismal outposts, or battles waged by Boer and Brit: Moedverloor, Douse-the-Glim, Bullet-trap, Nigramoep, Bowesdorp, Nababiep, Springbok. He'd learned in school that wars between the descendants of the original Dutch settlers and the British wanting to expand their Empire had started in the 1800s. Sure, he knew a lot of stuff.

The music done, Alex asked, "Pastor, you ever been up the West Coast? Port Nolloth, now there's an interesting town. Started out as a diamond mining town, with all the alluvial diamonds up in these parts.

Got dubiously incorporated by De Beers." But Pastor Heinz, staring out of the window, said nothing.

He tried again: "The Star of South Africa diamond comes from the Orange River, which incidentally flows from Lesotho. Eighty-three or so carats picked up by a Griqua shepherd boy in 1869. A Boer settler traded with him, offered five hundred sheep and ten oxen for the stone. Even the piccanins knew there was something special about the stones they played with. The rest is history. Set off the diamond rush. Cecil John Rhodes staked his first claim at the Kimberley field, formed De Beers in 1880. Built his Africa on the back of the diamond trade. Boasted of linking the Cape to Cairo, by rail."

Pastor Heinz contributed not a word.

So much for conversation. So much for making a connection. The silence exacerbated a pulsing throb at his brain. He pulled his vibrating cell from the dashboard, relieved he'd have someone, anyone, to talk to.

"Alex, all fine there?"

"Long drive, Boss."

"I want a word with Heinz."

Bloody Rocco.

"Sure thing." He handed back the phone. Heinz saying yes, all was well, he was comfortable, was looking forward to getting to the settlement, thank you. Then Alex heard the window drone down, looked over his shoulder the split second Heinz tossed the phone out the open window, Alex swerved, saw the phone explode behind them on the tarmac. Tried to hold his tongue, *you bloody madman*!

"What the—?"

"We won't need phones where we're going, Brother Alex."

Fuck! Cellphone gone, destroyed, just like that. He needed his fuckin' cell! This excruciating drive couldn't end a moment too soon. Alex pressed replay on the compilation—this was better at least than JP's current fave, *Payable On Death*—hoping Heinz, sitting as unbending as a pipe, his jaw clamped, would chill. When Alex checked again Pastor's chin had turned up slightly, his mouth moved as if in prayer, as if he was soaring high on the divine tunes in his own head.

※

JP detoured into Breda Street and parked. He got out the Landie, said, "Listen, you brain surgeon." JP handed the Taurus to Christoff. "The Chink so much as sighs, shoot him."

JP checked first. No neighbors out and about. Plan would spoil if curtain-twitchers spying out their windows saw him. But it was quiet, just wind for noise. And dark, the way he liked it, a bonus to have streetlights down after the storm. He sat on the bell, humming, "Tonight's gonna be a *great* night."

She opened the door, no chain on it. He pushed her inside, slammed the door closed with his foot, clutched the girl tight around the neck, mashing her lips with his mouth. The girl wrapped her arms like tentacles around his chest, thrust her tongue at his palate, coming up for air, asking, "Where've you been?"

"I'm here now, Stella." His cock was a keen lead pipe in his Levi's, itching to beat out. He carried her to the bed, dumped her, pushed her down, tugged at her baby-doll shorts. She groaned as he vampire-sucked at her neck, licked and nipped at perky breasts, rubbed her dyed-dark pubes trimmed to a neat heart shape.

"You like, JP?"

He could hardly pull his pants off. Missionary

would have to do; she guided him in, he pumped, pumped, pumped, dropped his load. "Hallelujah!"

He swiveled on the bed, wiped himself off on her PJs, pulled up his pants. Lit three of her Stuyvie Extra Lights, put the cigarettes in his mouth all at the same time, said, "May as well smoke air. Now put some clothes on."

"What's up now, JP? I'm done."

"I need a favor."

"JP, if you didn't notice, I'm totally fucked," Stella croaked. "That was, like, intense."

"Stella," he said deadpan, "put your clothes on."

"No way. What the hell time is it, anyway? I need my beauty sleep."

"You pretty enough."

Her nipples stiffened again, as she drew on the fabric of a clean nighty, then put on a gown. "No way I'm going out tonight, JP."

"Thing is, Stella, you're always willing to put out."

"What're you talking about?"

"Heinz Dieter, Pastor Heinz, he wants a woman. And you're it."

"No way. Buzz off," she whined. "What're you on about, anyway? Really, I'm done doing what you want all the time. I'm going back to Technikon. Gonna finish my Phys Ed diploma. Wanna do something with my life. And my mom's coming over early."

"You not making this easy, Stel."

"What about *us*, JP?"

"Baby, I need this."

"Look, JP, I don't know what you want any more. I let you in Sol's shop. You didn't have to nearly beat the old man to death. Trashing the place and hurting him was never part of the deal, and what about the ring I wanted? Where's my ring, JP? I thought I meant something to you."

"You do, Stel."

"You go too far, you know."

"You getting stroppy with me, Stel. Tell me, in any case, why you work for a Jewboy." The ugly snarl played at JP's lips.

Stella, sulking, her mouth a rosy pout, those full lips, pink and soft, opened the door. "Time for you to leave."

"I said put your clothes on, Stella, and don't fucking sulk."

"I'm not going anywhere"—she clutched her fleece gown tight around her—"and FYI I didn't even come!"

He lashed out, hit Stella full at the jaw with a closed fist, her head snapping back. "You needed a slap. One thing the Muslims have got right, at least the women know their fucking place!" He hit her one more time, a chop to the neck. Then he tossed her over his shoulder, went fireman-style down the stairs. "C'mon, girlfriend." He nuzzled his nose at her damp thighs, smelled the sex on her, the perfume, as he dumped her on the back seat of the Landie. "Yeah, Stella, you'll show the pastor a thing or two. Oh, Praise the Lord! Thank You for this pretty white arse!" Only the best for Heinz Dieter.

"One hundred percent," agreed Christoff. "Pastor won't wanna fool around with a half-breed when he can have quality pussy."

"Shut the fuck up, Christoff."

They got straight onto the N1, then left onto the N7, headed due north. Not a peep coming from JP's sweetheart, prone on the back seat, or from the PI in the boot.

※

...Pirouetting on stage, leaping in arabesques from one foot to the other, muscles in perfect sync...She floated, weightless...

The shrill ringtone interrupted Rae's dream. Groggy with sleep, where she'd passed out on the couch, she reached for the cellphone.

"Hey." She sat up, yawned, checked the time on the screen as she pulled it from under her hip. Nearly midnight.

"Rex Hawkins."

"Rex. To what do I owe the pleasure?"

"There's been a shooting at your offices."

Instantly awake: "Vincent!" *No no no, he's offed himself...*

"I'm afraid the victim is Mandla Ubuntu."

"Mandla? From the law firm?"

"Injured but alive. At Christiaan Barnard Memorial Hospital. He's had death threats on account of his civil rights work, could be the reason."

"So this's what doing good gets him."

"We're not sure. He's been in the news, working on cases of asylum, sorting papers for Zimbabweans, Congolese, Chinese you name it, the vulnerable needing protection."

"I'll be right there." She grabbed the Colt, locked up.

Crime tape and crowds, the two were synonymous. Hardly five minutes later she pushed her way through the gobsmacked kyk-daars on the street. Had never climbed the stairs quite so quickly. Burst in on Rex.

"What's going on?" The office was trashed, vandalized, her notes strewn all over. Drawers turfed out. Concentric burns on the leather desk. The computer was on, thank God undamaged. She didn't need Kinsey Millhone to tell her whoever'd searched the place had done a thorough job. She gasped at the damp blood stain on the floor.

"Anything you can tell us, Rae?"

"Not a thing. What the hell happened?"

"Got an emergency call about some trouble, got here, found the lawyer. May have confronted whoever was shaking the place down. Wrong place at the wrong time. Look around. Tell us what's missing."

The TV was old, the crime novels no one was interested in. Her laptop was home. Shit. Nothing to steal apart from Vince's Taurus. Christ almighty. Not in the drawer. The cops would have found it if it had been there. Unless he had it with him. What the cops had missed—no surprise with cops known to miss dead bodies stashed in attics, under beds—was this: Vince's cell under the desk. No one was looking. She pocketed the phone.

She stepped back from rookie CSIs, with their toolboxes and dust kits, struggling to lift prints, find slugs and casings, make sense of whatever had gone down. A young cop sealed an oily take-aways tray in a Ziploc bag. Probably would end up stored in a brown box for months, growing mold like some kid's science experiment.

"Where's your sidekick?" Rex asked.

"Most likely sleeping off an almighty babalas under a table at the Kimberley or on a park bench somewhere." Or in some woman's arms. Russian roulette with HIV all part of his slow death. Fuck knew. *Vince, for Christ's sake, you don't have anything to do with this, do you? Please, tell me it wasn't your gun Mandla was shot with?*

Rae nodded, sighed. "Something's not right here."

"You don't say? Look, you've been in this business what? Months? You've hardly got your nose wet. Still relying on Sue Grafton, I see"—he picked up a paperback—"for PI know-how. This's under control.

You cool it, you hear."

"Don't tell me to stay out of it."

"Look." He drew her aside, "I'll tell you this. There's plenty men out there who've come back to SA from Iraq, Iran, Ivory Coast, after earning a hundred thou a month as mercenaries, men who aren't interested in guarding Shoprites and Checkers. No one— not least the government—gives a rat's arse about them. They're pissed off. See the graffiti? This stinks of treason, or just plain hate. Mandla Ubuntu could well have been the target. This is more than you can handle, Rae. Go home. We'll look after things. Keep your cell on so I can keep in touch."

Rex's way of saying stay behind a desk, answer phones, look pretty.

Well, I've got news for you, Rex.

She'd be wasting her time begging the cops for more truth than they were willing to part with.

The truth was right there in red and black paint— the triple-seven symbol on the wall. Plus a childlike rendition of what had to be an eagle. Couldn't have been that long ago that this crew had desecrated her space.

Close to 2:00 am, she left the scene. Made it down the stairs, her fingers itching to check Vince's cell. She knew the passcode: 123. Vince couldn't care less.

In the Jeep, thumbing through the pics, she was treated to more of the truth: saw Trudie Kellerman on screen, one minute living, the next dead: puffy face, blue lips, vacant eyes.

She dropped in at the Kimberley. Deon's bar doing good business, but not with Vince.

Went home. Called the hospital.

"I'm enquiring about Mandla Ubuntu?"

"He's not conscious."

"But he'll live, right?"

"The bulletproof vest saved him. But there're complications."

"So tell me. Please."

"Vest stopped the bullet, but not the heart attack."

Whatever this was, diamonds had to be the least of it.

PART THREE

DIRT AND DUST

SUNDAY: RETREAT

Alex Silver drove through the night, the sky whitening as dawn crept closer. The scenery, all shades of gray as the sun promised to rise, kept changing—little gray hills and bumps, dotted with tufts of bush, showed up on either side of a road as straight as a gun barrel. Then morphed into a bleak moonscape of rock and craters, a seemingly endless stretch, till it was again relieved with splashes of growth, becoming cultivated farmland as they got closer to the river flood plain. He slowed down, pulled to the side of the road, got out the hand-drawn map.

He turned off the highway, stayed with the tarred road; there was a landmark now, a quiver tree, the kokerboom, the indigenous tree aloe, where the road forked right and turned to gravel and dirt.

"We're nearly there, Pastor Heinz," said Alex, the bumpy ride bringing Heinz out of a light doze. They passed a derelict windmill, an empty reservoir, a burnt-out tractor, a two-meter tall tree stump encasing a hive where a blanket of bees moved like silk caught by a breeze.

"Check that out." Alex pointed.

Heinz Dieter yawned.

Alex brought the car to a stop alongside a lone Namakwa fig tree at the edge of a clearing. He switched off his headlights, taken aback as he was by the illuminated eyes of ostriches in a pen, the birds squawking and ruffling their plumage. He got out, walked over to the passenger side and held open the door for Heinz. "Here we are, Pastor."

Heinz sat tight. Squirted disinfectant on his hands.

Alex sniffed, the pungent camphor rising to clear his sinuses. "Strong stuff."

"I like to keep clean."

"You're lightening up at last, Pastor."

"Where are we, Brother?" Heinz shivered. "Why have we stopped?"

"This is it."

"There has to be some mistake."

"Would I lie to you, Pastor?"

"But there is nothing here."

"Pastor, I'm also in the dark."

It was a camping ground of sorts. The land was barren, the soil dry and rocky, with clumps of veld grass poking through here and there from earth and stones, and small bushes sprouting after the winter rains. On the central grassy clearing, tree stumps were set around the remains of a campfire. Between two thorn trees was strung a makeshift washing line, near to it a green-topped formica table laden with utensils. Beyond this, from what he could see, the land rose slightly to form an embankment before dipping to what had to be water by the sound of the rush, had to be the meandering Orange River, the natural border between South Africa on one side and Namibia, with all her secrets, on the other.

"I thought we were heading straight for Aurora," said Heinz, his mouth set. He wouldn't budge.

"Orders say we have to wait for the others."

"I am ready to embrace my followers, my disciples who have placed faith in me. I have no desire whatever to prolong the journey."

"Come now, Pastor, this is God's own country. Have a look around."

"I insist on an explanation."

"Look, I've been told we'll be here a few days, that's all."

"A few days, you say?" His tone incredulous.

"To rest, sort out the supplies, gather our reserves."

The door of the shepherd's shed opened now, and in the breaking dawn the car's headlights cast an eerie glow on a thin brown man, with sinewy arms and high cheekbones, skin texture rough and tough as hide. He was wrapped in a leather kaross, under it a Green Party T-shirt and floral shorts, tradition meeting the contemporary. He made his way towards the two men. "Welcome, welcome!"

"You Johannes?" asked Alex.

The Bushman bared yellowed teeth and pink gums in a broad grin, thumbed his chest, said, "That's me. Ek het vir julle gewag. I have been waiting for you."

Truth be told the destination was a disappointment. Alex wasn't in the mood for camping. He'd hoped at least there'd be an ablution block. He wasn't in the mood for extending his stay with Pastor, or the Boyz and crazy Rocco a minute longer than he had to. He patted his jacket for his cell. Damn! An image flashed of the phone exploding into a million pieces on the highway. The loss of his cell was a proper bugger. Irritated, he ordered, "Come, Pastor, step out of the car."

Heinz gingerly rose from the Mini. He adjusted his bow tie; in the dawn chill, he buttoned the brown suit jacket. His breath came in small gasps. He bunched his hands deep in the pockets. He lifted his eyes to the granite-topped mountains on the horizon, his mouth quivering in silent prayer.

"Pastor, there is wood for the fire, there is water," said Johannes. "Everything you need." Johannes pointed to the table at the thorn trees, laden with pots, pans, an assortment of dishes and kitchenware.

Heinz asked, "How long will we be here did you say, Brother Alex?"

"Maybe two days, Pastor."

"But where will I sleep?"

"In a tent."

"A tent?"

"Gear's in the boot. There's deck chairs, there's supplies, a Weber barbeque, we'll make good food. You'll be comfortable, Pastor."

Johannes spoke up quietly, pointed to the shed. "If you like, Pastor, there's a cot and mattress in there. You are welcome to sleep inside."

"Now there's an offer for you," said Alex. "A roof over your head. Relative luxury out here."

"Come inside." Johannes moved towards the hut. "Put down your things, Pastor. Ja, kom rus. It is the day of rest after all."

"Rest? This is no time to rest."

This was not the time to show weakness.

He followed the San-man, stepping over the threshold into the shed, the pungent smell of farm slapping him in the face—the ripe, dank smell of dung, the ashy smell of an extinguished wood fire, the sweet-meat smell of strips of flesh on the cure hanging from a rickety wooden clothes horse held together with insulation tape. He stood still, scanned the room, saw in the dim light the floor of brushed dirt, the single brass and wrought-iron bed, the unpolished jongman's kas. Saw a framed graduation photo of a young woman in pride of place alongside postcards stuck to the wall. Saw in the corner the San-man's pet curled up in a straw dog's basket. His heart lurched as the devil in animal guise popped open amber eyes. A She-devil in a white and brown body with four awkward limbs and pendulous ears. But what held him were the eyes. Eyes that glowed. Rectangular pupils staring at him from the dark. The She-devil bleated.

"I'll take a tent," croaked Pastor Heinz, turning on his heels, stumbling back over the threshold with the San-man and his goat coming after him. As he lifted his hand to pinch closed his nostrils, he rubbed against a clay bakoond, the whitewash from the oven leaving a smear of powder on the back of his hand. On the brink of the abyss, he brought out his traveling towelettes, pulled one from its packaging and wiped away the sin.

"Whatever suits you, Pastor," said Johannes. "Nog iets. Another thing. The long drop, if you need it," he pointed with a gnarled brown finger, "is just over the ridge there."

"Long drop?" Struggling for breath, Heinz rummaged in his tog bag for the asthma pump, sucking at the tube as he squeezed, prayed: *Dear God, show me the way*. Brother Alex patted his his shoulder. He cringed at the touch.

Alex said, "Come sit, Pastor," leading him to a deck chair set up alongside the ostrich pen, a hand-fashioned enclosure of sorts made of branches and wire.

Heinz hobbled along, hoping this was all a nightmare from which he'd wake. He stared at the birds in the pen, one close to him, focused on her in particular, trying to talk himself down, to calm himself. He stared at her brown eyes, her deep brown eyes. He breathed deep to subdue his racing heart, steady his nerves.

"Spectacular bird, isn't she?" said Alex. "Stunners all. Two-toed, swift-footed flightless birds tall as men …Those sinewy necks, goggle-eyes, all date back to prehistory."

The ostrich blinked. Turned her head to stare at the San-man and his pet goat approaching, then turned her eyes back to Heinz. She was a mere foot from him.

Strangely, Heinz was neither afraid nor repulsed as the bird stood seemingly transfixed by his presence. He drew air into his lungs, he calmed himself. Seeing his image reflected in those dark pools edged with thick luxurious lashes, he softened, was compelled to whisper, "My love, Liebschen."

The bird ruffled her brown feathers. Dipped a coy head. Heinz gingerly held out a hand. Just short of touching the bird, the feathers so soft, he whispered, "Yes, I will practice my sweet nothings on you."

Johannes clicked. "Pastor is already making a pet of the ostrich. Aikona! Die wit mense, these white people!" he said to Nannie goat. "You see something new every day."

Many minutes later Heinz looked up to see the San-man cupping an ostrich egg between two palms.

He heard Brother Alex suggest, "Maak vir ons, cook for us, Johannes, asseblief, please. We are hungry. Vir brekfis."

"It is difficult to raise the chicks, maar die eiers, the eggs, are delicious."

Alex erected two pup tents on the clearing near the thorn trees as Johannes started a fire with Blitz then coiled stuffed sausage plump with dried apricot, herbs and spices, on a grid.

Johannes brought dented tin cooking utensils from the table at the tree. Pulled out a battered bowl from a cardboard box. He squatted, placed a pointed stick on top of the egg gripped between his knees, and drilled a hole through the hard shell. Then shook out the contents, watched the yolk and white dribble into the mixing bowl beneath. Whisked expertly, poured into the pan and stirred; within minutes the scrambled eggs were ready.

"Seasoned with oregano from my garden over the koppie, the hill over there." Johannes pointed towards the river. "Pastor must come see my vegetables and flowers."

"You gonna eat on your lap, Pastor?" Alex had set up another deck chair, at the fire, more comfy than the logs.

Heinz came away from the pen and Alex served him his share, the egg, the aromatic sausage, plus baked beans warmed in a tin pot and fried home-grown tomatoes, all of it on an enamel plate garnished with a sprig of parsley.

This is not Woolworths, shuddered Heinz, seeing the food types slipping into each other. The dirt, the smell of the penned birds, how could he eat watching the stranger, Johannes—he saw him from the corner of his eye—scratching the goat under the bearded chin, feeding it scraps from his own plate, allowing the filthy animal's tongue to lap at his fingertips. The She-devil folded its limbs under a rotund belly and settled near him, butting at his master's knee for another pat, another treat. Mutti did not allow pets. Heinz's breakfast turned cold.

Alex asked, "You not hungry, Pastor?"

Johannes offered Heinz goat's milk in an enamel cup. "Fresh from Nannie."

"N-n-no thank you." The pungent aroma rising with the steam, the icky cream skein forming on the surface, repulsed him.

"Dis lekker. It's tasty," said Johannes. "You don't know what you missing, Pastor." He burped, wiped the milk moustache from his weather-beaten upper lip.

Heinz watched the San-man wash the pot and saucepan in a plastic tub under the thorn trees. The goat at his heels peered back all the while at Heinz, fixing those black horizontal-strip pupils on him as if in a dare.

He held back a gag. He picked himself up from the chair, made for the pen, but the ostrich was no longer a distraction. He crawled into the bubble Disciple Alex had indicated was his tent, hoping to escape the rising heat of the mid-morning. The light filtering through the fabric walls was green, the color of toads. Heinz pressed his palms together, kneeled on the thin blue camping mat, and prayed.

I am reduced to a tent, as were the Israelites. Dear Lord, give me strength, I must not complain.

Then he rummaged in the pack Alex had given him, pulled out a head torch, a sleeping bag, bottled water. Was this it? He wanted—*no, needed*—to wipe the stench of adrenaline from his armpits, his crotch. But then he'd have to undress. He settled down on the mat, his head on a rolled-up cardigan he'd taken from his suitcase.

This was not what he had imagined.

Chief Disciple Rocco had said nothing about an interim stop.

Rocco had slept in the hangar, hadn't wanted to leave in the dark.

Now the Piper Warrior, even with strong cross-winds at first, made good time at a cruise speed of 115 knots. What Rocco liked about the Piper, it was easy to fly. With this model and her range of 625 nautical miles, he could make longer trips, carry a passenger or two if he wanted.

Turning the plane slightly to the left, he flew across the Orange River towards the interior, over the Namib desert with her rippling dunes stretching under him; he flew over the ghostly relics, what was left of roofs and walls, of the diamond-boom town Kolmanskap protruding from the sands which had overtaken the structures, then arced back towards what would soon be his new home.

He came in low over the coast, saw seals basking on rocky slopes; he saw the remains of bleached whale bones poking from the white sands, and a shipwreck held fast on the shore of a turbulent and deadly Atlantic Ocean. The wild and desolate landscape of the forbidden coast never failed to impress him. This land, with all its promise, was the future. He could never leave Africa, this Blue Sky country in his blood.

Ah yes, there was the building site, the spot set further down the coast from the string of holiday homes past Luderitz, marked by piles of sand, trucks, a cement mixer. Three men looked up as the plane flew low. The men, Dirk, Pieter, and Cornelius, securing the rooftop of red tiles, stopped their hammering and waved.

He'd live the good life here, oh yeah, *Praise the Lord!* A good life where Rocco Robano would rejoice in his role as hunter, king, god, living his best life of leisure, fresh oysters, African sunsets, pure pleasure! He might once again run safaris, but some other subservient follower would deal with the problematic staff, the demanding punters.

As the Piper crossed back over the river, he marveled at the waters of the Orange River that had transported diamonds from inland volcanic pipes to the sea; currents had carried them northwards and the surf deposited them into the dune fields of the Namib; exactly where Rocco, with new techniques and the men he could count on, would soon be sifting for them.

He laughed now, allowed himself a wild, unrestrained gleeful "Yes!" as he thought of his plan coming together. He'd nailed the cops in the silver camper, he'd see to Heinz. He had eyes in the back of his head. He had a handle on it all!

Heh, heh, heh, heh.

He spotted the runway on the farm, nothing more than a dirt track. He brought the plane down. He'd grown accustomed to the low sink rate, a problem for him at first; when the Piper fan stopped, he may as well have been flying a rock, and not something he'd appreciated after flying the Cessna 172. Though the upside was you didn't float around as you touched the ground.

Rae Valentine woke in a cold sweat. She'd hoped a couple of hours' sleep would ease her mind, show her the way, reveal the answers. At least provide the next step. But she'd tossed and turned with bad dreams and the breaking of another storm. Mid Sunday morning she lifted the blinds on lightning striking over Table Bay, a spectacular natural fireworks display as the punishing weather battered the peninsula. Her leg was stiff, her hip sore. She'd do well to go to the pool and do lengths, but bathed instead in near-scalding water to get her circulation going.

Refreshed, she called Vince. Voicemail.

She called Mrs. S.

"Vince there? He home for some tender loving care, Mrs. S?"

"My boy not at office?"

"I'll call him there, so no worries, Mrs. S."

Though she knew it was futile—more than mere sixth sense, she knew it in her marrow that he'd never head for help—she called rehab centers, private and state: Stepping Stones, Crescent Clinic, Valkenberg; plus police stations near the Kimberley, a couple of hospitals, the morgue. A Chinese citizen had been brought in, all panga'd up. Killed in his general dealership on the outskirts of Nyanga, but at five-foot-five the victim couldn't be Vince.

She was half-expecting a call from Rex telling her a neat pile of Vince's clothing had been found on beach rocks somewhere, or that Vince's rust-bucket had gone off Chapman's Peak. Said to herself, "That'd really piss me off, Vince."

Once up and about, the next thing was to visit the Christiaan Barnard hospital. She felt somehow responsible for Mandla's plight, and could only hope the unfortunate encounter had nothing to do with her or Vince or the job they were on.

She pulled in, parked. More than the fact that the wards had names like birch, cedar, oak—the kind of wood coffins are made of—what Rae hated most about hospitals was the smell. The antiseptic she could handle. It was something under the antiseptic, a morbidity, the smell of death, that had her on edge. Taking the elevator to the third floor, she stared at her distorted image in the stainless steel interior, flashed back to her days in trauma, breathed through a panic attack, getting it under control as the elevator door opened. The worst thing about the attack was she was just not ready to die, did not want to die, remembering she was taken completely by surprise that it might have been her time.

At the nurses' station she said, "I'm here to see Mandla Ubuntu."

"Sorry," said the matron on duty. "He's under

police guard. Only visitor allowed is his wife. And he's still not conscious."

"Is there cause for concern?"

"There's always concern when a patient is in ICU."

Sol's house, the address she'd looked up in the white pages—she'd learned something from Anthony after all—was perched on the rocks at Clifton at the cul de sac of a rustic pathway. The cottage overlooked the premier Blue Flag beach frequented in summer by beautiful celebs and fans alike, people like Posh and Becks and their hangers-on, and the general populace slaughtering sheep for sunset braai-meat. From the sublime to the primal. At Sol's, she peered though salt-crusted windows into empty space. Made out a cardboard box, a roll of packing plastic. What was going on? *Not you too, Sol...*

She stopped next at the Sea Breeze Pharmacy. Was told Heinz Dieter had taken a week's sick leave.

Then drove to the Dieter residence. Parked. No answer on cell or landline. Walked slowly and deliberately towards the house, scanning for anything out of the ordinary. Didn't want some surprise coming at her from the shadows, from the crawl spaces on either side of impressive condos.

She pushed open the garden gate. Vince was right: Frau Dieter and her son still lived in a dream world. Not even a simple security gate bought cheap from Makro secured the property, let alone a Trellidor which would stop a wrecking ball according to the TV ad. She pressed the brass bell. Rapped the lion-shaped knocker. House must be charmed. No street child had ripped the brass from the door. Where was Rosa? She rang again. Maybe Rosa was preoccupied with her early-morning brain gym or Sudoku or crossword puzzles, protecting her mind from Alzheimer's.

She rang a third time, but no luck. Rosa had to be out and about, was obviously not home preparing chicken soup for son Heinz's speedy recovery.

And where's your sick boy?

❋

Heinz Dieter felt trapped, as if in a body bag at the morgue. Hours had passed since their arrival and he could still not fathom the reason for being here. He couldn't bear to stay in the tent a moment longer. His pride intact—he had not removed his Hush Puppies or his jacket—he now ran a comb through his hair. He moistened his eyes with drops, unzipped the tent, adjusting his vision to the stark late-morning sun and bright blue sky.

He heard a low rumble—a plane?—and raised his eyes heavenward.

What test is this, to prove my commitment?

He stood straight and tall, reminding himself he was the Pastor, a Prophet!

The great King of Terror shall come,
Fireballs from on High will heat the sea like the sun.
Then comes the cold and dark...
But the Core will be safe!

Yes, while clouds of ash, dust, soot, toxic gas rained from on high in the northern hemisphere, only the most elaborate shelters in Africa would survive!

The San-man was suddenly at his side, talking quickly. "Come, let us walk, we'll get a better view."

Together they climbed the gentle rise from the clearing and descended to a grassy verge along the river.

"See there, Pastor." Johannes pointed his stick-finger to a painted rock set back from the reeds on the opposite side of the river. "R for Richtersveld."

So near to Namibia, to Luderitz, to the settlement, and yet so far. He would have liked to have paged through his scrapbook, to pore over the varied scenery; from flat, sandy coastal plains, to craggy mountains of volcanic rock, to the lush Orange River.

"Isn't this the perfect spot, Pastor?"

"I am surprised by this...domesticity. The river is tame, and crowded." Heinz pointed to a group of tourists floating by on branded canoes. The faint nattering of women and chatter of children as they cavorted carried across the river's breadth. Two youths raised their arms in greeting as their canoe, scraping over hidden rocks, came to a standstill. They pushed free with paddles, releasing the canoe from the grip of stones and disappeared around the bend.

"But there is so much beauty. See the fish eagles, Pastor!"

Heinz squinted into the sun, watched the pair lock together, a feathered Catherine wheel, till the brown female with her white hood broke free from the spin.

"Hear her call, Pastor."

A haunting, evocative cry.

Heinz's lips parted in prayer.

Then disturbed by footfall, he turned, stared hard at Chief Disciple Rocco.

"Apologies, Pastor, if I startled you."

"I've been expecting you, Brother. I heard your plane."

"Stunning here, isn't it?"

Heinz ignored the comment. "I'm owed answers."

"You're the one who wanted to leave, and in a hurry too, if I recall, Pastor."

"Why bring me to a patch of dirt in the middle of nowhere?" Heinz shouted. "I don't care for this interim-camp pit-stop rubbish. Only race cars at Kyalami need a pit stop."

"It's short term. The men are installing the finishing touches as we speak. You don't want to get to Aurora and be disappointed, do you? Aurora must be perfect for you, Pastor."

"So I'm forced to slum it." He stamped his foot.

"At least we're camped at a beautiful spot, surely you agree?"

"I'm disenchanted...And the river is...busy."

"Tibet, the Amazon, Kilimanjaro, there's foot traffic in every magnificent corner of the globe."

"I'd expected it to be more...tumultuous...turbulent..."

"Like what? Victoria Falls? Niagara?"

"Brother, do you mock me?"

"Never, never, Pastor...Would be more water if there weren't measures in place to regulate flow."

"But Nature, thwarted, will find her voice, not so?"

"You're asking me, Pastor?"

"The mosquitoes, the heat, the She-devil watching, I won't sleep a wink in that tent. You should have warned me. And after all these months, why isn't Aurora ready?

"Rome wasn't built in a day, Pastor."

Heinz sniffed. "God made the world in seven."

"The compound is impressive. It's incredible how it's shaped up in the last few months. Look again at the progress." He scrolled down pictures on his cell, Heinz's heart lifting at the sight of the windowless bunkers. "Seven units done, as a start. Scaffolding's been removed as you can see and the roof on the community center's going up as we speak. Your residence is splendid and the ablution block is complete."

Heinz peered at close-ups of exquisite bathroom plumbing, pristine, as he'd wanted, needed.

"See, Pastor, stainless-steel Cobra taps plus white tiles to the ceiling, as you wanted. There's a towel warmer. There's underfloor heating and air conditioning throughout. You have your own mini-fridge in your suite. Don't worry, everything's gonna be fine. A couple of days or so you'll be far from the madding crowd, living with every comfort."

"Tell me exactly when, when, when, Brother."

"Don't you fret, Pastor, we'll move ASAP."

"I want to go now, today."

"I explained to you the problem of cash flow…"

"Nonsense, Brother."

"We're a little over budget, you can't rely on builder's quotes, but I assure you, Pastor, you'll be well pleased when we cross over."

"Cross over?"

"We're gonna sneak across the river, Pastor. We can hardly announce ourselves at the border and apply for stamps in our passports now, can we now?"

Stupid sod, believing the Namib was a farm over which Pastor held title deeds. And what She-devil was he bloody babbling about?

Rocco's tongue was raw where he'd bitten down on the ridicule too many times, but the shock on the wackjob's face nearly had him split his sides. Cross over? Yeah, Heinz'd be crossing over all right—to hell. He controlled his impatience as Heinz brought out the spray bottle from his pocket, his lip trembling as he squirted into his palm the last of the sanitizing mist.

Just don't start bawling.

He was sick of this man who turned into an infant in two seconds flat.

He heard a commotion, men arriving in a vehicle, the Land Rover must be, screeching to a halt, doors slamming, men shouting.

"In fact there's the Boyz now. With your Regina as promised." *Yes, your dirty princess.* "It's all coming together, Pastor."

Heinz's eyes widened with instant joy, then a realization, a downer: "I was expecting to entertain in style, in at least some sort of grandeur."

"As long as the woman is at your side, Pastor, she'll be happy. Ecstatic." He laid it on thick, saw the blush creep up Heinz's neck. "Let's go say hi, and how about getting out of that suit." He slapped him on the back. "I'm suffering heatstroke just looking at you."

"At least the weather's more temperate here. A respite from the rain."

"Comes from being closer to the equator."

"The winter has been cold indeed, Brother."

"That's the spirit, Pastor, focus on the positive."

"First I must pray."

Heh, heh, heh, heh, went Rocco, watching Heinz hurry the short way back to the river, saw him spread his arms like a Prophet with a capital P, the luminary he believed he was.

"Sorely tempted by Satan's Lilith, isolated from the distractions of humanity, I accept my role in the wilderness with the wild beasts!" started Heinz. He gathered breath, his heart rapidly beating. "And now my angel will minister to my needs! Thanks be to God!"

He couldn't wait to see her. He adjusted his bow tie. Anxiety tickled at his throat. He swallowed, focused on keeping his breath even.

Walking back to camp, he noticed God's glory between rocks and stones, spring succulents beginning to swell with the last of the winter rainfalls, subtle hues of greens and blues. He took a moment to compose himself, to pick a treat of a posy from the Bushman's garden: pelargonium, lion's tail, desert daisies and cosmos. Placing it on a rock, he ripped from the sheath a refreshing towelette and cleaned his palms of any smidgen of dirt and sweat. He smoothed back his hair, cleared his throat.

"I am ready."

Holding the posy at his chest, an offering of sorts, he walked slowly, stiffly, his heart lurching as he thought fleetingly, guiltily, of resting his head on his Regina's plump breasts.

Whoopsie!

Johannes would do his nut when he saw the broken stalks of the flowers he'd so carefully nurtured. But this was love for you! Rocco accompanied Heinz to camp. Getting closer he heard Christoff strumming his air-Fender, belting out Bobbejaan klim die berg, baboon climb the mountain, giving way to the preferred anthem De la Rey, ay, ay, ay. "The Boers are coming! Ay, ay, ay! Coming to save the land!" The Boyz already settled at the fire, had popped open the giant cooler box filled with ice chunks and booze, were knocking back the beers before they'd even started unpacking the supplies.

JP gave Rocco a thumbs up, indicated towards Heinz's tent. JP, with a big fat smirk on his dial, downed another brewski and licked the foam off his upper lip as Heinz stood there, straightening his bow tie with one hand, clutching the flowers with the other.

"Well go on, then," said Rocco, "what're you waiting for?" He watched Heinz walk slowly, faltering, across the clearing towards his tent at the far side of the thorn trees, then slip inside through the opened flap.

Rocco got himself a beer, pulled the tab, settled in a chair. Yeah, he'd give the lovebirds some moments, then get down to business with Heinz. Then could only choke on his heh, heh, heh, heh, slopping beer on his khaki shorts, as a bloodcurdling scream shattered his peace. He saw Heinz running, stumbling from the tent, heard him squealing like a hyena, his teeth bared.

"Pastor." He dropped the beer, stood up. "What's wrong?"

"Where is she?" Heinz yowled, slipping on a streak of dirt, the flowers landing in a heap beside him. Propping himself up on all fours, he pushed back on his haunches, he stared at his grazed and sullied hands, whimpered, "You promised me, you promised!" He pushed his once neatly gelled black hair, now sweaty and stringy, off a glistening forehead, screeched, "Where is she?"

Rocco turned to JP. "Well lightning strike me, what have you arseholes gone and done?"

"We got a great girl–"

"But you didn't get *the* girl, did you? Is that it?" He couldn't believe the words coming out his own mouth.

"We thought he'd like this one better. She's cute, she's sexy. She's white."

"You fucking imbecile, JP."

"Jeez, sorry already." He grinned. "What's the big issue, hey? The chick'll show Heinz a good time. Guaranteed tried and tested."

Rocco pointed to Heinz tantrumming in the dirt.

"Our revered spiritual leader is swooning in love and you bring him the wrong woman, you fuckwit! And you ask me what's the problem? It matters."

JP saw the anger rising in Rocco, saw the balled fists, the thin lips like an underlined wrong answer; went into damage control. "So we give him a while to pull himself right. Don't worry, he'll like her, trust me." Then louder, addressing the tent: "Come on out, sweetheart. Show us what you got."

Stella Botha crawled from the tent, scratching at her tatty nightie. She stood up and tucked a blood-crusted blonde curl behind her ear. She brought up a small hand, waved, said, "Hi everybody."

Five minutes later, no progress. The two had hardly warmed to each other. JP nudged Stella from behind in the direction of the horrified pharmacist-cum-preacher, saying, "Go on, Pastor Heinz, seize the day. Step out of your darkness into the light and fuck... excuse me, make lurve to a white chick."

"I don't want her!" Heinz declared, turning away from Stella, fists tight at his sides.

"Stella's quality pussy, Pastor," said Christoff.

"Exactly!" said JP. "Where's the man's taste?"

"Shut up, you idiots," said Rocco, finally cracking amid the commotion, the sheer bloody incompetence. Taking out his Python, moving like an animal in the wild, he reached JP in three quick steps. He put the gun at the boy's head, muttered, "I fucking warned you," through gritted teeth, and let a bullet fly, the fuckwit yowling, grabbing the side of his head, ears ringing, drum damaged.

"What the fuck, you nearly shot my fucking ear off!"

His rage appeased, Rocco turned to Heinz, said, "Calm down, Pastor," taking him by the elbow, leading him to his deck chair. "Sit, relax. I'll sort it out. I don't want you upset."

"I want Rae Valentine," whinnied Heinz, pulling away, clinging to the side of the ostrich pen. "I want her..." staring at the birds, crying now, wiping snot from his lip, leaving dirt streaks on his face. Inconsolable.

"And what are we gonna do with him?" Alex heaved the tarpaulin off the body in the back of the Landie.

Rocco recognized the slit-eyed Chinaman, pulled himself once again back from the brink of beserk: "From bad to fucking worse! Not only do you bring the wrong girl, but you bring me Vincent fucking Saldana. Another motherfucking snag is all I need."

Vince moaned, rolled over.

"There was a problem. No way we could leave him there on the street, Boss," Christoff said. "He's ex-police, remember? Cops'd be all over this one."

"Spare me. Cops don't give a shit about their own. Would've been less complicated if he was dead."

"Then let's feed him to the crocs, man."

"Why kill him now?" Alex chipped in. "Let's put off the pleasure. You know the term delayed gratification, Christoff? Maybe not. Clearly you never studied geography." Alex wondered if carrot-top had actually got past primary school. "The Orange River flows from Lesotho and there's no crocodiles in it. Lots of other killers up here, though. Scorpions, snakes, sun."

"That's why you brought the factor 50," JP scoffed, sulking, still clutching his ear. "So you don't freckle your Prettyboy skin."

Christoff said: "I learned it's called the Orange 'cos of the color of the water."

"Actually," Alex said, "it was named in honor of

William of Orange, a Dutch prince. The only South African river named after a color is the Vaal—means gray."

Rocco had listened long enough to the jokers carrying on in the face of their fuck up. He interjected, "Well aren't you a mine of useless information, Alex. One thing for sure I can tell you all, is the river's hardly deep enough to drown in and there's no bloody crocs, nor alligators, piranhas nor killer eels likely to eat Saldana's corpse." He felt a zap at his neck. Slapped his collarbone. A bloody bee. "Hell, Johannes, pull out the sting." He felt the intensity of the pain as his adrenaline reacted to the toxin. He barked at the boys: "Just get the Chinaman out the back of the fucking Landie. Maybe he'll come in handy. Kom nou, Johannes, help these idiots."

Thank God for Johannes, thought Rocco. A special relationship they had, for ten years now, ever since Rocco'd bought this land on the river for possible development. Johannes swept the dirt, baked bread, polished Rocco's boots. He did what he was told. "And wrap the Chink's head in a towel or something," he shouted. "I don't want him bleeding all over everything. He's already made a right mess in the vehicle."

With Heinz sobbing at the ostrich pen and Vince Saldana chained to a tree, Rocco needed a strong drink. "Pour me a double, JP."

"Sure, my man. All okay with us?"

JP sloshed a ration into a plastic cup, the Klippies brandy bottle already half empty.

Rocco nodded at JP's feeble attempt at conciliation. "What can I say?" Showing no hard feelings, but smiling with satisfaction knowing Jean-Pierre had just moved to number one on his hit list. Would be first to get it, ahead of the bloody annoying Heinz Dieter.

"How long we gonna hole up here, Boss?"

"There's things to sort out before we head for the settlement."

Yeah, for certain sure. But without the woman as bargaining power, how would he get Heinz to part with the stones? They could be anywhere.

Think, Rocco, think.

And what the blazes now? He looked on as Heinz seemed to be chatting up an ostrich, his trembling fingers hovering at her neck as if he wanted to stroke her, calling the damn thing Liebschen.

Bloody unbelievable!

God Almighty! How the brain-damaged jokers had fucked up.

Things couldn't get any worse.

At which point Heinz lifted his head, face to the heavens and bayed like a mad dog.

All going pear-shaped!

Rocco buried his face in his hands, repressed the anger. Then got up, went over to Heinz, patted his shoulder.

"I'll fetch her in the morning, Pastor. First thing. I promise." He called Alex. "Bring the man here a drink!"

Then left him there, got in the Landie, needed to get away from the crew at the fire, and from crazy Heinz, his face grubby and stained with tears, staring into the orbs of his favorite bird.

On the edges of consciousness, Vince heard voices, laughter, loud popping, had to be ammo tossed into flames. He forced open one crusted eye, saw several men, looked like four maybe, or eight, sitting round a campfire, the flames lapping at a clear blue sky from what Vince could tell with the blurred vision of a single eye. He winced at the pain of the other, glued shut with pus and blood. The Boy Scouts were singing army songs, talking trash, telling bad jokes, sharing what looked like a bottle of Klipdrift Gold, tossing back healthy tots of the brandy, waiting for the meat.

Vincent's parched mouth couldn't work up saliva, even with the aroma coming at him of chops and sausage pinned in the grid, fat popping, sizzling.

He managed a harsh bark: "I need liquids." Brandy would do.

One of them got up from the fire, kicked him in the groin. Grabbed his hair, pulled his head back from his fetal spasm.

"That army jacket you wearing is the girl's, you moffie gaytard..."

Vince's instinct awakened, he kicked out, missed the guy's face; then came a knife-edged pain at his kidneys.

"You deserve whatever comes your way, you Chink A-hole."

He gasped as the blows landed hard and fast, in the gut, in the balls, the guy ranting, nasty with the booze: "Stop whining. Go back to China. Where you belong. Plenty of jobs there making cheap shit your kind ship over to us citizens as if we don't care. What happened to the good old days when the government classified you yellow bastards as non-whites? Land's gone to the dogs."

"Actually," rasped Vince, "us yellow bastards were Honorary Whites."

"Shut your bloody yap. You got a big mouth on you."

The one called Alex corrected, "Actually, it was

the Japs who were Honorary Whites."

Another kick to his side winded Vince afresh. He felt a searing rip, sucked in air, nearly passed out. He had to be dying.

"Whatever you are, you're at least half-dead. Gonna be a fun experiment to see how long you last without food or water in the blazing sun."

A hit across the mouth with what must be a gun; Vince spewed blood, teeth, saw sparks. Then nothing.

Alex, turning to JP and Christoff, said, "Wanna know something?"

"What now?" huffed JP.

"If you drink a lot of brandy, or whiskey, I mean a lot, then if you piss in a cup before you bed down and you leave it till the next morning, right, you'll see a clear layer on top, the way cream settles on milk. See, the alcohol rises. You can drink it off with a straw."

"S'truth?" said Christoff.

"Not that I've tried it myself. No way I'm gonna sluk my own piss," said Alex.

JP ordered, "Bring me lunch, Bushboy!"

"Meat's not ready yet," said Johannes, squatting at the edge of the fire.

"I wanna eat so's I can get outta this heat."

"Ek sê vir jou, I'm telling you, my brothers," said Christoff, "there's flooding in Cape Town, but here it's like forty-five degrees in the shade. Planet is befok like the guy says in that movie, you know the one where polar bears are drowning there at the South Pole?"

"It's called global warming"—you dumb specimen —"and you mean the North Pole, Christoff," said Alex. "North Pole's where polar bears live, and Santa. Yeah, I've seen that movie. Plus the other million flicks, a million scientists all proving the same thing, we're messing up our planet."

"Load a crap!" said JP. "Global warming's the biggest con there is. Wool pulled over our eyes is all. Far as this country goes, it's always been hot. This's godless deep dark Africa, man."

"That's why God put darkies here," said Christoff, remembering the story his ma had told him. "Darkies got burned in the oven of creation. God was careless."

"Check these bananas, JP," said Alex, lifting a blackened bunch. "You telling me this kinda heat is normal? This morning they were as yellow as the sun. They've cooked black as a sheep's face from just sitting in their skins."

"Cooked as black as a kaffir's face," Christoff said, "what d'you think, hey, Bushboy?" Getting no answer.

"Waste of good fruit, bro," said Alex.

"You're a stick in the mud, Alex. You probably buy organic."

"Could've enjoyed them fresh. Could still cook them in the pan with a splash of brandy."

"Waste of booze," said JP playing with his phone.

"You got signal on that thing?" asked Alex.

"Weak."

Christoff leaned in, getting in JP's space to look at the screen.

"Don't crowd me, Christoff, your breath smells like a damn corpse."

"You ever fucked a corpse, JP?"

"You dare imply I'm some kinda pervert, I'll moer you."

"At least a corpse lies still and doesn't nag you to get it over and done." Christoff laughed, but backed off.

Alex goaded: "Anyone know what the words on

the United States dollar bill mean? E pluribus unum?"

"You with your general knowledge bullshit again, Alex," said JP.

"That French or something? Or Spanish? They speak Spic over there, don't they?" slurred Christoff. "Ag, just gimme more brandewyn, man…"

"Let's toast, Boyz!" said Alex, cautious of pushing too far. E pluribus unum being Latin for the blending of many into one, from a Virgil poem. The blending of color to form a single, united nation where every citizen was equal. But he had self-preservation enough to keep that to himself.

"To the good life!'

"To Braaivleis! To Beer! To Brandy!"

"Brandy the porn star. Yeah! 'N' here's to Breast Implants on American Bitches!"

Christoff dropped the empty bottle at his feet. Went to get another. He looked over at Pastor Heinz. "You sure into birds, Pastor." To JP and Alex, he said, "Pastor's making eyes at that ostrich. First comes love, then marriage, ha!" Then to no one in particular: "So what's there to do here, besides get lekker pissed."

Rocco loved this stretch of land, the barren isolation, but the idiots spoiled it with their pathetic binging, their verbal diarrhea, no stopping the flow when they were sauced. The drive had done him good. Land looked mighty fine, stretching out in front of him, as did the infinite possibilities.

Back at the camp, post lunch, he summed up the scene pronto: the Boyz, in baggies with palm trees and shit on, as if they were on a beach someplace about to go surfing, headed for the river. Christoff lugged the cooler box. Alex had his sun cream and straw hat. JP, sunglasses on his face, a mean set to his lips, yanked Stella behind him. So much for Pastor's lectures on commitment, patience, discipline.

Heinz, still in a daze, stood forlorn at the ostrich pen.

Rocco had to make quick.

He unzipped Heinz's tent, crawled inside, nearly turning back as the stench hit him, of rank body odor and Doom pest spray. Heinz, the crazy, had conned him. No two ways about it. Heinz had the diamonds. Rocco wanted them.

He unzipped the sleeping bag, put his hand down towards the bundle there, pulled out a plastic Ziploc of meds. Nothing but vials of pills. He poured them out. In Heinz's tog bag was a store of antiseptic cleaning fluids; he held clear bottles up to what little light there was; squeezed tubes feeling for stones there. But nada. Packed it all neatly back.

He rummaged through wrappers piled in a corner of the tent, he unfolded used tissues and Wet Wipes, sorted through the stash of health bars.

He worked though every shirt and suit pocket. He patted down the side pockets of the suitcase. Could see no false bottom. Rifled one last time in the tog bag. Scratched under the edges of the groundsheet.

Niks. Nothing. Fuck all.

He left everything in order, as he'd found it, rolled down the flap of the torn tent and gasped for fresh air.

Johannes, keeping watch, said, "Find what you looking for?"

He shook his head. "You've been on this land a long time, Johannes."

"Been with you years now."

"We'll all be out of your hair soon enough. No worries."

Johannes nodded, clicked with his tongue, a sign of

impatience, and wandered off.

The campsite was deserted; even the pastor had disappeared somewhere.

Rocco stoked the fire, the heat of the coals rising.

Further upstream from where the Disciples lay on beach towels, a shepherd herded his straggly goats on the opposite bank with his shepherd's staff, a strange sort of knobkerrie with a handle like a fist. The goat-herd—was it Johannes?—raised his arm in greeting, then went back to prodding his precious pets to drink.

Heinz smelled the pungent odor of the devil's envoy carried on an almost imperceptible breeze. The largest, most monstrous, a bearded Billy, brought up the rear and kept the group moving. But Johannes's goat, the manifestation of Satan, stopped abruptly, turned her head to glare and bare teeth right at him.

Heinz fell on his knees, vomited a thin stream of bile into the river. He raised his head, squinted, but the San-man was gone as if he and his herd had never been there in the first place. He resisted the impulse to scratch at his scalp, to grab at a fistful of hair, to run to the dirt road, beyond the eye of the storm, screaming, screaming.

"I can't stand it, Mutti," he muttered, "the heat, the flies, the filth. Where are you, Mutti?"

Fear would not release the grip at his throat.

He retched another string of bile.

He staggered to the stretch of sand hidden from the river by thorn trees.

He shuddered as a length of wind-dried toilet paper hanging from a branch fluttered against his cheek. He swallowed his rising dread. He yanked out a clump of hair from just behind his ear. In the long drop he pulled down his pants, then couldn't bear to sit on the stained toilet seat, the rich stink of excrement so powerful he held his breath. Bees and flies buzzed, monstrous ugly flies with blue eyes, wanting to burrow up his anus, the sound of their vibrating wings accentuated to a roar in his head. He couldn't do it. He whipped up his trousers.

He hurried back to camp, picked up the spade. "Oh God, the trials I must endure!"

He went beyond the curve of the verge to a sandy hollow. Dug a hole. When he was done, he buried his feces, shuddered as he stomped the hole flat. He swatted wildly at a horse fly settling on his knuckles. Felt the panic rise again. He had to clean his hands. He ran to the river, to the water. The cavorting, the shrieks of pleasure, not lost on him, he wondered how the Core—his Disciples!—could possibly enjoy themselves at a time like this. He forced himself to dip his fingers into the murky waters, a reddish brown, like dirt and blood. He wanted his wipes, his sanitizing mist long empty.

He climbed the embankment, found himself back at the clearing. Back in his tent he scrubbed himself with the Wet Wipes. He rubbed at his hands, his feet, every inch of skin exposed to the She-devil's tainted breath. The air in the tent, so hot it burned his lungs, remained cloying, contaminated with Stella Botha's cheap perfume. Despite the intense heat, he lay on the mat, pulled his camping sheet over his body, trapped his hands between his knees.

He'd sprayed with Doom, the acrid after-smell comforting, but still spiders crawled, clinging to the insides of the tent, and the smell of Stella persisted, and the stench of goat he could not filter.

He tore a face mask of tissues to shield his skin

from creeping bugs. He breathed through his mouth, lay perfectly still, eventually losing track of time.

He longed for Aurora. The safety, the privacy, the like-minded; his haven that would be spared the rising tides. He longed for crisp Egyptian cotton sheets, for locks on the doors of his bedroom; he longed for the Peace of the Lord.

His fingertips tingled, his breath came in short bursts. Dizzy, disoriented. The flashes of a goat's accusing eyes, the feel of his mother's hands on him. The heat, the spiders, the flies. All too much. He patted down empty pockets, shook out the sleeping bag. *Where are my pills?* He threw about his few clothes. He searched in his tog bag, his suitcase, yes, he was breathing hard, but located them in the sleeping bag. With tears streaming, he spilled the vials of Valium, Vicodin, Stilnox. He twisted off the child-proof caps, threw a combination to the back of his throat, swallowed dry and waited for the panic—coming in waves, crashing over him—to subside.

"Deliver me from evil," he moaned, fingering the edge of his suit coat, comforted by the feel of the lumps in the hem of his jacket. The twenty-eight rough diamonds he'd sewn with meticulous, neat stitching into the lining, just as Mutti had told him they were sewn into the hem of *her* coat when she'd escaped Germany.

Chief Disciple Rocco has let me down. Oh God, show me the way!

Heinzie, good boy, kept his fists clenched in his pockets, kept his hands away from his piddler in case the troll was tempted to nip either fingers or penis. But his fingers would not stop twitching. He swigged back more pills, his head swirling like the water of the rapids; he felt the anaesthetic kick in, and at last he lifted out of his body.

When a sand storm hit the camp in the late afternoon and wind gusted hard and sharp and dust and grit blew through the openings of the tent, Pastor Heinz was knocked out, hardly dreaming of his Regina.

He woke in the dead of night, gasping, sweating, Mutti's voice echoing in his head: *The troll will eat your fingers! Will nip with jaws embedded with hundreds of razor-sharp teeth!*

He yanked his fist from his pants. By torchlight he inspected his once beautifully manicured hands. In the green light, reflected off the tent walls, the fingers, short as they were, that he'd looked after all these years were now damaged and dirty, the soft skin aging before his eyes. The heat in his tent was extreme. His neck was stiff. His body sore. The trapped stillness of the air like a pillow held over his nostrils and mouth. He clutched at the vinyl of the sleeping bag, screamed without making a sound, his mouth cavernous.

He sat up.

"Will you come soon, Mutti?" he whispered now, staring about wildly in the confined space. On his knees he retched up the mustard-magenta residue of the pills. Where was the respite? From the burning Hell in his brain. The high-pitched screeching of baboons down-river refused to end.

A new sound now, the She-devil teasing, bleating aloud about Heinz's lewd and nasty deeds. *What did you do to your mother, Heinzie? What did Mutter do to you?*

He bolted upright, battered the tent with his fist, broke the zipper, pulling at it wildly, gulped at dust and dirt as he escaped the claustrophobic tomb. Stumbled out. Smelled the stench. Saw the goat perched right there in a tree: sent by Satan himself to torment Heinz, to rub salt in his wounds.

He ghosted past rolled-up sleeping bags, tog bags, crates, supplies, past his comatose Disciples on their mats, heading straight to the rickety camping table at the thorn trees.

Easily enough, with his head torch on dim, he found the knife.

The She-devil cackled, staring him down from the tree, taunting, those flaccid lips drawn back from pink gums and yellowed teeth, eyes glowing in the dark.

Where's your Aurora, Heinzie?

What's happened to your New Order?

Your Queen? Your Rae? Your Regina?

"Shut up, shut up!" hissed Heinz.

He charged the tree, grabbed a hoof, hung on through the enraged bleating, with strength that could only come from God. He pulled the creature from the branches. The She-devil landed thud on the dirt, winded, momentarily stunned, silent. He stabbed at evil come to pass as mere flesh, blood and bones, stabbed at evil eyes till they were gouged and could no longer look back.

Hallelujah! The righteous shall prevail!

A vague memory came to him, of cutting through human flesh and bone.

He looked up at the Southern Cross, at Orion's Belt, at so many glittering stars, the constellations blurring as part of the spectacular mass of the Milky Way.

"Now is the time for resolution and courage!"

Vincent woke shivering in the chill that had descended on the night. Half-naked. His cheek hard to the dirt. His tongue, swollen thick, flicked at the dried blood at his nose and mouth. His hands and feet were tied tightly behind his back, his fingers were numb. He was secured by a chain to a tree. He wished he could pull

protection tight around his body, a woman's arms.
Vince had welcomed the beating: *I deserve to be annihilated, destroyed. Kill me, kill me!*

He saw a figure approach in the dark, holding
fingers to his lips, crawling closer, something in his
hand. He felt warm breath near his face. Amber's
sweet scent like a summer's day came to him then
from somewhere deep in his memory. God, how he
missed her.

For the first time since Amber's death, Vincent
Saldana cried, lapping at salty tears washing over red
ants crawling on his cheeks and all over him, tempted
by his raw and bloodied flesh.

Rocco's sweet dream...*hunting with a crossbow,
chasing human quarry in a city street, a homeless boy,
hearing the hiss as he let fly the arrow*...was disrupted
rudely by riotous bleating, then crying and sobbing.
"Christ!" he rasped, lighting his gas lamp.

He grabbed the Colt Python, zipped open his tent,
saw Heinz whirling about at the ashes of the campfire, his head torch drawing moths and miggies, Heinz
glassy-eyed and shiny-faced, limbs jerking, demented,
his eyes blazing, lit from that demented place inside.

"I want the woman! I want Rae Valentine!"

"I said I'll get her." His urge strong to put a bullet
between Heinz's eyes right then and there, shoot him
and be done.

I want the stones, you mad fuck.

"Why haven't you left yet?" Heinz's sobs morphed
into hysteria, hyena-like yelps escaping his twisted lips
as he held up his fist.

Rocco saw blood squirt from Heinz's fist as he
squeezed...saw the blood trickling down his face,

splatter staining his coat. *What was he clutching?*

"Well, strike me down with a feather!" His jaw dropped, as Heinz, his mad grin stretching from soft cheek to soft cheek, opened his hand, held out three severed fingers, the stumpy digits sitting like fat mopane worms in his palm.

Johannes came from the shed. Alex, Christoff and JP crowded around, stared at the Pastor's hands, illuminated by the light of Rocco's lamp.

"Tell me this is a horror movie," said Rocco, staring at the bleeding stumps, what was left of Heinz's left hand, the blood dripping into the ashes, his thumb and forefinger sticking up as if he was hailing a taxi. *Christ yeah, for a ride right to the loony bin.*

"Get me Rae Valentine, Brother Rocco, you promised!" An ear-splitting and querulous warning.

"I told you I would, Pastor."

I still want to search the camp, you fruitcake, before I have to mission the fuck back to Cape Town.

"Go now!"

"Not just yet, Pastor. Get the first-aid kit, Alex," he ordered. "Christoff, get the brandy."

"Look at the blood," said Christoff. "It's pouring outta the oke."

Rocco held open a Ziploc bag. Heinz dropped in the three fingers. Alex led Heinz to the deck chair at the pen. Heinz sat. Alex applied pressure to the stumps, mopping up the oozing blood. He pressed clean swabs to the wounds and wrapped tight Heinz's hand in a crêpe bandage. "Leg, penis or finger, treatment for amputation's all the same. Gotta get you to a hospital, Pastor."

Rocco thought: *No hospital for you, Humpty*

Dumpty. Agog, he wondered what had run through the guy's head to maim himself. If he'd ever had sanity in the first place, he'd lost it at last, had slipped over the edge, fallen off the wall.

All wrapped up, brandy poured down his throat, Heinz announced, "I have made the ultimate flesh and blood sacrifice."

"Must have hurt like hell," said Rocco.

"You know," Heinz said, suddenly pensive, "I didn't feel a thing."

"Yeah?" *You will soon, you madman.*

"I'm like Mutti now, I'm one of them," squeaked Heinz. "Give Ms. Valentine the fingers as a pledge of my love."

"You think that'll encourage her?"

"I want her. Go get her."

JP scowled. "Tell her the fingers are Vincent Saldana's. Tell her if she doesn't come, we'll chop off his hand next."

"Yeah, Pastor," chipped in Christoff. "Woulda made sense to chop off the China's finger's in the first place instead of your own. Jissis, why'd you do it?"

"I've always had ambivalent feelings about my fingers, Brothers, from the age of four," said Heinz in a split moment of clarity before his eyes clouded over, the truth of the pain setting in. He whimpered, "You'd b-b-better put my fingers on ice."

Too late for regrets now, thought Rocco, scooping up a handful of opaque chips from what was left of the cooler box ice into an empty margarine tub. He shook out the fingers from the Ziploc too bulky to fit in the tub, the fingers lying side-by side now, the seeping blood tainting the ice pink. "Now, Pastor." He escorted a stooped and moaning Heinz to his tent, settled him, kneeled down, looked into the spaced-out eyes and spoke to the excuse for a man as if to a child: "I'll deliver Rae Valentine, Pastor Heinz. I promised. But will I get what I want?"

"You're talking about the diamonds, Brother?"

He nodded patiently. "If we both get what we want, we can live happily ever after. We have to sell them. Make that last push to finalize the finishing touches at Aurora. Your Regina will love it. And you'll need medical intervention. Get these fingers sewn back on. It all costs."

"I don't have the diamonds."

Dear Saints and Archangel, surely Heinz would not have given the diamonds to the bozo Boyz?

Through clenched teeth, he asked, "What are you talking about, Pastor?"

Heinz shot him a crafty look. "I said, I don't have the diamonds."

"Who has the them then?"

"Mutti has them," peeped Heinz.

"Your dead mother?"

Crikey fucking Moses.

Too late to schedule a flight plan, Rocco took the Mini, sped into the night, refueled in one-horse Van Reenensdorp. He had plenty bucks stashed in banks, but he wanted those diamonds, and Heinz Dieter, insane in the membrane and so pathetically delirious, had to be telling the truth.

Rae had driven the streets, visited every homeless shelter. Even got an appointment at the morgue to see the short, dead Oriental. Still unclaimed. Definitely not Vince.

Back at the flat she took off her leg, leaned it against the coffee table, the leg looking out of place separated from her. The way Rae explained her disability to school kids: it's like wearing glasses, braces, that's just the way it is. The way she thought of it herself: *we're all disabled, in some way, each of us licking our wounds.*

She still experienced the sensation of having toes, felt as if she could wiggle them even though they weren't there, sometimes felt agony so bad she was tempted to over-medicate, swallow pain pills and wait for the wash of nothingness. Oblivion. But she was careful. One thing she knew: she'd never again go down addiction road.

The psychiatrist at Groote Schuur rehab had explained phantom limb pain, had called it residual pain, the severed nerves remembering the moment of the cut. *It's all in the brain. You think pain so you feel pain.*

She rubbed the stump now. Her mind set on massaging away the ache.

She'd phoned the police every hour on the hour. No word of Vincent.

She got to bed. Stared for a long while at peeling paint on her ceiling, thinking she had to get the place spruced up; finally she slept, just the wind for company.

MONDAY: TRUTH DAWNING

Rae's waking thoughts: *Have we been set up? Incriminated in fraud, now murder? By accident or on purpose?* Was only a matter of time before someone reported Vincent at the scene of Trudie Kellerman's demise.

She got up. Fried a minute steak, slapped on a slice of cheese, door-stopped it with bread. Brown at least. When in doubt, eat. Protein and carbs. With a glass of milk for strong teeth and bones.

She stared out the picture window. The street was quiet, the weather bleak, the wind chasing a plastic packet into the gutter. Shadows danced; a homeless man pushed a laden shopping trolley past her block. Beyond the sprawling city were the harbor lights, still visible, then the endless sea.

Her thoughts ran wild.

Vince, where the hell are you?

Frau Dieter, Rosa, what are you and Heinz playing at?

She called Rex. "Any word on Saturday night's shooting?"

"Ubuntu's still in a coma. Prints we'll have to wait on. The casing was found, the bullet shot from a revolver."

Jesus! Vince's gun. Had to be. What the fuck was going on?

※

Christoff, peeling apart his pink eyelids, hardly awake, checked the the cooler box for what wasn't there—booze.

JP came from Heinz's tent, said, "What's the nut-job gonna do next?"

"Pastor Heinz is fucking falling apart," said Christoff. He hauled out a warm beer from under the table, popped the lid.

"Least he's stopped calling for his mommy," said JP.

"He's delirious with fever," said Alex, helping himself to Johannes's strong black moerkoffie percolating on the fire.

"You a doctor now, Alex?" said Christoff.

"It's always the fucking mother," grumbled JP.

"Tell you what, soon as the Rocco's back, I want my cut 'n' I'm outta here."

"What'd you do to him?" asked Alex. "It's so quiet in there, he's okay, right? Rocco's not gonna take it as a favor if you've sorted out the pastor."

"Stop worrying," said JP. "I jacked him some extra meds, a couple of E tabs. Take his mind off his problems, and I loaned him my Samsung."

"Your pride and joy." said Christoff.

"I'm not sure that's such a good idea," muttered Alex, recalling the demise of his iPhone. Christoff had only an iPod, Rocco kept his phone in his top pocket.

"Anything to make him shut the fuck up," said JP. "Can't stand him grunting like a warthog. What did the guy expect, that hacking off his fingers with a cheap steak knife wouldn't be a bitch?"

"So what's he doing with the phone? You don't think he's gonna call someone?" said Alex.

"Please," snorted JP, "it's the last thing on his wigged-out mind. He's entertaining himself. You can always rely on the Net."

A forty-second clip showed a white-clad surgeon sawing off a leg. But the picture was hazy, the sound of the saw eating at bone distorted. He clicked on to a longer, three-minute clip of a pretty brunette doped on morphine, in hospital after her amputation—her family filming her, her one breast exposed, popping from the green hospital gown. Not the kind of woman who aroused Heinz's interest. Not at all. Tacky, dodgy, Jerry Springer trailer trash.

He tried Disability Heaven, Ampulove, Disabled Dating.

This was more like it. Disabledbrides.com: how

beautiful were the women in white with hooks, limps, leg braces. Women with one limb shorter than the other, with limbs in plaster casts.

He wanted his Regina!

Regina would touch him. She would relieve the ache in his heart and groin. He would celebrate his Regina, more lovely than any of the ladies on YouTube.

He couldn't wait to lead her to his sanctuary.

The phone battery, beeping at regular intervals, was low. He grasped the cell in his good hand, held it close as if his body heat would recharge it. He lay back and thought of her, Rae. Minutes later the tabs kicked in, the phone dropped from his grasp. Nursing his injured hand, he slipped into oblivion.

Rocco drove over a ridge of hills, saw Table Mountain, the spread of the awakening city at dawn under fading stars and streetlights. Coming into the city from the N7 never failed to impress as he saw Table Mountain as flat as tar under a road roller, with the gray sea at her feet. Swirling cloud threatened a downpour, the weather still lousy.

On the outskirts of Cape Town, coming into Milnerton, he pulled into a McDonald's drive-thru, got himself an early-bird double-cheese burger brunch takeaway, sat in the parking lot, slurping. He opened the plastic margarine tub, stared at Heinz's hacked fingers like a freaky-deaky Halloween trick, smears of crimson on the stumps like varnished paint. No way anyone, least of all PI Rae Valentine, would believe these dumpy digits, pale as cutworms, were Vincent Saldana's.

"Fuck this," he said, wiping ketchup from his mouth. From the open window he tossed out the fingers, Heinz's personal token of his love, to a stray dog scratching in the dirt near an overflowing bin.

"Enjoy your snack? Heh, heh, heh, heh," he chuckled as the hound wolfed down the treat.

Twenty minutes later, arriving at the Dieter residence, he pulled a drive-by, checking for surveillance. None. Why the cops had never cottoned on to Heinz himself was beyond him. Police had no idea Heinz was a charlatan, a fake, a fraud. A common criminal.

He used the key Heinz had handed over, let himself in. Fumbled around in the dark, turned on a weak light illuminating the passage. Creaked his way down and pushed open the door to Heinz the neat-freak's bedroom. He drew back the curtain to let in the bleached light. Looked out the window onto cars, trucks, taxis snaking along a wet Beach Road.

No one could know he was back in Cape Town. He'd come a circuitous route. Took detours.

Rocco Robano, you are indeed the invisible man.

The stench hit him even before he opened the door to Rosa Dieter's bedroom—the fruity, heady scent of perfume and death. The woman was stiff as a mummy. Heinz had seated her, wrapped a scarf around her neck, arranged her hands in her lap.

Heinz, you sneaky rat!

He panted. Saw what he wanted, got closer, said aloud, "Thank you, Jesus!"

Oh yeah! He licked his lips. Right there, gripped in her hands, was the velvet bag. He wrapped his hands in a towel and went at her brittle bones. Rigor had her holding fast. "You don't wanna let go, do you?" He broke her arm at the locked elbow, prised open her stiff paws, her fingers snapping like dry sticks.

Only one problem: the bag was empty. He balled the fabric in his fist. No stones. He felt the twitch at his cheek. He chewed at a whitlow giving him hell at the edge of his thumb. *What's the mad fuck playing at?*

He put his hands in her pockets, up her sleeves, in her bra—recoiling at the crinkle-paper texture of her breasts—and extracted used tissues. He forced off her shoes, a whiff of foot rot coming at him. No diamonds in the toes. He felt between her legs. No package wedged between Rosa's stiff thighs. The only stone on her was the Princess Kate sapphire on what remained of her ring finger, the token pressed there, on the stump, part of the haul Trudie Kellerman had handed back to Heinz Dieter. Showing it off now, as if to prove how clever was her Heinzie. He pulled the ring from the scarred stump, then unclasped a string of pearls from her neck. He slipped the consolation prizes into his pocket.

What he wanted were the diamonds.

And I'm damn well gonna find them.

Monday 9:15 am. Rae parked in Adderley Street, just outside Gold Extravaganza locked up tight, police crime tape still draped across the doors and windows.

What the hell were these people playing at? Sol and Rosa?

She'd done it again. Got a dead-end job. Would have to suffer Vince's resigned, "I told you so."

"I was thinking rent money," Rae said aloud. "My motives were pure."

Thanks, Frau Dieter, for the joyride.

The money had got just what Rosa had intended: nothing. Rae was sure of it. All that had happened was Vince had got caught up in Trudie Kellerman's murder, and had got himself somehow disappeared. This business, something that wasn't their business, the hate crimes, the bombings, the graffiti, she was sure too, had got Mandla shot, the good man still at death's door.

She returned to the Dieter residence.

Rae stamped her feet, exhaled warm breath, pressed the bell. She bent down and lifted the brass letter slot, strained to hear any kind of movement.

"Mrs. Dieter? Rosa?" she called through the gap, tentatively at first, then more boldly: "You there Frau Dieter? Heinz?" She rattled the door. Looked left and right at the buildings boxing in the house. She inspected the lock. A standard Yale. She knew there weren't infrared sensors or beams in the entrance hall, passage, or dining room. No alarm. Another thing pensioners didn't believe in. Trusted that a locked door would be respected. With an expired credit card eased between the frame and the door, only seconds of fiddling later the door opened easy as one two three.

She stood long moments in the dim light of the hallway, the pervasive smell of yesteryear coming at her. Of damp, of mustiness. And something else. Something rotten.

Listened to the sound of silence.

Hello darkness.

She drew the Colt.

Someone had beat her to it. Whatever "it" was.

The hatstand lay in the hallway; a smashed grandfather clock no longer tick-tocking accentuated the quiet of the house; on the floor were trinkets, household bills, papers, an umbrella. She crept along the passage. In the kitchen, every drawer'd been emptied: knives, forks, spoons, utensils dumped on the linoleum; pyramids of cake flour and maize meal heaped on the floor; split peas, pasta, lentils, bran, coffee granules, all emptied out. From the open defrosting freezer seeping water mixed up a mess with the spilled matter.

Someone had come looking for something all right. She scanned the dining room on the left. The dresser was bare; plates, glasses, cups, all smashed.

The wooden flooring groaned beneath her as she made her way further along the dark passage. The bathroom floor, slippery with shampoo, conditioner, creams, the contents of bottles and tubes squeezed out leaving an oozy slime, was dotted with pills.

In Heinz's bedroom, posters and pics were ripped from walls, the mattress and pillows sliced, all feathers and split foam, the school desk turned on its side; the shelf cleared of books, manuals, toy soldiers.

She slipped the Colt in the holster. Picked up a spiral-bound notebook, scanned hand-written notes in a minute and controlled script: notes on life in Namibia, coupled with hand-drawn maps of oil reserves and diamond deposits. Notes on the Apocalypse. Notes on Leadership. Photostatted essays on need and response, fascism, ethnic nationalism, religious fundamentalism.

Another notebook, one of several that had spilled from an open safe, boasted a collaged cover of natural disasters. She thumbed through the cuttings, pictures, clippings, from newspapers, magazines and printouts Heinz must have collected and pasted on the pages.

She stared at pictures of tsunami victims, earthquake damage, of floods and famine. Of a jet airplane that had ploughed into a skyscraper, billows of black smoke, people falling through the sky, the mass of rubble at Ground Zero that had been the Twin Towers.

She scanned paragraphs reproduced painstakingly in calligraphy, from the prophecies of Nostradamus, visions pertaining to the time of the Rapture and beyond, the collective information showing the visible power of God's hand.

"Great thunder will be heard in the city of God!

Dark ash-clouds blow over the city!"

"The day looks like night. Ash falls like black snow! There is nothing left."

"So many inundations. Land will be covered by water as the gates of the oceans are opened. A thousand other disasters will diminish the world. Burning stones will fall from a broken sky!"

She was compelled to read more.

"The Doomsday Clock is running!"

"At the time of the end, a body of men will be raised up who will turn their attention to the prophecies, who will rise in triumph, who will take it upon themselves to be the soldiers of God!"

All of it illustrated with naive drawings of volcanoes exploding, earth cracked and broken, waves drowning civilization, gesticulating stick men with faces reminiscent of Munch's Scream.

Under the notebooks was another revelation. She paged through several pharmaceutical mags, yellow Post-its marking specific explicit photographs, and stories penned of the trials and tribulations of amputees.

What a complex creature is your son, Mrs. Dieter.

And what of Rosa? Rae put the book down, closed the door on Heinz Dieter's deluded fantasies, and walked down the passage to the next room.

She stifled a yelp: there was Rosa Dieter, huge eyes in deep sockets reflecting back from the dressing-table mirror, a stone-cold Rosa propped in a chair, her twisted limbs mutilated, an ivory-handled weapon protruding from her chest.

Rae got out the cell, punched CONTACTS, R for Rex.

She felt cold steel at her temple, a strong grip at her shoulder, sour breath at her ear. "Don't you fucking press another button." The cell clattered to the floor; she hit out, bit, nearly passed out with her neck in a chokehold. So much for her fancy defense moves, and the Colt useless in the holster.

"Jesus, you're feisty." Rocco turned her, clutched her wrists, grabbed tight.

"What did you expect?" She kneed his balls, a glancing thrust.

He grunted, twisting one arm behind her back, pushing her to the floor.

"With a sense of humor too. Now, darling, behave." He yanked her up, pressed the steel circumference against her forehead. "Do what I say or you'll have a third eye." He forced the barrel into her waist, felt her give, her body slack against his. He frisked her one-handed, took the Colt off her. "Nice piece. Can't do better than a Colt 1911." He pushed her away, pointed both guns at her. Looked her up and down, liked her style: denims, boots, a "Vote for Evita Bez for Prez" slogan on her sweat-shirt under a purple velour jacket.

"I can appreciate what the men see in you, Rae Valentine."

His groot trek back to Cape Town not all for nought, the gods now on his side.

"You're looking for Heinz and Mommy, I take it? How perfect is this. Heinz Dieter stabbed her through the heart. Not that she didn't deserve it. Isn't the stench of death something?" He sniffed at the release of excrement and urine that had dried under her on the Persian carpet.

"Don't try anything now, Ms. Valentine." He put her pistol in his holster, kept his Colt Python trained on her. "You know better'n to argue with a gun. Let's go."

"Please. I know you didn't kill Rosa." *But I know who you did kill.*

"Am I correct in guessing you want to solve the whodunnit?"

"Something like that."

"Been reading too many detective novels, have you?"

"You're probably right."

"I said let's go."

"Police are on their way, you know."

"After you, Ms. Valentine." He stuck the metal in the small of her back, leaned in closer, ushered her out the door, closed it behind them. He chuckled. "Don't sprout bullshit."

He gripped her wrist as she activated her car alarm—how'd she get the beeper out her pocket?—said, "Damn you," as he grappled the keys from her, heard them drop to the pavement.

He gripped her arm. "Pick them up. Now switch it off. And now look around. See? No one bothers to check out a car alarm any more than they'd look out a window to see a bird singing. Now get in the fucking car."

"Why the driver's seat?"

"You know how to handle a Jeep, the Mini'll come easy."

"The Jeep is customized."

"I respect that about you. You shoot, you drive. You've got guts. You're coming with me, no question. This is an automatic. You can do it."

He rammed the gun into her shoulder, pushed her head down. "Now get in, I told you. Hands on two o'clock and ten o'clock, the way your daddy taught you." He tapped the dashboard with the Python, made himself comfy. "You'll do just fine. You know, that Durant was a donkey to dump a gorgeous thing like you. What a mistake."

"Wasn't it just."

Yeah, Rae Valentine might yet come in handy. He'd waterboard her if he had to, if Heinz didn't uphold his part of the bargain. He'd fucking hang, draw and quarter her, if needs be. *Where are the diamonds, Heinz?*

"D'you mind telling me where we're going?"

"Life's a journey, not a destination, Ms. Valentine."

"Call me Rae."

"Well, Rae, Rocco Robano at your service." If the name meant something to her, it didn't show.

"So, where's Heinz Dieter then?"

He went, "Heh, heh, heh, heh." Then: "You're into communication, it seems. He's safe, I'll tell you that, though the guy's not right in the noggin. Especially with all his mommy's attention over the years. Oh, you didn't know? Poor little Heinz Werner Dieter. Even his name has a story: Heinz the mixed-breed dog, a mutt, a mongrel, random-bred, his mother called him. She was raped, not so? She hated him. Yanked him around the house by the penis if he didn't listen to her, this when he was a little child. No wonder he offed her. You're looking a little queasy, Rae. And slow down. Something I said? Is it Heinz killing his own mommy that upsets you, or you don't like kids being abused, is that it?"

"Heinz Dieter means nothing to me."

"That's right. Rosa was the client, wasn't she? Durant, Saldana & Valentine working well as a team, are you?"

"You know something I don't?"

"I know the Chink's a nuisance, always pops up in the wrong places."

"Vincent Saldana. What's he got to do with this?"

"Wrong place at the wrong time."

"Tell me he's alive."

"My Boyz came looking for you, found him instead."

"I deserve to be filled in."

He raised a sardonic eyebrow. "Rosa tell you anything at all 'bout her son's interests? He wants a Queen for his settlement, which will, according to Heinz, survive the apocalypse around the next bend. He's the leader of the Core. You did your own research there back at the house, I take it. You saw those notebooks Heinz left behind. And let me tell you, he has, shall I say, a bit of a crush on you." He trailed the barrel of her gun down her cheek. "No doubt the feeling will be mutual."

At their first petrol stop, outside of town, he said, "You know what I'm gonna do if you lift a finger, your pinkie even, for help?"

"Shoot me?"

"Too easy. I'll put a bullet through the petrol attendant's head. What's his name? Goodwill? Imagine the call his mama's gonna get, his wife, his children. You want more blood on your hands? You already have your partner's blood on your conscience."

Ninety kilometers north of Nababiep, he pulled over at a deserted picnic spot, looked across at the vista of range upon mountain range, purple, blue, gray, as far as the eye could see. He gave her a Coke, a plastic-wrapped sandwich. Had to keep the driver awake and aware or he'd be dealing with Arrive Alive fanatics. Let her refresh herself. Ease the leg she said was giving her hell. All the time the Python trained on her.

"Now get back in the Mini," he said.

Yeah, he thought, tapping the barrel of her semi-automatic against the dashboard, a nice piece he'd enjoy trying out—perhaps he'd use it to kill. He'd get the diamonds, then he'd do this cripple a favor, and the madman: he'd put them out of their misery.

Oh yeah, he'd euthanize the lot of them. Her mag was full. Plus he had his .45 ammo. He just loved shooting big bullets.

"You really have no idea who I am," he said. "Do you?"

"You a D-List celeb or something?"

Behind the wheel again Rae looked fleetingly sideways at the straw-colored sac spider beside her, the hint of ginger at his hair, at his pale skin, the beard, his red-rimmed eyes, the irises almost colorless. *You're Trudie Kellerman's boyfriend, her murderer. The video on Vince's phone is proof.*

"Let's just say, we have…acquaintances in common …a couple of poachers out for vengeance…But your ex-lover killed them, a couple of would-be rapists. From what I hear they did you serious damage…"

She braked, swerved, nearly crashing into a vehicle in the fast lane as he pulled the steering wheel straight. She felt the gun behind her ear.

"Aw, I didn't wanna upset you. Now keep your eyes on the fucking road."

Couldn't be. This man connected to the scum who did it?

She got a grip. "Where're we going?"

"We'll get there when we get there."

The name came to her now, the memory of Tony pillow-talking of the poacher turned killer. She controlled her terror. Best to keep talking, engage, personalize herself. If it would make any difference to a psycopath like this.

She knew they were heading to the border; Heinz's notebooks had told a certain kind of story.

She'd clocked directions from the city; eyed the long, straight road ahead, kept her voice steady: "Don't you just love this drive?"

"Not too shabby."

"I guess this is the kind of beauty people have in mind when they talk about Africa. The vastness. Ruggedness. Something wild about the place. The purple mountains. The kind of beauty that gets under the skin."

He stayed silent, menacing.

Sick to her stomach, what she really, really wanted, the Spice Girls absurdly popping to mind, was to rewind her life. Give Vincent the benefit of the doubt for a change. Say *no* to Rosa Dieter. Now Vince might be dead.

She clutched the steering wheel tight, felt the sweat at her palms. This she knew without benefit of sixth sense: he'd have no mercy; he'd kill her with her own bloody gun when he was done with her. But he needed her.

There are reasons why I'm still alive.

For now.

She had to help Vince, if he was alive.

She had to help herself.

So scared she could smell her own fear.

The Disciples never stopped eating, drinking, partying. Eish!

Johannes had just done the breakfast dishes, now started on lunch.

The Disciples waited for Rocco.

Pastor Heinz waited for Regina.

"Sorry about your pet," Alex shared.

Johannes grunted at the prep table as he pulled

the skin from the goat, scraped off bits of fat with a paring knife. He chopped up the limbs, threw a heap of cutlets in a stainless-steel bowl. He trimmed the rest of the meat into neat squares, marinating the pieces in garlic, vinegar, salt and pepper. He hung the skin of the goat over the nylon lines, caressing it as if his sweet Nannie was still alive. The scapegoat. The sacrificial goat Pastor Heinz had pulled with superhuman strength from the tree and stabbed to death.

In the smaller cast-iron pot atop the fire, he stirred cabbage in a cream sauce. In the larger of the pots, the chunks of goat meat simmered now with diced potatoes. The tree-climbing boer goat was the tastiest, most succulent goat meat of the Namakwa. Johannes had come too late to save his garden. Pastor had picked the blooms before he could object. And poor Nannie. He didn't blame Pastor Heinz for her death. The illness cast a sheen over Heinz's eyes, Johannes could smell it on his breath. As he stirred the meal in the pot he prayed aloud, offering thanks to Mantis, for her, for Nannie. *What is life after all, without death?* One had to be practical. He fried up a sliver of her liver, savored the taste.

He brought the campers bread from the shed, fresh-baked from the oven, the Boyz pulling it apart now, stuffing their mouths with steaming crusts. He removed a butternut wrapped in tinfoil from the coals, and sliced it. The Boyz helped themselves to the goat-and-veg stew, a silence descending as the group focused on chewing, slurping, burping.

The one, Alex, nursing the delicious ginger beer Johannes had brewed, praised him: "Ten out of ten."

"Bushboy, you a good cook, I'll say that much for you," said Christoff. "Jou kos is darem lekker. I smaak to be a chef myself, have a TV show like Gordon Ramsey. Hell that Gordon swears, hey? Fok this, fok that."

JP winked. "You can be chief chef at Aurora."

Johannes looked over at Pastor Heinz, his head bowed, his brown jacket plastered to his damp skin. The only one who wouldn't eat or drink what was provided, the pastor nibbled a health bar, something from a wrapper, processed, preserved, brought out from his private store. Didn't know what was good for him. Too sick to care. But cared about his Liebschen.

Johannes shook his head as JP, full with food, booze and bluster, pushed aside his plate, walked over to the pen. He watched JP vault over the rickety gate opening on to the pen, fling himself at the birds, grabbing the gray female closest to him, straddling her back, holding on for dear life as she resisted.

"Leave her alone," screeched Heinz, rising from the deck chair.

"Bird's a fucking bucking bronco!" yelled JP.

He rode her, gripping the ostrich's flapping wings, till he slipped from the bird's back, sprinting away fast as the bird, coming after him, almost landed a club-footed kick to his thigh. He jumped the fence, the bird facing him, still going after him. Her feathers ruffled, she squawked, U-turned and lolloped back to the rest of the harem.

"Ha! Did you check that? How wild was that? Christoff, you gotta try it, man! What a hoot!" JP pumped the air with his fist, did a white-boy shuffle back to the fire.

"No way, not me," slurred Christoff. "I don't drink and drive."

JP downed more of the brew, inebriation the name of the game.

The Boyz carried on as if this was one never-ending holiday, but bored now, they threw .22 ammo into the fire, the Russian subsonic bullets popping like fire crackers, the *blam, blam* driving Johannes near-crazy.

JP threw on another handful of ammo. "I miss a good blast."

Heinz staggered over, stood gazing at the fire, cocking his head at the small explosions, his expression changing from anger and defeat to interest and wonder.

"Check this out, Pastor," said Alex, tossing a chunk of crystalline fluorspar, the magic pale-green mineral collected from a Richtersveld mine, on the flames.

Johannes watched Heinz mesmerized by the pyrotechnic display, Heinz rapturous, staring into the blue center of the blaze, his jaw hanging open.

Jirre, Johannes shook his head, *when will this lot leave?*

"See there!" Heinz pointed at the popping, sparking, fluorescent pebbles bouncing in the flames. "See the taste of the holocaust!" screeched a gleeful Heinz. "See the city crouching at the foot of the mountain, see the mountain, see the rock explode!"

"That so, Pastor," smirked JP. "The holocaust? That already happened to the Jews, man, or so they say."

"Right before our eyes, we see the world lose its shape, its structure!"

"Tell me one thing, Pastor, since you hail from over the seas, your mamma being Kraut 'n' all, why don't you head back? Don't tell me, I know. Even in your homeland the fucking immigrants are causing kak. Syrians, Turks, Gypsies, even South Africans taking over. Germany's finished."

Heinz, lucid for a moment, said, "I can get decent German pastry there in Namibia, kuchen, stollen, like

I ordered from Fritzl's Bakery in Sea Point."

"Let them eat cake is how it goes," said JP, over at the pot now, saliva pooling in his mouth at the thought of helping himself to more stew. But the pot was empty. JP's tone changed, his inflection mean, the intensity of a match flare. "Bushboy, there was plenty. You scooped up the rest for yourself, did you?"

He picked up the shepherd's staff and prodded Johannes squatting outside of the circle of the chosen, clattering his metal plate and his food to the ground. "Greedy like all the fucking blacks. Eating in the dirt, no better than a dog."

"Leave him be," said Alex.

JP poked him again with the stick. "You're a living fossil, Bushboy. The Victorians used to put your kind in freak shows. Now let's see what the dwarf earthman of Africa's made of." He prodded again, then jabbed at him with the pointy tip, blood appearing at a gash in his thigh. "What a surprise, I thought mud would come out since you belong near the ground where you dig for grubs. Answer when I talk to you!" JP barked, getting meaner by the second, now taking the Taurus from where he'd stuck it his pants, spinning the cylinder.

"Ja, my people dig for roots and bulbs," nodded Johannes, staring at his empty plate, at his spilled fare.

"Tell me," said JP, "how can a throwback from the fucking Stone Age exist in the age of computers? You're a century out of date, making fire with sticks when there's bloody Blitz to start 'em with."

"The scientists say–"

"What the fuck do the scientists say, Alex?"

"They say the male San is a genetic Adam." Alex nursed his beer, hesitated, then added, "That all humans can ultimately trace their genetic heritage to the San people."

"Lies, Alex, all twisted lies."

"True, I swear. Scientists say San were the first people in the Garden of Eden, then a hundred and fifty of them, descendants all, left Africa and populated the rest of the world."

"Shut the fuck up."

"Yeah, ain't that just crazy. But the San had a hard time too. When the Dutch settlers annexed the Cape in 1652 they hunted the San for sport, and then over the next two hundred years the Afrikaner settlers pushing north and west killed the San where they found them. Even until the 1930s the German settlers in Namibia practiced ethnic cleansing."

"Why the fuck didn't they finish the job?"

JP jumped up, delivered a series of blows to Johannes falling to his knees, putting up no resistance, Alex yelling, "I said leave him alone, leave him out of it!" pulling JP off him.

"I'm sick of listening to your wackjob info-bites, Prettyboy. You either with us or fucking against us." JP pulled the Taurus and rammed it into Alex's neck.

Christoff yelled, "Skiet hom!"

Heinz howled.

Was when the Mini Cooper appeared—Rocco, hooting, screeching to a halt, shouting from the car: "Stop it, the lot of you! Get a fucking grip! JP, pack that piece away before I use mine and blow you to kingdom come!"

Rocco kept eyes on JP, a full-on psycho with too much booze in his veins, with those brooding deep-set eyes, lips drawn back from bad teeth, JP a hyped-up attention-deficit drunk. "Calm the fuck down!" JP demurring just a bit now that the alpha male had returned.

"Prettyboy's soft. Why d'you keep him around, with his know-it-all bullshit?" He turned, the aggression an overflowing sewer; he squeezed the trigger, again and again, emptied the cylinder into a goat tethered to the nearby thorn tree, the goat dropping to its knees. "Now at least there's more bloody meat. For biltong, Bushboy."

"I don't bloody believe it," said Rocco, through thin lips.

"I want out of shitzville. What the fuck we waiting for? We pander to that madman's every need. When's it gonna end? I wanna move on. I want my money, Boss."

"We'll move out tomorrow. We gotta play the game to the end."

JP mimicked Heinz's rant: "*It's in the prophecies! Europe is has-been, America's broke. New Zealand's on the ring of fire. Namibia's the only place'll survive the Day of Judgment.* Doesn't say much for the whitey. That we gotta rely on settling in bloody Africa." He looked towards the Mini, said, "So where's Pastor's woman then?"

Rocco eyed JP, pissed and violent. He'd get rid of him ASAP.

Rocco yanked her out of the Mini, her right leg nearly giving way beneath her, the pain searing at her hip as she reeled forward. The skinny guy, lean-and-mean— with a shaved head and sinewy arms covered in ink, a skull, a snake, lightning bolts—stuck his revolver in his pants.

The sunset was vermilion gold, the last rays sinking fast, cool air taking the edge off the heat. But Rae felt the simmering tension. This was some sort of camp-site situated below the rise of a grassy bank, on flat land, dry and rocky. Tents and a table and a crate and boxes and deck chairs were set up near a semi-circle of thorn trees. On a line strung between two trees hung strips of cloth; on a second line was draped a skin of an animal, a buck maybe. Lean-and-mean sauntered over to two men sitting wide-legged at the fire, beers in hand, an open yellow cooler box between them.

A Bushman lay curled on the ground, injured.

Near a kraal, an ostrich pen, was another man, this one strangely familiar. *Who was that?*

She kept her lid on a rise of hot anger, swallowed back the taste of fear when she recognized the body of the half-naked man, bruised, battered, sun-blistered, chained, secured to a tree in sparse shade—Vincent.

She refused to believe he was dead.

She recognized Sol Anderson's young assistant—what was her name?—crawling from a tent, standing up, wobbly on her feet, tear tracks at her cheeks. *Am I hallucinating?* The first three minutes here like a bad movie, she knew she'd have to play this cool, pack away the façade of bravado.

The name came back to her. Stella. Plucking now at a soiled, torn nightie stained with smears of red dirt at her thighs. Or was that blood? She limply lifted her hand in lethargic greeting.

"In case you have any ideas of running away," Rocco spat, kneeling in front of Rae, "I'm taking this off."

Rae leaned against the Mini for support, begged, "I need my leg."

"You'll do just fine without it." Rocco was blunt. "At any rate, seems Heinz prefers you au naturel. I'd better warn you, Ms. Valentine, you try anything, you try hopping off into the wild blue yonder, to the desert, the mountains, it won't take me long to find you and bring you back. You've got a hot bod for a cripple. You notice the Boyz drooling, just waiting to take turns to do you, darling? They'd love nothing more than to rip right into you."

She heard the sound of flowing water beyond the clearing, recognized from afar a group of iconic halfmens trees, their distinctive tapering trunks topped with leaf clusters, at a glance human-like, typical of the Richtersveld.

"You're going nowhere."

Heh, heh, heh, heh.

☀

"So this is the cherry," leered JP, giving her the once-over. "Not too bad for a brown chick." JP was liking his thoughts all right, of having his turn with her, making her *pay* for everything her people had taken from him.

"Off limits, JP," clarified Rocco. "She's Heinz's bint, and you wouldn't anyway want to pomp a half-breed, right?"

JP bit his tongue on the words just about to leave his mouth: *all cats are gray in the dark.*

Johannes picked himself up from the dirt, wiped off the seeping blood at his thigh. He nodded in greeting.

"Stop with your clicking sounds, Bushboy," said JP. "Why you keep this dude around is beyond me, Boss. Nothing but a primitive life form. See what he's wearing, hey? A kaross, and carrying a stick for digging out roots from the dirt."

"You jollers been going stir crazy this last fifteen hours?"

"Whiling away the time, that's all," said Christoff, raising his beer.

Rocco ordered: "Go tell Pastor his Regina is here."

"His Vagina," cackled JP.

"Stop with the jokes, damn it!" snapped Rocco. Then to Rae he said quietly, "Heinz Dieter's over there." He pointed to a hunched figure in a brown coat, sitting in the deck chair at the far end of the ostrich pen. "If you know what's good for you, it'll be love at first sight."

☀

The man Rae'd half-recognized, feeding the ostriches scraps from a tissue, was indeed Heinz Dieter.

He turned, disheveled, grimy, unkempt. As JP pointed to Rae, Heinz straightened himself, walked slowly, unsteady on his feet, crossing over to the small group. His left hand was bandaged, resting in a sling fashioned from a bandanna.

"We meet at last." He bowed in deference, added breathlessly, "I have waited so long," and with his good hand he held out a posy of wilted flowers.

Rae stopped herself recoiling at the smell of him, the wet patches under the arms of his brown jacket testament to his anticipation. She stuck her nose in the dead cosmos and daisies, must have been pretty once, said, "Thank you. I too have been waiting…for a man like you to come into my life." Balancing against the Mini Cooper, she extended one hand, kept it still as he tentatively reached for it, bowed his head, and feathered his lips to the back of her fingers.

He stepped away from her, wiped back the matted fringe from his forehead, his lower lip trembling. He sunk to his knees, worshipping before her. He peeled off the bloodied pus-yellowed bandage. "Look, look!"

"What did they do to you?" She held back the retch

rising at the putrid stench released from his fingers.

"They didn't do anything. *I* did it for *you*! I am transformed!" He beamed. He held up his hand, then blushed, eyes down. "I'm like you now, I'm one of you!"

Rocco sniffed. "Ain't love sweet?"

Heh, heh, heh, heh.

With her hand on Heinz Dieter's bony shoulder, hopping the last ten meters or so towards his tent, she stopped for breath, had to act, whispered, "Heinz, there's something you must do for *me*."

"My love, anything."

She leaned in closer. "You are a great Prophet and I must ask your intervention, your mercy. The sacrificial victim over there, Vincent Saldana, is my friend. I cannot allow him to die, chained to a tree, suffering like Jesus on the Cross."

"Chief Disciple Rocco is in charge of running the camp."

"Sweethearts stick together, they look after each other, Heinz..." She lingered on his name. "I'd do the same for you."

"He looks dead already."

"Are we animals? Please, I beg you." She kept her voice soothing, gentle, her heart beating in her throat as she played her luck, squeezed out a tear, just one, felt it roll from the corner of an eye, down her cheek. "He must at least have protection from the sun, the cold at night. He needs food and water, his hands must be cut loose."

Heinz scowled. "Does he mean that much to you?"

"If you don't help him," she pouted, "I won't go in the tent with you, Heinz...I won't have a thing to do with you."

"Stop, stop! And don't cry."

"He must have a T-shirt and shorts, a cap, a space blanket."

Heinz set back his shoulders, shuffled back to Rocco. She heard a deal being struck, saw something pass hands. Heard Rocco order, "Stella! Bring some clothes and a blanket."

❋

Tony Durant rolled a joint in the kitchen. The harsh wind blew through the gap under the door. The kitchen was without heart or soul. He retreated to the lounge, reached for the ringing cellphone on the coffee table. Answered, "Yeah?" before he checked the screen.

Natasha Armstrong said, "At last you pick up."

He'd ignored her calls. Heck, he didn't want to talk to her. Had deleted her messages. Wanted no more of the third degree.

"So what's up?"

"I've got news."

He sat up, felt the chill, said, "Good or bad?"

"Are you ready for this?"

"As ready as I'll ever be."

"Charges have been dropped. I've been working round the clock. You're a free man. Magistrate says police didn't follow proper protocol. Your case should have been tossed out of court months ago."

Tony Durant toked long and hard on his joint. His mouth formed a circle. He released a perfect smoke ring, watched it wobble and disintegrate.

"You there, Tony?"

"So it's over. After all these months."

"You've got your life back. I'm coming over. I'll bring champagne."

"Natasha. What the heck, now? We'll make it

another time."

He flopped on the couch. Listened to the rain battering his tin roof. In this house that was going to be their house. His and Rae's. He stared at the paint curdling at the damp corners of the ceiling.

A banging at the front door disturbed his uneasy doze. He wiped sleep from his eyes, stumbled up, "Coming, coming."

He heard Rex Hawkins through the door: "I've brought something for you, Tony."

Once inside Rex handed him a cloth bank bag; in it his Astra Special plus two mags.

"Rex, good of you."

"You're legit once more."

"Guess so."

"Word travels fast."

"Come sit, Rex."

"You want an update?"

"You're gonna give me one."

"Mandla Ubuntu's conscious. Lucky he was wearing a civilian vest or the bullet would've gone straight through his big heart. His blood all over the place turned out to be ketchup from those little takeaway packets in his pocket. Guy likes his junk food, has high blood pressure, gave us a scare but turns out his heart attack was minor. He's been very helpful. Told us Vince showed him pics of a kinky-sex murder on Vince's cell. Cell's missing, so's Vince. Intelligence was onto the victim's double dealings. Trudie Kellerman's linked to the insurgents. Seems the case Rae and Vince took on—the missing diamonds—might be linked to the intel case..."

"What're you *not* telling me, Rex?"

Rex inhaled, let the smoke roll from his nose. He crushed the empty pack in his fist.

"I hate to break the bad news. Rocco Robano's

flown the coop."

"Christ's sake. You didn't shut him down?"

"Look, Intel had agents on it, were close to going in. Two good cops were shot dead in a caravan outside the Origin Street house before they could nab him."

"Jesus. I give you the info and this is what happens? A fucking shoot-out happens in my offices. Robano's gone. Cops are dead. You wanna get things done, you do things yourself, that's what it boils down to."

"Not your fault, man, you had no license, no legal weapon. Our hands were tied, and Moodley would've tied you in fisherman's knots if you'd done the vigilante thing. We're talking major arms movements across the border. Trucks, supplies, weapons. These men are planning war. Treason, the vilest crime. We couldn't do a thing without the say-so from upstairs. No ways Intelligence—hellbent as they are on knowing where their base is—would take kindly to us boys in blue shutting down Robano's operation. They're focusing on threats to national security."

"So, for the greater good, you turn a blind eye to the multiple murders he's done?"

...the game rangers, others...now cops...Robano's henchmen back in the day knifing and scarring Rae...

"Take it easy, I'm giving you the heads-up here."

"That so? What do you know then?"

"We searched the house. Found bomb-making material. Something big's being planned. And there's a lead. We have an address in Namibia. Problem is..."

"Spit it out, Rex."

"Rosa Dieter's housekeeper reported her dead this morning. Stabbed. Called one of her bridge buddies, a Mrs. Kapinski, who called us. We found diaries, notes. Frightening paraphernalia, all of it outlining future plans for the Core. More than that, hate to tell you, Tony. A pensioner peeped between her blinds when she heard a car alarm, saw a wiry blond guy bundle a woman into a Mini Cooper."

"A woman?"

"Rae's Jeep is parked outside the Dieter's residence. No sign of Rae."

Tony hit the coffee table with the palm of his hand.

"Intel are on it. We're heading to the Namib. If you want in, I'll be pleased to have an old hand like you along."

"We fly in?"

"No way, Tony. Protocol and bureaucracy's a pain in the arse. We'll never get there. And you're not police. Get your passport."

Heinz Dieter helped her through the torn flap of the tent. He patted his blue mat, offered her a blanket. Watched as she settled, cross-legged, her empty pant leg flat and loose on her good knee. He stared then at her lovely face, almond-shaped eyes, the irises he'd sworn were chocolate looked dappled green and brown—earthy eyes, the colors of a forest, and shimmering. He reached out with trembling fingers, to smooth a stray curl off her forehead, her skin soft as brushed silk. But stopped short of touching. He shrunk back and sat on his good hand, watched as she rolled up her pant cuff, exposing the sheathed stump. Then struggled to keep his eyes on her face.

Tentatively he asked, "A-A-are you pleased to be here?" He chewed his lip, anxious at what she might say.

"Of course, Heinz."

As she said his name, as she touched him lightly on his arm, a shiver ran through him of pure ecstasy.

"Does your hand hurt?"

"Not a bit. I've taken pills." She was so easy to be with. He knew she'd be patient, accepting, loving. "We are soul mates, you and I."

"Yes, I feel it too."

He felt the catch at his throat as she stroked his cheek, savoring the gentle touch of his pretty Liebschen. "Du bist eine schöne Mädchen. Du hast schöne augen...*what pretty eyes you have.*"

"Ah, you speak German?" she said, then dared ask, "Tell me, what happened to your mother?"— nearly spoiling the mood with her silly intrusion.

He frowned, his tone chilly. "Mutti will arrive later in Aurora, once her cottage is complete. But don't let her come between us."

"No, never." *Better not make that mistake again.* "Tell me about this Aurora."

"When will Armageddon strike? That is the question, Regina."

"You mean Rae."

He shot her a look of irritation. "Hold your tongue. There is no Rae, only Regina."

Rae felt bilious. But if Regina was what he wanted, Regina was what he'd get. She summed up the situation. Rocco was pandering to Heinz Dieter for reasons unknown, but there was one thing she did know: the pastor, mad as he was, was her only chance of survival, and Vince's only chance as well.

His voice gained strength, momentum, power: "The Apocalypse will soon be upon us as the prophecies warn. No man knows the day or hour the Great Tribulation will begin, but man is surely sleepwalking to the end of the earth. Melting Arctic ice, shrinking glaciers, oceans turning to acid, the changes are everywhere. Cape Town has seen the hottest summer on record, with fire and drought, and now the city is lashed by gale-force winds and drenching downpours as man turns on fellow man." Heinz drew breath. "From London to Tokyo, Bombay to New York, vast areas will disappear under tens of hundreds of feet of water as God punishes sinners. Cities will drown, valleys will become seas!"

Ah! The interest! His Regina hung on his every word. How gratifying to see adoration in her eyes. The awe he'd noticed in so many of his followers. "But no worries, dear heart," the endearment rolled smoothly off his tongue, "the Chosen will be safe from all chaos—all storms, fires, floods, earthquakes —in Aurora where you will be my Queen!"

Heinz Dieter stopped, a tap smartly twisted off. "But enough of that." He presented his soul mate with a health bar and an opened bottle of lemon-flavored water, then toasted: "Guten Appetit!"

Rae made sure her fingertips brushed his as he handed over the dinner; she saw the blush at his neck and she knew he was hers, utterly and completely devoted.

He did not take his eyes off her. He waited an eternity for his sweetheart to breathe evenly, regularly, finally asleep.

He rummaged around for his headlight. Found it in the sleeping bag with his other treasures. He tightened the strap around his head and switched on the central of three small lights, the illuminated red bulb casting a rosy glow over her face.

He wanted to lay his head between her breasts, perhaps palpate them, lead a nipple to his mouth and suckle.

But it was too soon.

He watched her for long moments, her eyeballs fluttering under the lids, the lashes resting lightly on her cheeks. He stared at her features, her toned skin.

An angel under the blanket. He could no longer wait to see more. He tweaked the cover from her body. She did not so much as stir. He ever so gently peeled the sock off her stump, held his breath as it came into view. He ran his tongue over his lips but could not wet the dryness from them.

He snapped pictures of her face with the phone. But the stump intrigued him, drew his stare, the skin there shiny, smooth, though bunched at the tip. The torchlight cast shadows, accentuating the bumps and crevices, deepening the mauve of the scar tissue to purple. The close-up photos, like alien landscapes, filled the luminous screen.

Done, he turned his gaze away from her.

He swallowed several Vicodin to ease the dull ache in his hand and arm. Switched off the torch. Fell asleep and dreamed of a white wedding.

She waited for sleep to take hold of Heinz. Replaced the stump sock. Stayed in the tent with him, listening to the men argue at the fireside and tell jokes and get drunk. She prised open Heinz's good hand, only to find the phone dead. So much for plan A.

Hours later all was quiet, the fire smouldering, the night insects asleep. A brisk wind blew, rippling the tent fabric.

With the Boyz out cold, and Rocco zipped up tight in his tent, snoring, Rae crawled from hers, moving forward on her buttocks as best she could with three limbs, slowly, guided by Heinz's torch and the light of the Milky Way. She moved along the grass and dirt, straight to Vince lying on his side under the silver space blanket.

"Amber, that you?" Vince croaked.

"Sshhhh…" Rae held the torch fleetingly to his face, saw Vince's eyes and nostrils crusted with sand, pus and blisters, blood at his parched lips. He had no conception of the ants crawling along his arms, his face, feasting. She fed him water from Heinz's bottle. His eyes brightened with—was it recognition?—before he closed them and once again lost consciousness. She wiped his face as clean as she could and tucked the sides of the sheet tightly around his body.

She whispered, "Hang in there, Vince, stay with me."

Slowly she made it to the table at the fire, all the time smelling the river water, an organic scent, and hearing only the rustle of goats in the kraal. She felt the restlessness in the camp, even in the dead of night, a pervasive malaise you couldn't ignore, a storm building, about to break.

She lifted the apron of cloth covering the table, felt around in the cardboard box for the kind of shape she knew could come in useful: corkscrew, skewer, preferably gun.

A cough sounded, a zipper drawn.

She stayed behind the table, shrinking back into the shadows, placed fingers at her throat, at the quickening pulse, as Rocco came from the tent with his Python held loosely. He tap-tapped the barrel on the aluminium frame of a camping stool, put the gun on the table, took a slash against a thorn tree. Rae, so still in the dark, so close to him, smelled the pungent urine.

As sure as Heinz believed in the Apocalypse, Rae believed he would kill her if he saw her. She was alive to appease Heinz, that much was clear. *But why?*

He shook himself off, lit a fag, smoked half of it, crushed it under boot, went back to his tent with the gun and zipped himself in.

She resumed her search. No firepower, only a butter knife. She had to find her prosthesis. She stifled a snort. She was in the wilderness, looking not for God but for her leg. No way she could get out of this on one leg but no way was she going to be a victim. Never again. This time she was determined to turn the tables.

Please God, there must be something, but she found only Worcester sauce, condiments, charcoal briquettes, toilet paper. Perhaps she would set their tongues on fire, set the tent on fire if she had to. Send up smoke signals in the new day. *To whom?* Found a sealed bottle of brandy. Picked up a piece of cold charcoal. *Where the bloody hell had they stashed her leg?*

Heinz Dieter sat up as she crawled back into the tent, mumbled, "Where've you been?"

"Sshhh, just out for a tinkle, Heinz," she said quickly. "I'm here now."

"Don't leave me, Regina. Promise you won't leave me."

"I promise, Heinz, now hush."

"Will we be together always?"

"For always and forever."

She'd do whatever she needed to, to keep him in love. She'd flash her stump Sharon-Stone style as often as she had to, to keep Heinz loyal.

He moaned, clutched her arm, and laid his head in her lap. She felt the heat of his fever, whispered, "Sleep, Heinz." With a measure of compassion, she wiped the sweat from his forehead, stroked his damp hair. "Everything will be all right in the end."

TUESDAY: TOWARDS DIVINITY

Not yet dawn, but Rocco was wide awake. With the birds shifting in the pen and the goats bleating as Johannes led them from the kraal, he knew sleep was done. This was D-Day. He stretched. Got up. Lit the lamp. Checked the Python. Sitting at the burnt out fire, his mind's eye on his Boyz, he practiced dry target shooting.

Click, click, click.

Grunted: "Heh, heh, heh, heh."

Back in his tent he slotted bullets into the chambers, put the gun down and power dressed in clean khaki shorts, a dark shirt, applied cologne for the feel-good factor.

He lay back on his mat, waiting for the light. If Heinz didn't hand over the stones first thing, Pastor and his Disciples would be lining up at the Pearly Gates. Every damned one of them.

Bam, bam, bam...

He'd shoot Heinz between his mad eyes. Next the ADHD jerk-off JP, then Christoff, Alex, the girls, all stone dead.

☀

Johannes !Xaba, silhouetted against the cerise and orange sun, came over the embankment with his goats. The men would be awake now, with the heat rising.

Sure enough JP yelled as soon as he saw him: "Don't be all day about getting my breakfast, Bushboy!"

Before the sun had cut the moon to pieces, before Mantis had packed away his blanket of holes, Johannes had neatened the site, had scraped together the dying coals of the fire and poured water on the embers, had secured the last of the wire at the top of the fence at the pen which the city boy had flattened after his wild ride scaring the birds half to death.

"Ja, kom nou, boy. Maak gou, get a move on," said Christoff. "I want my coffee."

"And where's my phone?" said JP.

Johannes clicked with disapproval at the way JP

ordered him about.

"Fuck, I can't find my phone. Bushboy, I asked where's my cellphone?"

As if he should know where the stupid boy's cellphone was! He wiped the Formica table, brushed the ground with a weathered broom, readied the wood for the fire. The men disturbed the balance, the way they headed straight for the drink, the devil's juice, as soon as they opened their eyes.

"Jissis, JP," said Christoff, "don't tell me Heinz still has your phone?"

Certain it had to be Rocco come to shoot her, Rae nearly wet herself when lean-and-mean ripped open the tent flap.

JP scrambled for the phone.

"It's dead," she said.

He smacked her. "Fucking bint."

Done rubbing her stinging cheek, she left the tent, the Boyz hooting at her crab-like gait, but JP, for seconds at least, had eyes only for his cell.

First thing she noticed: a scrunched space blanket lying in the dirt. But no Vince.

No way Vince was going anywhere. So what had Rocco done with him?

She said, "I need to pee."

"That's what the reeds are for."

JP watched her butt crawl to the bush. "Spread 'em," he called after her. "An act women are well practiced at. Even missing half a leg, I'm sure you'll do just fine."

"We won't look, will we, boys?" said Alex.

Christoff popped a brewski, said, "Not this time."

❀

JP sat in the purring Landie with the Samsung plugged into the cigarette lighter to recharge, scrolled through the photos stored there.

"Well, lookee here. Heinz ain't a half-bad photographer." He clicked onto close-ups, of long lashes on a soft cheek, the light intensifying the warmth of Rae's skin. Then the close-ups of her stump. JP shrieked, "Pastor's a pervert! Come check it out, Disciples!"

"Sies, obscene," said Christoff.

JP said, "Why the hell won't Rocco just off the fool."

Alex said, "Let's have a squizz."

JP and Christoff headed back to the fire, leaving Prettyboy to pore over the pics.

Back at the campfire Rae eased herself up, plonked her backside onto a log. Watched Johannes clear the last of the dead ash and stack wood for a fresh fire.

The lot of them, the Boyz, carried on, showing off, complaining, kept goading Johannes with their horrific words: she felt outrage at their blatant prejudice; felt disgust at JP with his bad teeth and hateful attitude; disgust at the slob Christoff with his red face and his iPod, listening to offensive lyrics, singing along, the words firing him up the way they fired up neo-Nazis the world over: *The world is a white world, my white world.*

She noticed the sprinkling of freckles on Alex's cheeks and nose—no one could escape the sun here— and the dimples so deep you could fall into them. Yes, a Prettyboy. A racist, a crook, possibly a murderer, who knew what else? And here she was evaluating his defined cheekbones, his spiky lashes, the sensual set of his mouth. *How'd such a good-looking man gone so wrong?* She knew a thing or two, about how easy it was to slip. All went down the drain—education, good family, people in your life who loved you—as your bad habits, whatever they were, spiraled out of control.

"I thought you loved me, JP," whined Stella as she came cringing to the fire, sat, with her knees pressed tight, on a wooden stool Johannes had brought from the shed. She turned to Rae. "I'm done with JP. He goes too far, you know?"

Rae glanced at her, felt empathy for Stella caught up with these bad Boyz.

"Shut up, you stuck record," snarled JP.

"Where's the brekfis, Bushboy?" said Christoff. "We want food."

"Ja, kleinbaas, yes boss," said Johannes, "dit kom." He stirred the bucketful of egg, scrambling a helping in a large saucepan, adding his condiments, and sizzling goat meat to a crisp.

"Where's the Klippies?" JP searched under the table, rummaging in the box, settling for boxed red wine.

"Camp grub, my favorite," said Rae, as Alex handed her a plastic fork and a tin plate piled with meat, egg, and a surprise ratatouille.

Rocco, strolling over, said, "Johannes is a superb cook. Enjoy. So how's your lover boy this morning?"

No comment.

She ate what was more than likely her last meal. Needed to keep up her strength if it wasn't. She wanted news of Vince, but wouldn't beg, wouldn't show her fear.

Half an hour later Heinz Dieter, encased in his creased and smelly brown jacket, emerged from the tent, God's lamb squinting in the sun.

"Good morning."

"Good morning, Pastor," the Disciples responded in unison.

He collected the rinds and crusts, and headed straight for the birds.

The long-legged Liebschen waltzed over to the fence, blinking her lashes.

He whispered, "Sehr schön." Every part. Her pock-marked thighs, her gray-brown feathers lightly springing, her sinewy neck undulating. Waiting for him to toss her another tidbit.

"So soft," he said, stretching over the fence, the bird bending and curving her neck, welcoming his hand stroking the downy feathers on her head.

Pastor Heinz beckoned Regina to join him.

※

Rocco strolled over with Rae hopping close, her right hand resting on his shoulder, his left under her elbow.

"We need to talk, Pastor." He'd been more than patient.

"It can wait, Brother."

"Your wounds certainly can't. It's time to change the dressing. Johannes has made up a special medicine just for you."

"My fiancée will do it." Heinz, expectant, looked up at Regina.

Right there at the pen, with Rocco watching, Rae cleaned the seeping raw stumps with cooled boiled water. Johannes helping, standing alongside, held out the pungent poultice he'd mashed with pestle and mortar. "If this doesn't draw out the bad blood," clicked Johannes, "then nothing will."

She smeared on the mix of animal fat and crushed

herbs, reapplied a strip of cloth Johannes had washed the night before, crisp as crinkle paper, wrapping it tightly around Heinz's hand, securing it at his wrist.

"Now I must wash, Heinz," whispered Rae. "Tell Brother Rocco, I must wash."

"I heard you, Regina. Of course, Pastor wants you to be clean."

Rocco handed her a cake of Lux soap, a striped hand towel. "Be warned, darling," he hissed, "if you feel the need to call out to any groups going past, rafters, canoeists, whoever, then your pal Vincent will cop it." He patted his Python at his hip holster. "On the upside, it'll be quick. A bullet to his brain."

If Vince was alive.

Could she trust anything Rocco said?

Where are you, Vince? What have they done with you?

Rae hopped alongside Heinz, leaned on his shoulder, Heinz a surprisingly strong escort; Alex helped them over the ridge. JP and Stella followed, arguing, Stella saying, "I'm done being your doormat." JP smacked her. "You love it, bitch." The joker Christoff, already playing around in the river, shooting the gentle rapids on an inner tube, toppled off into the reeds at the inlet, the calm point.

The mid-morning light reflected off the curves of flowing, rippling water; the fresh smells, of newly cut grass and farm earth, carried on a slight breeze.

The sun, rising steadily above rugged peaks of distant red mountains, turned the harsh bare granite on the opposite bank alluring russets, oranges, silver, gold.

If they killed her at least it was a beautiful spot to

spend her last moments.

"Water's warm as piss!" Christoff yelled. "'Cos it is piss!" He balanced on the rocks, pointed his pecker at the reeds, then pointed at a passing canoe, called out: "You gotta be Swedes you's so blonde."

The tinkling laughter of the booze-cruise chicks echoed as they floated lazily downstream.

JP said, "Man, those enhanced tits have to be from the US of A, I'm telling you. America's the place to be. No mozzie bites on American chicks. Yeah, I've got my ticket booked."

Rae spread her jacket over the top of a bush, made shade and settled in a space underneath. She looked over at Heinz praying at the river, his arms spread, then looked at the irrigation pipes on the opposite bank pumping water to hidden farmland just a walk away.

Alex, sitting on the verge beside her, explained, "Pumps feed grape vines, even a diamond concern just over the banks."

"So we're not far from civilization, then?"

The pollution, she wondered where did it all go? The effluent from guesthouses, hotels, farms and industry on both sides of the river. She thought of all the people just out of sight.

"Not too far," said Alex quietly. "But you were warned if you try anything, Saldana'll suffer the consequences."

"So he's okay?"

They locked eyes, Rae taking in his mint-green irises, his dimples springing into action as his mouth moved, before she turned away, looked towards the river. She was a sucker for soft lips.

"You telling me not to make a break for it?"

"Something like that."

She watched as Alex stripped off his shirt, performed a rudimentary wash and towel-dry, slathered his face and limbs with sunscreen, put the shirt back on, left it open. He wet a bandanna and wrapped it at his head, pulled down the straw hat to secure the cloth, obviously not into the kind of sunburn the others were suffering: Christoff, his skin burned intense pink like the flesh of an overripe guava, his eyelids the magenta of the color wheel; JP, deep-fried a sallow ochre.

"Want some?" Alex handed her the tube, watched as she rubbed it on her face, her arms.

"You my bodyguard?"

"Someone has to watch you."

She checked out his six-pack exposed at his unbuttoned shirt. Checked out the garden path to heaven, the track of hair running down from his navel. Limbs tanned to honey. Saw the muscles at his ribs as he stretched on the grass beside her and their eyes locked a second time.

She wondered now, with Heinz Dieter back, standing on one side of her, and Prettyboy Alex Silver settling on the other: *How can I use these men?*

Rocco counted on Pastor Heinz not getting back from the river any time soon. No way he'd leave hopalong's side, and she sure as hell wasn't running anywhere. Was a painstaking climb over the ridge, he'd seen, she'd half-climbed, was half carried by Alex. He fingered the trio of diamonds Heinz had handed over, "in exchange for care for the prisoner," he'd said, and had promised him the remainder. But surely the stones were for the taking.

The stench in the tent was overpowering, of something sweet and something rotten. Heinz had been sweating in his brown suit for three nights; the tent held a stink of adrenaline and fear and an under-the-radar bacterial infection. With all his dreams, all the time spent in awe of his Regina, he was unaware of the capillary action carrying disease from the swollen stumps of his fingers to the rest of his body.

"Heinz, baby, you ain't got long."

Heh, heh, heh, heh.

Then he scowled. He'd better find the diamonds before Heinz kicked the bucket. He repeated his search. Emptied the suitcase, threw Heinz's magazines onto the dirt, went through the pockets of his spare shit-brown jacket. Nothing. He found a corkscrew, a butter knife, plus the Klipdrift Gold JP'd been scrounging for. No diamonds.

Heinz, you mutt, where the hell have you hidden the stones?

Who knew what craziness he'd been up to while Rocco had taken off on his wild-goose chase looking for Regina—the wild goose not so wild now. He left the tent. Didn't bother tidying up this time. Knew where to come for the pilfered Klippies; he'd need a drink later.

That only left the clothes Heinz was wearing. The stinky brown suit.

He relished the thought of offing the joker. Yeah, he was moving out, flying to the heavens ASAP. He'd check the Piper now, and Johannes would help refuel her. Then the pleasure would be his as he dispatched the Disciples straight to Hell.

Rae pulled off her grubby sweatshirt, peeled off her denims. Heard Heinz's sharp intake of breath as he watched her dip into the knee-deep water, in T-shirt and panties, her stump—the proof of her penance, according to Heinz—breaking the water now.

Maneuvering herself onto a flat rock, she lathered the soap, scrubbed her hands and face, took particular care as she washed her stump, then splashed and rinsed her limbs.

She knew the Boyz had eyes on her. Her brassiere showed through the T-shirt, the tops of her breasts pushed up. She felt no fear. Was beyond fear, all those hours with the shrink finally paying off. She knew she could do this. *You have to find yourself, do it for yourself, whatever "it" is, show courage; know all emotion, joy, disappointment, fear, will come in equal measures.* She knew too, that men who raped, men who hurt women, did it as a power play. She was an object to Rocco and the Boyz, it wasn't personal. Her death would not be personal.

What is personal is you and me, Vince.

I need to get us out alive.

She submerged, the silence of underwater, the weightlessness she felt for seconds centering her, then she broke surface, striking out from the shallows past the reeds to the deeper water.

"Don't go too far, Regina," Heinz called as she swam to less turbulent water at the middle of the flow.

She let go the small meds bottle she'd hidden in her panties, let it loose in the downstream of the river, hoped it would carry to a tourist group, the message in it she'd scrawled the night before, with a stick of charred wood from the dead fire, on a piece of cardboard torn from one of Heinz's pill boxes: *SOS. Help. Orange River. Call Anthony Durant.*

Plus his cell number.

Her Nancy Drew moment.

Message in a bottle.

Or was it Sting?

Wouldn't Tony just love it!

She saw JP jump up, stand at the bank, heard him shout, "What the hell, Alex, why'd you let her swim out?"

"She just went, man."

"Shit," yelled JP, pulling out his Smith. "Which of you arseholes is gonna go get her?"

Rae considered briefly heading for the far shore, but the Boyz would be after her. She wanted to swim downstream, find a tourist camp, but the men would drag her back within minutes— volatile JP stood now, cursing; Alex pulled off his shirt, ready to dive in.

No way could she leave Vincent to their mercy.

She struck back for shore, back to Heinz and the Boyz.

"Look! She returns!" Heinz watched, blissful, as Rae, his sweet love, slicing the water as gracefully as a dolphin, made her way to him.

He handed her the towel, her fingertips settling on his as she said, "Please, stay near me."

She peeled off her soaked T-shirt, momentarily losing her balance, grabbing Heinz's shoulder to steady herself, felt the fire generated in his body. Saw Heinz's lips spread from soft cheek to soft cheek, across his baby face, transfixed as a wax figure at London's Madame Tussauds as he caught a glimpse of her breasts, as he reached out with a quivering hand.

She drew on the dry sweatshirt, said, "Let's go."

The fresh bandage was already filthy, the edges tainted pus-yellow. Heinz Dieter's face was on fire, as red as the sun, not only from sitting in the forty-degree heat and from fever, but from the flush of ecstatic love.

He held out his good arm and the two of them headed back to the camp, a natural combination, as

Rae hopped and Heinz helped, and Rae simpered, and Heinz blushed with unadulterated adulation.

❋

Back in the tent, momentarily disconcerted as he noticed a certain disorder, Heinz plucked from the mess one of his clean shirts, a pale blue to set off her silky skin.

"So much cooler than that grubby sweatshirt." He stared at the spot just below the rolled-up denim jeans, at the the stump right there close to him, exposed, as she settled on her mat.

Heinz stuttered, "I-I-I worship you, Regina! I have a surprise for you."

"What is it, Heinz? I love surprises."

So unlike Mutti.

He brought from his pocket a small parcel the size of a single ravioli. Ripped open the tissue packet with his teeth, picked up the item which fell onto the sleeping bag, the light glinting on the ring in the palm of his good hand. "Regina, will you be my bride?"

"Of course." Rae hardly skipped a beat. "Just when I thought I'd never get asked on a date, that men would be put off by my disability, someone like you comes along."

"May I?" Heinz pushed the diamond solitaire onto her ring finger, a diamond of the palest yellow, in a setting of pink gold, the ring identical to the one Rosa Dieter had described and reported missing. A ring she'd seen in a photograph snapped by Sol Anderson.

"You and I will reign in Aurora!"

"Yes, Heinz. Me and you, together." And as he stared at her she knew she had to do it now. "Heinz, Schatzie...First I need to talk to you..."

His brow furrowed, he blinked rapidly. "You accepted my ring."

"Heinz, a diamond is forever. Of course I want the ring. But the Boyz, I don't trust the Boyz."

He pulled his hand away from her leg as if singed by a flame.

"In their eyes I'm vermin, a plaything, not even human. An accident of tainted love. I'm afraid of what they might do to me...Schatzie..."

He turned away, fumbled with the cap of a vial, gulped down more pills with the last of the bottled water. "No one will ever hurt you, my Queen," crooned Heinz. "I am the leader of Aurora." Then spat, cross as a pre-schooler: "So like a woman. Paranoid. Mutti warned me. Do not forsake me, Regina."

She picked up on the harshness to his tone. "No, no, no! Now who's being silly?" she scolded, taking his good hand in hers and drawing it towards her.

She had wanted to ask about Vince. But took another tack, whispered, "You know, Heinzie, I'd give anything to have my leg back."

"What are you talking about now?" he snapped.

Rae saw anger flash, knew he'd misunderstood. What she wanted was her prosthesis. If she grew her limb back, he'd be out the door.

"My missing limb is what makes me special, yes," she agreed.

"Your missing limb is your beauty, your strength," he clucked, squeezing closer. "Never forget that."

One minute his voice severe, the next loving. Unpredictable mood swings. She was dealing with a fragile sanity. Clearly not going to get help from this quarter: no ally here, Heinz too delirious to believe Rocco and the Boyz had so blatantly obvious a different agenda to his own.

No gun, no leg, no hope.

But she refused to give up.

To restore a delicate balance she stroked his cheek. She wanted to draw back from the sweet stench like a visible mist about him, of adrenaline, of sweat, of Johannes's poultice, the smells so rancid she was near vomiting. She forced the words out, husky as possible: "Would you like to touch it?"

Heinz groaned in anticipation. "May I?"

"Yes. Of course."

"Will it hurt?" he squeaked.

"Scar tissue is the most elastic tissue there is. I promise it won't hurt. Go ahead, Schatz."

He reached out, the intact fingers of his right hand trembling, hovering over her thigh, the light filtering through the tent bathing her in a soft sea-green wash.

He gently stroked the rounded tip of the stump, the delicious fruit so full of promise. His fingers brushed across the scar tissue, then hesitantly upwards, touching her thigh, then back down.

Holding her breath against the reek of body odor mingling with underlying putrefaction, gingivitis and the oily pungency of filthy hair, she watched transfixed, as with bloodshot eyes aglow, Heinz knelt down before her and ran the tip of his tongue briefly over her stump.

There was no erection and there would be no ejaculation—just deviant and feverish obsession.

"Siesta time," she said. "Come, rest next to me."

He laid his head on her lap, and she soothed him, she stroked his forehead, noticing the bald patches on his scalp, one the circumference of a two-rand coin, and waited for him to relax and sleep, her senses tuned to the trouble brewing out there. If the Boyz were moving out, no two ways about it, they wouldn't be taking her along, or Vince or Stella or Heinz either.

If only you realized, Heinz, how expedient you are.

And me. Rocco will kill us all.

The tent was chaos. Someone had searched for something.

Great powers of deduction, Rae. Though Millhone might not be as impressed.

It had to be Rocco. He'd searched the house, now the tent. Only one thing he could be searching for.

If Heinz had a ring on him, then the chances were he had more.

"Does this feel good, Schatzie?" Rae massaged his forehead, seeing his eyelids grow heavy, his hand moving to the stump and settling there, as light as a moth.

With Heinz finally passed out, she shifted his head off her lap.

She poured the bulk of the pills from Heinz's stash into a plastic bowl, ground them with the back of a spoon to a fine gray dust. She had the Klipdrift. She screwed open the cap, took a swig before spooning the powder into the newly opened bottle.

The Boyz would start drinking as soon as their eyes opened after their nap. Any mistiness, any bitter taste, they'd blame on the heat. Alcohol was alcohol, and running out as they were, the piss-cats would drink anything.

Anthony Durant, Rex Hawkins, and Adrian Lombard sat in the car at the South African border post.

"No way to beat the wait?" said Tony, the heat rolling in and smacking him in the face as he left the air-conditioned unmarked vehicle, checked out the snaking queue in front of them. Asians from a tour bus snapped pics of each other standing proudly in wide-brimmed safari hats and gloves and face-masks under the signs printed HOPE YOU ENJOYED YOUR VISIT! COME AGAIN SOON!

Passport control was a ship's container. Harassed officials worked slowly—tourists the priority, Swedes, French, Brits, Americans. A kid said, "Africa's so cool! But when we gonna see the tigers, Mommy?"

Went without saying, the real hold-up was the multitude of refugees waiting to be shipped back by the dysfunctional government to their war-torn hellholes.

Detective Captain Rex Hawkins brought out a fat wallet, did the dirty, greased a palm. This was business in Africa. Tony and Adrian turned blind eyes.

The men flashed passports, filled in forms, got their stamps.

Rex saluted an autographed photo of the corrupt president high up on one wall, in a gilt frame.

Tony said, "The stud has at least twenty-five wives. Probably fornicates with lizards."

They crossed to the other side.

Now the Asians snapped photos of each other under a sign that read: WELCOME TO VIOOLSDRIFT! WILLKOMMEN ZUR NAMIBIA!

Adrian read out the address.

JP, horny as hell, wasn't into listening to any idiot woman telling him she had a headache, or it was that time, or it was afternoon, or any other fucking excuse, and she was lying right there in his sight, in that skimpy nightie. "Stella, come." He clutched at his crotch, the hard-on like cement. "This good enough for you?" He pulled her up.

"Do you have to, JP? I wanna go home," Stella sniveled, tugging at the elastic of the neckline.

"When're you gonna take me home, JP?"

Alex stood up, spat into the veld grass. "She's a mixed-up kid, JP. Come on, leave her alone. Give yourself a damn hand job if you have to." He had to hold back, but how could he stand by and let this happen? He couldn't. "Stella, get back to your tent."

"Mind your own beeswax, Prettyboy. As for you, slut, don't you look at me like that!" JP hit her, leered as she sprawled to the ground. He turned towards Alex. "And you're really getting on my tits. You're one goody-two-shoes know-it-all motherfucker and it's time you stepped up. Yeah, I reckon you go sort out the hoity-toity Queen of the camp site. I've seen the way you look at her. You've got the hots for her brown skin. So go on, Alex, give her what for." JP pointed the Smith at Alex's crotch. "I'll shoot your balls off if you don't do it. Let's see what you've got to give."

"You want it this way," sneered Alex. "Sure I'll teach the peg leg a lesson. Just fuckin' watch me. I'll show you how it's done, bro."

He swaggered towards Heinz's tent, JP watching every step, keeping the gun trained on his back. "I knew you had it in you, Al my pal."

Alex vanished for a moment then pulled a struggling, protesting Rae out through the flap, Rae demanding, "Where's Rocco?"

"Most likely blowing his Piper, he's getting out of here, didn't you know?" said JP. "So he ain't around to fix things for you, Queenie. Me and the Boyz here are gonna have a little fun with you."

"Hold her right here, JP," instructed Alex and he gave Rae a push in JP's direction. "I'm getting a sleeping bag, make it more romantic, you know."

JP pulled her close, grabbed her tit.

Rae twisted, bit JP on the hand, drew blood. She

clawed, tore, and screamed for Rocco, for Heinz, but Rocco was clearly off on a mission and Heinz, out for the count on the meds, couldn't hear a thing.

"Shut up, bitch." JP thumped her one, had her on the ground, rubbing her face in the dirt, as Alex returned with the sleeping bag.

He plucked JP off her. He picked her up as if she were a lightweight and swung her over his shoulder fireman style, carried her struggling over the ridge towards the grassed verge near the river, the sleeping bag bunched under his free arm.

"I want privacy," he yelled.

"We gonna go watch?" slurred Christoff, stoking the coals to blood red.

"Nah," said JP, "give the lovebirds some space. We gonna get going on the Klipdrift. You find that bottle yet?"

Oh God! No!

Victims often got the treatment a second or third time, but she wouldn't survive this, not after what Rocco's mates had done to her.

Alex dumped her in the shade on the grass at the water's edge. He held one hand over her mouth in a bruising grip, so tight she couldn't bite him. He gripped her wrists above her head, pinned her down with his body.

"Stop struggling, Rae."

She kicked out at him with her good leg.

"I don't do rape," rasped Alex. "You wanna get out of this intact, stop fighting me, Rae."

It was the repetition of her name, acknowledging her as a person, that did it. She lay still for a moment, uncertain, nodding.

"We're gonna do a deal here. Know what's inside the sleeping bag?" He didn't wait for a reply. "Your leg. Like I said, I don't do rape and I don't like seeing a woman so humiliated." He brushed the sand from her face.

If she could cope with Heinz inside the stuffy tent then Alex was pure beefcake. She felt his body warm against hers, his fingers stroking her neck. She felt a jolt of pure oxytocin, horrified now as a shiver of erotic thrill ran though her. "I want you," she whispered. She'd read about Stockholm Syndrome, about women falling in love with their captors. But this was survival pure and simple. In the sultry air, heavy with the smell of the river, she wrapped her arms around his body in a full embrace, kissed him on the mouth, felt his lips parting, the moist warmth, the softness of his tongue; she tasted brandy. *She'd do what had to be done to stay alive*, relishing his heavy breathing, the power she had over Alex Silver.

As if reading her mind, he said, "Not now. This's survival for both of us."

He rolled off her. He handed her the leg.

She cleaned her stump, dried it, pulled the sock from her pocket, rolled it on the stump and clicked the prosthesis back in place. Got dressed.

He came closer. He ripped open her shirt, hit her.

The unexpected strike across her face sent her reeling. Drew blood from her nose and cut the skin on her cheekbone. He half-dragged, half-carried her, over the rise and back to camp, as yelping and screeching she lashed out with her fists.

Her hair was matted with sticks and sand, her shirtsleeve torn almost right off.

She registered JP saying, "Good for you, Prettyboy. Now it's my turn."

"No, JP. She's done."

JP shouldered up to them. "What you saying, Alex?"

"I'm saying Jean-Pierre, neither you nor Christoff is gonna touch her."

"Hear that, Christoff?"

JP slammed Smith down on the camping table and unbuckled his belt. "You, boy, you spoiled my fun with Stella. I'm having it off now with the brown whore."

"You want her, you fight me for her." Alex threw her down; standing in front of her, he held his ground.

"Hey, look at that," interrupted Christoff. "Bitch is walking, she's grown a second leg."

JP, the tension gone from him, threw back his head and guffawed.

At the sight of his Queen come home, disheveled, her clothing torn, her face a mess, her leg restored, Heinz fled the tent.

Weeping and wailing, trapped in a tortured world of his own, paying Regina no heed, he sank into his deck chair at the ostrich pen and curled up like a fetus.

Monday afternoon Tony, Rex, and Adrian arrived at the town, a one-horse down from Luderitz. Had a narrow main drag, with Germanic style buildings, a corner shop, a petrol station. Didn't take long to find the place.

"This it?" said Tony, amazed.

Adrian checked the address. "This's it."

They faced a mansion with fancy gates, Tuscan pillars, double-volume entrance hall, a gleaming pool outside.

"Where're the mercenaries?" said Rex, holstering his gun. "Where's the electric fences, the guards? Where're our guys?"

The builders—their names Dirk, Pieter and Cornelius—showed them around. "Nice pozzie, hey?" said Dirk.

"For one Rocco Robano paying top-dollar for top-of-the-range finishes and our expertise," said Pieter.

"He's moving in any day. Why're the cops looking for him? He didn't pay his parking tickets or what?" asked Cornelius.

They gave Rex and Tony the grand tour, the place tiled white, with lots of light; took the elevator to the top floor to five en-suite bedrooms with picture windows, all glass and steel, every room overlooking sweeping sands, the view stretching over a treacherous and rocky coast littered with shipwrecks, towards a wild sea.

"How's this place?" said Adrian.

"We've stumbled into a live screening of *Top Billing*," said Rex, "the dream palace Robano's planning to disappear to."

"This whole thing's a con," said Tony. "We gotta move."

"What the hell, Johannes," said Rocco as he parked the Land Rover. Boyz were causing kak. Some trouble with Alex this time. With his plane refueled, he wanted to fuck off ASAP, but now had more drama to deal with.

"Heite aarde. Hell, can't leave the youngsters for more than a couple of minutes before there's trouble," joked Johannes.

"Get the coffee going." The moerkoffie as black as Rocco's mood, as black as Hades.

He saw Heinz, clearly delirious, back at the ostrich pen, sniveling, feeding his ostrich again, his Liebschen. From right across the campsite Rocco smelled his festering skin, saw tears flowing down the pastor's burning cheeks. He watched the other birds join the snack frenzy, their sinewy necks curving down to the dirt, guzzling the morsels Heinz threw in one by one. Yeah, indeed, it was time to put the mad fuck out of his misery. He turned away from the Boyz and their petty bickering, approached Heinz. "We need a confab, Pastor."

Heinz wiped away the snot smearing at his upper lip with his jacket sleeve. His tone tinged with anguish, he squeezed out the words, "They hurt my Regina."

"What are you saying? Tell me in plain English."

"It was him, he did it." He pointed at Alex at the campfire. "He pulled her from the tent. He did… things…I heard her screaming."

"Christ Almighty. He won't touch her again." He bit his tongue on the words, *yeah, he broke Regina in for you is all.* "Now, Pastor, I have no more capacity for patience. I want the stones."

"I see." Heinz sniffed, kept feeding the ostriches, the tears dripping off his chin.

"We can delay no longer."

"Yes, I understand. Did you ever think that maybe Mutti's diamonds were plucked from the alluvial deposits right here, Brother? That perhaps they came from right this spot on the Orange River?"

"Could be," he played along.

Heinz dried his eyes on his sleeve, tossed a titbit. "Yes, Liebschen, there you go." Dipped in his pocket for another.

"So where are they, Pastor?"

Heinz held out the closed fist. "A man is drawn to them, can't help wanting them, wooing them."

Enough of this bullshit.

"Stop the bloody sniveling, Heinz! Tell me where the fuck are the diamonds!"

Heinz opened his fist, tossed the handful of treats into the air, watched a rainfall of crusts and pebbles fall to the dirt, wondered at Liebschen herself scrabbling, gobbling—what a keen bird!—and the others, their placid brown eyes popping, necks bulging as they sucked up the morsels, like a collective vacuum cleaner, the glint and color, on the orange dirt, disappearing. The ostriches couldn't get enough

"What," Rocco laid patient emphasis on every word, "have—you—done—with—the—God—damned—diamonds—Pastor?"

"Why, Brother, do you forsake me?"

Rocco resisted the urge to smack him upside the head.

"Choose, Heinz." He pulled out the Python. "Regina over there or the diamonds. You can't have both. I'll shoot her, you know I will. Right fucking now."

Heinz stared listlessly back at him. "She's no longer mine. Do you not understand? She's been defiled. But the diamonds are still mine, my inheritance. There must be something that remains mine!" He sobbed with fever and broken dreams, looking to the heavens for answers.

Tears and sunshine, Heinz sniffed then, said matter-of-fact, "Ostriches need pebbles in their stomachs to grind up their food."

What's the fuckwit gabbing on about now?

Took a few seconds for the information to sink in.

"Hang on...What are you talking about?"

But Rocco didn't need a reply, he knew the truth as clear as day: "You fed the diamonds to the ostriches."

Heinz looked him straight in the eye, a sly smile breaking across his face.

Looney Tunes had fed the diamonds, stone by stone, to the birds. Right before his bloody eyes.

Played me for a fool!

Rocco had no clue whether he shot Heinz first, or pushed open the gate of the pen first, to stop the gobbling birds. He felt the recoil of the pistol. Heinz was in the dirt, blood everywhere. Before he could do anything, the birds, spooked by the gunfire, made for the open gate, wanting out the pen, making a bid for freedom.

He tried herding the panicked birds running back and forth, from side to side, a male glancing an almighty kick off his shin—"Jesus fucking Christ!" He lunged at a flapping wing, grabbed Liebschen around the throat, gun in one hand, couldn't hold her.

Rocco fired randomly at the squawking creatures, getting one in the neck, clipping another's wing as Liebschen flapped past him right out the pen, others following suit down the dirt track. He forced the pen shut, half the birds still in there, bouncing on meaty thighs, squawking, flapping; some lying in pools of blood.

He took control. Summoned Johannes. "Slaughter the birds in the pen. Do it now. Stomachs to one side. Dig a hole for the carcasses."

The Bushman startled.

"Do what I say! And JP, start the fucking Landie! Christoff, help Johannes!"

Alex came running. "I go for a bush crap and I come back to chaos!"

Rae, kneeling alongside Heinz, tended his hurt.

Christoff spat, "What an abortion, a right fokken mess." He almost wished he was home, watching *Generations* and snapping his fingers for Ma to make him food.

Rocco jumped in the passenger seat, JP accelerating zero to sixty in five seconds flat. JP whistled. "Didn't know these birds could take off so fucking fast!"

"Just bloody drive, I said." The vehicle bounced down the track. "Put fucking foot!"

"I've hit seventy already!"

"Just fucking drive. Mow them down if you have to!"

"Wait till we get you," JP crowed at the birds, "you're gonna fucking pay! All you's good for is handbags and fucking feather dusters!" Loving the handling of the Landie over the rocky terrain, JP chased Liebschen and the others along the fenced edge of the farm, back along the road they'd arrived on, past the windmill, towards the beehive and the quiver tree; with one hand on the steering wheel, the other out the window, JP kept shooting. "Like we cowboys! Except we have us wheels!"

Rocco aimed again at Liebschen. Let off another quick two shots. Missed.

The ostrich, tiring, slowed to a trot, turned, looked back, stopped maybe twenty-five meters from the Landie as JP hit the breaks.

Liebschen blinked.

JP said, "She's teasing us, Boss, flirting with us."

She came to a standstill near the beehive, stepping beyond it, as if for cover.

"She's the one Heinz is in love with. Stroking her, feeding her. Giving her what's mine."

"How does he tell the difference? All look the same to me. She gonna stick her head in the sand now and make it easy for us?" JP took aim.

"Old wives' tale that." Rocco kept eyes on his prey. "Though they do lie on the ground 'n' play dead. One thing for sure, any second now she's gonna be dead."

"Why the fuck we chasing one particular bird anyway?"

"Because I bloody well want to, I bloody well say so. Don't piss me off." He leaned across the seat and backhanded JP in the face. "Do as you're told and shut the fuck up for once."

Had been ages coming.

JP, shocked, scowled in red-faced rage.

Rocco left the Landie without taking his eyes off the bird, crept closer. He'd get her from ten meters, even fifteen would do.

The bird frozen, googly eyes bulging. Going nowhere.

Fifteen meters now, ten, seven—could walk right up to her, he reckoned. Said, "Who's your daddy, then, you beauty." The only part of her moving were the eyes, blinking, as he slowly lifted the gun and focused on the site picture.

Same split-second he pulled the trigger, he let go his two-handed grip, smacked his left hand onto his neck, felt the intense and throbbing surge of pain that took his breath away. The bird sidestepped with his miss and took off running.

"Damn you!" He swore and shot from the hip, right into one of her meaty thighs. "Thought you could get away?"

He grabbed at his neck again, pulled off the dead motherfucking bee right there between his fingers.

He put a shot through the bird's neck for good measure. Stuck the gun in his holster, pulled out his hunting knife. Bird still flapped her wings, those boggle eyes staring. Rocco kicked her, the bird lying in a pool of warm blood, the smell of rust in his nostrils. He brought out his hunting knife, unsheathed it, slit and sliced into her three stomachs. Didn't care that she was alive. He ripped open her lucky packets, saw the contents spilling: bottle tops, beer-can pulls, cigarette stompies, a watch face, spark plugs, what looked like a brooch, all coated with slime and bile and blood; getting his hands slippery as he sifted. No diamonds.

"Where'd all this crap come from?" he shouted. "Like a bloody junk shop in here."

"There's all sorts of shit in the veld, Boss," said JP from the Landie, still stewing. *And all sorts of precious shit in those birds.* Yeah, he knew what Rocco was after.

"I told you shut up." The only thing on Rocco's mind was the worth of the diamonds.

I'll kill every bird, every damn one, to get the stones...

Rae tuned in to Johannes's soft hum as he prayed over his dead birds.

...The day we die, a soft breeze will wipe out our footprints in the sand.

When the wind dies down, who will tell the time-lessness that once we walked this way in the dawn of time...

"Stella, pour the Klippies!" ordered Christoff. "Pastor's whore, you good for something after all."

Rae had dug up the brandewyn none too soon.

"Anything to keep you happy," she said, staying out of Christoff's way. He wanted to be boss, let him be boss.

She'd made Heinz as comfortable as she could

in Johannes's shed, alongside Vince, Heinz softly moaning but alive. Both alive. Vince accounted for. She'd wadded a shirt at Heinz's wound and applied pressure to staunch the bleeding. Vince was out for the count but still breathing.

"Bushboy," said Christoff. "What you doing, you communing with the dead or what? You Alex, take over the digging."

"Why the fuck don't you do it, Christoff?"

"Jus' you fokken get in there and dig the hole, Prettyboy." He aimed the Taurus JP'd left him, flexing his flab. "You give me any flack I'll shoot you. Ja, Prettyboy, the hole's too small for our feathered voêls. Dig the hole deep as the Kimberley Diamond Mine."

"Lazy bum, come bloody help."

Christoff jumped off the chair, lashed out with the gun, the crack resounding as the grip connected with Alex's skull; saw the surprise in Prettboy's eyes, saw him stumbling, sink to his knees, fall backwards, saw blood flow from his forehead.

Rocco ordered: "JP, stay in the Landie. I'll scare the rest towards you, you shoot from there. Understand?"

"Yes, sir."

In the searing late-afternoon heat, Rocco stalked the birds, circling the traumatized ostriches. Exhausted but still wary, the birds had all but stopped, were now closer to the koppie and the entrance to the campsite.

Rocco heard the gunshot, *blam*!

None of the birds went down.

Yelled, "What the fuck're you shooting at, JP?" He felt a sudden sting at his arm, another at his neck, pain shooting like electric shock through his veins. "Holy

Christ!" He smacked his neck, stamped his feet.

He smacked at the bees now buzzing at his head. Smelled the strong aroma of bananas. Heard the escalating sound of angry buzzing. He stumbled, swatting at the darkening swarm, bees at his body, creeping under his clothing, coming at his face. Could only mean one thing. Came back to him from army basics: when killer African bees attack, protect your face, find cover. No house, no shed, no bushes. River too far. *Get to the car!* He ran a zigzag back to the Landie, the gun dropping from his grip as he sprinted, the bees after him in mad frenzy.

"Holy shit!" JP stared from the car. In a genius-flash, he did the windows up tight. For good measure he snapped closed the air vents. Heard the satisfying clunk of the central locking system.

Rocco bashed on the window. Slapped his body against the door, his hands black with bees, swatting them from his face, pulling and scratching at bees on his neck, at his eyes, his ears, his nose, his mouth.

Wild with pain, Rocco screamed but no words came.
JP, help me!

He bashed on the window, hands, arms, the bees dripping off him, he scratched at the door handle, could hardly hold on with fingers swollen and numb.

JP accelerated.

Fingernails breaking, the handle ripped from Rocco's grasp.

Through the fury, it dawned on him: *JP shot the hive!*

Running blind, gurgling, flailing, he fell, rolling in the dirt, the bees creeping into his ear drums, into his nostrils, under his eyelids, stinging his eyeballs; he sucked in bees, his tongue stung, swelling,

his throat constricting, he couldn't stand the shooting pain through blood vessels throbbing fit to burst;
he clutched handfuls of russet earth, red dust sifting
through his fingers, his fists clamping on bees stinging;
a vice grip tightened, he pounded his exploding chest,
his last breath stuck in his throat.

His mouth: a black, heaving hole.

※

JP screeched up to camp and jumped from the Landie.
Christoff sat wide-legged in his deck chair, alongside
a hole, pointing the Taurus. JP heard the tail-end of a
barney between Bushboy and Christoff, saw Johannes
retreat and sit sullen alongside the dead birds. The
camp reeked of sweat and urine.

"Where's the Boss?" asked Christoff.

"Dead."

"What you saying? Jissis! Jy jok!"

"No jokes's" said JP, breathless, disbelieving, slapping his thighs. "Rocco thought he was the bees' knees
but he turned out not so sharp after all."

"Nah, where's he then? Don't pull the wool."

"Got stung to death." JP sang, "Rocco Robano the
great white hunter, bees did in the cheating punter!"

Christoff giggled nervously.

"I'm serious, you shoulda seen him, man, his face
covered, his back, his arms, bees piling on every bit of
skin, under his clothes, all over, stinging the life outta
him."

"Fokken A fine."

"Where's Prettyboy?"

"Down there," Christoff pointed the gun at Alex
lying in a shallow grave.

Now was JP's turn to be shocked: "You shoot him
then?"

"Rocco must've died of bee shock, bro," intoned Alex from the hole, standing up, groggy. "Apitoxin promotes histamine release. And no, he didn't shoot me."

JP almost choked. "Clearly can't keep a good man down!"

"Bees are spooked by loud noises, strong odors, fragrances, shiny jewelry, dark clothes. Worker bees do territorial patrols in a radius of thirty meters around their hive. They swarm if their colony's threatened. Better break some records running if the Africanized honeybee attacks."

"Africa even fucked up the honeybee," cackled JP. Then said to Johannes, "Tell you what you gonna do, Bushboy. You rural darkies are used to skinning shit. You've opened the stomachs. Put the crap in a heap and bring it to me. Then you gonna cut the meat off those plump thighs, for biltong, make sure you strip every bit. So get busy, Bushboy. While the girl, the maid—that's you, Ms. Valentine—is gonna cook!"

"Wait till you taste my stew, Kleinbaas," said Rae, eyes down now, demure, knowing her place. "You'll love it." All sorts of yummy condiments she could throw in. The remainder of crushed Trepeline, Valium, Zopiclone...

JP leered, coming right up close to her, whispered in her ear. "You smell nice, like spice." He ran the barrel down her cheek, under her jaw. "Meidjie, you gonna be good for something after all."

Rae held her ground. "Don't wave the gun about, Kleinbaas."

"Christoff, keep an eye on these two."

"Bushboy and the bint," Christoff toasted, downing another dop of Klippies. "Maggies, what a good team you two make. And what a sweet turn—Boss Man gone to meet his maker!"

"Alex, come," said JP, zipping up his windbreaker, pulling a baseball cap low over his eyes, grabbing a can of Bug Off. "We gonna bring him back."

And the birds. With their bellies full of treats.

Back at camp, JP pulled the wrapped bundle from the rear of the Landie.

Christoff unrolled the plastic groundsheet, ran a stick across the body, dislodging hundreds, thousands, of dead bees.

"Will you look at that, man." He prodded Rocco with his boot. "His face is one big bloody bee sting." A swollen red mass, his eyes puffy, the lids slits at which dead bees were embedded; his mouth open, a purple tongue protruding.

Then JP rolled the corpse into the grave. Kicked sand on ex-Boss Rocco. "Nice knowing you, arsehole!" he shouted into the blue. Then looked at Rae: "I want my lunch, girl."

Christoff slurred, "Stella, pour us another drink. Fokken A fine." Christoff, bleary-eyed, could hardly get the words past his numb tongue, as she sloshed more of the brandy into his tin cup. Throwing back the laced Klippies like water, he sank lower and lower into his seat.

JP pointed to the ostriches in the back of the 4x4. "Bushboy, don't forget to cut up these ones." He watched as Alex and Johannes pulled the birds from the Landie, piling them in a heap, their feathers matted with blood.

"While you do that, me and you, Rae, we gonna have some fun." He came at her at the fire, from behind, slithered the gun barrel between her legs. "I've been waiting, and now's the time."

Alex, coming up to him with nothing but his fists, said, "I told you *no*, JP. Leave her alone."

"Who died and made *you* boss, Prettyboy?"

"I said leave her out of this."

"Wake the fuck up. She's already in it. Pastor's whore, yours too. What's the big deal?"

"I said no way."

"I want my turn."

Alex flared. "Don't you dare touch her."

"I'll do what I fucking want. If I want to fuck the brown whore, I'll fuck her!"

"You ignorant, racist pig. You know, I live for losers like you."

"Look who's calling names now. Don't fucking dare call me stupid. And as for you, it's like you got Google tattooed on your forehead and I'm sick of it. We been seeing your true colors for a while now, Prettyboy."

"For months I've put up with your bullshit, your hatred." Alex got closer, poking JP in the chest, getting in his face. "That's it! It's over! I'm not doing this any more!" He lunged, landed his knee in JP's groin, connected his fist with JP's ugly mug.

With Alex and JP fighting, spit and fury flying, a rattle of fear ran up Rae's spine. The tingling at her fingertips intensified as the Boyz squared off against each other, oblivious to anything but their own aggression. The testosterone rising made them blind, made Alex careless.

JP had the Smith & Wesson, Christoff had Vince's Taurus. No sign of Rocco's Python. That left her gun, and there was only one place the Colt could be. She slipped unnoticed into Rocco's tent, all neat and tidy, the sleeping bag rolled tight. He'd packed, was clearly on his way out. And indeed miracles do happen. Her Colt was right there in his tog bag under his folded shirts and khaki pants. She picked it up, knowing the feel of the grip. Checked the mag, full; pushed off the safety, cocked the gun, gripped it, her hands steady, her eye in, oh yes, always. Knew this was the time, now or never.

She heard JP yell, "I knew it from the start, you soft, you never had the guts for this."

"I said she's mine," said Alex.

Rae stepped from the tent, her grip on the Colt firm, her sites on JP, concentration intense. She said loudly, calmly, "Drop the gun."

JP had Smith lined up on Alex; he half-turned, amused. "Or what, you gonna shoot me?"

His eyes shining, this was what he lived for, she knew: for confrontation.

"Yes, I'm going to shoot you."

JP sneered. "Women can't shoot. As for you, Prettyboy, for a brain surgeon, you're fucking stupid. Don't come to a gunfight with your fists. I shoulda put a load in you a long time ago. This time you're gonna stay in the grave. You'll stay bloody de–!"

Bam! Bam!

The same instant Alex flew backwards into the grave, JP screamed, stared at Smith on the ground, at the bullet hole in his hand.

"Reckon I can't shoot, JP? Check this out." *Bam, bam*. Rae shot a tin, the beans exploding, next a water bottle. She shot the dregs-empty Klipdrift bottle from Christoff's comatose grip. *Bam*. Trained the gun back on JP scrambling in the dirt for the Smith, shot him in the foot, the guy shrieking, clutching his bloodied Doc Martens.

"You ruined my shoes, you fucking half-breed!"

"Target practice, JP. You don't listen, do you? I warned you not to wave about the fire-power."

JP, a rabid dog, wasn't about to stay down. She kept her hand steady, her eye in, her promise in mind, when months ago the attacker had come at her with a knife, when her hands were tied, when she could do nothing. "Go on, make my day."

On the periphery of her vision Johannes unfurled from a crouch, a praying mantis twisting his body, leaping at JP, chopping at his torso with his knobkerrie. JP sprawled to the ground, his arms over his face, his head in his hands, squealing as Johannes delivered a series of perfectly executed blows to his body, cracking his kneecap, breaking his ribs, smashing his jaw. Then Rae put her Colt to the back of JP's head and he pissed his pants.

As JP's urine soaked into the dusty earth, he blubbered, "I'm begging you, please, don't kill me!"

She heard the wup-wup of helicopter blades. Had to be police. Alex had promised her it would soon all be over.

Alex!

She turned; seeing Alex rising from the grave, she nearly shot him with fright. He pulled himself out and floundered towards her, said, "Call me Lazarus! Had to rise from the dead twice today."

Relief. JP had missed.

The paramedics strapped Vincent Saldana onto a stretcher, carried him towards the helicopter. Heinz could walk. He whimpered about his Aurora, his Regina. Stella staggered along in handcuffs, sulky, complaining.

Rae squeezed Vince's hand, said, "See you in Cape

Town."

"Hey, Rae, I'm sorry."

"Hey, Vince, I'm sorry too. So sorry I got you into this."

"Nothing like forced detox." His voice wavered, his face contorted with pain.

A woman came over, Princess someone or other. Beautiful, with velvet skin. She said, "Ms. Valentine, no worries, I'm going along in the Medevac. Vince'll be fine. Bien sûr, I'll take good care of him." Princess waved—"Au Revoir, a bientôt"—and clambered into the helicopter.

Rae couldn't work it out. *For the love of God, who's Princess?*

Detective Captain Rex Hawkins flashed his badge as he passed river rafters pointing—"That way!"

Tony worked the paddle with urgency, felt the burn at his biceps as he sliced hard and fast into the water. He heard the crescendo of rotor blades, looked up. Saw a red and white Medevac helicopter rising, leaving.

Rex said, "Heck, this doesn't look good."

"Fuck it, we're too late!" said Tony. "So much for the stealth arrival."

At last they slid their canoe into the reeds, jumped over the bow, pulled it up onto the bank. Tony leopard crawled behind Rex to the bend up ahead, cursing under his breath as the torch, penknife, rope, all at the front of his tactical jacket, hampered his movement. They crossed over an embankment to a clearing. They checked the tents, nothing. No one. Found the remains of a goat and a heap of ostrich carcasses alongside a dug-out hole in the ground.

In it, Rocco Robano. Blistered. Flayed. Dead.

"My God, where's Rae?" said Tony.

"We'll find her," said Rex.

Tony, tense and ready, his Astra Special firm in his hand, smelled the aroma of grilled meat as he clawed and scraped his way up the next embankment. Sound drifted from the river bank, voices, music. He recognized the last chords of a distorted Locnville, the boyband singing about the sun and the moon and the stars...Electro-hop kids' stuff.

Clearing the top, he saw three figures on the river bank, a couple in deck chairs under a makeshift shade cloth of towels and shirts, and a Bushman at a barbeque.

Again he heard the tinny music, now Johnny Clegg searching for the Spirit of the Great Heart, the sound definitely coming from a cellphone.

He took in the scene.

What the heck?

He saw a dimpled blond shaking hands with Rex Hawkins.

Saw the Bushman stirring a mix in a three-legged pot, what smelled like a potjie of offal.

A woman's voice he recognized, asked, "Alex, how d'you want your meat done?" Rae Valentine, in T-shirt and denims, went into a clinch with the dimpled blond. A Greek God.

Rae waved him over.

"Tony! What took you so long?"

She dished up corn mash on paper plates, with a tomato salsa, plus the mouth-watering slow-braaied skewers. "I tell you, nothing can beat ostrich."

"Ostrich meat is better than beef, scientists say," said the Greek God. "Bird's low in cholesterol, low in saturated fat. Good for the ticker." He tapped his chest. "Healthier even than skinless chicken, or turkey." He held out his hand, introduced himself: "Detective Savalas, aka Alex Silver. Been working undercover."

Alex turned back to Rae, back to filling her in on the upside of carrying a Viper stun gun. "Like I said, you gotta get one, looks just like a cellphone there in its little leather nest at your belt. You put the tip on a man's skin, then push the button. 1,500 volt electricity shoots straight into the goolies. The perp'll shriek and fall to the ground, heavy and silent as a sack of stones. And it'll keep you out of court. Could've done with one today, hey?"

"Live and learn, right, Tony?" said Rae. "No use shooting the bastards considering all the damn trouble it brings." She pointed at two cuffed men, and at police, who'd arrived with Adrian Lombard in an armored van, about to take them away.

Alex said, "Justice prevails."

Tony rolled his eyes.

DAYS LATER

Tony Durant picked up a couple of voicemails.

From the doc and psych interns: "Please call" and "We need you."

From Sarah, the come-on in her tone: "Anthony, that glass of wine is on ice for you, any time."

From the Prof: "You added ten percent for a weekend delivery, Mr. Sugarman, and you didn't even have the common decency to deliver personally at the door."

Tony switched on the TV news.

…In the latest update, Khayelitsha residents have taken a stand against xenophobia as community leaders encourage the reintegration of refugees. And the spate of cold fronts is over as the sun comes out on a

sparkling Cape Town. But first the latest news on the foiled coup.

The last of a group of mercenary conscripts were arraigned, after arrest, for plotting against the South African government. The land earmarked for the new whites-only settlement, Aurora, from where massive military action was planned, has been expropriated by the Namibian government. This extravagant operation, in which hundreds of trained military personnel were enlisted to destabilize the region, has now been shut down...

He switched off.

So much for unbiased news reporting, could call it fake news. The revolution had turned out to be a couple of maniacs and a nutcase manipulated by a psycopath.

He picked up the vibrating cell.

"Heard of 'Cheese,' Mr. Sugarman? Make it up to me. I want to try some of that."

"For you, Prof, anything."

Cheese: super-excellent quality dope at a hundred-and-twenty bucks a bag. He'd charge double. He cut the connection. Another incoming buzzed almost immediately. Like a bloody train station in his hand.

"See the news?" said Rex.

"All's well that ends well. What's the latest?"

"Heinz Dieter's in the Valkenberg loony bin courtesy of the State. He'll never get out. Prosecutors are still deciding what to do with Stella due to extenuating circumstances. Seems she needs care and counseling more than incarceration. JP Cowart and Christoff Wessels are both awaiting trial in Pollsmoor prison."

"That's punishment enough. White boys last, what is it, eight minutes in those holding pens before they get jack-hammered?"

"Putting it mildly," chuckled Rex.

"You chat to the Bushman yet?"

"Seems Johannes !Xaba bought himself a round-the-world airline ticket. Just got on a plane for the States."

"Yeah?"

"He got security clearance plus a ten-year visa on account of his daughter's on a fancy PhD program at NYU."

"How's he afford it all?"

"It's a funny world."

"So that's it?"

"Adrian searched the farm if you can call it that. Brought back Rocco Robano's effects. It's the end of an era, Tony. Oh, here's a puzzle for you. That heap of ostrich carcasses with their multiple stomachs slit? Neat cuts. Contents emptied. What d'you make of that?"

"Probably some sacred San ritual."

"Must be…"

They said their goodbyes.

Tony weighed the phone in his hand. Got up and cracked a beer at the fridge.

Rae would love this story.

He dialed her landline. Listened to it ring, rocked on his heels, longing for the lilt of her hello.

"Yeah?"

He recognized the voice. One Alexander Savalas, aka Alex Silver. The undercover cop hailed for saving the day at the river, with an SMS. The Greek God. Hell! She was in bed with the toy boy!

He put down the phone, scrambled for the Bic. He lit a spliff, pulled on it long and deep. Slotted Johnny Cash in the CD player, lay with his feet up on the couch, in the dusk, settling into the long night. Yeah, with gravel-voiced Cash for company, croaking out an ode to the dark side of a man's soul.

I know the beast alright. God help me, a caged and restless beast.

※

Rae Valentine was more than pleased to be back in her apartment.

She'd already unrolled the prayer mat. Had started unpacking her crime novels. *Crackerjack* she couldn't wait to get her teeth into. She'd checked Facebook: 114 messages. Plus orders coming in already for her memoir. She'd get to her email eventually. She'd get to it all.

The phone rang.

Alex answered.

"Who was that?"

"Must have been a wrong number."

"You didn't check caller ID?"

Alex shrugged, leaned over, poured them each a glass of Retsina. "You ready for this quintessential Mediterranean vino? With its sappy pine taste? Early Greeks thought of it as wood nymph tears."

They clinked glasses.

"Yuck, Alex, tastes like turpentine."

Snuggled in his embrace, on the couch, she watched the tail end of the TV news.

...property and goods, including priceless jewelry which was to be sold to fund the Core, have been confiscated by the assets-forfeiture unit...

She fingered her ring. She deserved the diamond. Call it payment for finding the jewels. Too bad she couldn't report back to her client. Too bad for Rosa. Lucky for Johannes.

Rae checked her watch. "Johannes'll be halfway over the Atlantic by now."

They'd seen him off at the airport, in his natty suit,

with his pull-along carry bag, off to visit the apple of his eye, his daughter, there in the USA, doing her doctorate on Evolutionary Anthropology. Johannes had ways and means it seemed, had learned lessons from Rocco Robano. The recovered stones would buy his kid another whole chunk of education.

"Did you know," said Alex, reading the classic *The Covenant*, "that in San culture women are revered, the leader has limited power, that decisions are made by consensus…?"

Rae switched off the TV, plucked the Kindle from his hands, put it on the coffee table, said to her young stud know-it-all, "Shut the fuck up, Prettyboy," and sealed his mouth with a kiss.

THE END

… for now…

CPSIA information can be obtained
at www.ICGtesting.com
Printed in the USA
FSHW021645160520
70046FS